Sally Ann Voak has writter
and healthy eating. She has
and treatment of overweight people, and in 2003 she won the prestigious Roche International Journalism award for her special six month series on helping children get fitter and eat balanced meals.

This is her first work of fiction - and what a delicious mix of sex, conspiracy and calories it is too!

To Anne —
Hope you enjoy it!
Sally Ann
xxxxx

Thermogenesis

.... sex, conspiracy and calories!

Cover Design, Text and Illustrations copyright © 2007 Sally Ann Voak
Original Cover Design by Tom Bunning Design

First edition published in Great Britain in 2007
by four o' clock press - an imprint of discovered authors

The right of Sally Ann Voak to be identified as the Author
of the Work has been asserted by her in accordance with
the Copyright, Designs and Patent Act 1988

All rights reserved. No part of this publication may be reproduced, stored in a
retrieval system, or transmitted, in any form or by any means without the prior
written permission of the Author

All characters in this publication are fictitious and any resemblance to real persons,
living or dead, is purely coincidental

978-1906146-1-53

four o'clock press

Available from www.discoveredauthors.co.uk
All major online retailers and available to order through all UK bookshops

Or contact:
Books
Discovered Authors
50 Albemarle Street, London
W1S 4BD
+ (44) 207 529 37 29
books@discoveredauthors.co.uk

Printed in the UK by BookForce Ltd.

BookForce UK's policy is to use papers that are natural, renewable and
recyclable products and made from wood grown in sustainable forests where ever
possible

BookForce UK Ltd.
Alma Park,
6 Woodlands Drive
Grantham, Lincs
www.bookforce.co.uk

Thermogenesis

... sex, conspiracy and calories!

Sally Ann Voak

Chapter One

Case Notes:
Department of Dietetics, East Central Hospital.

The patient, Mr. John Barnard is 55 and morbidly obese. He is employed as a taxi driver. Sibutramine has been prescribed. This seratonin and noradrenaline uptake inhibitor reduces energy intake by increasing the sense of fullness. Mr Barnard has been advised to adopt a low-calorie diet, aiming for a reduction of about 600 kcal by reducing dietary fat and portion size. The most recent clinical trials show that this treatment plus lifestyle changes could give a weight loss of between 3 and 13 percent in three years. Prognosis: if there is no compliance, this patient will be given additional drug therapy or recommended for surgery. This is the best we can do.

The East Central hospital was like a small, nineteeth century industrial town; a mass of shabby grey buildings, dominated by four tall brick chimneys, people scurrying to and fro like the matchstick men in a Lowrie painting. Everywhere, there were large red and black signs. The directions on the signs were like commands from from a sci-fi computer game: "To Red Zone, " You are now in Blue Zone, " "This is Level 11", Caution: You are now entering the Scanner Suite. "

The main hospital had been erected over a hundred years ago on a five-acre site, then added to, piecemeal, whenever enough Government or Lottery funds became available. The multitude of outbuildings covered another five acres, stretching over the surrounding land like tentacles from a greedy octopus.

Inside the imposing iron gateway, the network of concrete roads and parking areas was choked by vehicles; over 5,000 cars belonging to patients and staff, as well as an assortment of laundry trucks, ambulances, taxis, and waste collection juggernauts.

Despite the hundreds of notices, there were no useful directions for patients trying to locate the department or ward they needed. If they were wise, they arrived at the hospital's large, impressive entrance hall (recently renovated, courtesy of Muffin 'n Burgers, the giant American fast food chain) at least thirty minutes before their appointment.

Susan Simpson sat in her tiny office tucked away on the third floor at the far end of " Red Zone", and tried to relax. She had ten minutes to spare before her next clinic, which gave her just enough time to glance at the morning newspaper and sip a cup of tepid hospital coffee. Then it would be back to the usual grind: an afternoon spent in five minute consultations with patients who either wouldn't, or couldn't take the advice she gave them.

The grey file on the table beside her coffee cup was stuffed with patient case histories and many of them made grim reading, especially the notes on John Barnard, a taxi driver whose daily life was a constant struggle because of his vast size.

As a state registered dietitian, with four years' training and six years of clinical practice under her belt, Susan sometimes doubted whether she had made any contribution whatsoever to the health of the nation. The vast majority of her patients at the hospital were considered to be clinically obese, and, because of this, they had been referred to her by their general practitioners. She often thought of herself as the "last chance saloon" for these supersized patients before they underwent major surgery to prevent them from absorbing high fat food.

It was up to her to help these unfortunate people lose weight by less drastic means, by encouraging them to eat a balanced diet. In most cases, their level of compliance was nil: it was almost as though they wanted to go under the knife. The surgeon could then take responsibility for their survival or death by drowning...in their own blubber.

Someone opened the door and Susan glanced up from her newspaper. Dr. Guy Johnson strode in, and slumped into the only armchair in the room.

"Seen the latest report from the Commons Select Committee on Health, Sue? It's the usual list of pipe dream ideas that will never be carried out by the Government. At this rate, we'll soon be feeding fatties low-calorie liquid food intravenously while they lie on beds in the hospital corridors. There are so many obesity-related cases on the wards that I'm finding it hard to locate beds for my road accident victims. I've just sent one amputee over to Wimbledon Hospital because I haven't got anywhere to put him. The poor bastard was packed up and despatched like a load of freshly butchered meat, but I had no alternative.

"I hate to speak ill of your precious fatties, but this place is like a beehive stuffed with bloated queen bees, being fed by just a few worker-bees: us"

Guy worked as Head of the Accident and Emergency Department, a job which was so appalling that the only way he could cope was by dispensing liberal amounts of sarcasm: his personal brand of pain-killer. His ideas on the treatment of obese patients were simple: they had brought their problems on themselves, so they should pay for the consequences by using private health care.

He was now fifty eight, and had struggled, mostly unsuccessfully, for twenty years to get improvements made in his own department. His disappointment showed: with his thinning grey hair, stooped shoulders and well-rounded paunch, he looked at least sixty five. His own ample girth made his remarks about "fatties" seem very unfair. Susan sympathised with Guy's problems, and admired his work, but the two colleagues had very different views on the value of dietetics and nutrition in medicine. Treating the "whole" patient, was just not one of Guy's priorities.

"I was just reading the article, " said Susan. "Frankly, there is no way that the Committee's recommendations will ever be implemented. I'd love to see a special obesity unit attached to every hospital, but who's going to pay for it? Did you see the other story about the drug company who are testing a "wonder pill" which is supposed to stop people craving alcohol and cigarettes as well as too much food? The trials have been good…but no-one knows what the long-term effects will be. That's the problem with drugs; you need time to test them.

"I really can't agree with you. Guy. Talking about "bloated Queen bees" is unfair. Obesity is an illness, and it should be treated with appropriate medical care, whatever the cost."

Guy pulled a face: " I wish those Health Ministry buggers would come here and see what we're up against. " he said. " The trouble is that no-one, from the PM downwards, actually dares to give us the truth: hospitals are full to bursting and the main reason for it is that people are being stuffed with food by multinational food companies and supermarkets who make huge profits from gluttony. It's a time bomb ticking away, and those self-important arses in Parliament are too blinkered, or corrupt, to see it. The latest issue of "Inside Information" has two stories about Government back- handers from big food firms. It's a disgrace." He got up abruptly and walked out of the room, banging the door behind him.

Susan picked up her newspaper and re-read the article. Most of what Guy had said was true, but his was the kind of outburst that occurred almost every day in the hospital, a form of release which stopped senior staff from throwing in the towel. Despite his angry words, Guy was dedicated to his profession. But it was all just so bloody frustrating.

The newspaper suddenly seemed full of depressing stories. Susan threw it into the the waste-paper basket under her desk, where it soaked up a dribble of coffee from her discarded coffee cup.

Come on girl, don't get upset, Susan said to herself, sternly.

You are doing your best, and a few people do take your advice and follow the diets you give them. You can't change the world. Look at what you're up against: every high street is full of fast food outlets, No wonder people are fat.

Susan reflected on the lack of progress that had been made since the mid-nineties, when the first warning signs of the approaching "fat crisis" had emerged. Countless conferences had been held, scientific papers published, books written and political speeches penned since then. Yet, the world population, even in Far Eastern countries, was growing fatter and fatter.

In the three years since the British Government had commissioned an investigation into the causes of obesity, little had been done to solve the problem. In fact, figures released just a month ago, in August, 2008, showed that 35% of British adults, 45% of Americans and even 15% of the more sensible French, who at least consumed medium-sized meals, were now obese. The diet industry was thriving: everyone seemed to want to make a fast buck out of people's weaknesses. They all wanted to repeat the incredible success of the Atkins empire, founded by American slimming guru, Dr. Robert Atkins. His ideas were seriously flawed and even the fact that he weighed 18st when he died in 2001 didn't put off the vast numbers of people who just kept on buying into his mantra: eat fat and grow lean.

The company had gone bust in 2005, but other get-fat- profits-quick diet firms had come along to take its place. The Glycaemic Index Diet, complex and not scientifically proven to help obese patients, was also still popular. In the last year, there had been an increase in "fad" diets, often rehashed from those published in the seventies. Even a "new" version of the Grapefruit Diet, was selling well. People's appetite for diet books was as healthy as ever. The same could not be said for their appetite for good, fresh, low-fat food.

Liquid diet supplements were now standard issue in hospitals, world wide, where they were used to bring the weight of morbidly obese patients down to obese levels. Consequently, the companies who made them were making lots of money for their shareholders. Despite attempts to take on the big multi-national junk food conglomerates by activists who criticised their products and manufacturing methods, giant junk food chains like Muffins 'n Burgers were still raking in huge profits. Supermarket marketing bosses now knew so much about their consumers, thanks to tracking products via special chips in the packaging, that they were able to target junk food addicts with promotional material, even before they set foot in their stores.

Efforts to improve the standard of nutrition in British state schools had foundered after a sudden rush of enthusiasm by the Government in 2005. Sadly, the promised increase in funds to pay for healthy meals hadn't materialised, and kids were still being fed re-constituted meat products disguised as chicken nuggets, plus the inevitable mounds of greasy chips.

Susan wondered whether she would have studied so hard to become a dietitian if she had known how much of her life would be spent trying, unsuccessfully, to stop fat people from eating themselves to death.

Even as a little girl, she had been fascinated by food and diet. Both were an important part of her family's "healthy living" culture: her father, Ralph, was a successful solicitor who played squash regularly, and, when Susan was in her teens, her mother, Jane, had been an enthusiastic aerobics teacher. She started one of the first aerobics classes in the town of Redhill, Surrey, England where Susan and her older brother James were brought up. The children had been raised on healthy, fresh food, much of it home-grown, and were encouraged to play tennis and enjoyed a family ski-ing holiday every year. Susan was a star of the local grammar school hockey team, and a brilliant student: chemistry and art were her top subjects.

In her teens, Susan's role-model was her mother: a tall, willowy, dark-haired beauty who, even in her forties and fifties had a taut stomach and firm thighs. Susan was always petite, but with a tendency to gain weight, so she had been extra careful about eating properly. Sometimes she was a little too careful. At fifteen, a delicate stage in her physical development, she had become too thin and attended an eating disorders clinic. Even now, she occasionally had to remind herself to eat properly, especially when she was under stress.

When she enrolled as a student at Queen Elizabeth College, Edinburgh, to take her degree in dietetics and nutrition, Susan imagined that her career would be at the more glamorous end of the business; sports nutritionist, or consultant to the ever-increasing number of TV programmes which focused on slimming, fitness and diet. Unfortunately, these "plum" jobs in the industry were few and far between so Susan decided to work in the British National Health Service for a few years. She was now thirty three, and still hoping, albeit half-heartedly, for a chance to prove herself.

At first, she had been full of enthusiasm about her hospital work, naively imagining that she could change lives for the better with good nutrition. Now, she seemed to be stuck in a very deep rut; a bottomless pit of glutenous fat cells, wobbling flesh, and globules of cholesterol. There was no getting away from fat people. The patients were huge, the hospital was run by overweight managers, doctors and nurses, and when she left work, she was surrounded by obese, unhealthy looking men, women and children. It was predicted that, in twenty five years' time, most British people would be obese. To Susan, it looked as though that day had already arrived.

Just occasionally, a patient would respond positively, reminding her why she entered the profession in the first place. One such patient was Brenda Jones, a 48 year old mother of three teenaged sons, who had been referred to Susan after experiencing acute breathlessness and panic attacks. Tests showed that the woman's blood pressure was high, and she was borderline diabetic. When Susan had first seen her six months earlier, Brenda, who weighed over 18st, had been in despair. She had given up a part-time job as a factory cleaner because she had fainting fits every time she tried to climb the steep, rickety stairs from the main floor to the offices. Her exasperated husband had walked out, and their three sons were bullied at school because they, too, were obese. Before seeing Susan, Brenda had even contemplated suicide.

After looking at Brenda's " food diaries", the daily records of her food and drink intake which she had carefully recorded for the past week, Susan had prescribed a 1700 calorie, low-fat diet, and some gentle exercises. Brenda had stuck to the diet and the pounds had started to drop off very rapidly. Until this week, she had lost an average of 4lbs weekly and had become a lot more confident as well. In total, she had shed 28lbs. Curiously, although the records kept during the last seven days were fine, at this morning's clinic weigh-in there had been a problem: Brenda's weight had increased by 2lbs. Susan hoped it was a temporary "glitch", as the foods listed in her food diary were certainly well within the low-fat, low-calorie guidelines she had set.

That morning, she had spent her allotted five minutes with Brenda convincing her that she must stick to the diet, and encouraging her to join a local authority-run gym, where the instructors were well-qualified and could provide her with exercise advice.

****

Susan glanced up at the clock and contemplated the heavy file on the table. At least 100 patients' notes to review. Fine. Tonight, she'd open a bottle of decent wine, cook something simple and tackle half of them.

That afternoon, she saw fifteen more of her "precious fatties" including some on the wards who were being kept on a controlled, liquids-only diet to help them reduce weight before surgery.

The dangerously obese male patient, John Barnard, was taking the drug Sibutramine, and trying hard to follow Susan's diet advice.

When he arrived for his appointment he was ushered into Susan's consulting room by a nursing assistant.

Susan could tell that all was not well: his many-jowelled chin was lowered into his vast neck, his huge sweatshirt and jeans looked wrinkled and dirty, and he was twisting a scruffy red baseball cap in both hands, with an air of desperation, like a drowning man clutching a lifebuoy.

" So, how's it going, then John? Is the cab trade still thriving?" Susan always tried to start her clinical sessions with a friendly chat, before getting down to the real business: weight and blood pressure checks, food diary analysis, possible further clinical referral. Many of her patients also attended a diabetic clinic in the same part of the hospital.

"I'm feeling fuckin' awful," he replied "I can't carry on with my job much longer. Last week, during the heat wave, I got stuck in the cab for an hour in a traffic jam, and thought I was dying. When's this bleedin' drug going to work? I don't feel quite so hungry but I still seem to be eating all the wrong things. The trouble is, the missus always has a big roast dinner waiting for me at home at night and during the day, I still fancy my kebabs and burgers. They keep me going. What's the point of living, anyway, if you can't eat what you want? "

He sat down heavily on the chair in front of Susan's desk, and put the creased baseball cap on top of a pile of recipe leaflets. Beads of sweat dripped down over his nose. Susan felt like crying.

"John, last week you weighed 24st. You are not going to lose ten stone overnight. It's going to be a long, difficult process. What happened to the menus I worked out for you? Did you throw them away? The drug can only help you if you make a real effort to eat good, healthy food instead of rubbish. I am worried about you, obviously, but this is something you are going to have to do for yourself. Otherwise, you could die. The cardiovascular specialist you are seeing has already warned you that your arteries are becoming blocked. Tell your wife that she must co-operate too and produce healthy meals for you. Come on, John, you can do it."

Even while she was speaking, Susan knew she was lying.

John couldn't, and wouldn't do it. He hadn't lost an ounce in six months. His days were numbered. She went through the motions of weighing him (24st 1lb), taking his blood pressure reading (high), and writing another prescription for the drug.

"Come back next week, and I want to see that you've lost some weight, John, " she said. "You must try, you know. "

"I will , but it's hard, very hard." John picked up his cap, struggled to his feet and lumbered towards the door. As he reached for the door handle, his legs suddenly buckled, and he clutched the door frame to steady himself, then, very slowly, he walked into the corridor.

Oh God...look after him.

Although not a religious person (at university, she claimed to be an "agnostic"), Susan often said a prayer to herself after seeing morbidly obese patients. In the last year, six had died: two from cardiovascular disease, one from lung cancer, and three from pulmonary disease.

If I can't cure them, at least I care about them, she thought.

The afternoon progressed with more of the same. There were some brighter moments as well. Twelve patients were making good progress. Unfortunately, only three of them had actually shed any weight that week, which was surprising. Susan had recently given all her patients some new low-calorie menus to try which included "ready meals" available from supermarkets. It was something she felt strongly about. Purists in the profession preferred not to recommend "manufactured" meals which can be quickly heated up in a conventional or microwave oven in case they were seen to favour one supermarket chain or manufacturer above another, but Susan felt that, in the real world, people eat processed foods and there was no reason why some could not be included in her diets. Still, it was worth checking tonight that she had calculated the calorie and nutrient values in these meals accurately in case it was her own fault that her patients weren't able to shed weight.

At 5.30pm, Susan gathered her notes, thrust the thick grey file into her old brown briefcase, and went into the small adjoining reception room. "Good night, girls, " she said, brightly, to the two nursing orderlies on duty. "See you tomorrow. "

"Meeting your boyfriend tonight, Susan? "asked Gladys, a large, jolly woman in her forties wearing floppy cotton trousers, a loose top and white clogs. Her companion, Cally, a plump young Philipino girl with dark brown eyes and short, shiny hair, giggled.

"We broke up. I'm footloose and fancy free again, " said Susan as she walked towards the door. "You'll have to find me a boyfriend, girls..so long as it's no-one working here. I need a rich bloke who'll whisk me off into the sunset!"

A few minutes later, as she eased her battered green Renault estate car out of the staff carpark, Susan reflected on how dedicated most of the staff of East Central were. Despite his sarcastic jibes, Guy was a brilliant, skilled physician who really cared about his work. Gladys and Cally were great: paid peanuts, but they obviously enjoyed their jobs, and were courteous to even the most difficult patients. There were more fat people in the country than ever before, and most of them had suffered verbal abuse in the street and on public transport. At least they got some sympathy at the hospital, even if it was only from members of the Dietetics Department.

During her 25-minute drive home she experienced the usual nightmarish mixture of stress, fear, and frustration: the hot weather seemed to bring out the worst in people. When she finally arrived in her street on the outskirts of town, there was just room to squeeze between two cars parked right outside her house.

My life is ruled by bloody parking spaces, she thought. There must be more to it, than this. God, I sound as though I should be signing up for one of those "What's it all about?" quasi-religious courses that seem to have sprung up since the May, 2005 General Election.

It had been a very strange three years.

After the lowest turn out at the polls in history, the Government had been re-elected, but with a new Prime Minister, Jack Barton. The previous incumbent of No 10 Downing Street had beaten a hasty retreat to a Caribbean island after a heart by-pass operation, and the new man, the former Health Minister, had been at the helm ever since. His three years in office had not been fun: the housing market had crashed, the FT index was at an all time low, and the world's terrorists were as active as ever. However, because most people were eating more, the food industry was booming. Surprisingly, the churches were doing good business as well.

Susan wondered why. Could it be that people really were fed up with materialism and looking for another way of living? Shame that they wouldn't have long to enjoy a simpler lifestyle. Despite new drugs, and signicant improvement in the care and treatment of cancer and heart patients, average life expectancy was actually gradually decreasing. She shuddered, and said, out loud, " We're all doomed, folks...didn't you know? "

Her tiny terraced house was in a narrow street, backing onto a railway line. Some owners had painted their front doors in bright colours. Susan's was turquoise blue with a bold, brass knocker. After letting herself in, she hung her coat on the peg in the hall and headed for the drinks cabinet in the snug brown and cream painted sitting room. Until a month ago, she'd shared the house with Mark: his favourite malt whisky was still in the cabinet. She tried to put him out of her mind. It was over, she had to move on. What she needed was a large gin and tonic, a hot bath, and a tasty meal. After that, she'd tackle those case histories.

An hour later, refreshed, fed, and dressed in a light white cotton caftan embroidered with orange flowers, she relaxed on her beige leather sofa with her file, an open bottle of chilled Sauvignon and a wineglass. She'd flung wide the French doors, so she could look out onto the tiny, paved terrace which was crammed with earthenware pots stuffed with the garish-bright flowers she loved:

geraniums, marigolds, and fuschias. Even though it was 8.30pm, the late September air was still warm and the last rays of sunshine lit up the tips of branches of the spruce tree at the end of the terrace like bright candles on a Christmas tree.

Susan opened the file carefully, and shuffled through the pile of case histories. She selected the notes on the twelve patients who were doing well, reasoning that she might as well cheer herself up with some positive stuff before looking at the disasters.

Six of the twelve people she picked out had visited the clinic that day. Unfortunately, none of them had lost weight that week, but, overall, they had been making good progress. As well as Brenda Jones, there were five more "successes":

Les Martin, a 52 year old who weighed 22st 3lb, was an angina sufferer. His wife Ann, a gutsy little woman, was determined that he should shed weight, and always came with him to his clinic appointments.

Valerie Tate was 45, and a heavy smoker. She had already suffered a mild heart attack. She had cut down her smoking habit, and was trying very hard to improve her diet, although tackling the two things at once was difficult. She weighed 19st 4lb.

Arthur Taylor, an amputee, was confined to a wheelchair, but had recovered well from prostate cancer and, at the age of 72, wanted to improve his quality of life by losing some weight from his twenty one stone frame. He was a great character, and despite his difficulties, Susan was delighted with his progress. He'd shed three stone in a year, which was a brilliant achievement.

The two youngest members of the group had both been referred to Susan by the same GP. Daryl O Brien was only fifteen but already weighed over seventeen and a half stone, and Gemma Hartley was just nineteen years old. When she had stepped onto the scales that day, they'd registered twenty stone, eight pounds.

The six are interesting, thought Susan, because they all weigh in on the same day each week, and I gave them all similar diet plans - tailored to each individual, but with the same basic foods. Now, why didn't they lose any weight this week? Maybe there's a common factor somewhere. Certainly, I did suggest the same supermarket ready-meals, so maybe I've made a mistake with my calculations and recommended double portions instead of single helpings.

She got up from the sofa, and, taking her half-full wine glass with her, walked over to the alcove where she kept her desk and computer. After logging on, she searched for her menu lists which were filed according to their calorie and nutrient value. When planning diets for patients, she could swiftly pull out suitable menus for each meal, knowing that they would be nutritious and within the patient's daily calorie and fat allowance.

Three ready-meal products had been eaten by all six patients: a vegetable curry, a chicken dish with rice and beans, and a ready-made spaghetti Bolognese, complete with low-fat cheese topping. They were all from the "healthy eating" ranges sold by well-known supermarkets and Susan's computer showed that each 550 gram portion contained under 400 calories, less than 2 grams of salt and only 3.5 grams of fat.

When she had written out their diet plans, Susan had advised her patients to add lots of vegetables and salad to "bulk out" the meal on their plate, and boost the amount of fibre and vitamins it contained.

Many of her dietetics colleagues believed that food shouldn't come in boxes at all, but should be cooked freshly at every meal. She agreed, but these days, people just didn't want to spend time searching for good produce, then cooking it at home. Many didn't have a clue how to prepare a meal from raw ingredients. If she was to have a chance of succeeding with her patients, she had to ease them gently into a healthier lifestyle.

It was plain that the calorie and fat content of these three meals was low: there was no way any of the three could be described as "fattening". She checked the rest of the ingredients in each pack, plus any additives included in each recipe. The list of "extras" was long and included such unappetising-sounding things as mono and diacatyltartaric acid, modified maize starch and milk proteins. Yummy, thought Susan. However, she was well aware that food processing techniques, hygiene and shelf-life requirements necessitated additives. Without some of them, the food would go bad, and people would get sick.

At least they don't contain many "E" numbers, she thought. These are the additives, such as colourants and preservatives, which can, sometimes, cause an allergic reaction. However, there was one ingredient common to all three products which she didn't recognise - GE203. As the products were savoury-tasting, maybe this was a flavour enhancer? Or perhaps it was a colourant? Whatever it was, it wasn't affecting the calorie content of the product, so it couldn't possibly stop her six patients from losing weight effectively. Maybe, they were all lying about what they'd eaten, a regular occurrence among overweight people, which Susan had to live with. She must tackle them about this next week.

She switched off the computer, closed the French doors, went back to the sofa and struggled through another twenty sets of case notes, making recommendations for additional treatment where necessary.

Two hours later, after glancing up at the clock, and down at the empty wine bottle, she decided that she had done enough for one night. Tomorrow, she would find out exactly what GE203 was, just to satisfy her curiosity.

****

Chapter Two

Press invitation:
Independent Food Manufacturers' Association Launch New Intiative to tackle Obesity Crisis.

Come to the IFMA offices, 27 Golden Square, London W1, at 9.00am on Tuesday 30th September, 2008, and meet Bruce James, UK Managing Director of FizzCo, who will explain the new initiative, present the results of an important, nationwide, survey on UK eating habits, and launch an exciting range of figure-friendly snack-foods.
   There will be a photo call at 10.30am., when England soccer captain, Phil Walker will be available for pictures in the IFMA gym.
   A "Continental-style" buffet breakfast of croissants, doughnuts, pastries and coffee will be served.

"You couldn't make it up, " muttered Caroline Dempsey after reading the invitation thrown onto her desk by the newspaper's Features Editor, Jim Dawson.

"They want us to go along at the crack of dawn tomorrow and give them a load of free publicity about their poxy junk food, thinly disguised as "figure-friendly snacks", and then they intend to feed us a high-fat breakfast. Still, the survey will probably make a couple of paragraphs for News, and maybe something for the health section, too. I'll go."

Caroline, who was sensitive about her own size 16 figure, wondered why the public relations people who advised FizzCo imagined that journalists enjoyed stuffing their faces with doughnuts at early morning press conferences. Frankly, these events were a pain. After struggling into London from the suburbs (in Caroline's case, from Chislehurst, in leafy Kent) you were forced to listen to some self-important industry boss waffling on about his or her company and products before they even got to the main meat of the story. Then they expected you to be thrilled because they'd paid trillions to the England Soccer captain to appear for five minutes and there were a few croissants to eat. It was pathetic.

Still, obesity-related stories still seemed to be going down a storm with the Editor. and if she played her cards right, this time next year she could get a chance to switch to political reporting. Now, that really was a meaty subject.

Caroline had been on the staff of the London Evening Echo for two years. After obtaining a 2-1 media studies degree, she landed a 6-month stint on a local, Kent, paper as a general reporter.

She started working night shifts for the Echo, and was then taken on, full-time, as a junior news reporter, covering less important daily stories; minor criminal cases, leaves on railway lines. Lately, her by-line had appeared on several news stories about the food industry and the obesity epidemic, and she had been helping the paper's features and health departments with longer articles on slimming and nutrition.

Hard-working, ambitious and attractive in a voluptuous way, Caroline was popular with her colleagues. She had quickly discovered that the only way to succeed in the male-dominated world of newspaper journalism was to wear the most glamorous office clothes she could afford, while maintaining a cool head and working longer hours than most of the blokes. Office romances were as common as cardboard coffee cups on the Evening Echo, but Caroline had decided that an affair with a colleague would be unwise at this , early, stage of her career. Later on, when she was in a position of power, she might indulge. Right now it was best to decline, politely, all advances, without deflating any delicate egos.

This was not as difficult at it sounds, Caroline found, so long as you got the timing right. The libido of the average male evening newspaper reporter can be measured on a scale of 0-10 according to the time of day: early mornings are a total flop and rate zero , there is a slight rise at 10am, when stories start to break , followed by another "low" when the boys are all working away on their computer terminals. After the first edition of the newspaper goes off just before noon, the male organ starts to rise again. Large portions of pie and chips from the canteen dampens the guys' collective ardour for a while, but once the final editions leave the presses at about 5pm, the pent-up emotions of the day finally climax - resulting in a rush of suggestive emails, and frantic mobile phone calls to the reservation desks at various London hotels.

So, in the mornings, it was safe to flirt away, while later in the day, a brisk, efficient demeanour was best. Glib one-liners and jokey put-downs could be used to defuse any embarrassing situations. It was essential to be "one of the boys" in the pub after work, matching pint for pint, but also wise to have a list of reliable mini-cab firms in your handbag.

Caroline's long, softly waving blond hair, ample cleavage and sparkling blue eyes, ensured that she attracted plenty of admirers on the paper, but she had decided that her current boyfriend was perfect for now: solid, reliable, not too local. His name was Tom, and they'd met at the London college where they'd both studied. Tom's degree was in accountancy, and he now worked for a large firm in Birmingham. They spent weekends together, and Tom occasionally came down to London during the week. The relationship was just fine; lots of laughs, good sex, no commitment, plenty of time for work.

Today's invitation from FizzCo was typical of the kind that dropped onto her desk most days. Sometimes, they were a waste of time, sometimes there was a story. In any case, there was always the opportunity to make contacts in the industry and a glimpse of a pair of well-rounded boobs could sometimes make those self-important food company bosses say more than they meant to. All you needed was a good quote, and you were laughing.

A few months previously, Caroline had helped the paper obtain a major scoop: the discovery of high levels of "trans fat", a kind of fat that clogs up the arteries while having no known nutritional benefit, in the products sold by a major high street fast food chain. This kind of fat is formed when manufacturers hydrogenate fat or oil, a process used to extend food shelf life. Research has shown that just one gram of trans fat eaten daily over many years significantly increases a person's chance of getting heart disease.

The scandal came to light when Caroline was asked to check out the fat content of a whole range of foods for a diet feature for the health pull-out section of the paper. Instead of simply checking the contents labels on the packet, she'd sent the items round to be analysed at a laboratory. The analysis had come back with the trans fat content separated out from the other fat in the products and a note from the lab technician saying that he was alarmed at the fact that one of them, a boxed takeaway meal of fried chicken strips and chips, contained 5 grams of trans fat.

It made a great story, and the company concerned had been forced to lower the amount of trans fat contained in the product. The British food safety watchdog, The Food Standards Agency, who were still smarting from criticism about their handling of a major health alert in 2005, when a chilli powder had been found to contain a carcinogenic colourant, had been embarrassed by the feature. Their reaction was satisfactory, as Caroline's Editor enjoyed a good old row; ministers getting hot under the collar was the stuff that tabloids thrived on.

Well done, me, thought Caroline, as she went through the rest of her post. The story gained Caroline plenty of brownie points with her bosses, even though the Health Editor, Gaby Stone, had made sure her own byline and photograph were prominently displayed above the piece.

As she emailed Gaby telling her about the invitation, Caroline indulged in a rare moment of vitriole. Sometimes, you couldn't make it up, she thought, bitterly. After I'd done all the donkey work, the ugly bitch wrote the introduction, pinching most of it from a health magazine, and didn't even credit me. She cheered up a little: despite Gaby's barefaced cheek, everyone on the paper knew who was really responsible. You've got to be philosophical in this game. Maybe I'll get a chance to interview the Health Minister next. My time will come.

Later that day, as she struggled through the commuter crush before catching her train home, Caroline planned her strategy for the following day's Press Conference. Dress: long denim skirt, low-necked top, strappy sandals. Perfume: Anais Anais. Attitude: soft and friendly...then in for the kill!

****

At 8.30am the next morning, half an hour before the Conference, FizzCo UK Managing Director Bruce James was pacing the floor in the steel and glass boardroom of the Food Manufacturers' Association Head Office in Golden Square. The forty nine year old executive was in a foul mood.

His company car had been thirty minutes late in picking him up from his Hertfordshire home, his wife, Ellen, had been moaning about the state of their four-acre garden, and his breakfast egg had been too runny and smelt like fresh sperm.

Worse, he had just received an email from the company's international headquarters in Baltimore, USA, telling him to ensure that media coverage of today's launch of the new range of "figure -friendly" snacks was favourable.

The email, from Charles Henderson, Senior Vice President, World-Wide, FizzCo Healthy Foods Division, was short and to the point:

Bruce - for Christ's sake get those bastard Limey journos to write something good about us for once. The C.E.O is fed up with reading knocking stories in the British Press. It's bad for business. Give them plenty of free samples, and if that doesn't work, threaten them with pulling our advertising pages from their papers. Got it? Join me for a round of golf when you're over next time. Charles.

Bruce's already-florid complexion went a deeper shade of puce. The C.E.O was fed up? He wasn't the only one. Bruce was absolutely pissed off with receiving stupid emails from the States. They had no idea what he was up against. It was all very well for Charlie Henderson; he had the US government eating out of his hand, and many of the American papers were onside as well. What's more, after the huge sales of their food and drink products Beijing this year, he knew for a fact that FizzCo-USA was currently negotiating sole rights for the 2016 Olympics, with plenty of freebies and trips for the committee members who made the decisions.

Unfortunately for Bruce, life this side of the pond was more complicated. Money certainly talked, but bribery had to be subtle. No amount of free goodies, or blackmail about pulling advertising pages would stop any UK journalist from writing just what they wanted to write; in fact, threats would make them more likely to dish the dirt. Unfortunately, any story knocking the food industry seemed to be incredibly popular with all editors, whatever the political allegiance of their particular paper.

Today's "Initiative" from the Independent Food Manufacturers' Association, of which FizzCo was a prominent member, was fine and laudable, as far as it went. It had been decided that the 250 members of the Association would be cutting the prices of "healthy" food ranges which were, at present more expensive to buy than ordinary food products.

The Survey on UK eating habits, to be launched that day, had been funded by the Association and carried out by an agency, who interviewed 5000 people in the United Kingdom. The findings were conclusive: overweight people wanted to eat healthily, but found many products too expensive. The Survey showed too, that there was a definite association between income levels and obesity: poorer people were likely to take less exercise, eat badly...and were therefore fatter than the well off. None of this was very surprising, but statistics gave the journalists something tangible to report. After all, 5000 people was quite a large sample.

Bruce tried to imagine what the press would do with both stories. There was something there for right and left-wing papers and journalists could hardly write knocking copy if the industry was really trying to cut prices - or could they? His worry was that they might ignore the most important part of the Press Conference, the launch of " Super Snacks", FizzCo's new range of breakfast bars, biscuits and packaged nibbles. Phil Walker, the England soccer captain, had been signed up for a six figure sum to help promote the new range, and had demanded an extra ten grand for today's short appearance. He would be wearing a "Super Snacks" T-shirt, but, these days, it was simple for picture editors to erase logos . The big disaster for Bruce would be a clutch of press cuttings with no mention of "Super Snacks", or, even worse, a knocking story of some kind.

All this conjecture was making Bruce feel decidedly hungry, and he helped himself to three packs of "Super Snacks" breakfast bars from the boardroom table where they had been displayed by the public relations girls. Containing just 150 calories, and fortified with six vitamins, these chocolate-coated, raisin-stuffed bars were delicious, and ideal for the whole family.

He almost believed his own sales patter. As Bruce knew, there was no substitute for a proper, balanced breakfast, but if parents hadn't got time...why shouldn't FizzCo cash in?

Bruce's own parents had been big breakfast eaters: most days, they enjoyed porridge with brown sugar and cream, followed by fried eggs, bacon, sausage and tomatoes, plus several slices of hot buttered toast and marmalade. Their eldest son didn't enjoy many of these fried feasts as he was sent away to boarding school at the age of seven. The breakfasts at school had been Spartan, but nutritious: porridge or bread, butter and jam with a glass of milk.

After enduring his formative years without the comfort of fatty fried breakfasts, or parental love, Bruce was now spending his middle age making up for his earlier deprivations. He enjoyed food - a lot of it , the greasier the better - and he also indulged in extra-marital affairs whenever the opportunity presented itself. Luckily, Ellen was too preoccupied with her two horses, and various charities to notice. Their three children were at boarding school, so didn't need much attention, apart from during the holidays, when the whole family re-located to their villa just outside Marbella, Spain. Even on holiday, the local golf club provided Bruce with a good excuse for spending long hours away from Ellen and the kids.

The best thing about Spain, he thought now, was the restaurants: you could get anything from a huge steak, the size of half a cow, to a vast plateful of paella with chips on the side, and the booze was brilliant, too. Life wasn't all bad while you could enjoy a long, lazy lunch in the sun. Or, in London, for that matter. He promised himself a large lunch at Simpson's on the Strand after this morning's press conference was over. He would deserve it.

Half an hour later, the publicity machine was in full swing. The vast boardroom was buzzing. Six pretty public relations girls, dressed in black mini skirts, were handing out doughnuts, croissants and coffee to a couple of dozen journalists, along with folders containing details of the nationwide eating habits survey, and the new "Super Snacks" products.

****

Caroline Dempsey avoided the pile of sugar-coated jam doughnuts, and took a cup of black coffee from one of the PR girls. Rows of steel and leather chairs had been set up at one end of the room, and she sat down at the far end of the front row, near the door. Experience had told her that it was wise to be close to the speaker at a Press Conference, but also important to have an easy escape route, in case she needed to phone the office quickly. One by one, the other journalists followed her, most aiming for end of row seats.

Her neighbour was an earnest-looking young man with a leather bag over his shoulder, tape recorder and notebook in one hand and a doughnut in the other. He sat down heavily and some of the jam from the doughnut plopped over Caroline's denim skirt, washed the night before and dried on the hot tank in the airing cupboard. Great start to my day, she thought.

At 9.30am precisely, Bruce James walked to the front of the rows of chairs and stood behind a small metal table with a glass, bottle of mineral and laptop computer on it.

"Welcome to the headquarters of the Independent Food Manufacturers' Association, " he said. "Some of you know me already as the Marketing Director of FizzCo, but today I am here as Vice-chairman of the Association. As you are aware, we have been working hard to help the Government tackle the obesity crisis. Our members have already lowered sugar, salt and fat levels in many of our products, and now we are altering the price structure of our healthy food ranges. The survey launched today shows that people want to eat healthier foods, but often find them too expensive - and the Association is rising to the challenge by making a commitment to cutting the prices of all foods in the "healthy eating" sector by 3% over the next three years. The supermarkets are backing this initiative by keeping their own profit margins at present levels.

"You might wonder how we can afford to do this, without upsetting our shareholders", he continued, with a much-practised wry smile on his lips. "In fact, we have decided that the health of our consumers is more important than profit. Although, of course, we hope that, by reducing prices we will sell more products."

This is all bullshit, thought Caroline. Profit margins are already so high that the billions made by big food manufacturers won't even be dented by a 3% cut over three years. They'll simply screw the people who supply the basic raw materials for their products, the farmers, and won't even feel the pinch themselves.

Unaware of the collective feeling of distaste among the journalists in front of him, Bruce was enjoying himself. The audience was paying attention, and the girl at the end of the front row had luscious breasts. He must make time to chat to her after the presentation. This was going better than he thought. It was the perfect moment for the hard sell. He pressed a key on the laptop on the table in front of him, and a large logo appeared on the screen behind him. The words "Super Snacks" in large, flowing script, were picked out in green and gold (such healthy colours!) on a blue background. Below the logo were images of a happy, smiling family of four on bikes, obviously full of energy and sparkling good health.

"This is our new brand label," said Bruce. "We are delighted that the products in the range are all made from the healthiest possible ingredients and are low in price, so they fit nicely into the Association's new, greener initiative. As you know, our company is already in the forefront of the world's movement to decrease carbon emissions, by running our factories with the latest, cleanest equipment. Many of our deliveries are made by barge along the network of canals in the Midlands and our fleet of barges will be featured in the television advertisements to accompany the launch of the range. It include low-calorie biscuits, fat-free crisps and the product which I think will be most popular of all - especially with the kiddies - crunchy, chewy "Super Snacks" Breakfast Bars. These have a delicious corn crisp base with nuts, raisins and yogurt, come in small, single packs and are ideal to replace breakfast, for lunch boxes or to eat after exercise.

"We will be giving you samples, and the publicity girls are here to answer any questions you might have. First, though, please enjoy the ten minute film about the UK Eating Habits survey which we have prepared for you . The full survey findings are in your Press Pack. At 10.30am, your photographers will be invited to the gym downstairs for some pictures with England soccer captain Phil Walker, who now uses the Super Snacks products as part of his training diet. We will also be donating some of our profits on this range to the London 2012 Olympic Games fund, with special on-pack promotional activity starting next year. Thank you very much for your attention."

Polite clapping from some of the PR team followed, and, before any of the journalists could chip in with a question, the lights dimmed and the film was shown. It was a collection of jolly interviews, TV news-style, with three overweight families talking about their food budgets. The glamorous female interviewer questioned members of each family about their efforts to slim down. The film was shot in their own kitchens, where the clutter of food cartons and empty cola cans indicated that interviewees were living on a diet of fast food and ready-meals. No fresh produce was visible. The "victims" also appeared to be exceptionally lethargic, barely moving an inch while being interviewed, and smiling uncertainly when the camera panned in for close-up shots.

This could have been caused by sheer terror at the ordeal of having a camera team in your home, thought Caroline, or possibly they were unable to move because of their size. One chap must have weighed 28st, and a teenage boy had three chins.

The Evening Echo picture desk had sent a photographer to cover the appearance of Phil Walker, so, after the film ended, she made contact with him. She was relieved when she saw that he was one of the older guys on the desk, a man who was equally at home in a war zone as he was photographing royalty (or a footballer who thought he was royalty). They followed the other journalists into the lift which took them down six floors to the gym in the basement of the building. Bruce and his entourage were waiting to usher them into the brightly-lit room where the England soccer captain was already waiting. Stacks of "Super Snacks" boxes were arranged between the various pieces of exercise equipment.

The photographer moved in swiftly for a close-up shot of Phil who was sitting on an exercise bike wearing a green, yellow and white "Super Snacks" T-shirt, and very tight dark green shorts, clutching a "Super Snacks" Breakfast Bar. Lean, muscular and tanned, with a diamond earring, and closely shaved head, today he was looking decidedly sulky. He had missed a penalty in the previous Saturday's match, and was still smarting after a telling-off from his club manager.

Caroline followed the photographer. She seized her opportunity: "How much are they paying you for this lot, Phil, " she whispered in his ear, sweetly, so the other journalists couldn't hear. "Enough to keep your ex wife in designer knickers for the rest of her life, I bet."

" Mind your own fucking business, " replied Phil, very softly. "It's more than you'd earn in a lifetime, darling, that's for sure. It all tastes like shit, but if they want me to promote it, they've got to pay.. that's the rule. Nice jugs, girl."

At that point, two large, ugly-looking minders ushered Caroline away, and, after that, Phil refused to say another word. Disgruntled, the other photographers took a few shots, and left, and the journalists went back upstairs for their free samples.

Caroline made a beeline for Bruce. He was a large man, at least 6ft 2in tall, with an ample gut, so Caroline had to stand very close to him just to hear what he said. This gave Bruce a chance to admire her chest, while she fired a few pertinent questions:

"Mr. James, do the "Super Snacks" breakfast bars contain all the nutrients a child would need in the morning?, " she asked, politely, gazing up at him from beneath heavily mascar-ed eyelashes.

"Well, they are not meant as a complete substitute for breakfast, "admitted Bruce. " There aren't as many vitamins and minerals in the bars as there would be in a bowl of porridge topped with fruit, for instance. Personally, I think porridge is the best breakfast of all, but then I'm rather partial to it. "

Caroline sensed a chance for a really good quote. She moved in for the kill, taking a deep breath which had the effect of making her breasts rise slightly. "How much exercise do you take, Mr. James? I expect you use the gym here whenever you're in town? FizzCo is based in Hertfordshire, I gather, but I'm sure you must use these facilities or have similar facilities at your factory?"

Bruce, transfixed by Caroline's bosom, replied without thinking: "Now, my dear, you must realise that I'm a very busy man. I don't have time for exercise. I confess that today is the first time I've ever been in the Association's gym. I know I'm overweight, but my doctor tells me I'm fit as a fiddle. However, we at FizzCo are very mindful of the duty we have to encourage our customers to eat well and take regular exercise. Of course, it's up to the individual how they tackle the problem, but with our new price structure and "Super Snacks" products we are doing our best to help the nation shape up.

"I do hope you will write a good story about our efforts. By the way, we are taking a few selected journalists to New York next month to the International Obesity Summit. I'll get the PR company to send you details. Here's my card."

Gotcha!. Caroline felt elated as she took the card from his outstretched hand. What a prat. The piece would write itself. She thanked Bruce, gathered up her Press Pack and bag of samples and leaflets, and made for the lift.

Outside the building, she hailed a taxi. As a fairly junior member of the Echo's staff, she was supposed to travel by bus or tube, but this was a special occasion: her story would definitely make a page three lead, and, if it was a slow news day, it might even end up on the front page. She reached into the goodie bag and selected a packet of "Super Snacks" biscuits. Only 50 calories each, so just one would be fine.

When the cab reached the Evening Echo front entrance twenty minutes later she had somehow polished off the entire pack. Never mind, she could make up for it by skipping lunch. She had a story to write.

Chapter Three

Our low-fat snacks are bad for kids' health - say FizzCo
Exclusive, by Caroline Dempsey

Bruce James, UK boss of the FizzCo soft drinks and snacks multi-national empire, stated yesterday that his firm's new line of "healthy" products are bad for children.

In an amazingly frank confession, very similar to the gaffe by jewellery boss Gerald Ratner who admitted that his baubles were "rubbish", Mr. James told me that the company's new "Super Snacks" Breakfast Bars are not suitable to serve up as a child's breakfast. He advises parents to give their kids porridge and fruit instead.

Yet, in the company's publicity material, the Bars are described as a "perfect breakfast in a wrapper".

England soccer captain, Phil Walker, who has been signed up for a six figure sum to promote the brand, is equally unflattering: He says the snacks "taste like s**t!"

Dr. Brian Donovan, senior lecturer in Nutrition and Food Science at The Royal College, London was already late for his 2.30pm. lecture to a group of first year students who were studying the effect of a very high carbohydrate diet on pregnant mice.

Flustered, he grabbed some papers off his desk, and thrust them into his brown leather briefcast, upsetting a half-empty mug of tea as he did so. He pulled a blue silk handkerchief out of his top pocket, and started dabbing at the mess. It had started to soak into the early edition of The Evening Echo which his secretary had opened at page three and placed by the side of his computer terminal.

She had stuck a yellow "post it" note at the top of an article by Caroline Dempsey. "FizzCo are on the list you gave me of firms which might fund research next year. Do you still want me to send them our usual begging letter?"

Dr. Donovan stopped mopping, and started reading. After the first four paragraphs, the article went on to give quotes from health experts on the dangers of high-sugar bars for kids', listing health hazards such as dental decay, obesity and diabetes. An accompanying picture layout compared the fat, sugar, and salt content of various snack foods.

The usual "shock, horror" tactics, he thought. However, that man Bruce James is a blithering idiot. The "Super Snacks" breakfast bars should have been promoted differently. Claiming that they were fine as a complete subsitute for a proper breakfast meal was stupid. As for using Phil Walker to plug the snacks, that was silly too. The Government had already published strong guidelines for the advertising industry, asking them not to use sports and pop stars to promote high-fat, high-sugar snacks aimed at children. Using celebrities to promote so-called "healthy" products only worked if the food really was nutritious, and as far as he could see from the figures quoted in the article, the snacks were sugar-loaded, and contained a fair amount of salt, and a couple of artificial colourants, as well. Thank goodness he hadn't been involved in the research for the product.

Research and consultancy work for food manufacturers, to help them develop, modify and test food products, was the life-blood of Dr. Donovan's department. Without sufficient funds from companies such as FizzCo, he would be unable to afford the computers and expensive lab equipment he needed. Foreign students bought in a lot of money as well, but it would be impossible to maintain standards without cash from the multinationals.

As he left his office, and strode down the labyrinth of corridors which stretched across the sprawling South London building, towards his lecture room, Dr. Donovan wondered if the few idealists in his current crop of PhD students who wanted to go into teaching realised that their biggest asset would be a good grasp of the art of writing effective begging letters. You simply had to kiss arse if you wanted to get the cash. He often cringed when he read some of his own letters, asking for much-needed funds in return for organising a scientific study which would prove that a product really was good for the health of the nation.

Unfortunately, all research has a commercial purpose, which was why it was so hard to give an unbiased result: the scientist operated from a clear brief, and no matter how many blind, double-blind and double, double blind tests were carried out, that purpose was always right at the top of the agenda. Even Government-funded projects invariably included a political goal hidden away behind noble-sounding objectives. No wonder nothing had been done to halt the biggest health catastrophy facing the Western world, when there were so many vested interests determined to make money from selling food and drink.

Stopping briefly at a vending machine to grab a paper cup of light brown, scalding hot coffee to replace the one he'd spilt, Dr. Donovan recalled how many times he'd read the results of dubious clinical trials published in respected nutrition journals. Often there would be two papers which directly contradicted each other. Not surprising, really, when the number of people studied was so small. How could you tell anything, he wondered, if you examined just 100 people in one small country community in Denmark or Sweden?

When he had left his college at a large North West university thirty years earlier, Brian Donovan had been full of enthusiasm for his profession. After gaining his doctorate, he was determined to combine teaching with research into his three passions: child nutrition, post-operative nutrition in hospitals, and the causes and treatment of obesity. These were areas which had interested him while he was at college in London and Liverpool. In the early seventies, he had seen plenty of under-fed kids roaming the back streets of both cities, and had witnessed the fall in standards of dietetics services in hospitals. Even in those days there were already signs that obesity would become a major world health issue. On an exchange trip to the University of California, he had his first experience of seeing 35 stone-plus men and women in hospital, awaiting gastro-bypass surgery, and visited a summer camp for overweight children.

Although he had been an A-grade student, and spent long hours studying, Brian had managed, somehow, to aquire a reputation for seducing college women. His gentle manner, tall, rather gangly frame, floppy fair hair and soft, faintly freckled, almost feminine skin, seemed to bring out the mothering instinct in his female fellow students. He came from a cosy, intellectual background: his mother was an English teacher, his father was head of Charlton High, one of London's top independent boys' grammar schools. He had three older sisters, two married and one working as a junior doctor in a big teaching hospital .

Grace, Brian's mother, had somehow contrived to bring up her family, hold down her teaching job, and create the kind of home which would never be featured on a TV reality show. It was just too civilised, and swear words were rarely heard. The spacious Victorian detached house in Cheam was warm, welcoming, furnished with polished antiques, exquisite faded Indian rugs and soft velvet curtains. There was a grand piano in the drawing room, a constantly used Aga in the kitchen and well-filled bookshelves in every room. As the youngest child, Brian was a little spoilt by his mother and sisters, and, quite naturally, he grew up enjoying the company of women. Unlike most men of his generation, he didn't think they came from another planet...Venus, Uranus, or anywhere else. So, at college, he talked to his female colleagues as if they were people, not sex objects.

This meant that he notched up far more conquests than his

male friends, who were envious and irritated. After all, Brian wasn't particularly good-looking, he had a scrawny physique and was useless at sports. When his contemporaries at college asked women students what they saw in Brian, their answer was invariably the same: he listens to what we say, he's charming, and he knows where the "g" spot is. Women's magazines had recently identified this spot as the key to a good love-making experience for a woman, and Brian's doctor sister, Cheryl, had sent him a useful cutting from a popular new monthly magazine complete with colourful diagrams. Sadly, the other men in his group didn't have the same advantage. At that time, there were no helpful "lad mags" to explain these delicate things.

So, when Brian became engaged to a brilliant young Scottish law student called Molly McFaddeon, the men were furious, and the girls were envious. After graduating, the couple were married in Edinburgh, and lived with Brian's parents for a year while Molly took up a junior position in a London chamber of solicitors, and Brian plunged into his first teaching post, as a junior lecturer at a North London polytechnic. They saved for a deposit on their first house, a semi in Barnes, and, for a while, were blissfully happy.

****

While he negotiated the various, almost impossibly dangerous manoevres that were necessary to obtain a cup of coffee from the machine without severely scalding his hands, Brian wondered if Molly was having a good day in her chrome and teak office in the newest, and, to his mind, most hideous-looking building in the City of London. She had always aimed high. Well, now she was a partner in a big firm, Dunmore and Partners, and spent her days sitting on the forty second floor of a glass carbuncle overlooking the Thames. You couldn't get much higher than that.

Her speciality was show business law, particularly contracts, and since so many minor (and a few major) celebrities seemed to get themselves into trouble these days, she was always busy. There was no doubt about it, Molly was brilliant, and very successful. She was also skilful at choosing classic designer clothes that flattered her slim figure, reddish gold hair and pale skin. She had been asked many times to appear in Sunday supplement articles as an example of a "powerful woman of the 21st century", but was far too discreet to allow herself to indulge in such vain self-promotion. For once, there was substance behind the image: Molly was energetic, clever, and a devoted mother to their two children, Amy, 15 and 17 year old Toby. Their north London home was immaculate, and their lifestyle was the envy of Brian's less affluent academic friends.

So why is it, he reflected, that some marriages just stagnate, while others seem to grow? I still love Molly, of course I do, but we don't have time to talk these days, except on holiday. Even our sex life has to be planned around Molly's case-load, and, the children's needs always come first with both of us. I have to express myself and is it my fault that I work surrounded by nubile young women on the threshold of their lives who want to tell me all their problems, both academic and personal?

Walking along the last twenty five metres of corridor to the lab, he very nearly dropped the half-full paper cup when one of these nubile young women came dashing along, overtaking him just before the glass-panelled lab door. She turned sharply, catching the delicate heel of one of her leather sandals in a knot-hole in the wooden floor, dropping two large textbooks. "Slow down, Jenny, " said Brian, stooping to retrieve the books, "I'm late as well, so we can go in together."

Jenny, a nineteen year old first-year student with blonde hair, a nervous laugh, and a passion for purple (her sandals, mini-skirt, cropped top and navel stud were all in shades of purple, from palest mauve to puce), was Brian's favourite "fresher". In her first year interview earlier in the summer, she had told him about her ambition to work with the World Health Organisation, helping third world countries to develop viable and sustainable nutrition programmes. He didn't have the heart to warn her that the three "wicked serpents" which accompanied all aid initatives, (red tape, corruption, and lack of funds), frequently crushed the life out of such projects. She would learn. Meanwhile, maybe he should invite her to his office later that afternoon to discuss her first essay, on the role of dietary fibre in the adolescent diet. She had written a thoughtful, well-researched 5000 word piece, and it certainly merited a half-hour of in-depth discussion and analysis. As did Jenny.

Brian's lecture style was laid-back, friendly, but firm. He explained difficult concepts clearly and spoke fluently. The two hour session passed swiftly, and he felt very satisfied as he walked back to his office at 4.45pm. Now he could get his mind around writing a couple of "begging" letters, and preparing a hard-hitting paper for the forthcoming International Summit on Obesity, to be held in New York in November. The crisis Summit had been called by the United Nations to examine the ever-increasing rise in world-wide obesity, and, hopefully, to come up with some kind of internationally-agreed strategy to deal with it. Delegates from over forty nations would be present: scientists, politicians, and industry representatives from North and South America, Europe, Africa and the Near and Far East.

Brian hoped that some kind of consensus would be achieved, and practical strategies agreed. Like the Kyoto Summit on Climate Change sixteen years earlier, this meeting could affect the future of mankind. He had decided to follow his conscience and write a paper that would make delegates sit up and listen. His paper, provisionally entitled "Obesity: the biggest health issue of the 21st Century", would be a shocker. Although it went against the grain, Brian knew that he had to risk his career by being controversial: for once, headlines were necessary. He would back up his argument with plenty of scientifically proven facts and figures, but the thrust would be - well, sensational.

His secretary went home at 4pm, but she had left another

"post-it" note on his desk. "Read your emails, Brian. Four sound important. See you tomorrow." He sat down at his desk , switched on his computer terminal, logged onto his emails and clicked on the "inbox" icon. There were six messages: one from the College Vice-chancellor asking him to attend a financial review, three from food manufacturers wanting meetings to discuss projects, one from Susan Simpson, a hospital dietitian requesting advice on a clinical problem, and the last from Caroline Dempsey, a journalist from a London evening paper who wanted a quote about diabetes in children.

Although the first four messages were probably more important than the last two, Brian decided to allow himself a few minutes of indulgence. He liked talking to people who were working in the field; it was refreshing after a day spent teaching or in the cloistered atmosphere of research. Susan Simpson's email was interesting. She sounded puzzled about the nutrient content of some products, and was obviously concerned about her patients. She had left a telephone number.

He also loved chatting to journalists, especially female ones. They were always amusing, and cut straight to the point. Their questions reminded Brian of the huge responsibility scientists had ; it was vital that people understood his work. Unlike many members of the scientific establishment, he always tried to give short, accurate answers to journalists and, consequently, was rarely misquoted. He had spoken to Caroline Dempsey before, and she was very witty and flirtatious on the phone. Perhaps it was time they met up for lunch. He needed some good tips if he was going to succeed in injecting a "tabloid-friendly" tone into his paper for the New York conference . Maybe Caroline could help.

Brian picked up the phone - he was going to enjoy both calls.

****

Chapter Four

<u>Le Bon Gourmet: Luncheon Menu:</u>

Fois Gras de Canard maison, et cèpes geratines au beaufort
ou
Vol au vent de Roquefort aux champignons flambés au Calvados

****

Fricassée de lapin a la Bière avec pommes de terre Lyonnais
ou
Medaillon de Flétin en croute
ou
Magret de canard entier, sauce poivre vert

****

Tarte au pommes avec Crème Chantilly
Assiette de fromages.
Price: £55, inclusive (Service non compris)
Calories: 3,982 Fat Grams: 567

The restaurant was a small, badly lit, pretentious French establishment in Covent Garden where the waiters were so off-hand that lunch could take up to three hours. However, it was popular because the food was excellent and the tables were far enough apart for serious, private conversation. The menus were hand-written daily in perfect, flowing script on pristine white cards. Like every other restaurant in the country, the *Bon Gourmet*'s menus carried calorie and fat gram details to comply with Government "anti-obesity" legislation which was designed to help inform people of the dangers of over-eating.

In reality, this information was ignored by complacent overweight male executives, and made business meetings less enjoyable for weight-conscious women. In 2008, the Bridget Jones's of the workplace were still wracked with guilt most of the time, seeking comfort in cream cakes, red wine and vodka.

As Brian Donovan sat waiting for his guest to arrive, he wondered which of the various companies for which he was currently carrying out research could be persuaded to pick up the bill. Probably the Kent Apple Growers' Federation: they were desperate for some good press, and Brian was in the process of setting up a study to prove that munching an apple before a meal can help you lose up to a stone in a year without changing your eating habits. It would definitely prove just that because the Federation were coughing up £50,000 to pay for the reseach. His guest, Caroline Dempsey of the Evening Echo, was bound to be interested even though she had phoned him about another topic.

When he'd returned her call, Caroline had explained that she needed a nutrition expert to give her some background about the dangers of sugar-loaded snack foods when fed to children on a regular basis. Could this kind of junk cause Type 2 diabetes? Brian had suggested that they have lunch, as the topic was a very complex one. He'd brought a lot of relevant scientific papers with him, but his real reason for the lunch was to meet Caroline: she sounded just the right kind of woman for a late summer liaison: warm, witty, exciting, the total opposite of his cool, organised wife.

This was going to be a fascinating week. There was the chance of starting something with the young student, today's lunch with a feisty, ambitious reporter was sure to be interesting, and tomorrow he was due to meet up with Susan Simpson, the young dietitian who wanted nutritional help. She'd agreed to his suggestion of an early evening meeting followed by a "working" supper. Sometimes, his status as a leading nutrition scientist really was an advantage. Even though his wife earned twice as much as he did, Brian was glad that she wasn't the only one with a prestige job. He sighed, contentedly, and sipped some mineral water.

****

Caroline was 20 minutes late for the lunch, thanks to a sudden email from the Health Editor (the cow!) who demanded 300 words on the subject of compulsory contraceptive machines for schools, another recent Health Department innovation. The short article was to be a "filler" for the weekly healthy living supplement. In ten minutes flat, Caroline polished off a concise think-piece on the various disadvantages of encouraging kids to have sex during school hours (the limited availability of desk space was one consideration), then grabbed her long, white linen coat from the peg near her desk and dashed downstairs to find a taxi. In the cab on the way to the restaurant, she repaired her make-up and sprayed herself with Chanel No 5, her chosen perfume for the day.

When she walked through the restaurant door, blonde hair flying, her coat swung open revealing an expanse of chest bursting out of a tight pink v-necked T-shirt . Brian nearly choked on his mineral water.

"Caroline, how lovely to meet you at last, " he said, getting up from his seat, while a waiter helped Caroline remove her coat. "This is a real pleasure. You write such well-researched pieces. I saw your story on FizzCo, and it certainly was hard-hitting . I hope I can help you. What would you like to drink?"

Caroline sat down heavily on the small French cafe style chair, (it was unusual to find such small chairs in a restaurant in these days of expanding backsides), bosom heaving, and leaned back, stretching her bare legs under the table. She was wearing a short, full, pink cotton skirt which matched her skimpy T-shirt. Around her neck was a large gold locket which rested on her chest . It was a hot day, and tiny beads of perspiration clung to her neck. A faint, silver stream of moisture was working its way down between her breasts. Brian was mesmerised.

"I'll have a glass of white wine, please Dr. Donovan, " she said, breathlessly. "Now, what I want to know is what eminent scientific people like you are going to do about the way our children are being poisoned by the fast food multinationals. The facts are right there: there's been a sharp increase in diabetes in children over the last few years, and now we're getting more and more stories about kids suffering heart attacks at the age of five and six because they are carrying too much weight. FizzCo are the perfect example of a company that should take far more responsibility for the junk they put on supermarket shelves. What have you got to say about all this? I'm sure you must be furious at the lack of action by the Government."

Brian had temporarily forgotten that journalists get down to the nitty gritty very quickly. A few pleasantries before they ordered lunch might have been more polite, but obviously this girl wasn't into small talk. He wondered if she was the same in bed. His preferred seduction routine was leisurely: lots of intimate conversation, livened with a few glasses of champagne, followed by plenty of touching, stroking, even a bit of tickling, then a sensual afternoon or evening of copulation in a pleasant country hotel. With Caroline, it would probably be "wham, bam, thank you.man, " and on to the next lover..and next story.

His ardour cooled somewhat by this thought, he spoke quietly, in measured terms (a technique which never failed with his female students). As he spoke, he put his elbows on the table, and placed his long fingers together. He'd allowed his hair to grow longer (much to his wife's annoyance), wore an open-necked blue cotton shirt, beige chinos and pale suede shoes, the effect was very professorial indeed. He gazed into Caroline's eyes :

"Miss Dempsey, I'm afraid it isn't as simple as that. The Government has already taken steps to encourage companies to lower the amounts of sugar, salt and fat in their products, and have banned TV advertising of junk food targeting children. I am undertaking a number of studies on school-children and diet, which will help provide valuable information and we are also looking at the whole issue of satiety - that is, which foods fill you up, yet contain few calories. Apples are a useful anti-hunger food, by the way, and I'm just doing some exciting work on how they can help in the fight against obesity. Such a simple food, a nutrition storehouse, really. Anyway, I digress.

"The problem is that all these projects have to be funded, and, of course, it is usually the food manufacturers who provide the funding. In my view, it's best to work with the industry, rather than against it. On the subject of diabetes in children, that really is a worry. Parents must be educated about the dangers of feeding children too many sugary snacks between meals. What would *you* like to eat, by the way? The luncheon menu is always good here. I recommend the terrine and rabbit, followed by the apple tart and cream. "

Brian was used to guiding young, inexperienced female students through the complexities of restaurant menus, so he genuinely thought he was being helpful.

"No, thanks, " said Caroline, sharply. "I'm trying to lose a bit of weight. I'll have the fish with a mixed salad, no dessert. Another glass of wine would be nice, though. I have to say that you sound more like a health minister than an independent scientist - all talk and no balls "

Caroline hesitated....maybe, just maybe, she had gone too far? Silly girl, she'd broken the first rule of journalism: insults are best left until lunch has been paid for! She leaned forward, smiled gently and continued:

" Please don't be offended, but surely you are worried? It's so easy to lay the blame on parents - a typical Government cop-out.

These companies are so concerned about making money that they want people to consume a lot of processed food. It's not in their interest to have a healthy nation that's lost its taste for Super Snacks, is it? Does it ever occur to you that while they pretend to co-operate with the Government on lowering sugar, salt and fat in their products, they could be beavering away to find something else to put in food which is indetectable yet makes us all overeat? It's something that has definitely occurred to me. After meeting the Marketing Director of Fizzco UK, who is obviously terrified of his US bosses, I truly believe that these companies would do anything to make people dependent on their products. Think of the cigarette companies, the burger people. What a load of crooks! Surely you have been approached to work on something like that?"

At that moment, a waiter appeared at Brian's shoulder, giving him a short breathing space. He ordered the fish and salad for Caroline and the rabbit for himself. Forgoing the starter and pudding would keep his bill down, although Caroline was now into her second glass of Chablis. After ordering the food, Brian sat back in his chair and watched his guest sipping her wine, while he thought about her comments.

His first reaction to her outburst was to feel deeply offended that she even considered that he might be working on research which would help make food manufacturers richer at the expense of people's health. His whole life had been devoted to helping people improve their nutritional standards. He had worked with one big company to formulate supplements to help post-operative patients to recover more quickly, had spent a year working on a project in Liverpool which encouraged breakfast clubs in schools (funded, naturally by the world's richest cereal company), and none of his current research could be described as simply for commercial gain.

Yet, Caroline might have a point. He knew that not all scientists were as scrupulous in their dealings with large companies as he tried to be. They were often vain, and easily seduced by money. Many of them weren't worldly wise in these matters either. They could easily be persuaded to embark on seemingly innocent projects which turned out to have highly controversial consequences. He sometimes wondered how pharmaceutical chemists could sleep at night, when their industry was making such vast profits out of so many drugs with harmful side-effects . Every few months there seemed to be a new story emerging of a drug which had been sold before sufficient checks had been made. Three years earlier, in 2005, one anti-inflammatory drug had been withdrawn after it was found to increase the risk of heart disease. Surely, somewhere, a scientist must have suspected that it wasn't safe? He shuddered slightly and decided not to rise to the bait. This lunch was proving to be more tricky than he had thought it would be.

"Sadly, no, Caroline, " he said, smiling. I've never been asked to get involved in any such research. I must be too ethical in my approach, and my reputation is based on my published body of work, which is all in the scientific journals for anyone to see. I couldn't compromise my integrity by taking on anything of that nature. In any case, it would be a difficult project to set up. It could be argued that simply over-processing foods, removing fibre and natural nutrients, does in itself encourage over-consumption, but actually adding something to stimulate the appetite is another matter. There is no natural ingredient, as far as I am aware, which would produce this effect. In any case, the Government do monitor food additives very carefully, you know. "

Caroline laughed out loud. "Oh yes? What about "E" numbered additives, like colourants? Several of these potions were gaily added to products, and then hastily withdrawn when it was discovered that they made children hyper-active. And trans fats are harmful too, yet there they are - large as life - in many processed foods. Don't kid me that sufficient checks are made. You know damn well that mad cow disease was caused by neglect. It's an extreme example, but, frankly, in this game you never take for granted anything the Government or boffins like yourself say. When the Sudan 1 colourant, which is carcinogenic, was discovered, there was a big outcry and products were withdrawn from the supermarket shelves, but what about the carcinogenic ingredients that the Government actually does allow in foods? If journalists like me don't keep on nagging away, we're not doing our job properly. "

She paused, dived down under the table and produced a large floral handkerchief from one of the many pockets in her enormous dark blue denim handbag. She mopped her forehead, and chest and took another gulp of Chablis.

"Look, I'm sorry Brian - may I call you that?- but you are living in cloud cuckoo land. I am determined to carry on digging into this whole business. After meeting the boss of FizzCo the other day, I wouldn't trust any of them. The amazing thing is that I wrote a really hard piece about his revolting Super Snacks and the very next day he rang me up and invited me on a jolly to New York. Strange, that. Apparently, there's an International Summit on Obesity and FizzCo are taking ten journalists over. I thought it sounded suspiciously like bribery or sheer desperation, but my Editor wants me to go along and dig more dirt. He loves this stuff - and, luckily, FizzCo don't advertise in the Evening Echo."

Brian was quick to pick up on this remark.

"So, Caroline, you're now telling me that if they *did* advertise, you wouldn't have trashed them in the paper? Sounds like the Press aren't exactly knights in shining armour protecting the nation from being poisoned, are they? Gotcha!"

Caroline threw her head back and roared with laughter. "You're absolutely right, of course Brian, but I still have my readers' interests at heart. I'm looking forward to the Conference, anyway. There are bound to be some great stories, and I can do some serious shopping as well. Will you be going?"

At that moment, the waiter returned with their food: a large portion of fish in a shiny puff pastry case for Caroline, and a generous helping of rabbit with delicious-looking, mashed potatoes for Brian. Caroline's salad was perfect: spinach leaves, rocket, slivers of celeriac and red onion and tiny tomatoes, all in a light vinaigrette dressing. A large basket of crusty bread with a stone dish containing creamy-looking butter was placed in the centre of the table. Caroline took three pieces of bread, and stuck her knife into the dish, digging out a liberal quantity of butter.

"This is gorgeous," she said, piercing the puff pastry surrounding her fish with her knife. "The diet starts tomorrow. Come on, Brian, you're the expert, should I try Atkins again, or something else? I want to shed at least a stone before going to New York. I don't want to know what's good for me, I want to know what really works."

"Well, if you want to pile all the weight back on again, and more, and possibly have a heart attack when you're forty, follow the Atkins high fat plan again," said Brian. "Otherwise, I would suggest you just try eating - and drinking - more sensibly. Of course, you must exercise as well. Do you manage to get to a gym?"

"You've got to be joking," she said. "I only get one day off a week, and I see my boyfriend then. He lives in Birmingham, so I take the train up to his flat, or he comes to London. It's a long-distance affair but it seems to work. No jealousy, no strings, no boredom. Are you married?"

"Yes, and I've got two teenaged children as well," said Brian. "My wife works in the city, so life gets complicated. Of course, the kids' needs always come first. Most evenings I like to get home after lectures, so I see as much of them as possible. Then, I work in my study. By the way, I will be going to the Conference you mentioned. I am actually presenting a paper there, so we'll probably meet up. I've been working at it for months. I thought I was being quite controversial and hard-hitting, but after talking to you, my criticism of the food industry will sound quite tame, I'm afraid!"

Caroline put down her knife and fork, carefully. Delicious though her meal was, with its wonderful aroma of perfectly cooked halibut and light, golden pastry, the smell of a good story was even better; in fact it was almost orgasmic:

"Can you let me have a look at your paper before it's presented?" she said, a bit too casually. "It will just give me a handle on the general thrust, and I promise I will respect any embargo put on the date of release to the press."

It was Brian's turn to roar with laughter. "Come on Caroline, what do you take me for? You'll have to wait for the Conference. I'll be honest: I was going to ask you for some advice on how to put some of my main points in easy language so the press would be able to interpret it properly, but after our conversation, I think I'd better tone it down!

"Now, let's get on to the subject of diabetes in children I've got a few interesting scientific papers here which you are welcome to study. Frankly, it is a time bomb waiting to go off. If cases continue to increase, we will run out of spaces in diabetes clinics, there will be more amputees in about 15 years time, and many youngsters will be on insulin most of their lives. This is serious stuff. Caroline, and you can certainly quote me. "

Caroline realised that this was all she was likely to get from Brian, as far as work was concerned. Of course, he was gagging for sex - all academics were - but she'd have to disappoint him. She had to get back to the funny farm, or the Features Editor would start sending her rude text messages. She stuffed one last piece of bread and butter in her mouth, took a long swig of wine, and stood up.

"Brian, I'm so sorry. I'm going to have to dash away. It's been a great lunch. Now, promise me that you will think about what I've said, and if you come across any dodgy bits of research, you'll phone me. I'm not kidding. I really do believe there could be a plot out there...or several plots!"

Brian stood up, and, on impulse, kissed her cheek. "You are amazing, Caroline, " he said. "Here are the papers I mentioned. Now, just relax. I promise you that we scientists are not scheming to fatten up the nation. No-one would do such a thing. What we all need is to encourage people to eat properly...and that includes you Caroline. Take care of that great body of yours. "

He wondered whether he might have gone too far with his last remark, but Caroline laughed. "Now, Dr. Donovan, you are flirting with me…I can't have that. But, thanks anyway. " She heaved up her heavy bag from under the table, stuffed the papers inside, then waved at a waiter to fetch her coat. She put it over one arm, looked back at Brian and waved quickly, then almost ran out of the door.

Brian sat down and ordered a coffee from the waiter, who was furious for being called out from the kitchen, where he had been enjoying a quiet cigarette and glass of Bordeaux left behind by a gent on table seven.

Luckily, Brian's next lecture was at 4pm, so when his coffee arrived ten minutes later, he was still able to spend fifteen minutes sipping it slowly while he recovered from the Dempsey onslaught. No, she definitely was not his type, but what a girl! The clothes were tarty and tasteless, of course, but she certainly knew what she wanted. Maybe she would be fun for a quickie in New York? After he'd presented his paper, naturally.

****

The stifling, Indian Summer had given way to cooler, blustery weather. Gusts of wind blew into the main entrance of East Central Hospital, forcing the double revolving doors to whizz around like a pair of glass and chrome spinning tops. Susan clutched her thin beige cotton trenchcoat around her body as she struggled out through the left-hand door. It was certainly getting a lot cooler, and storms were forecast for later in the week.

It was a familiar autumn pattern, she thought, as a particularly violent gust of wind caught her heavy leather briefcase, and almost wrenched it out of her hand. Crazy, sizzling hot temperatures, followed by chill winds, rain and 70 mph storms. Now, everyone accepted that global warming was to blame for the strange weather, but world governments still couldn't agree on how to deal with it. Susan took the view that, while the politicians dithered and seemed hell-bent on destroying the planet, all the ordinary person could do was to be prepared. There was a bit of loose guttering on her roof that she would have to get fixed, and she must wash some sweaters, and sort out a warmer coat to wear to work.

She had left her car in the hospital carpark and walked the short distance to East Central station before taking the train up to Charing Cross. The Royal College was only a few minutes away from the London terminal, so it seemed ridiculous to drive. Traffic was so bad between the hospital and the centre of London; in any case there was nowhere to park. Her car would be safe, she hoped, until she returned later that night to collect it.

Susan had made print-outs of all the diet menus she had prepared for the six patients who had failed to lose weight. Before going to work, she had visited a big supermarket and bought two packs of each of the three ready-meals that contained the suspicious ingredient, GE203. She was hoping that Dr. Donovan would be able to analyse the meals in his laboratory, and establish exactly what the ingredient was. If, as she suspected, it was something which might stimulate the appetite and make her patients overeat, she would approach the manufacturers and find out what the hell was going on!

On the phone, Dr. Donovan had sounded very sceptical about her idea that the ingredient might be anything other than a stabiliser or flavouring additive, but he had suggested the meeting, which must mean that he was interested enough to help her. As one of the top people in country in the field of nutritional research, he was definitely the right person to approach, Susan had met him just once before, when he had given a lecture to her college. She'd found him impressive, academically, and, with his charming manner and courteous approach, she had also rather fancied him.

It was only 4.30pm, but the platform was crowded with commuters, most of them going in the opposite direction to Susan. At least half of the men and women jostling each other to board the south-bound express to Brighton were very overweight. Susan breathed a sigh of relief when her train came in quickly. She stepped on board, and found a double seat, unoccupied, where she could stretch out and relax without being squashed up against someone else's huge thighs.

Although she didn't have a clinic to run that afternoon, she had attended two meetings about funding for her department, which had been depressing enough; in the first meeting, with the hospital governors, it was decided that there was no extra cash to pay for another dietitian to help her, even though her caseload was very heavy. During the second meeting, she had been criticised by the head of the cardiac unit for failing to provide individual diets quickly enough for post heart attack patients from ethnic backgrounds. As it took several interviews with the patients concerned .(often with an interpreter present) before she could even start planning their diets, she felt resentful and angry. Without an assistant to help, she was running around like a scalded cat.

It was useless to feel upset, she decided. What she needed was something to take her mind off the seemingly insoluble problems of working in the Health Service. An affair, maybe. Susan almost laughed out loud. Mark had only been out of her life for a few weeks, and she was already thinking about another man. It was too soon for anything like that, but if something turned up. Well, why not? She relaxed back in her seat, undid the belt of her raincoat, and smoothed down her black skirt. It was part of a businesslike suit, but today she'd left the jacket at home and worn it with a pale green shirt, black patent leather high-heeled pumps, and her beige trenchcoat. She opened a small black handbag and extracted a black plastic compact, then powdered her nose, automatically, without studying her face. With her short, dark curly hair, pale skin, and well-defined eyebrows, she was strikingly attractive but had never been vain enough to realise just how attractive. She was always on the thin side, and today, yet again, she had "forgotten "to eat lunch.

She thought about her ex-boyfriend for the first time in several days - great, she was getting over it! Mark was 6ft 3in tall, dark-haired, aged 39, and divorced. They'd met at the launch of a new baby food product; Mark worked as a marketing manager for the company . It had been lust at first sight. Within a couple of months, Mark had left the flat he was renting, and moved into Susan's house. Right from the start, the arrangement had proved difficult: the sex was wonderful, but their day-to-day relationship was strained. They were two, highly independent people who had been used to making their own decisions, without taking anyone else's feelings into consideration. They both worked long hours, and, during the week, they hardly saw each other. The lazy weekend mornings in bed were delicious, but just like the chocolate desserts Susan always tried to avoid, they were simply not sustaining enough to nourish their relationship.

Over the last few months, Mark had became more and more unreliable. On several occasions, he simply didn't come home for a couple of days, pleading work problems. They had parted amicably enough, but Susan suspected that the "work problems" had been another woman. She still smarted at the thought that he had happily spent Sunday mornings making love to her, while thinking about someone else. Anyway, it was over. No harm done. Apart from a dent in my pride, she thought, sadly. Her parents had been devastated by the split. They'd both liked Mark, and had assumed Susan would marry him. Her mother phoned several times a week, just to check that she was all right, and Susan had become adept at pretending she was leading a fantastic social life: in reality, she was spending most of her free time reading up on work subjects. She relaxed, and gazed out of the train window as the suburban homes flashed by. In some of them, she could clearly see people sitting round the table having their tea. God, what a sad sight: family life in South London; at least she'd escaped that.

She decided to take a holiday next spring, and to try and get back in touch with some of her female friends, who, to her shame, she had neglected during her two year affair with Mark.

By the time the train reached Charing Cross, Susan was fired up with plans for the future, and had pushed the reason for her visit to London to the back of her mind. As she strode through the station concourse, she noticed a billboard for the London Evening Echo: "Fat Kids Could lose Limbs". She bought a copy and tucked it under her arm to read later. No doubt it was another diabetes story. Alarmist, but with a lot of truth in it, too. Fat children were vulnerable to all kinds of illnesses, including loss of limbs if they became ill with diabetes. They could also suffer heart attacks, or choke on their own fat during sleep. The papers just loved those kinds of nightmare predictions, but Susan thought that this particular story was probably justified.

Everyone was far too complacent. It was time she brought her feet back to earth, and got on with the job. She was here to find out if people were deliberately being *made* fat by unscrupulous food producers. This was the real world and she had to persue this, even if Dr. Donovan turned out to be useless, she vowed she wouldn't rest until she found out what GE203 was, and what it was doing to people's health.

She tried to switch off her worries as she walked to the College, but found herself scrutinising passers-by; a somewhat depressing occupation, as so many of them were vastly overweight. The College was large, granite building, set round a large central courtyard. It was reassuringly solid; the kind of educational institution that looked as though it would turn out fine young professionals who would be an asset to the country. The reality was somewhat different: most of the graduates failed to find jobs related to their degrees, and those who did often found them abroad. In any case, at least sixty per cent of the students were from countries other than the United Kingdom because they paid higher tuition fees and the College needed the cash. Susan glanced up at the ornate clock set into the far wall of the curved building. Six o'clock, perfect timing.

Dr. Donovan's office was on the fourth floor, and the lift smelt of urine. So much for well-behaved, highly motivated, intelligent students, thought Susan. They're just as disgusting as any other youngsters. God, I sound like an old woman, she thought. Lighten up, Sue.

The office door was ajar, so Susan knocked gently, pushed it open and walked in. Brian Donovan was sitting at a large desk, facing the door, with what appeared to be a pile of old apple cores on a large aluminium tray in front of him. He was wearing a light blue roll-neck pullover and his fair hair flopped into his eyes. He looked up and smiled:

" No, I haven't turned into an apple junkie since we last met, Susan. I'm going to send these to be weighed in the lab, so we can work out how much fibre has been consumed by my group of third year student volunteers. If they're starving hungry by 9am tomorrow morning , I'll know that apples aren't much use for preventing hunger pangs. Anyway, enough of that. How are you? I remember meeting you six or was it seven? years ago after some lecture or other. Do sit down and take your coat off and I'll get rid of this lot."

"It's good to see you again, Dr. Donovan, " Susan replied."I still refer to the notes I took during your lecture: it was on the subject of child nutrition. Apples featured strongly - so you obviously still believe in the importance of fresh fruit. "

He laughed and got up, revealing slim-cut grey trousers and brown leather loafers. He placed the dish of apple cores in an old-fashioned, large white fridge standing against the wall at the far end of the room. When he opened the fridge door, Susan could just see a bottle of Moet & Chandon champagne in the door compartment. Nice touch, but was it for solitary consumption or for visitors, she wondered? Dr. Donovan was just as she'd remembered him; tall, thin-ish, and boyish looking, even though he must have been pushing forty five by now. She wondered whether he was happily married. He was wearing a thick gold wedding band on the third finger of his left hand, but, then, so did many unhappily married men. She glanced around the office.

It was furnished with a comfortable, padded brown leather sofa, a couple of straight-backed chairs, and floor to ceiling book-cases on two sides of the room, stacked with hefty scientific volumes, including bound copies of The International Journal of Obesity and Science. There was a modern, flat TV screen on one wall, and a pile of videos, DVDs and CDs on the floor next to it. A slightly incongruous touch for a male professor was the untidy stack of women's magazines on one chair. Susan sat down on one of the chairs, in front of Professor Donovan's huge mahogany desk. He must have noticed her staring at the magazines, because he walked over and picked one up before sitting down behind the desk on his own, swivel chair. The magazine was Vogue, the fashion monthly. As he placed it on the table, it fell open at an article entitled "The Last Diet You'll Ever Need".

"I read all the slimming features in women's magazines, because they provide a fascinating insight into the health of the nation, " he said. "No wonder people are confused about what to eat when there are so many mixed messages out there. This one for instance, sounds as if it's recommending starvation as the "ultimate solution" to overweight. What a stupid title. What does it mean, exactly? God knows.

" I check through the tabloid newspapers every day for the same reason. There's no point in teaching and doing research into such a popular, and important health subject unless you know exactly what your students and the general public are likely to be thinking. Of course, you're on the cutting edge at the hospital. I just wished there were more people like you to help obese patients. It's a nightmare.

" Now, what's the story again? You mentioned a suspect additive on the phone. Let's get it straight. Have you got some sample products with you? As I said to you when we spoke, I would be very surprised if anyone had come up with a ingredient that could alter appetite." He leaned back in his chair and continued, hardly pausing for breath.

" I won't talk down to you Susan, as I know you are highly

qualified, but I have been trying to think this thing through and I hope you will bear with me if I share my thought processes with you?"

He carried on talking in measured tones, punctuating each sentence by tapping a red pencil on a photograph of a nude model which illustrated the Vogue article. As he tapped away, he gradually covered the gorgeous young girl with red spots until she looked as though she had a bad case of acne.

"We all know that the basics of human energy expenditure are pretty simple: the human body is like a car which needs fuel , or energy, to function properly. Once that energy is in place, it is expended in one of four ways. These are: Basal Metabolic Rate, the thermic effect of food, adaptive thermogenesis and physical activity.

"BMI is used to measure the energy required to maintain all bodily functions like respiration, circulation and so-on. In sedentary types this can account for about 75 percent of total energy expenditure. I have a theory that there is a "cut off" point when the subject becomes so immobile that they expend very little energy indeed and their calorie requirements fall so low that even as few calories as 1000 a day make them put on weight.

" Then, there is the the thermal effect of food. That's the energy needed for digestion, absorption, metabolism and the storage of food. It accounts for about 10 per cent of daily energy expenditure, and is affected by the calorie content and composition of a meal. So, if your suspicions are correct, and there is an additive in some foods which encourages weight-gain, I suppose it could reasonably be something in the composition of a meal which would do this. However, even if this were so, it would affect a very small percentage of the energy expended, so would only be a problem for people who were already very sedentary, or overweight or both.

"The other two components, I think we can forget about. Adaptive thermogenesis is the energy needed in times of environmental and physiological stress; in extreme changes of temperature, for instance. Physical activity is the most variable component of energy expenditure of all. While a couch potato may only burn off 100 calories in one day by simply getting up and down from the sofa to turn on the TV, an athlete could easily burn 2000 calories, or more, and a healthy sex life is another good way to use up energy. Not a great deal, I admit...but it adds up!

" From what you told me on the telephone, the people you believe are affected are already overweight, which makes sense, but why would food manufacturers want to make fat people even fatter? That section of the market is already hooked on food. So, logically what we are looking at here is an ingredient which would encourage slim people to eat more than before. This means an ingredient which affects the appetite centres of the brain. I know our drug regulations are far from perfect, but I can't imagine that such a powerful substance could, somehow, manage to infiltrate the food chain without someone, somewhere noticing! That's why I'm sceptical about this".

Susan liked the way he spoke: straight to the point. There was no ridiculous inuendo or stupid sexist remarks which were often used by male academics when confronted with a female. It was refreshing. However, he obviously was going to take some convincing that her theory had some substance. What was needed was careful analysis of the suspicious products.

"I have the actual meals with me, " she said. She opened her briefcase and produced an insulated bag containing the three packet meals. By now, they had become rather soggy.-looking Brian spread a couple more magazines on the desk, and placed the packages in front of him.

"Let's check through the ingredients listed on the back of the packs." he said, removing a large magnifying glass from the centre drawer of his desk. "The one that you are suspicious about is GE203, but although I'm not familiar with that one, it could simply be a natural flavour enhancer or a harmless natural colourant. Many of these pre-packed meals contain a certain amount of non-animal protein to bulk out the meat and reduce costs, and it could be contained in such a substance. That is not unusual and certainly not harmful to people's health. The meat subsitutes used are carefully controlled and mainly produced from vegetable sources, so you could argue that a products which is "laced" with one of them is actually better for your health than one which contains more meat, especially if the meaty product would otherwise contain re-constituted slurry instead of the lean stuff."

He leaned forward in his chair, and examined each package, taking notes as he did so. The desk was wide, so Susan stood up and leaned forward as well, staring through the magnifying glass as the enlarged images on each of the three boxes. As she did so, she suddenly felt that Brian Donavan was staring straight at her chest. To her embarrassment, she realised that the top two buttons of her green silk shirt were undone and he was gazing at her white lace bra. The buttons must have popped open when she took off her coat, which was now on the back of her chair. She sat down hastily, and tugged her shirt down: to re-fasten the buttons would look very obvious, so, to hide her confusion, she gabbled:

"That's all true, of course, Dr. Donovan, but I really do think there are powerful ingredients out there which can affect the brain and have yet to be regulated. Even you must have come across plant extracts, from China, for instance, which had very potent effects? Anyway, the proof is in the products themselves. I know you have a heavy workload, but could they be analysed in your laboratories here? "

Brian Donovan appeared to have slipped into a trance. He was looking at her so intently that she could feel herself flushing. He put down the magnifying glass and stood up.

"Before we discuss that, would you like a glass of champagne, Susan. I was going to suggest a drink afterwards, but why not have one now? It's nearly seven o'clock, and I think my secretary has left a couple of glasses in the kitchen. Just hang on and I'll get them. " He got up rapidly and went out of the room.

Susan decided to take the initiative and got up from the chair, intending to move over to the sofa. As she crossed the office, she glanced at the pile of old videos, DVDs and CDs. She read a few labels: copies of TV programmes on obesity, conference proceedings, various gastro-abdominal operations and even a few films. To her surprise, one of the videos was the '60s French soft porn movie, " Emmanuelle". She was holding it in her hand when Brian returned, carrying two elegant, heavy champagne glasses on a plastic tray. He nearly dropped it when he saw what she was holding. "Sometimes, watching a light film helps me switch off when I'm writing a serious book, " he said lamely. "You know how it is."

Susan laughed. "There's no need to explain, Dr. Donovan. It's a good movie. I saw it years ago. How about watching it again, together? We can always carry on our discussions and have supper some other time. It would be fun!"

Brian thought his birthday had come early. Here was an attractive, intelligent female who obviously fancied him. Of course, he was used to it. Most women enjoyed his company, but usually he had to work a bit harder than this to get them to have sex with him. Unless, of courses, she was playing games.

"Great idea, Susan. You make yourself comfortable and I'll put the video on and pour the champagne. I'm sure we'll both benefit from a bit of relaxation. It might make our brains work better when we try and solve the nutrition mystery. "

Brian inserted the video into the recorder, poured two glasses of bubbly, and sat down next to her. He raised his glass. "To finding an answer to the world obesity crisis. Let's hope we can do it, Susan."

"I've got another toast, Dr. Donovan, " she laughed. "To thermogenesis - the process of burning off calories. Every activity helps keep us slim, even lifting a glassful of champagne." After the first gulp of the delicious liquid, she felt even bolder. She edged closer to him and clinked her glass against his.

The film was a surprise. Despite being so old, and fairly innocuous by present-day standards, it was incredibly sensual.

The heroine's preoccupation with her own body was mesmerising. Every gesture and caress was controlled: if you added the effect of the champagne, thought Susan, the whole thing was a complete turn on. They watched it, in silence, for the next half hour, without moving.

Emanuelle was enjoying yet another erotic moment when Susan decided that the time had come to make the big decision: should she let things follow their natural course and have sex with Brian, here and now on the the sofa - or should she take the heat out of the situation before things reached the point of no return?

As much as she fancied him (and although she felt extremely aroused, both by the film, and by Dr. Donovan's lemony scented cologne, and long, cool fingers which were, by this time, resting lightly on her knee), Susan decided that it was more important to maintain a working relationship with Brian - for the moment. She moved away, slightly, turned to face him and spoke softly, trying hard not to giggle:

"Brian, I'm just about to utter the biggest cliche in the book, sorry. However, it's the only thing I can think of to say at the moment, so here goes: we're both adults, and I think we both feel very turned on by this film, but we do have work to do. What's the next step? Shall we watch the rest of the movie, or do you think we should talk some more about GE203?"

Brian smiled and then burst into loud laughter (which effectively drowned the sound of Emanuelle's throaty shrieks as she acted out a convincing, multiple orgasm).

"You are absolutely right, Susan. There's no point in denying that I find you very attractive, but it would be crazy to get carried away by a saucy French actress and a few glasses of champagne - it is good, isn't it?- so let's just relax and save anything else for another time. I promise faithfully that I will get GE203 analysed as quickly as possible. Meanwhile, let's have another glass of champagne and enjoy the rest of the film."

For the next forty minutes, they sat, giggling like a couple of students as Emanuelle continued to explore her libido...and other things as well. Off-screen, the atmosphere was now cool and companionable, instead of hot and steamy.

After the credits had rolled, Brian switched off the TV, helped Susan into her trenchcoat, gathered up his own papers, and escorted her down the four flights of stairs (the lift was now switched off to save electricity) to the deserted college courtyard. Outside the college, he hailed a taxi for Susan, and kissed her lightly on the cheek before she climbed into the cab. "I promise I will be in touch shortly, " he said. "I am preparing for the Obesity Summit in New York, so there's a lot on at the moment, but this is important stuff Susan. Well done, for bringing it to my attention. I will be thorough, don't worry. If there is something strange here, I won't hesitate to expose it. "

The word "expose" struck a funny chord with both of them, and they started to laugh. Susan was still laughing when she arrived at Victoria Station to catch her train home. Dr. Donovan was certainly a charmer, but was he telling the truth about his scientific integrity? Or, was he a just a pawn in a game that was being played by the big boys...the international companies and governments who control our lives. She stopped smiling, and shuddered.

It was an awful thought, but she had no choice. For now, she had to trust him.

****

Chapter Five

Email to all Marketing Staff, FizzCo UK.
From: Bruce James, Marketing Director
Subject: International Obesity Summit, New York, November 6th-9th, 2008

As you are all aware, FizzCo will be part-sponsors of the above Conference, which is being held in the new Eastside Arena. FizzCo will host a dinner on the opening night, install a major display area in the foyer of the main conference hall, and supply drinks and snacks for the participants. Delegates are expected from all over the world and I am taking a party of ten journalists with me.
    Although most of the on-site work will be carried out by New York Head Office staff, input from the UK arm of the company is vital: and could affect funding from our Baltimore Head Office for upcoming UK strategies.
    I want a shit-hot marketing or promotional idea from every single one of you by 3pm today. I am calling a meeting in the Marketing Pod on the 6th floor at 4.30pm, so cancel any engagements which conflict with this.
    Don't forget: we are cost-cutting at the moment, so no job in this organisation is secure.
    Bruce.

That should get them off their fat arses, thought Bruce, as he clicked the computer mouse onto the "send" button of his home PC. He took a quick swig of coffee, sat back in his antique swivel chair and laughed. There were times when his job was fun - and this was one of them. It was only 6am, so when his staff arrived at the FizzCo UK offices in Hemel Hempstead, Hertfordshire in a couple of hours' time they would switch on their terminals and see his message. Today was Friday, so he imagined that there would be a flurry of phone calls cancelling lunchdates, outings to the theatre and cosy dinner parties. Very satisfactory!

There were ten brand managers, twenty assistant brand managers, and a promotional and advertising staff of eight in the organisation, all under Bruce's control. It also employed various outside companies: designers, PR specialists and media consultants. It was a costly business to market and promote the various products produced by FizzCo. The soft drinks arm of the organisation faced stiff competition from two other major international companies, and the food products were contantly being changed and reviewed to keep pace with market trends and the demands of the powerful supermarkets who stocked them. The giant Allardyce chain were the big boys..and FizzCo UK had to be on the ball to produce exactly what they wanted.

Bruce had worked his way up through the company from a lowly Assistant Brand Manager in the soft drinks division, to his present job. It had taken 15 years of hard graft. During that time, he had spent five years in Baltimore at FizzCo's world-wide headquarters, enjoyed a short posting in Central Africa to oversee a fizzy drinks plant , and another four years in Rotterdam. Ellen had been happy during their time in Baltimore where they had lived in a company-owned house, and enjoyed a great social life. But after their first child, Robert, had been born, things had become more complicated. Ellen missed her parents, and resented being a company wife. The constant entertaining and the long hours alone while Bruce played golf began to get on her nerves. She opted out of the posting to Africa, where Bruce set up a drinks bottling plant which managed, somehow, to deprive the local villages of thousands of gallons of water. His clever handling of the bad publicity this generated earned him promotion, and he asked to be sent back to Europe, to please Ellen.

By the time her husband was posted to Rotterdam, Ellen was pregnant again, with Joanna. After a short spell of living in another company house, this time in a very dull suburb of the Dutch city,

Ellen had had enough. She persuaded Bruce to buy a run-down period house set in twelve acres just north of Rickmansworth. It had taken all their savings, and they had a hefty mortgage, but Ellen loved doing the place up, and Bruce became used to his weekly commutes between Rotterdam and London. Their third child, Andrea, was born, and Ellen was quite content to be occupied with domesticity while Bruce persued his career.

When he was promoted to his present job in 2003, and could actually live permanently at home, the couple's relationship became strained. Their "weekends only" marriage had been perfect for both of them, and it was difficult to adapt to a normal life. These days, Ellen's main interests were the house, children, and her two horses. She left Bruce to his own devices.

His large, airy study was on the third floor of the house, and he had a small bedroom and bathroom next door so he didn't disturb Ellen if he came home late. The marital bedroom was on the second floor, together with the children's rooms, and on the ground floor there was a large drawing room, a dining room, and enormous kitchen, together with another office where Ellen planned numerous charity events and gymkhanas.

Sometimes, Bruce thought Ellen preferred her horses to him. There was a certain equine air about her. She certainly did look wonderful in the saddle: with her strong, wiry body, mane of dark hair worn in a hair-net under her riding helmet, and well-developed thighs, she was quite stunning, in a horsey way, of course. When they had first married, their sex-life had been marvellous: Ellen had been frisky, earthy and natural, and they had enjoyed plenty of romps in the hay. These days, sex was a bit like the Grand National: all over in 15 minutes.

He sighed at this thought, got up from his desk, went to the open study window and stretched. He was still in his crumpled navy and red striped Harrods pyjamas, and as he flung his arms upwards and took a deep breath, the buttons on the jacket strained alarmingly and his stomach expanded until it looked like a large, white balloon hovering over the top of his low-slung trousers. The white pyjama cord was under strain as well, and his flacid greyish-pink penis was clearly visible through the long gap in his trousers. A passing pigeon paused in flight, almost as though it was surprised at catching sight of this strange object dangling in mid-air. Unaware of the pigeon's interest, Bruce lowered his arms, and looked down towards his feet. Unfortunately, he couldn't see them as his stomach was in the way. Sadly, he couldn't see his penis either. He would simply have to go on a diet.

The horrible thought of cutting back on the boozy lunches he enjoyed stayed with him as he bathed and dressed. Frankly, dieting was a bore, but it was simple enough: all you had to do was to stop eating. It was strange that so many people seem to believe that eating low-calorie snacks and breakfast bars would make them thin: logically, this could not be so as all foods contain calories, and it's the sum total of the daily calorie intake that counts, not the calorie value of individual items. However, thank God people did believe that scoffing two or three low-calorie bars and fizzy drinks, plus a load of fatty junk every day would, somehow, make them lose weight. If they didn't, he would be out of a job.

He dressed carefully for the day ahead: blue and white Turnbull and Asser shirt with vertical stripes to make him look thinner, charcoal grey Hugo Boss suit, Church's black leather shoes and Armani belt. Naturally, he would wear his gold Rolex watch and monogrammed cufflinks. The final touch, a pale blue tie to match his eyes. Although he weighed over seventeen tone, Bruce was still a good-looking man: over 6ft tall, with well-cut silvery-grey hair, and broad shoulders. His complexion was pink, tending towards red when he had been drinking or was upset, and his once-firm jawline was now jowly, but he didn't look at all bad for a man of 50. Before leaving his bedroom, he admired himself in the long mahogany mirror on the wall next to the door: Brucie, boy, he thought, you look terrific: mean, keen. lean (maybe not lean, but that would be addressed), and ready to whip the FizzCo marketing staff into shape.

****

At 3.45pm, he was less confident about his ability to "kick arse" successfully. His usual way of dealing with this kind of disappointment was to order a Danish pastry to be sent up from the firm's restaurant. Mindful of this morning's vow to shed weight, he replaced this temptation with a temper tantrum; his face went the same colour as one of Ellen's precious peonies, and perspiration dripped down his neck.

It was a disgrace. His "tough" email had produced only four replies, all from brand managers who had most to lose in terms of salaries and pension provisions if they were fired. One suggestion, from the young upstart who looked after the "Super Snacks" Nibbles range was, frankly, laughable. His idea was to run a competition with a national newspaper to give free trips to the Obesity Summit for the ten fattest people in the country, and to get an independent TV company to film them during a week's stay in New York.

Bruce almost cried with disbelief. The ten fattest people in the country were probably in hospital, and even if they could travel by plane, the cost of their travel insurance would be enormous. Doubtless, some TV company would love to film them struggling to cope with the journey, and possibly even dying a painful death in New York. They would also love blaming Fizzco for the whole disaster. Reality TV had reached such heights of tastelessness that anything was permitted; they would probably make a follow-up film of the litigation process when FizzCo were sued by grieving relatives.

The other three suggestions were slightly more sensible, but lacked any real flair: goodie bags for each journalist in their hotel rooms, a special FizzCo fitness lounge for all delegates to use during the conference, a large donation from Fizzco to Third World Countries, announced at the Conference, to help them fight poverty and malnutrition, and, finally (from a bright girl who was capable of better things), a suggestion that FizzCo should make a gigantic balloon painted to look like the earth (with FizzCo logo, naturally). This could then represent the world's obesity crisis and would be launched it into the sky as a symbol of the Conference's determination to help people lighten up. With the US Air force on constant alert for terrorist attacks, it would probably be blasted out of the sky within minutes.

By 4.30pm, most staff members had managed to email a marketing or promotional suggestion of some kind, and Bruce was wading through them as they starting arriving at the Marketing Pod. This had been set up so that FizzCo's suppliers could put on presentations, thus keeping the company's personnel in the building. It consisted of a raised platform, with semi-circular seating, covered by a huge orange circular ceiling. Inside it was dark, and rather cool, which made it feel like a large, circular prison. Which, in fact, it was: a corporate slammer for deliquent executives.

Bruce sat at a desk on the platform and gazed down at the people in the "audience". He was delighted that, yet again, the Marketing Pod was being used so effectively. He did not believe in allowing staff to notch up travelling and hotel expenses, while they enjoyed themselves entertaining suppliers. After all, FizzCo was the big player, and small firms who supplied ingredients for breakfast bars, bottle tops, and labels, should travel to Hemel Hempstead. The only exception to the "no travel " rule was the occasional presentation to the offices of the big supermarkets who were at the top of the chain. Without them, no FizzCo. He adjusted the clip on microphone on his lapel and spoke:

"Well, gang, we're really up against it, I'm afraid. I hope none of you have any urgent appointments tonight. Looks like you'll be spending Friday evening with Brucie. Won't that be cosy? I've ordered in some Super Snacks and FizzCo drinks for later, so you won't starve. Ha Ha."

Bruce usually adopted a jokey, avuncular attitude when addressing his staff. He believed that this was good for "bonding".

He had read in one of the American "How to Succeed in Business" books which he devoured during his holidays in Marbella, that it's important to keep people on the edge of their seats if you want to get the best work out of them. Switching from "fond uncle" mode" to "piranha" mode was one way of ensuring that no-one became complacent. The element of surprise always worked!

"I have to say that most of your ideas are pure, unadulterated shit, but there is one suggestion that does have some value. Gina Boyle from Group Publicity has come up with something that might work, if it was handled correctly. Gina, stand up and tell everyone your idea."

Gina, a pretty freckle-faced redhead wearing a pair of tight black trousers and a green Indian top with long, floating sleeves, got to her feet and looked around, uncertainly. She was obviously terrified. Praise from Bruce could mean one of two things: either he genuinely liked the idea, or he was about to humiliate her by letting her outline her plan, then pouring piss on it. Bruce loved playing mind-games with staff, another ploy intended to keep them on their toes.

She shuffled some papers in a blue folder, dropped one, picked it up and began to speak.

"Well, as we know the British Prime Minister, Jack Barton, is due to be in Washington for a couple of days at the time of the Obesity Conference, for a meeting with the President of the United States." she said, as boldly as she could manage. "He has already declined to put in an appearance at the Conference, unfortunately. Our perfect photo opportunity would have been a picture of him nibbling one of our "Super Snacks" breakfast bars...I wish!"

She paused, and looked at Bruce...he was smiling. Fond uncle or fiendish piranha? Difficult to judge, but it was too late. She was committed to her theme:

" However," she continued, her voice dropping slightly. " My suggestion is that we invite Elizabeth Collins, the Junior Health Minister, along instead. Rumour has it that Jack is very fond of her (no innuendo meant there, but I'm sure you all know what I mean), and might change his mind about attending if she was there. Other countries are sending representatives from their government health departments, so I would imagine that Mrs Collins would be up for it. We wouldn't, of course, suggest that she comes as our guest, which would be sure to be met with a polite refusal, but we could send her the list of speakers, and a letter from the President of FizzCo, USA inviting her to visit the New York kids' AIDs clinic we help fund in Brooklyn while she's over. As you all know, Mrs. Collins' background is in hands-on health care. She was born in London of Jamaican parents, and worked as a nurse for some years before entering politics.

" She has a particular interest in sick children, as well as obesity problems, so that would make her look good, and give her an excuse for the trip and maybe she'll be able to fit in a rendez-vous with Jack. It would also give us some good PR. Our logo is all over the Conference, and we would be able to schmooze her and get some good pics. We could also pick her brains about the Government's intentions as far as any new legislation about snack foods and TV advertising is concerned, and maybe plant some ideas in her head about using our low-calorie products in hospitals and schools. Anyway, it can't do any harm. "

Gina sat down abruptly, and waited. Was she about to be praised..or fired?

There was a short silence. Everyone knew, of course, that sexy, forty two year old Elizabeth Collins was the PM's favourite Minister. No newspaper had been bold enough to suggest that there might be anything romantic going on between them, but a recent diary column had reported that Mrs Collins had been helping Jack Barton's wife to research a book on recipes from historic dinners at Number Ten Downing Street.

The trio had become very pally, especially since Mrs. Collins had divorced her husband Gerald, a high court judge with a fondness for wearing ladies' stiletto heeled boots. At a House of Commons reception for the UK Bengali Association, Jack Barton had been photographed looking deep into a laughing Mrs' Collins eyes, while eating a plateful of curry. Mrs Collins' high, rounded, honey-coloured bosom had been displayed to perfection in a white chiffon gown. The tabloids had had a field-day with witty captions for the picture. "Hot Stuff for the PM", "Enjoy Your Spicy Nibble, Jack" and "Tasty Dish of the Day", had been typical efforts from sub-editors. Rumours were certainly bubbling along about their relationship, but nothing had surfaced - yet.

Bruce broke the silence by leaning back in his chair and roaring with laughter. "Well, I don't think we need to speculate about the Prime Minister's love life, " he said. "But, I like the way your brain works, Gina. It's an excellent idea," said Bruce. Gina almost fainted with relief. Her job was secure, at least for another twenty four hours.

"Now, what we need is someone to set the ball rolling, and take responsibility for making this happen. Gina, it has to be you, under my command of course. Let's have a break for some delicious FizzCo food and drink and then I want you to select a small team to help you."

Gina, who had been almost comatose for the last few seconds, jumped to her feet, dropping her file of notes onto the floor. Oh my god, she thought. I've now got to upset most of my colleagues by selecting a team to help me with this. The others will hate me, of course, and I will have to carry the can at the end of the bloody day. If it goes well, Bruce will take the praise from the US office; if it all goes pear-shaped, I'll be fired.

Two hours, and many cans of FizzCo pop and low-calorie snacks later, Gina had selected her team and endured withering looks from the associates she hadn't chosen. She hoped that her ordeal was over, and the meeting would soon break up. No such luck. Bruce insisted that all Marketing Managers should give an overview of their plans for the next 6 months. It was 10pm. before the meeting ended. Before Gina could leave the Marketing Pod, she was button-holed by Bruce.

"Your strategy is good and you are developing nicely in the organisation, Gina...I really liked that idea. How about coming up to my office for a quick bevvy before you go home? We could toss a few more thoughts into the pot while we sip some of my vintage claret. What do you say?"

Gina hesitated. It was late, she had a husband and young son to go home to, and Bruce was clearly after a quick screw. However, sexual harrassment litigation was increasing to the point where bosses had to think twice, or even three times, before coming on too strong. Bruce wouldn't dare to risk his pension and become a laughing stock. He was far too vain. She decided that, after surviving the double ordeal of presenting her ideas in front of her colleagues, and then having to upset so many of them, she could handle this situation.

"Delighted, Bruce, " she said, coolly, "but let's keep this strictly professional, shall we? Mike, my husband, is expecting me home at 11pm, and I don't want to irritate him, especially as I'm going to be away for a week in New York in November. There will be time for more socialising then, I'm sure. " Perfect, she thought. A gentle put-down now, but the promise of, perhaps, a bit of action later on. That should keep him at arm's length, at least until November. Then, I'll have to think of something else to put him off without losing my job.

Bruce looked disappointed, but led the way out of the Pod, into entrance hall and pushed the lift button. Gina stepped in and said three "Hail Marys" to herself as the lift rose to the tenth floor. A committed catholic, she hated lying, but there were some situations where lying was the only way to save your soul. If Bruce really thought he stood a chance with her in November, he was sorely mistaken.

****

When Bruce arrived home, Ellen was already asleep. He walked into the hall, turned off the lights, and went upstairs to his study. He poured himself a large scotch and sipped it while he checked his emails. The Baltimore Head Office was just coming to life, and he had six messages, all from various company vice-presidents, asking for sales figures, projections, costs, and other business operation details. He sighed. Not a brilliant day. Some progress with plans for the Conference, which was a plus. A definite minus was being turned down by Gina. Bruce decided to be philosophical: you win some, you lose some, in this game. It's another day tomorrow, and it's Saturday. Maybe a round of golf in the morning, followed by a few snifters in the clubhouse? That would be good, and would make up for the fact that Ellen was hosting a dinner party for eight of her charity chums, and had told him to be on his best behaviour. Damn!

Slowly, he removed his working "uniform," and pulled on his striped pyjamas. As he stepped into the trousers of his pyjama suit, he caught sight of his reflection in the long mirror on the wall... Old John Thomas was looking a bit unloved. Never mind, there would be other opportunities. New York - now *there* was a city that never slept: he would have to get one of his mates to escort him round the hottest spots for gorgeous totty...all the girls were up for it there. He got into the single bed, turned off the light and turned on his side, determined to start the next day afresh. He slept soundly, dreaming that he was sitting in a bath of champagne, eating a large steak, while his back was being scrubbed vigorously... by the gorgeous femail TV newscaster whose website was the "soft porn" choice of UK top management.

****

Chapter Six

25 Lower Street,
Kings' Cross,
Sydney,
S,. Australia.
October 6th, 2008

Dear Mum and Dad,
Hope you are both well, and Dad is taking his diet plan seriously. I know it's hard, Dad, but you must try and follow the advice you're being given...we all want you to enjoy your retirement, you know! Anyway, I have some brilliant news. Remember I told you I was going out with a really great bloke, a colleague of mine called Shaun? Well, he has proposed - and I have accepted. Yes, your independent daughter is getting hitched - isn't it amazing? He wants to do the gentlemanly thing and refuses to buy me a ring until you've both given us your blessing, but I know you will. You'll love him, honestly.

We have so much in common: our teaching careers, sailing, travel, everything. It's right, I know it.

Anyway, we've decided to get married in March, next year, when the weather is a bit cooler out here. Of course, you must both come over. No excuses, Dad. You can leave that taxi cab of yours for once.

We'll be phoning in the next day or so. Take care, both of you.

Love, Jemma.

John Barnard read the letter carefully, almost unable to take it in. It seemed only a few years since Jemma had been a tiny girl with tousled curls, sitting on his knee; a little cracker. Bright as a button, as well, and passed all those exams with flying colours. John and his wife Peggy had been thrilled when Jemma had decided to become a teacher. When she had announced that she was going to work in Australia it had been a blow, but she'd been back home several times, and wrote regularly. Now, his little girl was getting married, and she wanted her mum and dad at her wedding.

Still clutching the letter, John heaved his twenty four stone body out of the large, shabby brown velvet armchair. His heart was racing, and his legs felt like two lumps of lead. Sweat was pouring off his face, so he put the letter on the mantlepiece, next to a large black and white photograph of Jemma, and her twin brother, Trevor, taken on their first day at school. They looked so young and innocent in the red and grey uniform; bright smiles, curly fair hair, identical gaps between their front teeth.

He wiped his forehead, cheeks and nose with a large handkerchief. It was a chilly autumn night, and Peggy had lit the fire before he had arrived home from the West End and parked his cab in the paved area outside the house. The front room of the terraced, North London house was too hot for John but Peggy felt the cold, so he sometimes lumbered into the kitchen and opened the door into the garden, where he would enjoy a smoke and some cool air.

Since Jemma had left for Australia two years earlier the couple had lived a quiet life. Peggy helped out behind the bar of the local pub and John worked from 10am to 5pm, arriving home about 6pm most evenings. He had given up lucrative night shifts because of the danger: it was impossible to deal with villains or drunken passengers when you couldn't move very fast. Working during daylight hours suited him fine, now, and he would never go out to work on a Sunday again. Life was too short.

The irony of his last thought almost made him smile as he

walked out of the room, and climbed the stairs one at a time, leaning on the banister as he made painful progress up to their bedroom, where Peggy was getting ready to go out to the pub. Yes, life was indeed short. Trevor, Jemma's twin had been killed at the age of 17 in a motorcycle accident. John and Peggy had helped him pay for the machine but, within a month of his seventeenth birthday, it had killed him. The accident happened outside a school, near a bus stop. Tangled wreckage, a weeping lorry driver, screaming mothers and children, the long hours at the hospital, and the awful, awful funeral. The memories flooded back.

As John tried to switch his mind off from these dark recollections of the tragedy, other upsetting, thoughts took their place. Life expectancy, now there was a big subject, especially if you were -what did they call it? - morbidly obese. That nice young dietitian lady at the East Central Hospital was always nagging him about his "life expectancy". On a scale of one to ten, it was about minus twenty. What she didn't mention was the fact that his pension fund was pretty healthy, and the insurance company would be paying out even more when he chose to retire because they didn't expect him to live very long. Another irony. Eat more, grow rich. Ha, flippin' ha.

The weight had started to pile on after Trevor's death. At first, John had simply started having a few extra beers on a Saturday night, and a fish and chip supper after the pub, the Rose and Crown, shut. It was a friendly local, and everyone knew about John and Peggy's tragic loss. They were quietly sympathetic, and the subject was only aired when the couple wanted to talk. Otherwise, there was simply an understanding that their pub pals would be there for them, come what may. The Rose and Crown became their refuge. On Sundays, while Peggy was working, John would pop in for a big lunch of roast beef with all the trimmings, apple crumble and custard, a nice dollop of Stilton with a glass of port, then he would drive home and help himself to a few cans of beer from the fridge. When Peggy arrived home she was usually hungry, so they'd have supper too - beans on toast, teacakes and butter, or scones and jam. Later, John would sink a few more pints while she sipped a gin and tonic.

As his stomach got larger, he began to wear his trousers lower on his hips, with a giant-sized sweater pulled down over his shirt. Today, he had abandoned the struggle to look reasonably smart and was wearing a pair of ancient navy blue tracksuit trousers, and a faded Arsenal Football Club sweatshirt, both in extra, extra large size. At least this outfit was comfortable to wear in the taxi cab, although it didn't look too elegant. It was safer too: he'd got into the habit of unbuckling his trouser belt while he was driving! The cooler autumn days meant that he no longer had to wear a baseball cap to prevent the sweat from running into his eyes.

At first, Peggy had joked about how "cuddly" he was becoming, but when the doctor advised him to attend an obesity clinic, she stopped joking and started worrying. Poor John, he just couldn't lose weight. It was a tragic shame. She was desperately sorry for her husband, but she didn't want to upset him by nagging. Her own figure was "comfortable" rather than fat, and lately, she had lost a little weight because she had taken over a lot of the physical jobs that John used to do happily, such as gardening and decorating.

The bedroom was exactly the same size as the sitting room below. Peggy liked it to look "feminine"; soft grey carpet, rose-patterned curtains and matching bedspread, white paintwork and a pale grey paper border which ran all around the room, half-way up the pink and white striped wallpaper. Every time he entered the room, John felt like the proverbial bull in the china shop: except that he was more like an old, clapped-out elephant than a bull. Only a few days earlier, he had knocked over one of Peggy's precious china figurines. The expensive piece of porcelain, moulded and painted in blue and gold, to look like a Dresden shepherdess, had been decapitated and John had stuck her head back onto her body with glue. The angle was all wrong, though, and she now looked slightly tipsy.

As he advanced, cautiously, through the centre of the doorway, the shepherdess seemed to be looking at him with a disapproving eye, willing him to trip over the synthetic white furry rug by the side of the brass double bed.

"Did you read our Jemma's letter, love?" Peggy was sitting in front of her kidney-shaped dressing table, applying lipstick. Breathing heavily after the exertion of climbing the stairs, John moved painfully over to her, and placed his hands gently on her shoulders, looking into the mirror at her pale, pretty face. The pink colour on her lips made her teeth look whiter. She smiled up at his reflection "I know what you're thinking, John, " she said, gently. "It would be a difficult journey for you to make now, but you do have four months to try and lose some weight and get fitter. Have a word with the hospital and see what they have to say. You can do it you know…and you now have the perfect reason to slim down. I'll stop giving you all those roast dinners, and buy salad instead, and you must remember to take your tablets, too. We'll go for more walks together. "

As she spoke, she looked down and picked up a bottle of John's favourite perfume, and removed the stopper. Miss Dior. Well, she wasn't exactly a "Miss" any more, but John loved that fragrance and it reminded her of their young days, when the twins were babies… such a very long time ago. As she glanced upwards again, she saw that there were tears in John's eyes. "I really will try, Peggy, " he said, gruffly. "Jemma is all we've got now, and it will be her special day. Promise you'll help me? I know I am my own worst enemy with food and drink, but life has been tough for us. This wedding will give me a goal to aim for. Thanks for being so patient with your fat old husband, Pegs."

He sat down heavily on the bed, and watched while Peggy finished applying her make-up. She dabbed a final touch of powder onto the end of her nose, and got up, smoothing down her skirt as she did so. She was wearing her pub "uniform" of black skirt and white blouse. The blouse was slightly transparent, and John could see her pretty white lace bra and petticoat underneath. She looked lovely; much too good for a fat old git like him. It hadn't always been like this: fifteen years ago, before Trevor's death, he had been fit, and not bad looking. Their sex life had been wonderful. Every week, they had somehow managed to snatch a couple of hours in bed while the children were at Sunday school. Peggy was warm, willing and very playful and John's lovemaking was tender and caring. Their sex sessions always ended with a good old giggle and a nice cup of tea.

The awful accident, and John's weight problem, had changed everything. Now, achieving an erection was becoming very difficult, and finding a comfortable position for sex was virtually impossible. John worried constantly about crushing his wife's neat body under his own huge bulk, or falling over or, worse, having a heart attack during the act itself. Then there was the acute embarrassment. He had no doubts about how ugly his body looked when he was naked. Even though he knew Peggy loved him dearly, it was appalling to think that she had to share a bed with someone so gross. He shuddered.

Peggy got up from the dressing table, and went to the white wooden wardrobe which was built into an alcove by the bed. She opened the door, and selected her black leather coat and the pink velvet scarf he'd given her last Christmas. After putting them on, she took her handbag and car keys from the bedside table, leaned over and gave him a big kiss on his forehead. " Lean back now, and have a nice rest, John, then go down and eat your supper, " she said. " I've left some salad and cold potatoes in the fridge for you, and there's a packet of vegetable curry that simply needs heating in the microwave oven - it's the curry that's on your diet sheet. Now, promise me you won't overdo the bread and butter; there's no point in me organising low-calorie meals if you sabotage my efforts, you naughty man!"

She was laughing as she said it, but the message was serious enough.

John suddenly had a vision of Peggy at work, being chatted up by Charlie, the local builder who was a regular at the pub. He was fifty three, very fit and recently divorced. He also had the gift of the gab. Peggy was a lovely, sexy lady; one of these days she was going to be tempted. It was a terrifying thought.

"Peggy, you know I'm really going to try this time." he said. " I'll stay here for five minutes or so, then I 'll eat and watch some telly. Do your usual thing and phone me just before you leave the pub, so I know when to expect you. Take care, my pet, I love you so much, you know." She went downstairs, and John heard her open the front door, and bang it shut behind her. A few seconds later, the car engine started. The house suddenly seemed empty without her.

He gazed up at the bedroom ceiling and thought about Jemma's letter again. The more he thought about it, the less likely it seemed that he would be able to attempt such a long journey. At the rate he was going, he would be lucky to lose a couple of stone in four months. He would still be classified as dangerously obese, and the prospect of spending nearly a whole day sitting in an aircraft was too awful to contemplate. No, he would have to tell Peggy to go alone, or take her widowed sister, Irene, along instead. Somehow, he would find the fares for them both. Peggy certainly deserved a break, after putting up with him for so long.

Maybe it would be easiest if he pretended to go along with her idea of aiming to shed weight for the trip, and then break it to her in January or early February. Christmas was in just a few weeks' time, and he couldn't see how he could possibly stick to his diet with all that food and drink around. They usually had Christmas lunch in the pub, and Peggy's mince pies were a dream; light as a feather, and lovely with a glass of sherry to wash them down.

"There I go again, thinking about food, " he said, out loud. "I'm a total failure. My arteries are furring up, I can't make love to my wife any more, and I feel like hell. Talk about a boring old fart. It must be like being married to a windy bull elephant. Poor Peggy, she deserves better. "

Leaning back, eyes closed, he tried to concentrate on something positive. His cab needed servicing, so he would organise that tomorrow. While it was off the road, he'd get some exercise; go for a walk, as Peggy had suggested. Tomorrow, he'd write back to Jemma, telling her he was hoping to come to the wedding. It would be a lie, but it would please his wife, and his daughter. He drifted off to sleep for half an hour or so, then woke suddenly - shaken by the sound of his own rasping breaths. This was a familiar sound. During the night, he would often wake up when his breathing became difficult. They'd called it "sleep apnea" at the hospital. It was apparently a very common problem for overweight people. Thank God he did wake up...otherwise, he could suffocate.

He took a few, deep breaths and sat up very slowly. This wouldn't do. He must go downstairs and eat his supper. Maybe he would have just one slice of bread and butter tonight instead of six. Painfully, he eased his feet off the bed and onto the floor. He paused before attempting the difficult bit: standing up.

He pressed his hands, palms down on the bed and pushed, trying to shift the weight from his hips to his legs and feet. As he struggled to raise twenty four stone of flesh, bones and blubber into an semi-upright position, he felt a sharp pain in his left shoulder and arm. For an instant, he thought the pain was caused by the weight of his body. He pushed again. The pain became more intense, and spread right across his chest. His upper body crumpled, he fell forward and hit his forehead on the dressing table stool, where Peggy had been sitting just half an hour earlier.

In the fraction of a second before he died, John knew that he was suffering a massive heart attack. Well, that settled it then, he thought, just before he lost consciousness. I won't be going to the wedding. It's sorted.

Three hours later, the telephone rang. It continued to ring for a minute, then stopped. The bedroom was silent again.

Next morning, Susan was sitting in her small consulting room in the East Surrey Hospital when the call came through from John Barnard's GP:

"Miss Simpson? It's Peter Galbraith here. John Barnard is one of my patients - I referred him to your clinic. I'm sure you remember. Anyway, I've got some sad news, I'm afraid. John died last night. Myocardiac infarction, of course. Unfortunately, he was alone in the house at the time, but I don't suppose his wife could have done much. It was a massive attack. Poor lady, she is distraught. She came home from work and found him there. What a terrible shock. I'd like to thank you for all your efforts with him, Miss Simpson. It is so difficult to make these people understand that they have to toe the line with their eating and it is so often too late. The damage is done. Keep it up, though, Miss Simpson. I have a feeling that you'll be getting more referrals from this practice: we have a number of very overweight patients. "

"I am so sorry to hear about John, " Susan replied. "He was a nice man, but seemed to have given up on things lately. I know he had family problems. His wife was lovely, and she really did try to help him, but the roast dinners seemed to win every time. It's tragic. I will be writing to her. Thanks a lot for the offer of more patients, but I'm afraid this unit is straining at the seams....like most of my customers! Goodbye, and thank you for letting me know."

After putting the phone down, Susan sat quietly for a moment. John had been a sad case, and probably her suspicions about the additive in the ready-meals would not have affected him at all because he had been referred to her so late. But, it was the kind of tragedy that was happening more and more frequently. She thought about John's wife and family, then took a deep breath and tried to concentrate on her work.

That morning, Brian Donovan had rung to give her the interim results of his analyis of the three products which she had brought to his office. The ingredient listed on each package, GE203, appeared to be a plant-based substance which was blended with the meat substitute, which was also plant-based, and was used to "bulk out" the real meat in each item. The Food Standards Agency had promised to get back to him about the precise meaning of GE203, but, so far, nothing.

Since re-constituted slurry-type meat products had been restricted a year earlier, it was common practice for manufacturers to add non-meat protein-based ingredients to meaty dishes. This was cheaper than using good quality chicken, lamb or beef, and so increased the profit margin on the product. These ingredients were impossible for customers to detect in made-up dishes like curries, because of the composition of the recipes. Brian hadn't managed to work out what role GE203 played in this meat substitute: but it certainly wasn't a colourant, or a flavour enhancer. He would need to have more long-term tests carried out to find out.

Thinking about Dr. Donovan made Susan smile, and she was suprised to find that she felt aroused as well - which seemed an inappropriate response after receiving such bad news about a patient. She poured herself a glass of water from the jug on her desk, and tried to calm down.

She swallowed a long draft of water. She was so glad that she had stopped things from going too far in Brian's office. Brian was married, after all. She didn't need that kind of complication in her life. However, despite her resolve not to start an affair with Brian, one thing had happened which might bring them together again. She had received an invitation to the World Obesity Summit in New York, the following week, which she knew Brian was attending. It came from a university friend who worked for a large nutrition research clinic and couldn't, herself, attend the conference. Although Susan would have to pay her own fares, the Regional Health Authority had agreed to let her have five days' unpaid leave, with a locum stepping in to run her clinics. Of course, she would be expected to give a full report, and run a couple of seminars for interested staff when she returned.

Despite her sombre mood, Susan had to smile. Other countries would be sending health professionals to the conference, all expenses paid, but she would have to fork out her own money for the privilege. Well, she thought it was worth it. She would stay in a cheap hotel, and get the lowest air fare she could find. Maybe there would be someone at the conference who could help with identifying GE203, and she would be able to discuss the implications of adding this substance to food with Brian, and other experts. It would also do her good, professionally, to hear the latest papers on treatments for obesity, and to meet other people in her field. She would be able to talk to people in the food industry too. There might even be a career opportunity to follow up.

She sighed. As much as she wanted to help people, there was obviously no future in working for the Health Service. No money was available to set up the nationwide chain of obesity clinics which was so urgently needed; everything was being done piece-meal...a "sticking plaster" approach to a problem which was haemorrhaging the country's healthcare resources. Were the Government so stupid that they didn't realise that the collective expanding girth of the nation was potentially as dangerous as the black death? Or were they so deeply in collusion with the food and drink industry that they simply didn't care, or dare, to act? Had John Barnard been a victim of his own stupidity and ignorance...or was he set up, to help put more money into the vast coffers of the food industry? Now *there* was a disturbing thought.

Gladys, Susan's nursing assistant, popped her head round the door. "Next clinic's about to start, Susan. Come on love, get a move on!". Susan gathered her files and briefcase, and got up. As she walked to the door, she vowed to do everything she could to expose any wrong-doing. If, of course, she could combine her researches with a little sex and recreation in New York, that would be fine, too. She was still feeling upset about John, but felt a new sense of purpose. What was the saying? Variety is the spice of life - that was it. Quite.

Chapter Seven

2008 INTERNATIONAL OBESITY SUMMIT, NEW YORK

November 6th, Afternoon Session, 2pm- 5.30pm

PROGRAMME:

2.pm Gene Profiling in Human Adipose Tissue: Dr. Heinrich Walter, Hans Johanneson, Humbold University, Berlin.

3.30pm Type 2 Diabetes in North American Obese Children: Dr. James Taylor, Laval University, Quebec, Canada.

4.30pm Obesity: the Biggest Health Issue of the 21st Century. Dr. Brian Donovan, Royal College, London

Note: all European delegates to the conference are invited to a Reception and dinner at 7pm. tonight, at the Waldorf Astoria Hotel, hosted by Charles Henderson, Senior Vice-President, FizzCo Healthy Foods Division.

Caroline Dempsey gazed down at her (nearly) flat stomach. She was feeling very smug. She had managed to shed 10lbs in weight on the Cabbage Soup diet before flying out to New York. Last night, after checking in at the Waldorf Astoria hotel, she'd spent an hour clothes shopping at the city's hottest fashion store, Barney's, before having dinner with the FizzCo executives and the nine other British newspaper and magazine journalists on the trip.

The best thing about American clothes, she thought, was the fact that their size system was so flattering. In England, she would now be a size 14, here in New York, she could fit into a 10. Maybe size zero was a long way off, but who was complaining? It had definitely been worth the agony of living on cabbage soup for ten days. She was delighted with her chosen outfit: long green cotton skirt, cropped, close-fitting beige suede jacket and matching high heeled boots, plus a stunning heavy silver and agate pendant: smart, yet interesting.

From her seat in the crowded East Side Conference Hall (in a strategic position at the end of a row) about half-way back from the large platform, she looked around at the delegates who were still settling themselves into their seats. They were a mixture of health workers, academics, business types, and journalists. The majority were obviously from Europe and North America, but she spotted a few oriental-looking men and women in the front row. After the huge amount of food and drink consumed during the Beijing Olympic games, obesity was now becoming a big problem in China, and a lucrative business as well. There were plenty of new business opportunities for American and European diet food and drink producers. Caroline wondered how much FizzCo had spent on flights and hotel accommodation for the Chinese delegates and journalists .Megabucks, probably.

She studied a few of the women nearby. It was easy to tell which of them were health professionals; nurses, pyschologists, physiotherapists. They were mainly dressed in drab suits and were, almost without exception, overweight. The scientists and academics, male and female, were easy to spot too: mostly thin, middle-aged, wearing glasses and carrying battered leather briefcases. Working with people with weight problems obviously makes you hungry, thought Caroline. Carrying out research into the causes of obesity leaves you with little time, or inclination, to eat rubbish. It was logical, really.

Only the journalists looked glamorous. There were three

camera crews in the hall, with lean-hipped young men in T-shirts and jeans manning the cameras, each accompanied by a woman presenter. The three women were almost identically dressed in sharp, well-cut, brightly coloured suits, all with immaculate hair and flashing white teeth.

The British press contingent, consisting of five men and five women, were all together, sitting in the same row as Caroline . The blokes were all young and a couple of them weren't bad looking: Caroline had already made a mental note to chat to the tall, beefy Social Affairs Editor of BBC Radio Four's Today Programme, who was a charmer. The women were attractive, too, apart from an middle-aged, hatchet-faced biddy from Nutrition World, but even she was stylishly turned out in a white jacket and short pinstriped skirt.

Officially, the group was being shepherded by a FizzCo PR girl, but Caroline predicted that they would soon stop being polite to their hosts and start working properly: sniffing out stories, seeking exclusive interviews, and, hopefully, stuffing the opposition.

She knew for a fact that the two women from The Sun and The Mirror had already filed similar stories gleaned from a bit of gossip at last night's dinner when that stupid prat from FizzCo, Bruce James, had revealed that he was signing up a very minor soap opera actress to promote a new mineral water brand.

They were keen, but would soon learn that it's not wise to draw attention to the fact that you are swanning around New York unless you file a story that's red hot. The trouble with a trip like this, she thought, is that most of the people in your department are jealous of you. What's more, your Editor is quite likely to tell you to go off and cover something completely different if a news story breaks.sWell, she intended to file at least one, maybe two cracking pieces from this Summit, and, if something else was going on in the Big Apple this week, she would be on the case! Minor soap opera actresses didn't count - and the story was probably all bollocks, anyway.

Her thoughts were interrupted by her neighbour, a bespectacled, chubby young man who worked for a food industry trade paper. "Do you think the first speaker will have anything printable to say?" he said. "If would be great if he came out with a good line like "Fat People are Programmed to be Obese by their Cave Man Ancestors". My readers are fed up with being blamed for the fat epidemic, so it would make a good piece for me. "

"No chance, " said Caroline, "He's just going to waffle on and show boring slides. The next session should be better, though. Plenty of shock, horror statistics to quote. Overweight kids are always good for a few paragraphs, maybe a whole feature. From your point of view, it will be best if the speaker blames parents rather than food conglomorates. I don't mind either way; believable statistics, plus a good old rant always goes down well with our Editor, whatever the angle. "

She felt safe in talking so openly: the trade papers were no threat to her, and this boy looked as though he was wet behind the ears. In fact, the second lecture would probably be fairly run-of-the-mill. She was counting on the last session, Dr. Brian Donovan's talk, to give her the big story she needed to impress her editor. After all, when they'd had lunch together, Brian had almost told her that he was going to make waves. What a pity he hadn't allowed her to look at his paper beforehand. Never mind, if he said anything earth-shattering, or potentially earth-shattering, she would collar him straight after the lecture and get him to give her some off-the-cuff quotes. He could hardly refuse to speak to her, after practically eating her alive when they had lunch. Maybe she should have led him on a bit? Well, it was too late now...she would just have to turn on the charm when she interviewed him later on. In this outfit, no problem.

Further down the hall, in her seat near the platform, Susan Simpson was trying hard to re-adjust to New York time. Eight hours in an economy class airline seat, followed by a restless night on the hard bed in her dingy downtown hotel had left her with a thumping headache, and cramp in her left leg. After the usual two hour hold-up at JFK, she had arrived so late that the restaurant had closed, and she had only been able to grab a burger and fries from the hotel bar. Although she had washed it down with a large brandy (which kills all known germs, according to Dr. Guy Johnson, her colleague at the East Central Hospital) her stomach was churning.

Getting away from work had been a nightmare, with extra clinics to take and a locum to instruct. Was this Summit going to be worthwhile? She sincerely hoped so as she had taken a week's holiday to attend, and paid her own air fare and hotel bill. Despite his promise, after his first phone call, Brian Donovan had not come back to her with any further information about GE203, and she felt bitterly let down. Obviously, he had been busy preparing his paper for this afternoon's lecture, but surely, if he had some results to report, he would have contacted her? Maybe there was nothing sinister about the mystery ingredient. In that case, why not say so? Or had he simply dismissed her as unimportant, a mere clinician with a bee in her bonnet?

She had a perfect right to try and do the best for her patients, and if she was worried about something that might affect their chances of recovery, she should be taken seriously. Bloody professors..all they thought about was where the next industry grant was coming from, and their own self-importance.

This train of thought made Susan very angry, but the sudden surge of self-righteousness and accompanying adrenaline rush had one good effect: she suddenly felt a lot less queasy. She sat up straight in her seat, did a couple of deep-breathing exercises to wake up her system, and took a swig of water from the small bottle in her briefcase. She made a decision: she certainly wasn't going to be fobbed off by Brian, and would approach him after his lecture for some answers. Even if he didn't give a toss about ethics in the food industry, she did.

When she had arrived at the hall, she signed in at the lavish reception desk manned by FizzCo staff in bright red mini skirts. As she pinned on her obligatory security badge, she decided that she would never work for them, or any other food and drink company as long as she lived . Her pay might be pathetic, and the East Central Hospital was the pits, but at least she was helping people, unlike Dr. Donovan.

However, she would definitely attend the dinner FizzCo were hosting at the Waldorf Astoria that evening: it was almost a pleasure to take advantage of their tainted hospitality, and she might even glean some inside knowledge about the dubious manufacturing and marketing methods used by them and similar companies.

The first lecture was about to start, and Susan was forced to switch from campaigning to professional mode. The subject of genetic profiling had always interested her, and these speakers were at the top of their field. They had just walked onto the platform and were taking their place at the podium. It should be fascinating stuff. She pulled her notebook out of her briefcase, sat back in her seat and concentrated hard.

****

"For god's sake, Gina, where the hell is she? She spent the morning at the Brooklyn AIDS Clinic, and was supposed to be here by 2pm. There are three American TV stations here, and ten UK journalists, including a man from BBC Radio Four, but no Elizabeth Collins for them to interview or photograph. This is a complete cock-up. "

In the foyer of the Conference Hall, a distraught Bruce James was fuming. His face was dark crimson, and the buttons on his lilac shirt were straining against his heaving stomach, which was even more inflated than usual after a night of daiquiri cocktails washed down with gassy American beer. The target of his wrath, the hapless Gina Boyle, was talking on two mobile phones at once, trying to find out if the British Junior Health Minister, Elizabeth

Collins, was en route for the Obesity Conference, or had been sidetracked or (even worse!) had escaped.

Ever since Gina had suggested that Elizabeth should be invited to the Obesity Summit, the FizzCo UK Group Publicity girl had been working her socks off to make it happen. Until this afternoon, things had gone well. Elizabeth had been sent a list of the distinquished speakers who were due to appear at the Summit, plus, in the next post, a letter from FizzCo USA President, Herbert Willis inviting her to visit the kiddies' clinic which was funded by FizzCo. By a lucky co-incidence the date of the Summit corresponded with the UK Prime Minister's visit to Washington and, as the two were rumoured to be having an affair, it seemed logical that she would decide to cross the pond for a few days.

Whether she was motivated by lust for the Prime Minister, Jack Barton, concern for AIDS victims or felt there was an urgent need to explore ways to combat the world obesity crisis, was not Gina's prime concern (although she suspected, that, like most politicians, Mrs. Collins was always up for a trip to the US, at the British taxpayers' expense, especially if it included some good photo opportunities to lift her profile, plus a bit of nooky on the side). The important thing was that Elizabeth had decided to come to New York, and to attend the Summit.

Gina's next job was to make sure that the Minister would be photographed with Bruce, preferably in front of a FizzCo logo, and gave some interviews praising the Summit and - fingers crossed - FizzCo's involvement with it. Unfortunately, as she hadn't yet turned up, there was a strong possibility that Mrs Collins had either been recalled to London after visiting the AIDS Centre, or she had taken a plane to Washington to visit her (rumoured!) lover and boss, Jack Barton.

"She definitely left at 1pm, in a car heading for the Conference Centre? Where can she have got to? It's now nearly 2.30pm and there's no sign of her." Gina was speaking on one of her two mobile phones to her opposite number in the New York FizzCo office. She tried not to sound desperate. "Don't worry, she's probably stopped off for some lunch or shopping. I am sure she'll be here soon. I'll get back to you." Switching off one mobile phone, she yelled into the other one - this time, without trying to disguise her panic.

"Jim, get down here immediately, and wait with us in the lobby. If she suddenly comes in, we have just got to get some good snaps. It might be our only opportunity." Her photographer had popped into the Conference Centre restaurant for some lunch, but food would have to wait. Gina just couldn't afford to miss out on this one. Her job was on the line, yet again.

"You heard that, she's definitely on her way " she said to Bruce James, who was now hopping from one foot to the other, and making loud panting noises, like a camel on heat.

"Why don't you go outside and stand on the steps so you are ready to greet her? The FizzCo publicity girls are all lined up, and they will release their red and green " Super Snacks" balloons into the air when she arrives. Bring her in here and Jim will get some really good pictures. You can talk her through our ranges, and then escort her into the Conference Hall. The first British speaker is Dr. Brian Donovan from The Royal College, London. His lecture is at 4.30pm. She's bound to want to listen to what he has to say, and then we can take her into the Press Room for interviews. We must make sure that none of the other companies here get hold of her, though. Turn on your charm, Bruce. She won't be able to resist you. "

Bruce stopped panting and smiled at Gina. "You're right, of course. I'll go outside now and wait. Once I've made contact with her, she'll stay with us. You've worked hard, Gina but now it's up to me to do the corporate bit. The last time I met Mrs. Collins it was at a very stuffy industry do, but she's bound to remember me. Most women do"

He walked through the revolving glass doors and took up a position on the Conference Hall steps, just in front of six miniskirted PR girls, holding their " Super Snacks" balloons. With their low-cut t-shirts, and bouncy accessories, the girls were an uplifting sight, and Bruce congratulated himself on deciding to go along with US style razzmatazz at the Summit. Just because obesity was such a serious subject, there was no need to skip the glamour. Unfortunately, while he was pondering the value of sex as a selling tool, the New York skyline darkened, and it started to rain. An hour later, the PR girls were looking jaded, and their balloons had started to deflate. The knife-sharp creases in the trousers of Bruce's new pin-striped suit had disappeared, and his shirt was covered with dark, wet patches.

Just as he was beginning to think that the four thousand dollar outlay on this reception was a waste of company money, a sleek green Lincoln saloon pulled up in the road at the foot of the steps. The uniformed driver got out and opened the rear door. A pair of feet in shiny black high-heeled shoes appeared, attached to the longest legs Bruce had ever seen in his life. He forgot about the rain, and dashed down the steps, just as the rest of the Junior Health Minister's curvacious body appeared. Elisabeth Collins was stunning, far better looking than Bruce remembered. Those legs! When they'd met before, she had been wearing a long evening dress which showed off her amazing breasts, now she was in a simple grey suit, with a knee-length skirt, and severely tailored jacket over what looked like a white lace shirt. With her tawny skin, and short, curly black hair, she was magnificent.

"Eat your heart out Condoleeza Rice, you don't hold a candle to our Liz. What a cracker", thought Bruce, as he side-stepped a large puddle, and thrust his hand out towards her. "Hello, Minister, I'm Bruce James from FizzCo UK - we met last year at the Guy's Hospital fundraising dinner, if you remember. I'm so glad you have managed to fit the Summit into your schedule after your visit to the AIDs hospital. The obesity crisis is something we need to tackle with world-wide initiatives like this. Can I have the pleasure of escorting you inside?"

"Fine, yes I do remember you Mr. James, " she replied, ignoring his outstretched hand. " But I haven't got a lot of time. The Prime Minister has asked me to take this evening's red-eye flight from Kennedy to Washington where he is in talks with the President. I gather that he has health issues to discuss with me. It's most convenient that we are both in the US at the same time. However, I do want to hear what Dr. Brian Donovan has to say, and meet some of the more prominent people here. Do you think you could arrange that for me?"

Bruce resisted the urge to take her arm. Instead, he turned and led the way up the steps , through the revolving glass doors and into the lobby where Gina and her photographer were waiting. "Do you mind if we take a photograph here, before we go into the Conference Hall, Mrs. Collins? It wouldn't take a moment, and we can send it out to the British papers tonight. I gather you are addressing a meeting of the Royal College of Nursing in London next week. I am sure they will be delighted to learn that you are attending this Summit. They have huge challenges to address about the problem of obesity-related illnesses. Although, perhaps "huge" was an inappropriate word. Ha. ha."

Her reply was terse. "Mr. James, you certainly seem to know an awful lot about my schedule. I'll be frank with you - I'd would rather be photographed with a leading scientist such as Dr. Donovan than with you, especially as I see that you have your company logo displayed everywhere. I noticed your girls outside. Lovely touch, but they did look damp and miserable. Big multinational companies such as yours are not very popular with the British electorate, I'm afraid, but you are welcome to make up a threesome and appear in some of the pictures with Dr. Donovan and myself. Try to organise something after his lecture. "

A threesome...I wish! By now, Bruce was entranced by Mrs. Collins , and could well understand why Jack Barton might be prepared to risk his marriage, and job, for the sake of bedding such a gorgeous creature. The pictures would have to wait. He shoo-ed away Gina and her very hungry photographer, as if they were a couple of rabid dogs sniffing round a particularly succulent pork chop. "Not now, Gina." he muttered, glaring at her. " Mrs. Collins and I are busy. Get her a copy of the Summit Programme, and organise some tea in the Press Room after Dr. Donovan's lecture."

****

The seat reserved for Elisabeth Collins was in a second floor box overlooking the Conference Hall platform. Two members of the European Union Council for Health, and the head of the US Food and Drug Administration were already in the box, and stood up politely as Bruce and the Junior Health Minister entered. Bruce made the introductions and they both sat down. The second speaker had just left the platform.

"Your British scientist is the next man on , ma'am, " said a short, fat man, who looked as though he lived on junk food, but was apparently the boss of the FDA, the powerful governing body that monitors all drugs and food in the US.

He continued, politely: "I hear he is going to shake a few people up here. We have started some radical moves in the US to attempt to slow down the spread of obesity such as getting big food companies to fund special clinics for overweight people, and, of course, we have stopped most of the supersizing, the practice of selling huge amounts of food at cheap prices. Several states have now banned the sale of junk food in schools. And we're telling companies to be more accurate about measuring the calories and other nutrients in their food. Maybe you people in the UK should start being more radical?"

"The problem is obviously very serious, " said Elisabeth, carefully. "But our Prime Minister is also aware that people should not be treated like children. We don't want to inflict a "nanny state" on our citizens, but they should, of course, be able to choose healthy meals and the supermarket chains have a responsibility to produce them. We believe in education, good medical treatment and choices...that's the key word, choices."

At that moment, Brian Donovan walked onto the stage. He was dressed in a dark blue suit and carried a laptop PC and a clipboard. He strode to the centre of the stage, and placed his laptop on the sloping lectern. He opened the PC, and pressed a switch. The screen behind him lit up. "Obesity: the Biggest Health Issue of the 21st Century." He smiled at the audience, and started to speak.

Down in the main part of the Hall, Susan clutched her notebook tightly. There was no doubt about it, Brian was a very attractive man, she thought. Now, let's hear what he's got to say.

****

The first half of Brian's lecture consisted mainly of statistics, illustrating the scale of the world-wide explosion in obesity. He also produced some horrifying slides of overweight people, including several of very young, hugely obese children. It was shocking, certainly, but fairly run-of-the-mill stuff. His audience had already experienced similar themes at other conferences. Susan began to wonder if he was going to say anything interesting at all.

After about fifteen minutes, his tone and body language changed. He loosened his tie, and closed the lid of his laptop computer.

"So, who is actually to blame for this appalling epidemic? " he said. "When I was preparing this lecture, I explored the usual "culprits": social change, lack of nutrition education, genetic influences, the increase of affluence with its accompanying greed, the role of the food industry, stress, sedentary lifestyles, TV advertising, the automobile - the whole lot of them.

"I also looked at trends such as the American Heart Association's study in 2005 which showed obesity is increasingly hitting prosperous Americans with incomes over $60,000 a year. They concluded that it should no longer be assumed that poor people are more likely to be fat. The same is true in European countries. In the UK, we have seen a rise in obesity in all income groups, but the so-called "Middle Classes" seem to be getting fatter more quickly - with a 2.5 per cent increase since 2004. Strange that so many surveys have shown that this group are more likely to be following slimming diets than any other!

"Of course, all these things are part of the picture but, during my research I came back, time and again, to instances of deliberate manipulation of our eating habits by the food industry to make huge profits. Many of you here today work for multinational food and drink companies, and I'm afraid you are not going to like what I am going to say next. In fact, I don't much like it myself - but my theory is simple. We are being made fatter by the "fat cats", and I have some pretty strong evidence to support this."

He paused and looked directly at Susan, who was sitting on the edge of her seat, all thoughts of tiredness and tummy bugs completely obliterated from her mind. How on earth did Brian know where she was sitting? She then realised that he didn't: the hall was quite dimly lit, and, as Brian was standing in the full glare of the platform lights, it was impossible for him to see her. She felt the hairs on the back of her neck prickling. Had he discovered something sinister about GE203 after all? She listened intently to the next part of his lecture.

"If you go back twenty five years to the very beginning of the rise in obesity, you will see quite clearly that this co-incides with the proliferation of fast food sold cheaply, and the start of mass-marketing of foods in supermarkets. Since that time, obesity has grown by over 400%, world-wide. Many studies, including several which will be presented to you by eminent scientists in the next few days prove, beyond doubt, that ingesting high fat, high sugar foods on a regular basis can cause dependency, rather like drug dependency.

"This been exploited by the commercial sector, with the practice of selling very large cartons of chips, fizzy drinks and extra large burgers, huge strings of doughnuts, vast "family sized "packets of crisps. The linking of fast food with sports events such as the

Olympic Games in Beijing, and in 2012 in London, is another insidious way of getting people to consume huge quantities, and, of course, the money big firms put up as sponsorship for these events means that governments are dependent on them for revenue.

" The question is, do they use these very clever marketing practices just in order to sell more product in the immediate and short term, or are they a cynical ploy to produce a whole world full of junk food dependent zombies who have to get a regular "fix", and will pour more and more money into their coffers over months, or even years?"

There was a collective sharp intake of breath in the audience. In their box to the right of the platform, Bruce James and Elisabeth Collins glanced at each other. Neither spoke. Bruce was sweating profusely. He tried to read Elisabeth's reaction to Dr. Donovan's comments but she turned her head quickly, without registering any emotion.

Brian continued: "Although the practice of supersizing has now been curtailed, particularly in the US, food manufacturers and supermarkets have other weapons in their armoury which they can use to hook people into spending more money on eating and drinking, and - let's not beat about the bush - dying young. Supermarkets, particularly, now use radio frequency identification to "tag" their customers, so they have an incredibly detailed picture of us all and our buying habits. They can then target our weaknesses, position high-fat foods where they know we won't be able to resist them, formulate products which pander to our appetite for bland, sweet rubbish, and fool us into thinking we are eating healthily. Just let me show you some of the items I found in UK supermarkets just last week and analysed before I came here today. "

Brian's voice had changed , thought Susan. His usual measured tones were still the same, but he was speaking with passion, and conviction. For the second time, she wondered what had happened to make him take this line? He was virtually doing himself out of thousands of pounds of funding from big businesses which invested in his research. His bosses at the university would be furious with him. It was a huge risk. She would have to speak to him after the lecture ended. It was extraordinary. Surely, he wasn't about to reveal the identity of GE203 here and now before even talking to her?

The next section of the lecture was visual: Brian re-opened his laptop, pressed a few keys and a series of images were shown on the screen behind him: greasy-looking fast food, sausages, cream, cakes, processed protein-type "chicken" nuggets, jam doughnuts. "These are all high-fat, or high-sugar foods - or both - and you will see from the analysis on the screen just what they contain. " he said. "Not surprisingly, they are packed with fat and calories. But now look at these, so-called "healthy " foods. Are they really healthy? Not at all. The food manufacturers even lie by using touched up pictures on packaging, and by working just inside the food labelling laws which allow them a 20% tolerance on the nutrient measurements given on the pack. Just look at the true analysis. So, who's being fooled? We all are!"

The following images were of meals targetting overweight people: ready-meals, drinks, snacks. All were promoted on the packaging as "healthy", yet contained a cocktail of additives, often a lot of sugar, and some were even high in fat. Surprisingly, the selection also included an apple.

"You might wonder why I have included a piece of fruit among the items, " said Brian. "Well, I have to tell you that during a simple piece of research undertaken at my own university, I found that a sugar substitute had been mixed with a preservative which coated some of the apples I selected for the research. So, if you don't wash apples thoroughly, folks, you not only risk being poisoned by insecticides, you are also given a shot of sugar-subsitute which could increase your desire for more sweet foods. Nasty, or what?

"I must add that there also seems to be a proliferation of non-specific food additives which seem to be appearing in some foods without being properly tested or regulated. I am currently undertaking very careful analysis of one such additive. At the moment, I cannot say any more than this, but if anyone here from a food product company has used this additive, they will know which one I mean."

"My final point on all this is a very strong one. Why are Governments being so slow to do anything to curtail these practices? Apart from the crack-down on supersizing, which is an obvious one, and a certain amount of "voluntary" restriction on TV advertising of junk food to children (which doesn't prevent each child in the US from seeing over 10,000 advertisements for junk food in any one year!), nothing is being done to curb the power of the people who make money out the one basic, human necessity which we cannot live without: food and drink. I can only speak for my own country, but I can assure you that Ministers in the United Kingdom have had plenty of evidence put before them by various Government Select Committees about this cynical, and highly profitable manipulation of people's health. Yet, very little, mostly ineffective, action has been taken. Why? I think we should be told."

He gathered up his computer, and left the platform. The audience were silent for a moment, and then most people applauded politely. The lights were switched on, and people got up to leave the Conference Hall. An excited Caroline Dempsey strode purposely down the central aisle of the hall and tried to get onto the platform but was told firmly by a conference official, that she would have to wait to speak to Dr. Donovan in the Press Room, like everyone else. She shrugged, undid her suede jacket to reveal a tight, bright purple, low-cut shirt and some impressive cleavage, and headed for the back of the hall. The Press Room was just through the lobby. Look out Brian Donovan, she thought, I want you to name some names.

In the box, Bruce James turned to Elisabeth Collins and said "Can I escort you to the Press room for some pictures, now Minister? In view of Dr. Donovan's comments, I'm sure a lot of people would like to question you. I think that he is somewhat ill-informed, and would love to tell you more about FizzCo's work in the fight against obesity. Our products are the finest quality, and we certainly do not aim to confuse people."

The junior health minister got up abruptly, and picked up her briefcase. "Sorry, Mr. James, I can't stay. Dr. Donovan's very interesting talk went on longer than I expected. I must catch the 7.30pm. flight to Washington. My car will be outside. I'll probably see you in London some time. Goodbye."

****

Chapter Eight

Dinner Menu for United Kingdom Delegates to the International Obesity Summit Conference.
Hosted by: FizzCo UK

Boston Crab and English Stilton Beignet in Lobster Bisque Sauce

Terrine of Duck Confit and Foie Gras with Blueberry sauce and warm Brioche

Beef Wellington with Madeira and Truffle Sauce

Iced Knickerbocker Glory with red berry compote and Green Chartreuse Syrup.

Petit Fours   Calories: 3,258 Fat Grams: 275

"Would you like champagne or Buck's Fizz, madam?" The tail-coated waiter spoke in a soft, Mid-west drawl. He was tall, with a tanned face, dark curly hair and regular features. Normally, Susan Simpson would have chatted to him, perhaps even asked him if he was an actor working between theatrical jobs. He really did look as though he should be in the cast of "Friends" or "Desperate Housewives."

Tonight, she was far too worried for small talk. It was ironic, really. Here she was, standing underneath a large palm tree on the amazing Starlight Roof at Waldorf Astoria Hotel, with its stunning art deco mirrors and impossibly large flower displays. She was among people she had come all this way to meet: the fifty or so British delegates to the conference, who shared her interest in health and nutrition matters. The views of New York City from the long windows were truly sensational. She should have been enjoying herself, but it was hard to adjust her jeg lagged senses to fully appreciate the splendour of her surroundings. She was also feeling agitated for a very good reason: Dr. Brian Donovan had disappeared.

After his lecture that afternoon, he had simply walked off the stage and gone missing. He had failed to appear at the Press Conference, and had not been in contact with any of the Summit organisers. Susan had enquired at the conference registration desk, and found out that he was staying at the Paramount Hotel, near Times Square, together with three other British nutrition experts.

When she'd put in a call to the hotel, she was told that there was no reply from his room. The switchboard operator then put her through to the message service, and she left a brief message, including her own hotel details. Maybe he would contact her later, maybe not. It was all very odd, and rather sinister. His lecture had been hard-hitting, certainly, and there would be plenty of people wanting to speak to him, but surely he was not so frightened that he couldn't face the world's press and the top industry executives at the conference? She had been surprised that he had referred to the "mystery" additive without detailing any definite evidence that it was, somehow, affecting peoples' health. That was hardly professional. He obviously did it because he wanted to encourage discussion, and now he had his big chance to follow through. Yet, he had chickened out. Why?

"I'll have sparkling mineral water, thank you, " she replied, forcing a smile. With jet lag, a stomach ache and now, a dose of acute anxiety knawing away at her insides, she decided not to risk drinking any alcohol. She'd already glanced at the dinner menu displayed on one of the dozen round tables at one side of the huge room, just in front of the open terrace. Beignets, Beef Wellington,

Knicker bocker Glory. It sounded like the perfect prescription for acute gastric strain, indigestion, flatulence and instant weight gain. Just the kind of food that the experts at the Summit spent their lives avoiding. Obviously, FizzCo, USA, did not believe in setting an example.

"Hello, are you from one of the British hospitals or universities?" An attractive blonde girl in a long suede skirt and low-cut purple top, which left little to the imagination, breezed up to her, waving a tape recorder. "Can you spare me a few minutes for a quick chat? I'm Caroline Dempsey, from the London Evening Echo."

"I'm not a doctor or a professor, I'm afraid, so probably not important enough for you to interview ," said Susan, quickly. "My name is Susan Simpson and I work as a dietitian at the East Central Hospital. I'm here to find out if there are any new treatments or initiatives that could help my patients. We are facing a huge problem at the hospital. I've just lost one patient who died from an obesity-related heart attack, and the numbers of acutely obese patients waiting to come to my clinic is growing daily. It's a ghastly situation, and I don't think the UK government is doing enough to address it. Let's hope this Summit wakes them up. There are certainly some shocking statistics coming out of it. You must have plenty of good stuff for your paper."

Susan surprised herself with her own, unusually candid approach to Caroline Dempsey. The girl looked like a typical, brash journalist, yet Susan felt very much at ease in talking openly to her. There was something warm and friendly about her face and attitude, although her clothes were rather flashy and she wore far too much make-up.

Susan was wearing her best black dress, by the American designer Donna Karan and knew she looked good. It was made from soft jersey, cut knee length, perfectly plain at the front, but with a low-cut, draped back. On one shoulder, she had pinned a large, thirties syle diamante broach which she had found in a charity shop. The effect was elegant and understated, and perfect in the slightly decadent, over-the-top setting of the Starlight Roof. With her dark hair and pale skin, she looked as though she should be sitting for a Tamara de Lempicka painting.

In direct contrast, the girl standing in front of her appeared to have dressed to get the maximum attention from the male delegates. The combination of long green skirt, pointed boots, purple silk top, and an aggressive-looking agate pendant dangling suggestively between her breasts was definitely "fuck me" gear. In the middle of this, somewhat unkind, observation, Susan pulled herself up short, and made a mental note not to be so stuffy: good luck to the girl; it was obviously the perfect outfit for the job she had to do: brown-nosing self-important men and getting them to give her good quotes. Clever, really.

"As usual, the newspaper journalists at the conference were pipped by TV and radio, " said Caroline. "A short item went out on BBC Radio Four News about overweight children at 11pm, and I think that they will be following up the story about the multinational food companies being responsible for the world obesity crisis on the Today programme tomorrow morning. Some of the live film has already gone out on Sky; just a clip, though. The follow-up stuff depends, of course, on whether, any of us can find Dr. Donovan. He's disappeared without trace. I've been over to his hotel, the Paramount, and he hasn't checked out yet, but hasn't been seen since the lecture.

"I'm working on the theory that he has been abducted by the Muffins 'n Burgers marketing department, bumped off and buried in a concrete flyover somewhere in New York State; his lecture was powerful stuff, and they will be gunning for him. I exaggerate, obviously, but I have been writing a lot of consumer features about the food industry lately, and I wouldn't put it past them to try and shut him up. I had lunch with Brian a couple of weeks ago, and it seems to me that he's shot himself in the foot as far as getting lucrative grants for his research is concerned. His university bosses must be furious. The mysterious ingredient he referred to is interesting. I'd love to know more. Coating apples with sugar substitute is a strange thing to do as well What, in your professional opinion, could be the reason for such a thing?"

This mixture of hard facts and conjecture swept over Susan like a tidal wave. After years of working with academics and health professionals, she just wasn't used to the upfront style of this colourful, outspoken journalist. In a couple of seconds, she had learnt that Caroline knew Brian, that the journalist had been one step ahead of her and actually been over to the Paramount Hotel, and that she, too, suspected some kind of collusion in the food industry to make people eat more rubbish. Even Mark, her former lover and a top marketing executive, hadn't been so forthright (come to think of it, he had been devious as hell). Susan took a sip of her mineral water before replying, carefully:

"The sugar substitute could, I suppose, be part of the special coating apple growers use to preserve picked fruit before it's packed up and sent to the supermarket. We always advise people to wash apples thoroughly to remove this coating, and any traces of pesticide before eating them, but I think many people ignore this advice. Also, apples used in restaurants and given to school children probably aren't washed properly. So, a lot of people could be ingesting the coating.

"There is definitely evidence that sugary tastes on the palate can make people crave more sweet foods even if they don't contain sugar. For instance, fizzy drinks which contain aspartame, and other sweeteners, may be low in calories, but they often taste even sweeter than sugar-loaded drinks, and many people trying to shed weight actually find that they eat more chocolate or biscuits if they consume these drinks. That's why we advise them to drink water instead. Why a fruit producer should want people to crave sweet foods is a mystery, though - unless they have a massive shareholding in a confectionary or biscuit firm. Which, I suppose, could be the case...although, please don't quote me on that one!"

Caroline appeared satisfied with this reply "I will be following this up with Dr. Donovan, when I can track him down, " she said. "I want to know which fruit producer these particular apples came from. Of course, I also want to know precisely what he was talking about when he mentioned the suspect additive. Did he really mean that some manufacturers put stuff in our food to make us eat more? How could this work, Susan? You must have an idea. Off the record, if you like. I promise I won't quote you. My editor would think I'd gone barmy anyway if I produced this story without making it stand up with a proper interview with Brian Donovan, and at least one or two other scientists and manufacturers. Like most newspapers, we don't worry about upsetting advertisers if it's really hard fact, but there's no point in doing it if there's no evidence. What do you think?

Susan made a rapid decision. This girl was good. She remembered seeing her byline over the Evening Echo story about kids and Type 2 diabetes. The piece had been scary, and designed to shock readers, but at least it had been factual. Caroline obviously had access to health bodies and government departments which she didn't have. If there was something fishy going on, perhaps they could investigate it together.

"Look Caroline. I'll be straight with you. I do know something about this additive. In fact I was the person who brought it to Dr. Donovan's attention in the first place. I am not a research scientist, but I know about people, and I can tell you that I have patients who, I feel, are being put at risk by the food industry. I've also been trying to find Brian, although I didn't actually go over to his hotel. Let's get together after the dinner tonight, and take a cab round there. Even if nothing sinister has happened, it's all very odd. He wanted to stir things up with his lecture. I can't for the life of me understand why he did a runner, if that is, in fact what he's done. This is all on the condition that you don't write a word about any of this - yet. What do you say?"

Her companion's eyes opened wide, her nostrils twitched and her heavily glossed lips parted slightly, like a horse being offered a particularly juicy carrot. "You're on Susan. We'll meet by the flower display in the central lobby at 10.30pm. You can't miss the floral concoction - it looks like the exotic species greenhouse at Kew, minus the glass. I'm sure there are a couple of elephants hidden inside it. Americans just have to supersize everything.

"I've got to schmooze some of these delegates now: there's a leading pediatrician over there who is going to talk about special hospitals for fat kids with diabetes being set up in Manchester and Birmingham. She's promised me a run-down of her paper. Sounds useful stuff for a couple of features. See you later."

She turned rapidly on one high heel, and strode off, grabbed a second glass of champagne from a passing waiter, and then disappearing into the crowd. Susan moved towards the open lobby doors, where she tried to appreciate the view. It was truly breathtaking: the Empire State and Chrysler Buildings, the Brooklyn Bridge; Maybe, some day, she'd come back here for a holiday and explore Manhatten properly. Now, there were people to talk to and work to do. She decided to put Brian out of her mind for the moment, and circulate. After all, that was what she was here for.

Half an hour later, with several useful business cards tucked into her black leather handbag, she made her way towards the circular tables where dinner would be served. When she checked the large table plan, set out on an elaborate gilt stand the size of a small football pitch, she found that she was seated next to Bruce James. Well, she would have to be polite, although she felt, like Brian Donovan, that it was Bruce and his kind who were killing people off. Admittedly they had a "healthy foods" division, but most of their profits came from sugar-loaded soft drinks. One of her young patients, Daryl O'Brien, was drinking five litres of FizzCo's Fruity Pop a day when he had first started attending her hospital clinic He was diabetic, and weighed seventeen stone, ten pounds. Susan was suddenly very glad that she had decided not to indulge in any champagne. Speaking to Bruce James would be interesting.

****

By ten o'clock, Susan was regretting her decision to keep off the booze: a glass or two of wine might have eased her through the meal. It had turned out to be less interesting than she expected. Bruce James seemed to be in a very bad mood. He had asked Susan one or two questions about her job, told her how much FizzCo donated to health care in the UK (£2 million, mainly for cancer research, raised by high sales during their sponsorship of the West Country marathon), then turned his back on her while he chatted up a thin young blonde journalist from Glamour Magazine dressed in a low-cut sequinned shift.

Susan's other neighbour, Professor Stanley Harwood, was at least seventy and very deaf. He was an endocrinologist from Leeds, due to deliver his paper on glandular disorders the following afternoon. It was a fascinating subject, but, as Susan soon found out, it was hard to discuss it with him. After pitching a couple of questions, very loudly, and receiving no answer to either of them, she resorted to smiling and nodding while he held forth on which drugs were most efficient in dealing with under-active thyroid conditions. He then repeated the same inpromptu lecture to the elderly woman doctor on his other side and Susan was left in peace. The meal was magnificent, but so rich that she gave up before her Knickerbocker Glory was served. Her digestion had suffered too much already.

By the time the coffee and petits fours arrived, she had had enough. Bruce had stopped talking to the pretty girl from Glamour, and was tucking in to a couple of petits fours, so she seized her opportunity:

"I hope you'll forgive me, Mr. James. I'm going to make my way back to my hotel now. It's been a long day, and I want to be fresh for tomorrow's seminar. Thank you so much for your hospitality."

Bruce stuffed a miniature chocolate profiterole in his mouth, and wiped it carefully with his white linen napkin. "Of course, Miss Simpson. What I would very much like to do is to have lunch with you when we get back to London. Our new "Super Snacks " healthy eating ranges could well be incorporated into your hospital's treatment programme for obese patients. Fat people love them."

"I'm sure they do, Mr. James, " Susan replied, and added, without a trace of sarcasm, "That's probably why they are fat." Luckily, Bruce was too wrapped up in his persuit of the Glamour journalist to notice the remark. As Susan rose from her seat, he said: "Gilly and I are off to a club later on for a bit of a boogie. See you tomorrow, perhaps. Great stuff!"

Susan made her way to the Powder Room, which was so luxurious that she wondered if she could creep back in there later and sleep on the floor. Her own, rather dingy, hotel was a converted brownstone house, which had seen better days. Her room was on the fourth floor, and tiny. She collected her beige trenchcoat and made her way to the lifts. She wondered if Caroline would meet her, or whether she would get side-tracked by another "story". Maybe she wouldn't turn up. In any case, Susan made up her mind that she would go to the Paramount, alone if necessary, and try to find Brian. She had some serious questions for him.

When she stepped into the lobby, she checked her watch and found that she had ten minutes to wait. She took the opportunity to sit and watch people walking by, from a vantage point on a padded leather bench near the enormous flower display that Caroline had described so graphically. It was a fascinating experience.

Over half of the people she saw were obese, and probably around a quarter were so fat that they had difficulty in walking. A group of elderly, very overweight tourists were checking in at the desk, and most of them used wheelchairs or walking sticks. In twenty years' time, when the current generation of junk food-guzzling teenagers reached the age of forty, most of them would be unable to walk properly, she thought. How appalling.

Just then, the lift doors opened and Caroline Dempsey strode into the lobby, carrying a purple handbag the size of an airline carry-on case. She looked a bit dishevelled, and her skirt was creased, but she had a big smile on her face. "Hi Sue, " she breezed. "What a hellish dinner. All those delicious courses. It must have been specially planned to ruin my diet. I've put on at least five pounds. Never mind, I made some good contacts and fleshed out some of the stuff I did earlier. I've been fleshed out as well...my god this skirt feels tight. I've already filed a couple of pieces, and the laptop's in my bag, so I can do some more copy at the Paramount. Let's go, shall we? "

The black doorman, magnificent in his green and gold uniform, hailed a cab, and the two women were driven to the Paramount Hotel, just a few blocks away. As the cab made its way down Broadway, Susan tried to concentrate on the amazing colour and razz-ma-tazz of New York's entertainment district. She couldn't stop looking at the food joints: flashing signs promised cheap deals on every kind of food from traditional burgers and Chinese noodles, to take-away blinis and caviar. These days, there was no need to sit in a restaurant for longer than 15 minutes, and most people on the street seemed to be eating as well. When did they stop? Only while they slept, probably, with late-night refrigerator raids as a safety valve.

Food dominated the lobby of the Paramount Hotel as well. Visitors returning from a night out at the theatre could indulge in a late night snack at the Mezzanine Restaurant, grab a nibble at the gourmet speciality shop (sandwiches and drinks) or fill their stomachs at the Library Bar (cocktails and "lite bites").

The hotel receptionist was polite and concerned. She said that there had been quite a few calls for Dr. Donovan, but he had been out all day. She told them to sit down while she tried to contact him on the house phone. If there was no reply from his room, he could possibly be in the Business Centre, or the gym. She tried both and then beckoned them over to her desk. "He is in the Business Centre, sending emails and will come down shortly to the Library Bar to meet you both," she said.

Susan felt some kind of relief. At least Brian was here. He hadn't been abducted, jumped off the Brooklyn Bridge or been knocked down by a car. She was surprised at how much she cared about his fate.

"Good, a result at last," said Caroline, as they settled into a cosy booth in the panelled bar. "The drinks are on me. I am sure my editor would approve of a bit of investment. I could get a series out of this. What will you have - a cocktail or champagne?"

Susan was horrified. It was obvious that she had to curb the enthusiasm of this journalist. There was yet, as far as she knew, no evidence that GE203 was harmful, or even sinister. Brian obviously had his own reasons for hinting that the ingredient was a "fattener" in his lecture, but he hadn't named names, or given the slightest indication of how the substance would work to encourage overeating, where it came from, whether it was plant-based, or synthetic. He was too good a scientist to say anything at all without proper, clinical evidence about the substance.

"Look, Caroline, I like you, but let's get something straight otherwise, I'm leaving. I can assure you that Brian is too well versed in the machiavellian plotting of journalists like you to talk to you without me being here. You either swear, in front of both of us, not to write anything until we say so or you are out of the picture. Geddit? God, I sound like Glenda Slagg. It must be catching. "

Despite her anger, Susan burst out laughing.

She continued: "Sorry, I didn't mean to be rude to you. I'm sure you are brilliant at your job. But, this is science, Caroline. It affects peoples' health, and therefore it is political too. If you are clever, you will swear not to go ahead with an article until Brian gives his consent. Otherwise, you'll land him in the shit. He is a nice guy, and, despite having to toe the line as far as his college sponsorships are concerned, he has done some brilliant work in the field of nutrition for the elderly, and for children. His research on the importance of folic acid during pregnancy has probably saved thousands of couples from the heartache of producing a kid with spina bifida. Don't destroy his life, please."

"You win. The tape recorder is off, and I will keep my mouth shut until you both say so. But, I will definitely be writing a series on the hidden ingredients in food that can make you fat and pose a few questions on just why food producers want us to get fatter - apart from the obvious one of making us all spend more money. I'll limit it to things like sugar, hidden fats, the way sugar subsitutes make people crave food, and that kind of thing. I will leave out the "mystery ingredient" bit, until you say so. That will give you both time to harden up on the evidence. Please, though, do keep it exclusive to me. That's not much to ask, is it?"

Susan's reply was short and succinct. " Talk to Brian, he's the scientist."

****

Chapter Nine

China Science News.Com November 6th, 2008
Total export to the US from China for US store group Morley Mart Holdings announced today, exceeds the figure of $25 billion. As well as goods in the technology sector, exports to Morley and other US supermarket chains now include confectionary and food ingredients. The Changjia Food Company, which has its HQ in the new Chongqing Technological Park, announced that their profits are likely to rise by 35% over the next year, thanks to continuing good business with the US. Chairman Tang Liu said today: "Our new candy range inspired by computer games is proving particularly popular with American children." Click here for more*.

When Brian walked through the long white curtains at the back of the Conference Centre platform, he felt drained but curiously elated at the same time. He had given a lecture which would set people talking and might even persuade the British Government to do something positive to halt the rise of obesity. The US was already taking steps, but they needed a shake-up as well. He just hoped that the Vice Chancellor of his University would be sympathetic to the stance Brian had taken: if not, he could lose his job.

As he made his way down the short flight of steps behind the stage, he was astonished to see three, oriental-looking men in dark suits barring his way. The aggressive looking character in the centre of the trio was wearing fine-rimmed glasses, and carrying a large, expensive looking black brief-case. Thick-set, with very broad shoulders, he appeared threatening, despite his lack of height.

Brian spoke quickly and firmly. "Excuse me, gentleman, I must go round to the front of the auditorium. There's a Press Conference which I am due to attend."

"Sorry, Dr. Donovan, but we insist that you join us for tea, first" said the thick-set man, taking a step nearer to Brian.

"It will only take an hour or so. Mr. Tang Liu, the Chairman of the Changjia Food Company, for whom we have the honour of working, is waiting at the Plaza Hotel to greet you. I have a letter here from the Vice Chancellor of your University promising that you would meet up with him to discuss funding for a piece of research on the importance of carbohydrate in children's diets. If we decide to offer your college the research project, it will be worth many hundreds of thousands of pounds. Mr. Liu flies back to Beijing tonight, so I am sure you would wish to see him."

Brian thought quickly. At their last meeting, the Vice Chancellor had mentioned a Chinese company which could be sending delegates to the Summit, and the possibility of making contact with them.

Chinese food and technology conglomerates were now interested in using European and American scientists to undertake research related to their products. This was part of their export marketing strategy. Despite thousands of years of Chinese medical expertise, it was still deemed valuable to have a piece of Western research to back up the efficacy of a product line, especially where overseas sales were concerned. The Chinese economy had the fastest growth rate in recorded history, moving 300million people out of poverty, but they were still hungry for more...and more. They already manufactured two thirds of the world's copiers, toys, DVD players and shoes, and now they were after the food market. Not just food outlets like Chinese takeaways and noodle restaurants. They were after the big supermarket money-spinners: confectionary, chocolate, packaged foods.

Brian tried to remember the conversation at his first meeting with the Vice Chancellor, sentence by sentence, word for word. Nowhere could he recall his boss mentioning that a letter had been sent to the Chairman of the Changjia Food Company. He supposed that it could well have happened afterwards, and maybe there was an email waiting for him which would confirm this.

"If you don't mind, I will just check my emails before we go. I want to be certain about this," said Brian. "As you are aware, sometimes the awarding of research grants can be quite a sensitive issue. I do need to have some authority before I meet Mr. Liu. If you can wait a minute, I will just go along to the Press Room, and join you outside. Presumably you have a car?"

"Sorry, Dr. Donovan, there is no time for that. You can check your emails when you get to our hotel. Our car is at the back of the Conference Centre. Come with us - now. " Something about the cold, uncompromising delivery of the last four words, made Brian's stomach turn over. The speaker's two companions had now moved either side of Brian, and turned towards the back entrance to the Hall. Thick-set man turned around as well, and and led the way.

Flanked by such a solid "ring of steel", Brian had two choices: either he could run backwards up the platform stairs, and probably be caught, or go along with the men. As his lecture had been the last of the afternoon, there was no-one about in the dark area behind the stage, so he had to make his mind up rapidly.

He decided to go with the "gang of three". After all, what could they actually do to him? If he made polite overtures to their boss, the mysterious and obviously very high-powered Mr. Tang Liu, the Vice Chancellor could do the rest. If they offered his University the contract for the research, fine. If they didn't, so what? They could hardly bump him off in the middle of New York. Questions would be asked, and Chinese-American relations would be affected. The Chinese food manufacturers wanted to do business with the US and Europe, so what possible gain would there be for them if they harmed a prominent British nutrition scientist? It was unthinkable.

When they reached the heavily barred steel back doors of the Centre, the two men either side of Brian stepped forward, and pulled them open easily. Despite their height, they were obviously very strong. Outside, a sleek black Cadillac with blacked-out windows waited, with the engine purring. The chauffeur who stood by the side of the car was also Chinese. He wore a collarless jacket and dark glasses. Brian was hustled into the back seat by Thick-Set man, who sat down beside him. The two other men sat in the middle seat, leaving the front seat, next to the driver, empty. For one moment, Brian considered opening the offside door and making a dash for it. Unfortunately, the late afternoon traffic on the freeway was dense, fast, and unrelenting, and there was no traffic island or other safety area to run to. Brian decided to stay put, but seize the initiative. He tried to speak calmly:

"Gentlemen, I think it's about time you introduced yourselves to me. As you are obviously well aware, I am Dr. Brian Donovan, from the Royal College London, a scientist and university lecturer who specialises in the field of human nutrition. You are - whom, exactly?"

His muscle-bound neighbour grinned, and spoke, very softly. "I am Mr. Hok Deng, and I am in charge of the confectionary section of our business. My colleagues are Mr. Hu Zhang, and Mr Mao Wang, from the financial services part of the company. We came over to the Summit as we, too, are worried about the increase in obesity: since your fast food became so popular in our country, Chinese people are getting fatter. This, we do not want as it will interfere with their productivity. Fat people become lazy. Your lecture was interesting, Dr. Donovan, but you did not mention that personal discipline is necessary, too. No-one forces people to overeat. It is a question of control."

This was not the proper time for Brian to start a reasoned argument about the causes of obesity in China. He had never been to the country, and suspected that, whatever he said, he would be in trouble. He was already beginning to feel like a prisoner. Hok Deng was sitting uncomfortably close to him, and the two men in front of them were staring straight ahead. It's like being in a James

Bond movie, he thought. Maybe Mr. Tan Liu will be wearing a long white caftan and stroking a grey cat. Or, he'll be surrounded by nubile young Chinese girls wearing skimpy shorts. Most likely, he would be sitting at a huge desk with machine guns in the arm-rests of his chair.

He smiled to himself, then shuddered. This was no joke. Thank goodness he had spoken to Molly before his lecture. At least she knew that he intended to go to the FizzCo dinner, and then back to the hotel this evening. She would be sound asleep by now, though. Maybe Susan Simpson would be concerned if he didn't turn up at the dinner? He found himself sinking into an alarmingly fearful state, and pulled himself up sharply. This situation was becoming ridiculous.

When they arrived at the Plaza, the three men moved into "ring of steel" formation once again, and the odd-looking foursome made their way through the lobby and up in the lift to the 24th floor. The door of Mr. Tan Liu's suite was slightly ajar, as if he'd been expecting them, and Brian was ushered in. The room was the size of a small ballroom, decorated in shades of white and beige with a large window overlooking the city. The panorama of skyscrapers behind the window, which had long gold and cream curtains, looked like a set from a musical comedy.

The big boss of the Changjia Food Company was standing by the window, looking out at Park Avenue below. As Brian, and his companions entered the suite, he turned and walked towards Brian. "I am Tan," he said, smiling broadly, "It is so good to meet you, Dr. Donovan."

Brian was so taken aback by Mr. Liu's appearance, that he could only stutter "and you, sir".

Tan Liu definitely did not look like the kind of man he imagined would head up a huge food conglomerate.

He was very tall, well-built, and appeared to be about sixty years old. Semi-casually dressed in a turquoise blue and white striped shirt, harlequin patterned tie and grey slacks attached to his body by a pair of bright red braces, his outfit stood out boldly against the muted beige and white of the immaculate suite.

His very dark, luxuriant hair looked suspiciously like a wig. The giveaway was the tuft of hair over each ear which appeared to anchor his dark, horn-rimmed spectacles to his head. The sleeves of his shirt were rolled up to elbow-level, exposing a huge gold Rolex watch. On the index finger of his left hand was a chunky gold signet ring emblazoned with a ruby-eyed dragon. The whole effect was extraordinary.

"Wall Street meets the World of Suzie Wong, via Andy Pandy" thought Brian, his worries vanishing. How could such a ridiculous, pantomime figure be a threat? He decided to cut the meeting as short as possible.

"Now, Mr. Liu. I gather that you want to talk to me about a possible scientific study on children and their dietary needs, especially carbohydrate. How did you see this working and what is the object of the study, exactly? As you make confectionary, I assume that you want me to try to establish that children need high levels of carbohydrate in their diet for energy and growth, and these can only be obtained if they eat sweet foods? We know children are being discouraged from eating chips, another good source of carbohydrate, because of the high levels of fat these contain, so they have to get their carbs from somewhere. So, and this is just a hypothesis, it could be argued that eating a few sweets every day is a good idea? Is that the kind of thing you are after?"

Brian surprised himself. It was usually unthinkable to tell a potential client that you knew just what they wanted a scientific study to conclude. The normal routine was for everyone to pretend that the study would be undertaken in a completely open-minded way, then the results would be carefully screened and if they proved to be advantageous to the client, that would be just dandy. Maybe he shouldn't have been so blunt.

Tan Liu looked pained. His smile vanished, and he sat down, heavily on one of the four cream leather sofas in the room. His three "ring of steel" henchmen remained standing by the door. "Come, sit down, Dr. Donovan. I know your reputation and I am sure you would not want to conduct a study which was biased in any way. I am very surprised indeed that you should imagine that I had that in mind. We are currently finalising our marketing strategy following this year's highly successful Olympic Games in Beijing, and this study would be an important part of that. We achieved huge sales during the games, and with such a large international market available to us, we feel we have a responsibility to our customers to ensure that our future products are well-researched."

Brian sat down on the matching cream sofa, opposite Tan Liu. He decided to try and repair the damage he had done by being so blunt. "I am sorry, I didn't mean that the study would be biased. However, it is obvious that children do need enough carbohydrate, and there have been worries expressed that cutting back on some fast foods could leave a gap in their diet, even though it is desirable to reduce fat. Sweets, in small quantities, are not harmful, and do supply simple carbohydrate which is easily absorbed.

" I firmly believe that kids should eat a wide variety of foods. Once I know exactly what you want, and what funds are available, I would prepare a protocol for you before undertaking the research. What figure do you have in mind, and how wide would you require the study to be? Would it be conducted in China, Europe or the US? If you can give me some idea now, then send me a written proposal, I will prepare the protocol."

Tan Liu beckoned to Hu Zhang. "Give me the costing you worked out for this study, please. I know it is quite substantial, and I am sure we can do business with Dr. Donovan's university."

Hu Zhang opened his briefcase and took out a small electronic notebook, which he switched on, then handed to his boss. "Before we discuss figures, you must have some tea, Dr. Donovan. It is well past the hour for your English tea-break, ha ha. We Chinese will drink it at any time."

He pushed a buzzer, and a slim, attractive Chinese girl dressed in a black suit appeared, pushing a trolley. "This is my personal secretary, Connie. She will serve tea. I took the precaution of ordering Earl Grey for you. Is that a good choice?" For some reason, Tan Liu seemed to think that was hilarious, and laughed heartily, his luxuriant hair (or wig), wobbling dangerously as his head nodded up and down.

Brian looked at the cream and gold cup placed in front of him by Connie, wondering if Tan's ludicrous wig was glued on or would soon be slipping off his head. Liu's own tea was served in a small bowl, decorated with gold dragons. From time to time, he placed it on the glass-topped table between the two sofas and looked at the electronic notebook.

The long pause, and the smoky taste of the tea had a strange effect on Brian: he suddenly started day-dreaming about his mother and sisters at home in South London. His mother had loved Earl Grey tea, always serving in thin china cups. Molly, his wife, preferred coffee and he had become used to drinking copious amounts of the dark brown college brew. Sitting here, facing this extraordinary looking man, sipping the delicious tea, everything seemed unreal. He felt as though he had stepped out of the present and was stuck somewhere in space, perhaps on a parallel universe. The whole experience was bizarre. None of this could be true.

He was pulled back to earth abruptly when Tan Liu placed the electronic notebook on the table, got up from the sofa and strode across the room to the large window. The floor to ceiling curtains, and lights from the buildings behind him provided the perfect stage set for the next part of his speech:

" Our corporation will pay your university a million dollars to cover the cost of setting up the protocol, Dr. Donovan, then a possible three million to carry the project forward. "

Now, Tan Liu was smiling, and waving his arms about in excitement, as if about to break into a dance routine.

"There is a proviso, of course. You will not do any more research into the substance called GE203, which you touched upon in your lecture this afternoon. There is no need for me to elaborate on my reasons for this. I will be writing to your Vice Chancellor and yourself to confirm these arrangements. Now, I am sure you would like to get back to your hotel. It must have been a tiring day for you. My three colleagues here will take you back to the Paramount. Connie, can you order the car for Dr. Donovan, please?" Tan Liu bowed deeply, as if confident that his audience-of-one would approve of these arrangements.

Brian was so shocked by Tan Liu's incredible offer, and the menacing sting in the dragon's tail, that he didn't even pause to wonder how on earth the Changjia Food Company boss could possibly know what substance he had been referring to in his lecture, or where he was staying. He mumbled a brief "thank you" and allowed himself to be escorted out of the suite and to the lift by the "heavy mob."

As the lift descended, Brian suddenly felt very tired, frightened and hungry. Tan Lui might look like a pantomime figure, but he obviously wielded a lot of power.

A million dollars was a ridiculously large amount to offer simply to set up a protocol for a fairly routine piece of research. Even if the protocol was approved, the research itself might never be commissioned. The whole thing sounded suspiciously like a bribe - a bribe to stop him from continuing to delve into the GE203 mystery. The very thought made Brian shudder.

"I expect you are looking forward to going home on Friday, Dr Donovan? " said Hok Deng, softly. "I am sure Molly, and your delightful children Amy and Toby are longing to see you. They are both doing so well at their school in Harrow. With such a marvellous combination of talent in the family it will be interesting to see where their own career ambitions lie. Children are so vulnerable nowadays. It is so hard to be a parent. I have six children of my own, and I worry about them every day. "

Before Brian had a chance to reply, the lift stopped on the

first floor, and Hok Deng bowed and got out, leaving him with the other two men. When it had descended, almost noiselessly, to the ground floor, they escorted him out, through the revolving doors of the hotel, and into the waiting cadillac. By now, Brian was shaking with fear. He gripped his laptop computer tightly, and prayed that he would get back to the hotel safely. Then, perhaps, he would be able to collect his thoughts.

When the car drew up at the hotel, the driver opened the door, and Brian got out, still shaking. As the sleek black automobile slid away into the darkness, Brian stood on the hotel steps for a moment. The lights in Times Square seemed crude and threatening. He collected his key from the concierge, and took the lift to the Business Centre on the 17th floor, which was empty. He sat down at one of the computer terminals and tried to clear his mind. First, he must contact his family to make sure they were all right. Then, he must email the college. If the Vice Chancellor wanted to take money from the Changjia Food Company, it was only fair to tell him what the real cost would be.

****

"Brian, we're over here. You look as if you've seen a ghost." Susan was shocked by Brian Donovan's pale, drawn face. The usual jaunty confidence was definitely missing, and, as he walked into the Libary Bar, he stared around at the few occupants as if he feared that one of them would draw out a gun and attack him.

Susan and Caroline were waiting in their comfortable booth drinking coffee. Caroline had suggested champagne, but Susan was worried that the over-enthusiastic journalist would forget her promise to hold fire on publishing a sensationalist article if she had too much to drink.

Brian sat down in the booth next to Susan. He smiled at the two women, weakly. Susan continued: " Your lecture was brilliant. Why did you disappear? We missed you at the dinner. What happened? You can speak in front of Caroline. It's all off the record until you say so."

"I've just spent an hour in the hotel Business Centre, trying to make sense of it all, " said Brian. "It's too early for any of my emails to have been read in London yet, but I have already received several from the media, asking for interviews, and from four other Summit delegates who would like to meet up with me. They were nutrition researchers from two of the drug companies.

"Something very strange and frightening happened after my lecture, which I can't talk about, yet. It makes me feel certain that I have hit the nail on the head about the multinational companies using any method they can to make people buy their products. Caroline, you must not quote me on any of this at the moment. Please swear that you won't do so. It would be stupid to rock the boat until I have proof. Believe me, after what happened today, I am determined to carry on with my research into GE203 and find out what is going on. It could involve more than big business; governments, even. God, I'm tired. It's after midnight, is there anything to eat in this place?"

"This is the Big Apple, Brian. Food is served all night, every night. I'll order you a sandwich." Susan got up and walked over to the bar.

Caroline seized her chance. She leant over the table, displaying so much cleavage that an elderly man sitting nearby stopped peering at his theatre programme, and took off his reading glasses. His grey-haired female companion nudged him in the ribs, and he put his spectacles on again and looked away.

"Brian, I want to persuade my editor to run a hard-hitting series on the way supermarkets and junk food manufacturers conspire to make people eat more. Obviously, it can't involve the research on the ingredient you mentioned in your lecture as that is not complete, but there is plenty of other material out there, as you know. Will you help? I'm going to ask Susan, too. The three of us could get together to make a really great three-part feature. Who knows, we might get a TV series out of it. All the telly companies are looking for this kind of thing. Please say you will do it?"

At that moment, Brian was not in the mood to be excited at the heady prospect of appearing on TV." Look Caroline, I will help. Right now, I can't even think straight. How about a chat tomorrow evening with Susan as well, so you can produce an outline for your editor?"

"Great, I'll be round at about 7pm. See you then." Satisfied with the promise of a good story, Caroline picked up her purple handbag, squeezed herself out of booth, and marched out of the bar, waving to Susan on her way out.

When Susan saw Caroline leaving, she ordered two large brandies from the barman, and took them back to the booth.

"Here, drink this, Brian. You need it. Your club sandwich is on its way. Now tell me what's happened. I've been worried sick about you. "

She was surprised at how much genuine concern she did feel. Away from his safe, university environment, Brian seemed vulnerable and even more boyish-looking than when they'd met in his office. His floppy hair fell over his forehead, and his blue silk tie was askew. His long thin fingers clasped the huge brandy glass tightly, and she could see that his hands were shaking. Despite her worries, Susan felt very turned on. What they both needed now was the best known cure for nervous tension: sex.

"Well, it's a strange story and sounds like something out of a "B" movie. If I told you that I was hijacked by three menacing Chinese men, forced to go to a hotel and offered a bribe to stop investigating GE203, would you think I had gone mad? I hope not, because that is exactly what happened.

"Now, I suggest that we take these drinks and my sandwich upstairs and continue this conversation in my room Sorry, Susan, that is not the most romantic pass I've ever made at a woman, and I really didn't mean that we should sleep together. Can you forgive me?"

Susan looked worried for a second, and then her features softened and she laughed. " Yes, I do believe you, but you can give me the details later. My own hotel is a dump, so I'm only doing this so I can get a decent bed for the night, and bathe in a luxurious bathroom in the morning. Is that understood?"

When they arrived at Brian's large double room on the 20th floor of the hotel, Susan was impressed by the black and grey chequered carpets, the dark panelling, and the view over New York's theatreland, but the item that really caught her eye was the huge double bed set against the wall facing the long window. It was at least 7ft wide, and covered with a soft brown "throw". She suddenly realised that she was absolutely exhausted, and sat down heavily on the bed, swinging her legs up onto the soft cover. Brian placed the brandy glasses on the bedside table, and took the wrapped club sandwich out of his pocket where he had stuffed it.

He put the sandwich next to the glasses, and sat down close to Susan: "Fancy a picnic in bed, and then a long sleep, Susan? You look tired, and we could both do with a good night."

"You're joking, of course, Brian. I have to know just what happened to you when you left the Conference Centre. Come on. Sit down here next to me and tell me the lot. It's important."

Half an hour, and two brandies later, Susan knew everything about Brian's disturbing adventure. The story triggered shock and sympathy from Susan. This time, she didn't hold back when he put his arms around her. The Club sandwich remained uneaten, and the couple were soon naked in bed together.

Mark, Susan's former lover had been tall and muscular. With Mark, sex was efficient and energetic: orgasm guaranteed, but no afterplay. Brian's body was narrow-hipped, and, in truth, rather boney. What he lacked in physique, he made up for with his love-making. Afterwards, they both fell asleep quickly.

Chapter Ten

Email to Mrs. Elizabeth Collins. I will be in the Georgetown apartment at 10pm. tonight. Please have a report on the Obesity Summit ready for me plus an overview of the strategy you would like to see in place in the UK to combat this increasing problem.

I would also like to go through your figures for the the Health Department's expenditure on anti-obesity drugs for the past six months. I have had discussions on this subject, and other health-related matters, with The President today. As I must go back to London first thing tomorrow morning, please make sure you are available for a fairly lengthy debriefing.

Jack B.

Elizabeth had just checked into the Hyatt Regency Hotel on Capitol Hill, Washington, when she received the email from Jack Barton. As a junior minister, she was not important enough to be given a room at the British Embassy, but her room on the 12th floor was comfortable, and had a computer, fax, and a large bathroom. After all, it was just for one night.

Her small, black carry-on suitcase was on the bed, and she had been unpacking some new cream silk underwear when she noticed the "message alert" signal flashed up on the computer screen. When she read the message, she burst out laughing. "Debriefing" indeed! Jack was getting careless: that kind of joke could be interpreted in the obvious way by one of his aides; emails were becoming a very dangerous method of communication. She would have to warn him about it later.

Meanwhile, it looked as though she would not be spending very much time in the hotel room. She glanced at the neat gold Cartier watch on her wrist: it was now 9pm. The shuttle from New York had been on time and she had had a smooth journey from the airport to the hotel. She would take a quick bath and have a change of underclothes before ordering a taxi to take her over to the Georgetown apartment. Her grey business suit would be fine for the meeting: she probably wouldn't be wearing it for very long, She smiled again, at the thought of seeing Jack. So far, their short affair had been conducted in her own London flat. The danger had been intoxicating but they both realised that it would have to end soon. Even if it was their last night together, tonight would be special; they would be able to relax and enjoy a few hours together without worrying about being disturbed.

Elizabeth was a person for whom the noun "pragmatist" could have been invented. She believed in using every experience as a lesson. Regret, sadness, and shame were sentiments in which she didn't have time to indulge. Even her appearance was uncompromising. She had a splendid, statuesque figure, long legs, broad shoulders and impressive, naturally rounded breasts, but they were the only "soft" thing about her. At forty five, she was in remarkable shape; she was one of the few Ministers to use the gym facilities at the House of Commons, and she hadn't produced any children which might have ruined her figure.

Her short, curly hair style could have made her look mannish, but Elizabeth made sure that her make-up was sensual: glossy dark red lips, eyes heavily outlined in kohl, well-shaped brows, and long, elegant nails painted to match her mouth. She wore Armani suits, Charles Jourdan shoes, and her underwear was made to measure by Rigby and Peller, the Queen's corsetiere. Her Jamaican-born mother had always believed that a lady should wear good underthings in case she was knocked over in the street and a doctor was called. Well, tonight there wouldn't be a doctor present, but her bra and knickers would definitely be seen to advantage by Jack. Sex in a foreign country was exciting enough, sex in the most exclusive love-nest in the world with the Prime Minister of the United Kingdom, was something else.

The Georgetown flat was a refuge for top UK government officials who required somewhere private to meet when doing business in Washington. Only a few people, including the Ambassador, knew of its existence. He, of course, was discretion itself ; if a visiting UK minister needed privacy for one reason or another, the apartment was always used and no questions were asked. Its exact location was kept secret to prevent press and FBI interest. Security at the third-floor apartment was tight; the entry code number was changed every day, and the walls were re-inforced with steel plating. There were no windows, and anyone looking at the outside of the neat terraced house could not possibly guess that the apartment existed. Elizabeth knew that the code for that day would be a seven figure number: the day of the week, followed by the month, then the time of entry. Simple, really.

She switched on CBS news, walked into the bathroom, and turned on both taps, adding some of the hotel's own scented bath essence. Lavender wasn't exactly her first choice of fragrance for a romantic night with Jack, but she would spray on plenty of his favourite perfume, Chanel No 5, before leaving for the apartment. Meanwhile, she had to be quick.

As she stepped into the foaming, lavender-scented water, she heard the male CBS presenter's voice, smooth as treacle, coming from the TV set in the bedroom:

"British premier Jack Barton met with The President today. It is believed that they discussed world health issues and also the problems faced by Britain and the United States on supporting the aging population of both countries. In the UK, as in this country, a number of large corporations have recently gone to the wall, leaving elderly people without adequate pensions. The recent protest demonstrations by senior citizens in New York and London have given this matter a degree of urgency. Tomorrow morning's press briefing by the President will, no doubt, provide more information. Your CBS news team will update you when it happens. Now, back to Chicago for the latest report on the fire which has broken out in the city hospital."

The word "pensions" in the news report caught Elizabeth's attention: there had, indeed, been a demonstration in London the previous week. Over a million elderly people had marched through Whitehall, demanding to know what the government intended to do about safeguarding their pensions. The state pension was woefully inadequate, and now that more and more companies were unable to fulfil their obligations to pay former employees, things were getting very serious. A TV documentary had forecast that, within 20 years, there would be thousands of old folk on the poverty line.

What a pity people are living so much longer, thought Elizabeth. Quite frankly, it was indecent. Measures to prevent doctors from treating elderly people when they were clearly too weak to recover, had already been in place for some time, but old folks' homes were full to overflowing. During her years spent working as a nurse she seen how degrading it can be to be sick and helpless. She would never allow herself to endure such indignity. When she reached retirement age, she would be fine, financially, thanks to her investments. It had been a good idea to buy a flat in Dubai with some of the money she had received from that drug company. The directors had been so grateful when they were awarded the exclusive contract for their bird 'flu vaccine. Clever girl.

Elizabeth had not gone into politics to improve life for the British people: she had gone into politics to improve life for Elizabeth Collins. She had started on the political career ladder by involving herself in local council work, then, bitten by the power drug, had studied for a law degree, eventually quitting hospital nursing. For a while, it had been hard to make ends meet, even though she took on private nursing work. Living at home in Tottenham, North London with her parents was inconvenient, and produced a lot of tension.

Then Elizabeth had a stroke of luck. She had met her husband, Gerald Collins, during a weekend seminar on racial diversity in the judiciary. Her striking good looks caught the eye of the elderly judge, who, despite his fondness for dressing up in lady's footwear, promptly decided that he needed a "trophy" wife. Elizabeth was stunning, intelligent, and a brilliant hostess. They married quietly, and settled down in his Chelsea home. It amused Gerald to encourage Elizabeth's political ambition. After she became an MP, and then a Junior Minister, she grew tired of pretending to be the perfect wife. Five years after their wedding, when Gerald's high heeled leather boot collection began to take up more closet space than her own, Elizabeth asked for a divorce.

The settlement was as discreet as their marriage. Gerald bought her a flat in Victoria, which was very handy for the House, and gave her a generous settlement. They kept in touch, and he was following her career success with great interest.

Good old Gerald, she thought now, as she stepped into her new pale cream silk knickers and bra. He might be a mad old buffer, but his money did help kick-start my political career. I could never have fought, and won, the seat for Brixton, West, if Gerald hadn't supported me. Those early years spent slogging away on the hustings are paying off now.

If I play my cards right, Jack could give me a Minister's job in the next reshuffle. The Health Department has been fun, and so handy for extracting favours from mega-rich drug companies, but I really fancy something a bit meatier: Foreign Secretary, perhaps? What a coup for Jack: the first black British woman in a top cabinet job.

She unwrapped a silk suspender belt and a pair of extra long, sheer, coffee-coloured nylon stockings, turned and performed a mock high kick in front of the TV. Tonight was going to be fun, and great for her career. She just loved combining pleasure with business...

****

At the Georgetown apartment, the British Prime Minister, Jack Barton, was sitting in one of the black leather armchairs in the large sitting room, sipping a glass of champagne and thumbing through the early editions of the New York Times and the Washington Herald. His driver was keeping a discreet vigil at the opposite side of the street, and all the security checks had been done before Jack entered the apartment. To all intents and purposes, he was alone. After days of being tailed by American security people as well as his own Special Branch detectives, it was a great feeling.

This afternoon's meeting with the President of the United States had been his first as PM; it had gone well. The President had been a big buddy of Jack's predecessor, so he had been anxious to make a good impression. Self-confidence was not a problem with Jack - he had bucketloads - but his advisors had warned him to let the President lead the discussion, and to speak in simple terms: America's leader was not known for his appreciation of subtleties, innuendo or clever jokes. Irony was a definite no-no.

The papers both gave a favourable report of the visit. Jack particularly liked two phrases used by the papers' journalists: "Jack Barton , Britain's young, good-looking new premier" and "Jack Barton, who carries on the tradition of friendship between our two great nations".

Details of their meeting would not be revealed until the President's early morning press conference. He had cleared the official press release with the White House before leaving the meeting. It was suitably bland, referring to "mutual concern" over the rising problem of pensions, and also the major health issue of the day; obesity. There were a couple of good lines. Both leaders expressed "shock" at the increasing number of deaths from obesity-related diseases, and "grave concern"about the pensions crisis. Action would be taken although exactly what kind of action wasn't mentioned. No doubt the President would come up with a few ideas for the conference.

Jack smiled. He had learned a lot from his predecessor, especially about controlling the media. It was quite easy to fool the press. Just give them a headline for tomorrow's edition. Then, tomorrow, find them another one. If it contradicted the previous day's offering, it didn't matter one jot. "President pushes obesity and pensions to top of Congress agenda" would do.

If the press knew the real substance of the President's discussion with Jack Barton, they would have enough headlines to last a week. Over half of the two leaders' conversation had taken place off the record, while they were taking a teatime walk in the White House private garden. They were both in agreement: the biggest social problem facing both nations was that of life expectancy: there were just not enough resources in the US or Britain to cope with the increasing numbers of elderly people. Hospitals were being overstretched, pension funds depleted, the quality of life of younger people was being eroded: all because people were living too long.

It's a double whammy, thought Jack, as he drained his champagne glass, and poured another one from the Moet and Chandon bottle on the low black laquered table beside him. Medical advances mean that people live longer, and now there are so many of them that we haven't got the resources to treat or look after them in old age. No wonder the President is worried.

Standards of integrity of politicians, even those of Presidents and Prime Ministers, fell into the "you couldn't make it up" category, but even the most hard-bitten hack might have considered these two leaders' views somewhat extreme.

Jack was used to speaking openly with his own advisors, but when the leader of the free world actually confides that he "wants people to die younger", you wonder if you have actually heard him correctly.

Jack recalled the conversation. It had started with a stunning admission from the President:

"Jack, we've got to help people to die with dignity. I really mean this. We just can't afford to keep paying out to old timers sitting around all day scratching their balls. Like you folks over in the old country, we have already instructed doctors to use their descretion about resuscitation and treatment for the elderly, but now I think the time has come for voluntary euthanasia. The obesity epidemic has been helpful, in some ways: at least people are going to their rest sooner. Agreed, fat people put more strain on health resources, but if we could just put these big bastards into special hospitals and gradually put them out of their misery, we would save a lot of money. What do you think?"

Jack had agreed, and gone even further. "The way to do it, and keep big food businesses happy - the ones that support us both, Mr. President - is to encourage even greater consumption of fast food. We have to do it subtly, of course The euthanasia question is more difficult: there is a lobby for this in the UK, but the vast majority of people would be horrified if it was given as an option. I think the best way forward is to offer it for the terminally ill, then take it from there. Some well-placed press stories and initiatives should smooth the way towards this idea."

At that point during their conversation, the President had received a note from an aide, which provided a temporary embarrassment for Jack. He read it quickly, then sent the aide away and gave Jack a resume of its contents. Some stupid British professor had given a lecture in New York, where he slated both governments for lack of action on world-wide obesity. He had even hinted that some manufacturers were putting appetite enhancing additives into "healthy" foods.

"You'll have to get rid of this son-of-a-bitch, Jack, " the President had said. "If not, you'll find that he could make waves which would make people suspicious of the quality of the food they are eating. We cannot have that…a lot of these appetite enhancing substances come over from China, you know. Those little yellow fellows are getting very uppity these days, Jack, and we do have to curb their exports, but this is not the way to do it. Remember, their army is now bigger than ours. If they can supply something useful which it would be embarrassing for us to produce ourselves, we should encourage them. Get to it, Jack."

Jack put down his glass. It was still half full. Even thinking about the rest of their chat made him feel a bit queasy. Well, he had wanted to join the league of big players. It was time to act bravely and positively. He would prove his good faith by dealing with the British professor. The other measures outlined in their conversation could be more difficult to put into place. Because of the government's small majority in Parliament, it wasn't always easy to get legislation through. He would have to look at different options.

Elizabeth Collins was the girl to help him. A great woman: no scruples, but plenty of energy. He liked that. She provided a welcome intellectual challenge as well; his wife, Marigold was a good sort, and marvellous at protecting their two children from the inevitable press scrutiny, but her conversation was confined to domestic and family matters. Elizabeth was someone to bounce around ideas with. Yes, he liked that about Elizabeth. "Bounce" was a fairly apt description of her charms. He forgot his queasiness, and downed the rest of the champagne in one gulp: this was no time to waver. He could deal with anything.

The door buzzer sounded, and Jack heard a soft voice, which sounded slightly muffled and off-key, through the metal grill: "Jack, it's the woman who's so good for your health, here. Can you let me in? " Jack grinned and got up, instinctively smoothing down his slightly creased trousers. On television, he appeared to be a shortish, cuddly-looking man with unruly brown hair, a crumpled suit and tired eyes. When he had taken over from the former Prime Minister who had more chiselled features and a glassy stare, most pundits had welcomed the fact that Jack looked like the bloke next door: approachable, forthright, honest.

In the flesh, he was taller, at least 5ft 11in, and the "tired" eyes showed flashes of passion and anger. There was nothing remotely "cuddly" about Jack's brain either: it was razor sharp. His sometimes untidy appearance gave young upstarts in the party a different impression. They were rapidly brought to heel. For this trip to the US, Marigold had made him buy two new Saville Row suits, and he had, so far, managed to keep them in immaculate shape. Tonight, he was relaxing. He had removed his grey, tailor-made jacket and now stood in his shirt-sleeves, with his red and white patterned tie undone.

"Elizabeth. Good. I'm pressing the entry button now." He heard the 2in thick, bullet-proof lift clang as it descended to the ground floor, stop, and then hiss smoothly upwards. A few seconds later, the door, which opened directly into the apartment, slid back.

There was no doubt about it, Elizabeth looked magnificent. There was something about the way she dressed: mannish outfit, feminine, high-heeled shoes and strong make-up, which was challenging and sexy at the same time. Jack wondered what she had on under her grey skirt and jacket. He felt himself becoming aroused. This would not do. Instead of kissing her on the cheek which was his usual greeting, he shook her hand. She got the message instantly. Business first. Sex could wait.

"Sit down over here next to the desk and let's discuss what's been achieved today. Your visit to the Children's Aids Hospital went well?

"Yes, Prime Minister. I gave an impromptu speech to the medical staff there, stating our Government's commitment to the fight against Aids, particularly in Africa. Luckily, there were reporters and photographers present, and the agency pictures have already gone into some of the first editions of the British papers. Here are some prints."

"Great stuff, Elizabeth," said Jack, thumbing through the photographs of his Junior Health Minister posing with sick babies and overweight nurses. "This is the kind of thing that we need to soften the party's image: the public need to know we care about these issues. It will look good in the health journals, too. Now, I must come onto a really serious topic. I gather that you went to the Obesity Summit, and were actually present at the lecture by Dr. Brian Donovan?"

Elizabeth was surprised that Jack already knew about Dr. Donovan's outburst:

"Yes. It was embarrassing because the conference was attended by so many top people from British food manufacturers, the US Food and Drug agencies, and the press. This Dr. Donovan is accusing manufacturers, and, more importantly, the British Government, of deliberately jeopardising peoples' health in order to make profits. He seems to believe that we've entered into some kind of pact with the food producers to make people fatter. It's ridiculous: we have already stopped them from advertising junk food on TV early in the evening, and they are reducing fat and salt content in so many foods. What more does he want?"

"He is a fool, but he has to be stopped." said Elizabeth." Luckily, I was able to get away from the conference before being railroaded into a press briefing by a marketing idiot from FizzCo. I could have handled any difficult questions, as you know, but my quotes would have been used in their reports, linking the government with Dr. Donovan's rantings. Did I do the right thing, Jack?"

She looked at him seriously, glossy lips slightly apart, brown eyes shining, like a sleek animal waiting to jump on her prey. Jack made a rapid decision: the rest of their conversation must take place in bed, otherwise he would have to take a cold shower.

"You always do the right thing, Elizabeth. That's why I think so highly of you," he said. "There are huge issues at stake here, which could have very important consequences for our relations with the United States. I will explain more later. Meanwhile, let's recharge our batteries. We've both had a long day. This flat has a marvellous, if slightly eccentrically decorated, bedroom, let me show you."

He stood up, and pushed open a large folding door which divided the sitting room from the bedroom of the apartment. While the sitting room was decorated in restrained, muted tones of grey, black and white with heavy leather armchairs, a mahogany desk and a selection of tasteful prints of views of Capitol Hill on the wall, the bedroom looked like an illustration from "Hello" magazine.

The king-sized teak bed against one oak-panelled wall was

adorned with a white silk cover and a selection of animal-print cushions. The false ceiling was much lower than the one in the sitting room, which prompted Elizabeth to wonder if it concealed a camera or viewing area. Although the wall-lights were dim, she could just make out an ornate japanese lacquer cabinet opposite the bed. and one large chair which looked like an oriental throne. It was upholstered in gold silk and stacked with yet more cushions. A discreet door, set in the oak panelling obviously led to the bathroom.

"I know, it looks like a brothel - sorry," Jack smiled apologetically. "Apparently, my predecessor liked it because he could relax here and feel like some kind of Eastern prince. Not many people realise that he is a bit of a romantic. Wonderful prime minister, but strange tastes. People do say that he's bisexual, you know. I intend to get it re-decorated. Am I forgiven?"

Not usually lost for words, Elizabeth simply nodded. She was now feeling incredibly turned on by the thought of romping on this outrageous bed with Jack. He turned towards her, and pulled her towards him by her jacket lapels. "Now, Minister, shall we get down to business? "

Elizabeth kissed him full on the lips, and let her tongue explore his mouth, while he unbuttoned her grey jacket. They both sat down on the bed, Elizabeth pulling him on top of her. Discarding her jacket, she let Jack unzip her skirt, and pull it down over her hips. She kicked it off, and resplendent in her stockings, high heels and silk underwear, she pulled herself up on her hands and knees on the bed and struck a pose like a panther.

"You didn't know that I've been asked to pose for the House of Commons pin-up calendar for next year," she joked. "These awful leopard-print cushions would be brilliant as props for the pictures. What do you think." Jack roared with laughter, and grabbed one silk-clad leg. "Come on Lizzie, no teasing," he said, playfully. "You know what I like. "

****

Chapter Eleven

STARTS TODAY; HIDDEN KILLERS IN YOUR FOOD!
Feeling ill? Overweight?
The Echo has discovered that food manufacturers are stuffing your food with hidden fat, sugar and other junk which will make you more prone to life-threatening health problems like hypertension, heart desease and cancer.

In our exclusive series, Caroline Dempsey reveals how the big companies are fattening you up.

It's shocking and it makes a mockery of our food and nutrition regulations. But, it's happening - and the proof is in a supermarket near you!

See page 25 for Caroline's report from the International Obesity Summit in New York.

It was 10.30am on Tuesday November 12th, 2008. The Evening Echo's offices in the East End of London were quiet; the rows of computer terminals gleamed brightly, like cybermen demanding to be fed with facts, ideas, sweat and tears. The journalists looked pale and washed out as if their blood had already been drained by these permanently hungry electronic tyrants.

There were six long windows on one side of the huge room, which overlooked a narrow, dank canal. They were kept fastened permanently, for safety reasons. One joker had pointed out that this level of security was to prevent people from escaping and it was certainly true that working in this vast, overlit space was like being a rabbit caught in the glare of headlights. If you made a mistake, you could be yesterday's meat.

Caroline sat at her desk, legs crossed, leaning back in her swivel chair as she feasted her eyes on the early edition of the newspaper: at last, she had her name on the front page. It looked just great. She had gained half a stone in weight while she was in in New York, but it had been worth it. She had come up with the goods: a meaty, three-part series which her Editor just loved.

Dr. Brian Donovan and Susan Simpson had helped her research the series, which kicked off in today's paper. She had stuck to her bargain: no mention of GE203, but there was still enough material to make a great splash about the hidden fat in food plus plenty of facts and figures about the world obesity crisis, and a whole page of product pictures revealing their calorie and fat content - which, in every case, was up to 20% higher than quoted on the pack. Susan had recommended a top nutrition laboratory to analyse the foods, and they had managed to do it in just a few hours. It had cost, but was worth it.

Caroline had managed to write most of the hard copy before she left her New York hotel on Saturday. She finished it at home on Sunday and Monday. Now, she was putting the final touches to tomorrow's double page spread: *Our Kids are Forced to Eat Sugar.* That should knock 'em for six!

Her phone rang, and she grabbed it quickly: she was expecting a call from the Press Officer of a confectionary company.

"Hi Caroline, this is Tom. Remember me? You said you'd call from New York. You could have at least left a text message to let me know you'd got home safely. Are you dumping me? If so, I'll fucking well dump you first. What have you got to say for yourself?"

It was amazing how mild-mannered accountants can turn exceptionally nasty when you ignore them for a few days. Tom was obviously pissed off. Well, her job had to come first.

Caroline partially covered the mouthpiece with her hand, so her close neighbour, a mini-skirted fashion stylist who had an ear for gossip, couldn't tune into the conversation.

"Sorry, babe." She spoke softly." I got involved in a big story in

New York, and had to run with it. How are things in 'Brum? I've got a great splash in today's Echo. Take a look on the newspaper website later. It's a beaut! We can meet up next week, if you like. Things will be less hectic then. "

There was a loud raspberry from the other end of the line. Tom was obviously very pissed off indeed. "You selfish bitch. All you bloody well care about is that sodding job. I am not going to be your plaything, mate. If you just want regular sex, get yourself a vibrator. Our arrangement is over, finito, finished...get that? I'm seeing someone else, and, wait for this Caroline, she is size eight with long legs and ginormous tits. Eat your heart out..babe! I'm sure you'll have a whale of a time without me...that's very appropriate, because you look like one! Goodbye."

Caroline put the phone down and started typing, fast. The call hadn't been unexpected, but she would have preferred to do the dumping herself. Caroline was ready to move on. She would survive Tom's insults. The most upsetting bit had been his rude comments about her figure. When they had been in bed together, the bastard had pretended that he found slim women a turn-off. Size eight, indeed!

"Got a problem, love? Boyfriend trouble?" Janice, the skimpily-dressed fashion journalist, was leaning over their shared desk, dangling a pair of fluorescent green knickers under Caroline's nose. The flimsy fabric was embroidered, in red sequins, with the legend: "No entry: woman at work."

"These are really useful if you want to stop blokes asking for a shag at lunchtime," said Janice. "Just one flash gets the message across. We're using them in the "Bad taste fashion" feature next week. I'm looking for someone in the office to test them. Could you oblige?"

Despite her anger, Caroline laughed. "Not me, Janice. You know I never wear knickers. They'd be wasted!" A pimply-faced officer messenger who was collecting empty cardboard coffee cups, overheard this remark and went bright red. The two women collapsed into giggles.

Caroline pulled herself up sharply. This would never do. She had to get on with her work. She took a swig of water, reached into her top drawer for a soft, rather stale FizzCo "Super Snacks" bar, and started running through the list of facts and figures she still needed. She had to make her story stand up with quotes from the big sugar producers, and possibly from someone in the Health Ministry: that sexy-looking junior minister Elizabeth Collins would be perfect. Getting hold of her would be difficult, but she could try.

The features section of the paper was at the far end of the vast, open plan editorial floor, well away from the news and picture desks. With around seventy people working away, the atmosphere could have been even more oppressive: but each journalist managed to work in his or her womb-like space, without treading on each others' toes too much. Egos were another matter. The energy generated by collective angst during a bad news day could have been harnessed and used to power the fleet of vans which delivered the paper all over London.

Robertson Kelly, the Editor, known as Rob or Robbo to his staff, was a tough, frog-like little man with a bald head, paunch, and chronic indigestion caused by irregular meals and nervous tension. As a boy, he had been a keen amateur boxer, and he still enjoyed a scrap, although, these days, it was likely to be verbal fisticuffs only. He had a simple philosophy about how to handle his staff: "Keep the buggers at each others' throats, then they won't have time to stab *me* in the back!"

It worked. There were feuds, upsets, and frequent drunken spats in local hostelries between various heads of department, but the journalists universally looked up to, and admired, their editor. He had to deal with shit from the paper's proprietor, board of directors and various pillocks from the Government on a daily basis, so Rob calculated that he could do without any enemies from within the paper. He was therefore careful to be fair to all his staff. Any necessary bollockings took place within his office, which was next to the news desk, and were usually given out at about 8am in the morning, or after the paper had been put to bed, to spare embarrassment.

This morning, Rob was in an unusually irritable mood. He had already taken an early morning call from the proprietor of the paper demanding to know what the front page headline would be; a question which, at this stage of the day, Rob was unable to answer for the very good reason that three or four good stories were breaking all at once. Lord Galbraith would have to be patient. Although he was irritating, Rob had a soft spot for the hugely overweight, avuncular peer who owned the paper. The Echo had been through some tough times, but somehow, Charlie Gilbraith had always found a way to keep it going. With press advertising sales declining, and more companies putting money into TV and on-line selling activities, times were hard indeed.

No, it wasn't Charlie who'd got up Rob's nose today; it was that awful little shit Ronnie Adams, the PM's personal spin doctor. His call, which had come through just as Rob was taking the first of his daily quota of indigestion tablets, had been the usual mixture of venom, rudeness and thinly veiled threats. Being phoned by Ronnie was rather like being hit on the head with a sledgehammer, while being flayed alive: to minimise the agony, the best plan was to hold the telephone at arms' length and let him rant on.

"Rob, you are a fucking idiot. God knows why Galbraith keeps you on. What the hell are you playing at by running this libellous series on food? The PM is going apeshit. It's the worst kind of tabloid scaremongering, and a load of bollocks, to boot. I've had three top food company bosses on the line this morning asking me if I can get you fired. If you don't pull the rest of the series, or at least soften it up, your head will be served up on a platter, surrounded by a pile of chips. Fuck the bloody calories! It will give me a lot of pleasure to see you go down, Robbo, mate. I've never liked you. Get it sorted, do you hear?"

Although it was difficult to contain his anger, Rob remembered his old mantra: keep people confused, and you'll always have the upper hand. He spoke very slowly, as if talking to the Westminster village idiot:

"Ronnie, it's so good to hear your charming voice so early in the morning....and such flattery, too. Any chance of letting me get a word in here? We all know that the junk food merchants are a load of double-dealing, greedy sheisters who don't give a toss about people's health. Remember how the burger chain used dirty tricks to suppress the truth in that defamation case? What a load of shits. This is a good series; well-researched, and we are standing by it. I suggest you go and choke on a double cheeseburger. I suppose you never eat such rubbish? Well, matey, let me tell you that it's all some people can afford. It's time your blinkered boss woke up to the fact!"

Ronnie spoke quietly, this time: varying his vocal decibel level was one of his techniques for catching his "victims" on the hop:

"Rob if you don't tone it down, three major advertisers will pull out of the Echo. In these difficult times, that seems a shame. I've already spoken to Charlie Galbraith, and he thinks you should play ball. If you want to keep your job, you need a paper to edit. Enough said?"

The line went dead. Rob slammed the handset down, got up from his desk, and aimed a blow at the medicine ball he kept in one corner of the office for occasions like this. His fist made contact with the shiny leather with a satisfying crunch. "Mary", he roared to his secretary who was sitting at her desk in the outer office. "Get me Charlie on the line, now...and I'll have a large coffee with three sugars.

By the time Lord Galbraith was put through, Rob was back behind his desk, sipping his coffee. He knew it was bad for his heart, but this was an emergency.

"Charlie, has that arsehole Adams been on? He has just been having a major rant about our killer foods series. What do you think? I reckon we tell him to get stuffed?"

Normally, Galbraith backed Rob in his decisions, but this time he was hesitant: "Rob, I'm sorry but what he says is true. I've had Archie Davies on this morning saying that Underhills, the supermarket chain and Allied Sugar Mills are both threatening to cancel six month's worth of advertising. That's over two million quid down the pan. We can't afford it, sorry. You'll have to can the rest of the series, or soften the angle. I also got a call from Jack Barton's diary secretary asking me to fit in a meeting at Number 10 next week. One to one, apparently. Very casual, but obviously a summons. There is more to this than we realise, Rob. "

Archie Davies was the Echo's advertising manager, and Rob knew that he would only call the proprietor in if there was an emergency. The PM's summons was odd: newspaper proprietors were often asked over to Downing Street, but usually in a group for lunch, or to meet foreign dignatories. A one-to-one meeting spelt trouble.

Well, today's piece had been good. Maybe Caroline should change her angle tomorrow. Rob was deeply suspicious, too. Why was the PM frightened of the food moguls? He was a greedy, ambitious devil and, in Rob's opinion he spent too much time sucking up to the US President, and the multinational corporations. There was a big story there somewhere, but, without any evidence, it was useless to try and stir up trouble. He assured Charlie that he would try to soften the series and put the phone down.

"Mary, get Caroline Dempsey in here at 1pm, sharp. Ok? I'm going for a slash. Get the News Editor to give me the best lines in the three top stories: I'll work on Page One when get back. My bladder is bursting "

****

When Caroline received an internal call from Rob' secretary, Mary, asking her to pop down and see the Editor at 1pm, she was very surprised. Even though she knew she was doing a good job on the "Food Fatteners" series, Rob's usual way of giving a compliment was to breeze over to a journalist's desk and tell them to "keep producing stuff like this, and one day you'll be a reasonably competent journalist." Praise indeed.

Her first thought was utter irritation with herself for not taking her usual care with her appearance. She had been busy and jet-lagged for god's sake, but there really was no excuse for turning up to work in a dowdy black suit and white shirt. At least she had washed her hair and could tart up her appearance with some more makeup. Fifteen minutes in the ladies' room would do the trick.

Her second, somewhat disturbing thought was that Rob was going to pull the first part of her series in today's late edition of the Evening Echo. It was too late to take it out in the early editions, but maybe a big news story had broken which meant that he had to clear the front page and needed space inside for the late afternoon and evening editions.

That was par for the course on a newspaper, and she would normally have been told about it by the features editor. A quick check online showed that the three top news stories were still bubbling along, but no agency had reported anything major in the last few minutes. No, it couldn't be that. Maybe the £500 she had spent on the laboratory bill when the junk food products were tested was being queried, although she had obtained permission to go ahead and use the lab. Well, she would just have to wait and see.

At 12.30, she stored her work, shut down her computer terminal, and wandered over to the subs' desk, where the features section of the next evening's paper was being laid out. Her piece was being given a lot of space. On the right hand page was a compelling image of a fat boy, about seven years old, sitting on a park bench, eating a chocolate bar and drinking cola. His face was in shadow so he couldn't be identified. Probably hired from a kids' model agency, thought Caroline. Poor little sod, he's earning cash for his parents by posing for "fat" pictures. They probably feed him sweets to keep him working. God, what a life.

"It's looking good, Mick, " she observed to the Chief Sub, a sixty year old journalist with a grizzled face and sandy hair who had been on the paper for over 30 years. "Hope it stays as a spread,"

"It should be safe, Caroline. Robbo loves it . He told us to give it a good showing. What do you think of the picture? Apparently, the kid is the brother of one of the messengers here. He gets loads of work. Very big demand for fat models these days. Oversized kids can make a fortune. Times have certainly changed. "

Caroline forced a smile, resisting the temptation to give her views on parents who allowed their children to be exploited for cash and newspapers who paid them to do it. She continued walking towards the ladies' loo, inconveniently situated near the predominantly male sports section of the paper. Two secretaries were having a quick smoke in the unwelcoming, white-tiled toilet. Caroline ignored them, and started a rapid make-up job: red lipstick, lots of kohl round her eyes, pale powder and blusher gave her a strong, sexy look, nicely set off by her long wavy blond hair.

The black suit was basic and boring, so she extracted a long immitation jet cross and chain from her handbag and put it around her neck, making sure the 3inch crucifix dangled between her boobs. Rob was one of the few top tabloid editors who didn't believe in sleeping with his staff, but it didn't hurt to look sexy. After all, she wanted a job on the Political Desk, and MPs were notoriously easy to nobble if you were clever. Appealing to their vanity helped, and gving the impression that you had some kind of spiritual mission was always a winner...it confused the poor dears. It was an image she would cultivate.

****

"What's this, Caroline. taking the veil? Or do you want to be our new Religious Correspondent? That piece of junk round your neck makes you look like a naughty nun. Nice one. Come in and close the door."

Rob's office door was always kept open, unless he was in conference with the proprietor, dealing with a major crisis or story, or he was firing someone, so Caroline was shaken by this simple request. She turned and closed the door carefully, then approached Rob's huge desk which was in front of two long windows overlooking the greasy, grey-brown waters of the canal. The editor was sitting in a leather swivel chair, both feet on the desk. His bald head gleamed in the swathe of light from the windows, and his freckled hands clasped a half-eaten cheese sandwich. All he needed to complete the image was a trilby on the back of his head and an empty whisky bottle on his desk. The array of indigestion pill bottles and framed photograph of Mohammed Ali rather spoilt things, but otherwise, it could have been a scene from the American movie, *Hold the Front Page*. Caroline pulled herself up: come on girl, stop your mind wandering. What on earth can you have done wrong?

"Don't look so pale, Caro, I'm not firing you. That's a great piece today. Well done. The pictures and captions showing how people are being fooled into thinking food is less fattening than it really is, were excellent - worth the cash you spent on getting the fat-loaded crap tested. Professor Donovan's quotes were good too. He seemed to have rattled a few cages at the Obesity Summit. Stick with him.. he's a great contact.

"Now, the reason I called you in is to tell you that I'm going to have to cut tomorrow's spread to a page. The picture space will have to be reduced, which is a pity. It's because the PM is going to tell the House about a new road tax which is coming in, and we really need that page for a hard piece from the various road lobby groups. Sorry, but readers are barmy about their cars, so we have to run it.

" Cut down the medical stuff linking sugar intake with diabetes and cancer, and can the shot of the fat boy. Let me have a look when you've finished. Part Three of the series will now go on page 43 on Thursday. So most of the interviews with the fat diabetics and cancer sufferers will have to come out. Use just one, with a good picture, and include some quotes from sweet manufacturers defending their products. We have to be seen to be fair. That's all. Get on with it, Madonna!"

Caroline was stupified. Her eyes filled with tears. Her hard-hitting, well-researched, fantastic three-parter was being reduced to a run-of-the-mill, pot-boiler of a series. By Friday, readers would have forgotten about today's piece. The two follow-up articles would successfully "dumb down" the whole series. It was so unfair. She blinked quickly, stood up and looked straight at Rob, who was now taking a large bite out of his cheese roll.

"Rob, with respect, I think it's a bloody shame to ruin the series. We're hitting these food manufacturers hard...and they deserve it. We could even get the Government to do something about setting and enforcing higher standards if we keep pressing hard enough. Our readers are being exploited. OK people love cars, but they've got to eat...which, to my mind, makes my series more important."

Her voice started to rise, and there was a pink flush on her neck. She had gone too far. Rob hated whinge-ing journos. He finished chewing a mouthful of cheese roll, then pulled a large red and blue plaid handkerchief out of his pocket and, very slowly, wiped his mouth. He took his feet off the desk, and leaned forward.

"Listen, Mother Theresa, I'm the fucking editor of this fucking paper, and I decide what goes into it. Get out of here, and get on with it. Understand?"

Rob swung round on his chair, and began banging out an email on the keyboard placed to the right of his desk. She was dismissed.

****

After leaving Rob's office, Caroline headed straight for the ladies' lavatory, and locked herself in a cubicle. She sat down on the closed toilet seat and took a few deep breaths. At least she hadn't cried. She was astonished by Rob's decision. He was known for his campaigning style and risk-taking. How could he be so pathetic?

It was all very curious indeed. She would obviously have to toe the line and make the changes he had demanded, otherwise she would be given the boot. This wasn't just about the road lobby, or any other lobby, it was something deeper. Maybe a cover-up. Surely her whiter-than-white boss didn't have shares in FizzCo, or any of the other companies she had attacked in her piece? He always maintained that newspaper Editors who courted TV producers, accepted freebies from politicians, or played around on the stock market were fools because, sooner or later, they would find themselves in a compromising situation: it just wasn't worth the hassle.

She emerged from the cubicle, checked her make-up in the mirror over the solitary, cracked white basin, and smiled at her reflection. Great, no smudges. She'd be a true professional, but she would also ring Professor Donovan and meet up with him at his office tonight. Maybe he had been "warned off" as well. Suddenly, she felt a lot better. This was just the beginning. She now felt sure that she was on to an even bigger story, which might, or might not be published in the Evening Echo but would be published somewhere. She was damned sure it would.

****

While Caroline had been polishing her story for that day's paper, Professor Donovan was clearing up the mess in his office: while he was in New York, there had been a break-in. It must have occurred some time on Saturday or Sunday night. The university cleaners had found his door, locked by Brian's secretary on Friday night, forced open, and papers strewn all over the office. The flimsy metal safe where he kept computer disks containing copies of his research and lecture projects had been smashed open, and the contents stolen. Police had been called, but no fingerprints had been found. On Monday, they had questioned students and other teaching staff, but, so far there were no leads.

There won't be any, either, thought Brian, grimly, as he stacked a pile of exam papers on his desk. Those Chinese bastards were too clever for that. They now had copies of every research project he had ever supervised, and would know everything about his work. The police had given an undertaking that they would carry on with their enquiries, but told Brian that, as nothing valuable had been taken and no-one was injured they would have to prioritise accordingly. The officer in charge of the case, a plodding sergeant with a beer belly and bad breath, had been quite dismissive, even suggesting with a loud laugh that it must have been some kind of prank. Brian had wondered, briefly, whether to tell this bumbling idiot about what had happened in New York, but thought better of it. The policeman would think he was off his trolley.

"Some prank," said Brian, out loud. "Years of work was stored on those disks. They knew exactly what they were looking for."

The phone rang, shrilly, and Brian let the answering machine pick it up. "Hello Brian, Caroline here. Did you see today's Echo? Thanks so much for your help with the story. Listen, something odd's happened here. Can we...?"

Brian picked up the receiver. "Something odd's happened here, too. Presumably, you want to meet up? Come over to the college now, Caroline. I'll meet you in the lobby. Phone me when you get there."

"Fine. I'm on my way. Bye."

Brian considered whether to see Caroline in his office, or not. Better to go to a noisy pub, he decided. Maybe the Chinese food mafia had bugged his office. He put in a quick call to Molly to tell her he would be late home. She had been concerned but sceptical about his experiences in New York, and dismissive about the break-in. Thank heavens she didn't know about his night with Susan Simpson. As he dialled Molly's direct line number, Brian wondered if she would actually care very much. To Molly, the high powered lawyer, a hospital dietitian was hardly any competition.

His wife sounded her usual efficient, no-nonsense self: " No problem, Brian. The kids are fine, I've just spoken to them, and I will be on my way home soon. Have you cleared up your office OK? If you will swan off to New York and leave all your precious stuff there, you've only got yourself to blame if someone breaks in. Probably the work of a student, high on drugs. All your papers have been published, darling, and we've got bound copies of the journals in the library at home. You are OK, which is all that matters. I honestly don't think you need to worry so much. This isn't China, you know."

Her sarcastic tone grated. All right, his meeting with Tan Liu hadn't actually resulted in any physical violence, but Brian had no doubt that he was being threatened. If he didn't accept Tan's thinly disguised "bribe" and drop his investigation into GE203, he would be in trouble. He felt certain that he, and his family, were in danger. Molly had, grudgingly, allowed him to get a security expert to come in and re-check their home alarm system but refused to let him tell the children about his suspicions.

She'd been almost dismissive: "You can't make their lives a misery just because you are out of your depth in the big, bad business world, Brian. All large public corporations have executives who behave aggressively. I deal with them every day. The Chinese are just throwing their weight about, as they can afford to in the present world climate. Don't worry."

Caroline phoned, and after a few words with her, he went down to the college lobby. She looked as attractive as ever, but plumper than she had been in New York. She must have gained at least 10lb since their last meeting. The poor girl was a binge-eater, that was obvious. Brian was glad he hadn't told her about his meeting with Tan Liu.

"Let's go to the Coal Hole pub along the road, and talk in one of the upstairs booths."she said, urgently, removing a pair of large black sunglasses, and grabbing his arm. "I have to tell you: something very strange is happening."

When they were settled in the pub booth, with a couple of

half-pints of beer, she told him about her interview with Rob. "I spent the rest of the afternoon cutting swathes of good stuff from my copy and getting bland quotes from bent PR people, " she said. "What is going on Brian? Could Rob have been nobbled by the Government on this? Are they getting so much cash from the food companies that we can't even criticise these people in a legitimate, well-researched newspaper article? You work with a lot of food industry people. You must know something. It's not just GE203, it's something bigger. The additive, of course, is a massive story. You must find out where it's coming from, and how it gets into the food chain. Even more importantly, who is behind it and what have they got to gain from fattening up the population?"

In full, passionate flow, with the jet crucifix bobbing up and down between her breasts as she spoke, Caroline cut a striking figure. A group of City boys sipping stout and champagne at the bar had stopped their conversation, and were staring at her.

"Calm down, Caroline," said Brian, very quietly. "We're being noticed. Look, the thing is I agree that we are into something odd here. Let's be sensible. I must re-think my own position. I want to continue looking into GE203, but I must be cautious. We won't be able to do anything if we lose our jobs, will we? It could be just as well that your editor has made you tone down your articles for tomorrow and Thursday. We can go on digging into this without making waves. Like you, I am beginning to be very suspicious. There is much more than mere profit involved I'm certain."

He sounded calmer, and more rational than he felt. He had gone out on a limb with his lecture in New York, and had expected flak, but now things were getting out of hand. First, Tan Liu's "torture chamber", next a break-in at the college, and now newspaper editors being nobbled by government officials. Whatever Molly said, it was all very frightening.

"Caroline, my advice is to carry on digging into the story, but in a subtle way. Don't let the big boys in the industry find out what you are up to. I'll help where I can, and maybe, between us, we will find out more.

" Susan is the one with the real problem: her patients are dying."

****

Chapter Twelve

Email to: Mr. Tan Liu, Chairman, Changjia Food Company.
From: Dr. Brian Donovan, Department of Nutrition and Food Science, The Royal College, London.

Following our very interesting meeting in New York regarding the effect of dietary carbohydrate on children's growth and development, I will be seeing the Vice Chancellor to discuss things this afternoon.
    The object of the meeting is to establish whether it is possible to set up a protocol, funded by your company, for research into this important subject. I will be in contact later this week to give you his decision. Regards, Brian Donovan.

Brian clicked onto the "send" icon on his computer. He wondered if Mr. Liu would detect the hidden sarcasm in his message. Probably not. Or, even if he did, he wouldn't care one bit. In this game, Mr. Liu definitely had the upper hand, and he knew it. Money was the universal language of business, and the Changjia Food Company was very profitable, and expanding rapidly. The Chinese food mogul knew that there was no way that the university could refuse his offer: he had the money, they needed it.

The university could certainly use a million dollars. If he looked out of the window of his office, Brian could see the shabby central courtyard of the college. Several of the beautiful statues depicting Greek philosophers and mathematicians were pitted with age, flaking and dirty. Pigeons had been using the white-spotted brown sill as a toilet for the last twenty five years and poor old Aristotle had lost his head. Inside, it was just as dingy: the grey carpet in his office was threadbare, and the lab where he would be lecturing this afternoon was like something out of a museum. The equipment was so basic that any detailed or complicated food analysis work had to be sent to a special food tech' laboratory in Slough. That's where the initial work on GE203 had been carried out, under Brian's instuctions.

The lab staff had established that the substance was plant related and a non-animal protein compound was being used as a carrier. The carrier compound was being added to many foods, including ready-meals, sausages, puddings, cereal bars. Many of these products were directed at the "healthy eating" market.

Now, they had to isolate the substance itself, and test it on laboratory animals, probably rats, to find out if it caused weight-gain, and, if so, whether this was as a result of increased appetite or some kind of chemical reaction which affected the appetite centres of the brain.

It was entirely possible that the plant extract could work in two, or more, ways to "fatten people up". Many plant-derived extracts were sold as "slimming " pills in the Far East, but banned in Western countries because of powerful side-effects including hallucinations, high blood pressure, increased heart rate. Maybe this substance worked in the opposite way, without the side effects. The only way to find out was to set up a proper study.

The lab staff were now waiting for Brian to give them the go-ahead, and the cash.

****

The high-pitched tone of Brian's mobile competed urgently with the cooing of the pigeons on the filthy window sill. He pulled the phone out of the deep inside pocket of his green tweed jacket.

" Hello Brian, it's Susan. I'm alone in my surgery at the hospital, so it's safe to talk . When is the lab going to start testing GE203 on rats? We need to follow through quickly with this. Sorry, I sound stupid. Of course, you know that more than anyone.

"My next obesity clinic is this afternoon. The four patients I'm seeing have all been eating products containing GE203 so it will be interesting to see if they have lost or gained weight. In all consciousness, I'll have to take these products off their next list of menus, otherwise I'll never be able to live with myself. The trouble is that many foods sold in supermarkets don't even include a complete list of ingredients on the packet: there are still so many loopholes in the labelling laws. It's all so bloody stupid.

"Oh, and are you OK? I was very worried about you in New York. Did you tell Molly about it? Not about us, of course, but about your Chinese experience? Sorry, there I go again. It's actually none of my business, is it?"

Although she was sitting alone in her tiny office, Susan blushed deeply. The short trip to New York had been one of the most confusing experiences of her life. The Summit was fascinating, and worth every penny she had saved to pay for the air fare and her horrible hotel. The night with Brian was incredible: great sex and so much to talk about. They obviously shared many of the same ideals and concerns about nutrition. She had no false illusions, though: he was married, so that was that.

Meeting Caroline Dempsey had been a real eye-opener: the girl was brash, and madly ambitious, but she was caring, at heart, and had a weight problem herself, so she could identify with her readers' anxieties.

Susan took a sip of water and continued, more calmly:

"Caroline's piece in yesterday's Echo was explosive, but today's is more muted, less powerful. I liked the stuff from you about the dangers of heart disease, and at least all the fat and calorie figures she quoted were correct. I checked them for her. It's a pity she had to devote so much space today to the usual stuff about parents being totally responsible for their kids' sugar addiction. As we know, parents are up against an insidious, brain-washing campaign by confectionary companies. You can't buy a packet of sugar-coated cereal without being asked to shell out for a beach ball or other toy.

The firms who use sugar substitutes are even worse: they pretend that their products are "healthy", when they are stuffed full of additives.

"The bottom line of all this, Brian, is that the three of us agree, and we are in a position to do something about it. I've made up my mind to carry it through to the bitter end, and, after your lecture, I believe you have too. Caroline has another agenda; the persuit of the big story. Underneath, though, I think she is as disgusted as we are about the way people are being manipulated, particularly the poor."

"Now, what about the next step, Brian? We have to get proof that GE203 is dangerous, and we have to find out who is encouraging its use and, more importantly, *why they are doing it.*"

Brian listened carefully. It was interesting that someone who came across as so calm and controlled could be so passionate. People like that can be hurt easily. He would have to tread carefully.

"Look Susan, I have to tell you something very important. My office was broken into over the weekend. Computer disks containing details of all my research were stolen. The police are being very slow and unhelpful. I'm certain that it has something to do with Tan Liu and his merry men. I didn't tell the Vice Chancellor about their heavy handed tactics. It all sounds so ridiculous. Even Molly thought I was over-reacting. The break-in has convinced me that I was right to be scared...and so are you.

"The official line about the burglary is that it was probably a student after exam papers - no chance, they are all locked in the central college strong room - or someone who wandered into the building, looking for cash. There has been an investigation, of sorts, but I believe that the Vice Chancellor will try and hush it all up. With no-one hurt and nothing of value taken, the police simply aren't interested. I have copies of all my papers at home, but I am wondering what the purpose of the break-in was. Maybe Tan Liu's henchmen were looking for blackmail material.

" Well, I think they will be disappointed. The only piece of research I've ever been involved in that was at all dubious was a study on twins and liver disease funded by a soft drink company. Each pair of twins consisted of one heavy drinker, and one non-drinker. We came up with the conclusion that the heavy drinkers displayed more evidence of early liver damage than the ones who didn't drink...now there's a surprise! The only snag about the piece of research was that it was a very small sample, only ten pairs of middle aged female twins, which proves absolutely nothing. Other academics like me do similar stuff, so I can't imagine that they would just use that to discredit me. Which makes me worry even more: if they couldn't find anything to use against me, they might try other tactics: attacking Molly or the children, for instance.

"Look, can I ring you back? I'm due to see the Vice Chancellor in five minutes to discus Tan Liu's proposition. One of the big problems is that the college needs the money. My own research budget has just been cut, which makes it hard to justify my GE203 expenditure. I know that the old boy will want me to accept the Chinese company's money. If I do, and then I carry on trying to investigate GE203, I could be in big trouble. I will ring you back, I promise.

"Listen, Susan, what happened between us in New York was very special, but, as you know I am married, and have children. Can you forgive me if I say something really crass: can we be friends, rather than lovers?"

Brian heard a click, and his mobile phone went dead.

****

" Come in, Dr Donovan, and close the door. Sit down, my boy. We've got a lot to discuss." Sir Dermot Browne, vice-chancellor of the college, always spoke to staff as if they were recalcitrant students. Even the most distinguished professors were treated like naughty adolescents; Browne loved telling them to wipe their shoes, pay attention, or stop fidgeting. It was a quirk of behaviour which his staff and academic colleagues tolerated with stoicism.

As Browne was now sixty five, and had had a distinguished career, he felt entitled to talk down to people. His suite of offices on the top floor of the college was decorated like a gentlemen's club: rich oak panelling, red carpets, antique furniture. In a way, it *was* a club, because Browne frequently entertained his cronies to luncheon, followed by copious glasses of port, in his own private dining room.

His friends included retired politicians, scientists and company chiefs, many of whom now held lucrative directorships. Browne chaired a number of Government quangos; each post carried a small retainer, which he augmented by playing the stock market, using tips from his pals to get the best return for his investments. He was a hands-on college boss; nothing escaped his notice, and, despite various attempts to get rid of him, he clung to the job. His wife had died five years previously, and the college was his life. He was determined to stay on until he was 70, like his close pal, the High Court judge who dined with him every Friday evening, Gerald Collins.

Brian sat down obediently, opposite Browne, who was behind a huge, mahogany desk in front of a long window overlooking the river Thames. He observed, not for the first time, that Browne needed to trim his white beard, and the curly white hairs which protruded from his nostrils like strands of fluffy angora knitting wool.

"I won't beat about the bush, Dr. Donovan." said Browne. "This piece of research for the Chinese company would bring in enough money for the College Building Fund to help ensure that we can renovate the entire central courtyard, and some of the laboratories. Devising the protocol for the research is a simple piece of work for you. Do it. I have also heard, from my contacts in the House of Lords, that the PM is keen on co-operation with this company. Our funding is due for re-appraisal by the Education Department later this year, so any research we undertake will be scrutinised. "

He paused, and tugged his beard, then reached for a pair of wire-rimmed spectacles, which he rammed on his large, hooked nose. He looked at a piece of paper on his desk, then peered over the top of the spectacles, and stared hard at Brian.

"As you know, it has been my policy to co-operate with and assist the food industry in this country where possible. After all, we have some of the finest scientific minds in the college, and our expertise in the field of nutrition is absolutely unsurpassed. We must, and should, use those assets to assist our own food producers. As one of our top brains, Dr. Donovan, it is encumbent on you to help the industry where possible and appropriate. After all, they are the future employers of many of our students. So, I advise you not to proceed any further with your researches into an ingredient called GE203. I have been assured by the Food Standards Agency that it is a perfectly harmless herbal flavouring which many manufacturers use. There is nothing to look at. I gather you used university funds to commission an outside laboratory to analyse it. This invoice for £650 has just been handed to me by the accounts section. A complete waste of money.

"I will overlook the misappropriation of funds on this occasion, but if you do this again without personal clearance from me, I will have to consider your position in this College. You are a valuable member of staff, Dr. Donovan, but not irreplacable. Understand?"

Brian got up, nodded, and walked to the door. There was nothing to say. It was perfectly clear that if he continued to investigate GE203, he would be fired.

Outside the suite, he stood still for a moment and considered his options. He was tempted to march straight back into Browne's office, and tell him to stuff his job. If he did that, Molly would be furious, and the academic grapevine was so strong that it was doubtful whether he would pick up a similar post at another leading university. Why not just go along with Browne, Tan, and all the rest of them? They called the shots, after all.

****

"Had you forgotten my tutorial, Dr Donovan? I'll come back after your lecture if you are busy now."

Brian had left his office door ajar, and was sitting, deep in thought, at his desk. Five minutes earlier, he had sent an email to Tan Liu confirming the Vice Chancellor's approval of the new piece of research, and requesting full details of the work required, plus a proper contract. So, he had committed himself to the project, and to accepting the "bribe" from Tan. He knew he had failed Susan, Caroline and himself, but there had really been no alternative. Tonight, he would tell Molly that he was being "sensible" for once.

The voice from behind the door was soft, and hesitant. The door opened wide, and Jenny, the student with the long blonde hair and passion for purple appeared. Her thin legs were encased in tight jeans, and she wore a deep fuschia-coloured crochet sweater and pink shoes. Her peony-coloured bra was clearly visible through the holes in the sweater. Despite his worries, Brian's intimate knowledge of female underwear, gleaned from years of sharing a house with three sisters, suddenly "kicked in", and he judged, correctly, that she must be a size 36D.

"You're absolutely right, Jenny," said Brian, "I had forgotten. I've got a lot on my mind. Come in, and pull up a chair. I have half an hour to spare now, and we can continue to talk later on this afternoon. How are you getting on with the project on takeaway meals? Have you managed to produce some interesting results? How did the fat and calorie analysis work out?"

Jenny sat down and opened a large pink file, covered with gaudy paper pansies which looked as though they'd been cut out from a piece of wrapping paper and stuck on with glue.

She began to speak, nervously: "Well, I looked at various kinds of fast food meals. I chose six in each category, analysed the calorie and fat content in each meal then worked out the average.

" For example, I found that the average calorie content of a chicken nugget takeaway is 707, which is about 30% higher than if you had cooked a similar meal yourself. A quarterpounder burger with cheese contains an average of 826 calories, about 52% higher than a tradional cooked meal. About 40% of the calories in all the meals came from saturated fat.

"Honestly, Dr. Donovan, this is so awful. When you think that our children are eating this rubbish, and becoming obese, it seems amazing that the Government don't control the amount of fat and calories in these meals. It would be easy enough to do it, I'd have thought. It seems as if these kids are almost being groomed to provide a lifetime of vast profits for the food industry. By the way, Dr. Donovan, I hope you don't mind me mentioning it, but I was so sorry to hear about the break-in. Was anything of value taken?"

Jenny looked genuinely concerned, and Brian was touched, both by her worries about children's nutrition needs, and his own, more immediate, problems. He found himself becoming very attracted to this pretty student.

"Thanks Jenny. No, there was nothing taken that can't be replaced. The police aren't being very helpful, though. Meanwhile, it is good to hear that you are making such excellent progress with your project. I suggest you expand it a little to include soft drinks served at these outlets -look at the sugar content. I like the colour scheme, by the way...very cheery on a grey November day. Did you stick the pansies on your folder yourself?"

Jenny laughed, throwing back her head. A curtain of straight, fine blond hair swung in front of her face, and she lifted a finger, tipped with glittering purple nail polish, to ease it back behind her ear. The smile suddenly vanished, and she became very serious:

"No, my little sister did it for me. She's only eleven. I think she'll get a place in art college. She's really talented. The poor kid is also very overweight, which is one reason why I'm so concerned about the effect of fast food on children. I'm trying to persuade her to eat more sensibly, but she just seems to be addicted to junk meals. My parents are so worried. I feel so ashamed of myself. If I can't help my own sister to eat healthily, how can I expect to get a job abroad, helping with nutrition programmes for underpriveleged kids? I'm useless."

To Brian's consternation, Jenny's eyes filled with tears. He got up and walked round the desk, and put his arms around her shoulders. "Come on, Jenny. It's not your fault. Come back later on and bring me the full print-out of all your statistics on the project and we'll talk again." He loosened his arms, and stepped back.

Jenny stood up, pulled a handkerchief out of her jeans pocket, and wiped her eyes. She threw her arms around Brian's neck and kissed him, full on the mouth, pressing her warm chest against his denim shirt. He could smell her scent: violets, of course.

"Dr. Donovan, you are such a kind man. Thank you." she said. "I will be back at five with all my data. Is that OK?"

"Absolutely wonderful, Jenny, " said Brian, with a smile. "I'm sure we'll have lots more to talk about. Now, off you go to your next lecture. See you later."

When Jenny had closed the office door, Brian sat down again. He decided he had make the right decision. It would be foolish to lose his job in the college. After all, there were so many hidden benefits.

****

When he put his key in the lock of the heavy oak door his home in North London at 9pm that evening, Brian was feeling less confident.

After her emotional outburst earlier in the day, Jenny had obviously recovered quickly, and, somehow transformed herself into a vamp. She had returned to Brian's office as promised, with the crochet sweater hanging, provocatively, off once shoulder, and dumped her pansy-patterned folder and spreadsheets on his desk. Five minutes later they were making love. She turned out to be both energetic and fiery. His back was covered with tiny, livid purple half-moons where her long nails had dug into his pale skin.

Their 5pm rendezvous had certainly been a learning curve, for Brian as well as Jenny. The springs on the old brown leather sofa in his office were probably still vibrating. Brian just hoped that Jenny had other colours in her wardrobe: he was definitely suffering from a surfeit of purple.

Now, he had to face an evening with Molly, Amy and Toby. Molly would be in her study, working on her latest case, a contractural muddle between a famous, extremely successful middle-aged actress and her American agent. The actress wanted to get rid of the agent, who was grabbing a higher and higher percentage of her income. She feared that there would be nothing left if, and when, she decided to retire. The complicated issues involved would keep Molly in designer suits for several years.

The children would probably be doing their homework or fighting, or both. Like most teenaged siblings, Amy and Toby were going through an "awkward" phase. Put simply, they hated each other's guts. Fifteen year old Amy was, tall, gangling and fair. She was an excellent student, and wanted to be a doctor, like her aunt Cheryl, Brian's sister. Toby, two years her senior, was red haired like his mother, but had not inherited her self-control and clever, analytical brain. He was short for his age, thickset, and punchy. Some of this aggression was worked off on the school rugby field, but a lot of it seemed to spill out over his family, especially his younger sister. Brian just hoped that he would grow out of it: at the moment, Toby seemed to have a permanent chip on his shoulder.

"Brian, can you come up here please?" Molly called out from her study, on the third floor of the elegant, Georgian terraced house. Brian's study was an attic room on the fourth floor. "I want to talk to you about something important."

Brian hung his coat on the antique hatstand in the cool, spacious hall, and walked across the elegant, natural quarry-tiled floor and up the three flights of stairs to his wife's blue and white painted study. She was wearing jeans and a stylish green roll-neck sweater, and sat in a large beige leather armchair, sipping a glass of white wine, a pile of books at her feet. For a moment, Brian remembered why he had fallen in love with her at college: the combination of fragility and toughness was extremely erotic. He went over and kissed her cheek, then sat down, cross-legged on the floor by her side.

"Ready, and waiting, Mol," he said. "What's up? Before you start, I must tell you that I have decided to stop stirring up trouble and become a good boy again. I had a meeting with Browne today, and we're going ahead with the Chinese project. Sorry, if I've caused you any worry, love. I just felt I had to take a stand against the big food conglomerates. Well, I've said my piece. Now I'm going to toe the line. OK?"

"Yes, Brian, that's great, but I must tell you something really exciting." Molly spoke quietly, but, as she so often did, sounded impatient, as if she felt that her husband's work was far less important that her own.

"Patrick Curtis, the New York MD has offered me the chance to go and work in his office for a year. You can come too - there are plenty of opportunities for scientists of your calibre in American universities. It will be brilliant for Amy and Toby. They'll be able to study at the British college over there, so their work won't be interrupted. They'll have a wonderful time. Toby needs an outlet for all that energy: the sports opportunities are marvellous. If you give in your notice now, we could go over in March. Maybe Browne would even give you a sabbatical. Isn't it all exciting?"

It was typical of Molly to have worked out all the details before discussing anything with Brian. He opened his mouth to speak, but, because of his acute physical and mental tiredness, he could only utter one word: "Really?"

"Yes, really. I am thrilled, of course. The money is wonderful, but the prestige is the best part. I'll be handling top clients: Hollywood and Broadway stars. It will be a huge challenge. You'll have fun, too, darling. There's a lot going on over there for you to get your teeth into, and so much more funding for your research projects. We can rent out the house, the three of us can go over after Christmas, and you can join us as soon as you've worked out your notice or they've found a replacement. You'll be in heaven."

Brian found enough strength to protest, albeit weakly: "Well, it does need thinking seriously about, Molly. It would be a big upheaval for us all. Let me sleep on it, darling. I'm dog-tired, and can't think straight. I'll go down to the kitchen and grab something to eat. What's in the fridge?"

Molly took a sip from her glass of wine, and tapped her free hand on her knee, a familiar sign of impatience:

"You don't sound very enthusiastic. By tomorrow, you'll see how brilliant it will be. Amy and Toby are really keen. By the way, there's a large parcel for you downstairs. I didn't open it, in case it's a bomb from one of those Chinese villains you met in New York."

She laughed; Brian's worries about his family's safety really were ridiculous; he was a lovely man, but so unworldly. It was pathetic.

Brian got up quickly. "Don't be sarcastic, Molly. I was only thinking about you and the children. In any case, I still don't understand how they managed to find out so much about us. It was bizarre. As we have now decided to take their thinly-disguised bribe, and I am not persuing my research into GE203, I imagine that we are off their hit list. I'll go down and fix myself a meal, and have a look at the parcel. If I think it's suspicious, it's going straight to the police. Understand me?"

Angry now, he heaved himself wearily up off the floor, walked quickly out of the room, and downstairs to the kitchen. Sometimes, in fact quite often these days, he wondered if he should leave Molly. He had fallen in love with her because she was so cool, and confident. Nothing phased her. The coolness and confidence now irritated the hell out of him. Compared with Susan, who was passionate and dedicated to her patients, or even Jenny, with her concern for her poor little fat sister, Molly seemed like a selfish cow.

Maybe he would wait until the children were at university then suggest a separation. She would probably welcome it.

The white polystyrene parcel was on the kitchen table. It was about a metre square, and Brian could see that the two halves of the package were bound with four strips of metal. It looked like the kind of box that would contain food samples or laboratory chemicals which needed to be kept cool. From time to time, food manufacturers would send Brian new products for testing or review but they were usually delivered to his college office, not his home. This one was clearly addressed to him at this house, with the exact postcode. On the side of the parcel was a large label bearing the words: "Overnight delivery. Fragile. Foodstuffs. Keep Cool"

Brian decided that he would rather open the parcel and be blown up than risk incurring Molly's scorn. It was an absolutely stupid thought, considering that the parcel looked very inoffensive, wasn't ticking away, and probably contained nothing more threatening than a couple of samples of a new sports drink which he had helped to develop.

He opened a kitchen drawer, took out a bread knife and sawed through the metal strips, one by one, removing them carefully so as not to cut his hands on their sharp edges. When he had removed the strips, he lifted the top half of the polystyrene container and placed it on on the table. Inside the box was a silver-grey cool bag, which had obviously been frozen before the parcel was sent. It was of the type used in picnic hampers. Innocuous enough.

He lifted the bag, and stepped back quickly, gagging at what he saw underneath. Lying, head to tail, in the cavity under the bag were two large, dead rats. Their throats had been cut, and dark brown congealed blood had dried on their fur. Their eyes were sunken, and glassy. Brian was used to seeing dead rats during his work in the university laboratory, but these two were horrible: they looked like two small children, brutally murdered, lying in a cold white coffin.

Something written on the underside of detached lid of the box caught Brian's attention. It was in very small print, on a tiny white label, stuck to the polystyrene. The message said: *Rats die. People die, too...*

"What was in the parcel, darling - a boiled bunny?" Molly was coming downstairs. Her slightly high-pitched voice sounded a little shriller than usual; mocking him.

Brian stuffed the cool bag on top of the rats, replaced the lid, and put the breadknife back in the drawer. If this was the work of the Chinese food "mafia", it was obviously designed to frighten him into abandoning his research into GE203. Well, they could have saved themselves a lot of trouble: he had already decided to forget the whole thing. He would not be returning Susan's calls, or meeting Caroline again. His mind was made up.

When Molly marched into the kitchen, holding her wine glass in her hand, and grinning broadly, Brian was opening the back door which led out into the garden, the box tucked under one arm. "It's from a lab, darling: a tissue culture I needed for a lecture tomorrow. I'll bung it straight in the car. Sorry I over-reacted. Sit down and join me for a bite to eat. Open another bottle of Pouilly Fuisse, and I'll be right back."

****

Chapter Thirteen

Case notes:
Department of Dietetics, East Central Hospital:

Daryl O'Brien, who is 15, 5ft 4in tall, and weighs 17st 10lb, is now being treated in the Diabetic Department after being diagnosed with Type Two diabetes. This is a condition associated with the health problem commonly referred to as "Syndrome X" He has other symptoms, including breathing problems, and high cholesterol. Treatment includes oral administration of the drug, Orlistat, which helps excrete excess fat from the body. It is essential that patients on this medication control their intake of fat. Daryl is finding this very difficult as his parents manage a fish and chip shop.

Susan was trying hard to concentrate on the notes in front of her. In ten minutes' time, she was due to see a young patient, Daryl O'Brien, and his parents. Somehow, she had to convince all three of them that, unless Daryl changed his eating habits, he could die. It was not something she relished, but it had to be done. She had decided that it was no longer good enough, or fair to patients, to tell half-truths about their treatment. The range of drugs currently available for treating obese people was limited, and none of them worked unless the patient made serious lifestyle changes. Surgery was becoming increasingly popular with many doctors, and patients, as a way of limiting food intake, but the side-effects were often unpleasant.

She believed that it was up to her to try and convince her patients that a healthy diet and increased exercise were preferable to surgery, apart from in the most serious cases: where a patient's life was in immediate danger, for instance, or where they were totally unable to cut back on fatty foods because of their limited intelligence or social background. It was a stance that often provoked heated arguments with medical colleagues at the hospital, especially Dr. Guy Johnson, whose favourite remark about such operations was that, apart from liposuction, they were "the quickest and most efficient way to get the fat off these obese bastards."

After her call to Brian Donovan, Susan had been, at first, furious, and then depressed, then furious again. She had told herself the emotional roller-coaster ride she was experiencing was caused, not by his intention to limit their relationship to "friendship", but because he had obviously gone soft on his promise to persue the GE203 investigation. Well, whatever he had decided, she was determined to carry on, even if it cost her her job.

"Susan, Daryl and his mum and dad are waiting outside. Shall I fetch them in?" Gladys was standing at the door, looking worried. "His mum has a couple of canned fizzy drinks and a chocolate bar in her string bag. I hope they are not intended for Daryl's lunch, poor kid, otherwise he'll be ill this afternoon. Good luck."

The O'Brien family entered the office singly, for the practical reason that that doorway was too narrow to accommodate two of them together. Paddy O'Brien was of medium height, with a large stomach, blotchy face and eyebrows like two grey scrubbing brushes. His dark hair was plastered to his forehead with grease, which could have been chip fat or brilliantine. His blonde wife, Maureen, wore a man-size black sweatshirt to cover her ample body. Incongruously, her legs were encased in red tights, and she wore gold high heeled shoes on her plump feet. Daryl, who entered last, wore a red, white and navy blue England soccer tracksuit, white trainers, and carried a turquoise and black mobile phone. He looked extremely tired, with dark circles under his eyes. His complexion was greyish, and there were two large red bumps on his chin.

"Sit down, everyone," said Susan, brightly, gesturing to three chairs which she had placed in front of her desk. "I think we need to have a good old chat before Daryl is weighed and measured. How is the diet going, Daryl? Have you filled in the food diaries I gave you? Are you taking your tablets every day?"

Daryl showed no sign of hearing Susan's questions, and continued to fiddle with his phone, which he gazed at lovingly. It was painfully clear to Susan that this small plastic and metal object wasn't just a means of communication, it was the teenager's best friend and "comforter".

"He's been trying, dear," said Maureen. "We were doing fine on those ready-meals you recommended, as they were so quick to cook in the microwave. But, now you're expecting me to make casseroles and things, it's more difficult. We have a business to run, you know. I clean the shop in the mornings, so there's no time for breakfast, and we never eat supper together. Me and Paddy reckon that Daryl should be enrolled at one of those fat camp places, or have an operation to stop him eating so much. I've told him that if he hides one more bar of chocolate under his bed, his father will take a strap to him."

Susan spoke calmly, but firmly: "Look, Mrs. O'Brien, I can understand how difficult it is for you to monitor what Daryl eats, but you need to make sure that the correct foods are available in the house. I understand that your own kitchen is upstairs, above the shop, so try to make it the "healthy" zone. If he's going to get well, your son needs regular meals: starchy foods like cereals for breakfast, lots of vegetables, lean meat and fish that's not coated in batter. It would be a good idea if you could stock up with these items. Then, when Daryl fixes his own meals, there will always be something suitable for him to eat. Is the cola and chocolate in your bag for you and your husband?"

"God no, me and Paddy will be having our dinner before we open tonight, probably some nice fried halibut and sausages. These are here in case Daryl has a wobbly - you know, a hypo-thingy - you told us to give him some fruit juice and a something sweet if he has a funny turn. I keep them with me, just in case. It happened yesterday, as a matter of fact, when we were at the pub. He was sitting in the pub garden and came over all funny. Right as rain after he'd had some cola. He'll probably have these at lunchtime, just in case he feels a bit funny, like."

Susan wondered if Maureen had read, let alone understood, the booklet on the management of diabetes and the diet sheets which she had been given.

"Maureen, first of all, it will be less likely that Daryl experiences a "funny turn" if he has regular meals - which I don't think is happening at the moment. Secondly, it is not a good idea to give him the sweet food and drink as a preventative; those are the foods that actually cause hypoglaecaemia, or "hypo" for short, by pushing up blood sugar levels. Daryl can't produce enough insulin to deal with this, which is why he feels wobbly. All you need to carry around with you are a small carton of sweetened fruit juice and a couple of biscuits. They should only be given to Daryl in an emergency, and should be swiftly followed by a sandwich or bowl of cereal, to prevent his glucose levels from dropping again. Do you understand?"

Paddy decided to speak. His son continued to look bored.

"We're not thick, you know, Miss Simpson. I've been reading up on Daryl's illness, and I reckon he needs surgery. He obviously has a big eating problem which isn't his fault. It's in his genes. He's being slagged off at school about it which makes him eat more. There is nothing his mother and I can do about it. We have to make a living. I demand an appointment with a surgeon. We've had enough of your advice. It just doesn't work."

Susan tried, once more, to get some kind of response from the patient. "Daryl, this concerns you. Tell me, honestly, do you think you could try to stick to the diet I've given you? Your mum and dad are obviously very busy, but you can do it by yourself. Want to give it a try?" Daryl shifted his gaze, very briefly, from the luminous screen of his mobile phone towards Susan. His tired, slightly hooded eyes looked like two small doughnuts in his large, spotty face. "I'm fed up of it Miss, I want to go to a fat camp where I can be with other kids like me, who won't laugh at me because I'm fat." He turned towards his mother. "Give us a drink, mum. I'm ever so thirsty."

Maureen's fat fingers started to unravel the cord which fastened her string bag, but before she could offer her son the can of cola, Susan poured out a beaker of water from the plastic jug on her desk.

She passed it to Daryl. "Here, drink this, Daryl. You mustn't have cola. I'm sorry. I will put you all in touch with one of the special centres for overweight children and also talk to your GP about the possibility of getting some kind of grant for you to spend a few weeks there in the summer holidays next year. Meanwhile, Daryl, you simply must try to eat properly. We'll weigh and measure you and then I suggest that you all go to the canteen here and get a sandwich. Could you pop outside and sit with Gladys for a moment, Daryl? She's got some really good football magazines out there. I'd like to have a quick word with your mum and dad. "

Sluggishly, Daryl lumbered to his feet, carefully cradling the mobile phone in both hands, and left the office. Paddy folded his arms and glared at Susan. Maureen spread her large legs wider apart, and leaned forward, scowling. Susan stared straight back at them as she spoke:

"Mr. and Mrs. O'Brien, I must tell you that surgery for Daryl would not be considered in this hospital. It could be dangerous, given his condition, and even if he survived the operation, the outcome would not necessarily be satisfactory. Forcing a boy of his age to undergo such a procedure would be cruel, to say the least. His condition is treatable, and I don't think you are giving his care enough priority. While I appreciate that you have a tough job to do as you live on your business premises, he is your son, for goodness sake. I suggest that you both re-read the information I have given you and try to organise your lives so that Daryl gets the food, care and understanding he needs. It would probably do you both the world of good to follow the same diet. You are both overweight. If there is anything you don't understand, you can phone me at any time. You've got to help the poor kid, overwise his future looks bleak, believe me."

A split second too late, Susan realised that she had gone too far: the personal remark about Daryl's parents was unprofessional, and would only make the situation worse. It did. Tears welled up in Maureen's eyes. Whether she was upset about her son's plight, or Susan's criticism of her figure, it was impossible to tell.

Paddy stood up, the hairs on his stomach clearly visible though the straining buttons of his denim shirt: "How dare you talk such bollocks about my wife. She has a lovely figure. It's all in proportion. You are supposed to be treating our Daryl, and you are obviously bloody incompetent. Come on, Maureen, let's get out of here. She hasn't got a clue. We'll go private, even if I have to work my balls off for years to pay for it."

****

At roughly the same time that Susan realised she had made a big mistake with her outspoken remark to Daryl's parents. Brian came to the same conclusion about his own conduct towards the girl he had mentally pigeon-holed as "Purple Jenny". He'd chosen the name, not through unkindness, but because of her purple clothes and passionate nature.

How damned stupid: he had started an affair with a vulnerable young student just when his life was a mess, and he needed to smooth things down at the university. He must nip this latest sexual adventure in the bud with as much dignity, kindness and humanity as possible, and then try and keep a low profile for a while.

It was a free period for Brian, and he was sitting at his desk in his college office, pretending to prepare a lecture. In fact, he was trying to think sensibly, giving his "fine, analytical" mind a chance to work on the various problems he was facing. He had a lost a little weight, and his already thin face looked positively gaunt. His dark blue jeans hung loosely on his hips, and his bony, freckled hands clutched nervously at his coffee cup.

If it wasn't all so frightening, it would be ridiculous, he thought. Here I am, with two revolting dead rats in a box which is sitting in my office fridge, a bunch of mad Chinese after my blood, a wife who thinks I'm pathetic, and two young women upset because of me. It is stupid. I need a few bullet-points for action.

One: get rid of the rats - take them to the council tip after work. Two: ignore the Chinese Mafia. After all, I can't do anything else. Three: go along with Molly's idea of a year in New York. It will get me out of the country, and I won't have to work with Tan Liu or put up with the whims of mad Dermot Browne. It will also distance me from both women: Susan and Jenny. Four: give Jenny the brush off, with as much compassion as possible.

"Would you like me to tidy up the fridge before I go, Brian? I've got the afternoon off if you remember. I've left a file of letters on your desk for you to sign." His secretary appeared at the door of her office, which adjoined his room.

"No, Ruby, thank you very much. I'll do it. Off you go. See you tomorrow." Close one. The phone on his desk rang. "I'll take the call, Ruby. Cheers, now."

The voice on the other end of the line was soft, and breathy. Brian could almost smell the violets. "Brian, I must see you urgently about one of my projects. Are you alone? I'm calling from the phone in the canteen in the basement , so I can't speak much longer. Can I come up?"

"Well Jenny. It is Jenny, isn't it? I'm pretty busy right now. Aren't you supposed to be going to a lecture? You're such a bright student that you mustn't miss out on anything while you are here. I've got a high regard for your abilities, you know, but I do have my own work to do. I'll see you for your usual tutorial tomorrow. "

Brian tried to sound matter-of-fact. This was the best way to talk to girls like Jenny. Be friendly, and concerned about their welfare, but pretend that you have completely forgotten about the sex. They were usually too embarrassed to mention it, and the incident could be pushed to one side. In some cases, an avuncular chat was necessary, but mostly, Brian found that girls these days were perfectly happy to enjoy a one-off sexual experience without any strings attached. It was almost part of the university curriculum.

Unfortunately for Brian, Jenny had other ideas.

Ten minutes later, she burst into the office like a purple rocket, her hair flying, and slammed the door behind her. Today, she was wearing a long black cotton skirt, covered in purple sequins, a cerise coloured t-shirt, and, round her neck, various strings of mauve, purple and red baubles, which jingled together like a bead curtain in an Indian restaurant. Brian wondered if his life could get any worse.

"It's usual to knock, Jenny. What can I do for you?"

"You know damn well what you can do for me, you bastard," she said. "Did you or did you not enjoy yourself yesterday afternoon? I'm not some kind of prostitute you know. Believe it or not, the sex meant something to me."

Brian didn't hesitate for a second; he had been in this situation before. His brain clicked into automatic, and produced one of his standard responses to besotted students:

"Of course you're not, Jenny. You are a wonderful girl and it meant a lot to me as well. You must realise, though, that we can't all have everything we want in this life. Some moments are very special, but can't be repeated for a whole variety of reasons. You have your studies to persue, and I have my own life to lead. You are young, and must look for partners among your own age group. Forgive me if I have hurt you. I didn't mean to. I hope we can still be friends?"

She was silent for a minute, then spoke slowly. "I get the message, loud and clear Brian. I will consider my position. Good afternoon, professor." She turned, sequins swirling and glinting, beads jangling, and strode out of the office.

The summons came just two hours later. "Brian, it's Liz here. Would you come upstairs immediately to see Sir Dermot, please? He needs to speak to you urgently."

Browne's secretary's measured tones gave nothing away. Maybe she didn't know anything. Unlikely, but still, since the college grapevine worked very efficiently. If Jenny had decided to shop him to the Vice Chancellor immediately after leaving Brian's office, the story could be all over the world by now. Students and staff were strictly forbidden to use emails for their own, private messages, but this rule was very difficult to control.

In academic circles, a professor enjoying some recreational sex with a female student was hardly unusual, so Brian tried to convince himself that he would be given a rap over the knuckles and told to keep his flies zipped in future. There had been several similar incidents in the last year, and none of the staff involved had been dismissed.

If the worst happened, well, he had decided to resign during the next month or two anyway. He had already written the letter. He put it in his pocket, ready to produce if necessary, pulled on his brown tweed jacket, and the old college tie which he kept in a drawer ready for meetings like this. He checked his reflection in the mirror hanging by the door, and practised various expressions. Stupid to look too serious and contrite. Best to be breezy, and somewhat bemused by the whole thing. At home, his mother had been able to forgive Brian's various misdemeanors because he always looked so puzzled when she chastised him. It was hard to be annoyed with someone who truly didn't understand what he had done wrong. Perhaps the same strategy would work with Browne.

****

"This is a tricky business, Dr. Donovan." For once, Browne came straight to the point. He was standing behind his desk, looking as though he had just eaten a bad oyster at the Savoy Cocktail Bar.

"A first year female student, Jenny Lewis, came up here an hour ago in tears, accusing you of all kinds of ungentlemanly things. She says she will give the story to a television production company. Apparently, they are filming a series entitled, most graphically, Britain's Bonking Professors. It consists of a series of interviews from girls, and boys I must add, who have been seduced by their university teachers. Quite disgusting. What have you got to say for yourself? You know our policy on this, Dr. Donovan. Your private life is your own, so long as you never bring the college into disrepute. Well?"

Brian tried the quizzical look that had worked so well with his mother. "Sir Dermot, I am absolutely astonished. Jenny is a lovely girl, and a bright student, but she must have misinterpreted my actions. I simply comforted her when she told me about some problems she is having at home. What on earth has she been saying?"

" Dr. Donovan, you might as well tell me the truth. The girl made a tape recording during her sex session with you. Sordid affair, isn't it? I suggest you make your peace. She gave me one copy of the tape which I had to listen to, for obvious reasons, although it was very distasteful indeed. There may be others, so be careful.

"I have, of course, warned her that she will be dismissed from the college if she takes part in the television programme. The young seem to want their five minutes of fame these days, so I am very doubtful whether she cares much about that. It's very disappointing. My only hope is that she realises what she is throwing away, and, with you gone from the college, she will come to her senses and forget the whole, disgraceful episode. She is a volatile girl, so I am very afraid that she might not see sense." He paused, looked down, and shuffled some papers on his desk, then looked up again."You used a French Letter, I hope?"

The old fashioned term for a condom sounded so bizarre

coming from Sir Dermot's lips that Brian very nearly forgot his awful predicament. He turned his chuckle into a cough, pulled his letter of resignation from the inside pocket of his jacket and placed the long white envelope on the desk in front of the Vice Chancellor.

"Of course, sir. As it happens, I was about to tender my resignation anyway. My wife is going to New York on an assignment next year, and the children and I will be accompanying her. Here is the letter. My contract was up for renewal in January, but I could work until you find someone to replace me if you like. There are not many highly qualified nutrition scientists with sufficient teaching experience in this country, but you will probably find someone from abroad: the University of Kuopio in Finland has some fine lecturers, and they all speak good English."

"Dr. Donovan, I can assure you that the problem of replacing you has already been addressed. The Chair you are vacating is one of the most prestigious in the world. I think you are forgetting that. Under the circumstances, I think it is unlikely that you will find a similar post anywhere in this country or America. If I were you, I would spend the evening checking out the junior posts at Northern universities.

" It is nearly the end of term, so I suggest you leave today. The usual arrangements will be made by the Bursar as far as your salary is concerned. He has a copy of your contract, and I can assure you that the university will honour it. You can take this envelope away with you, as I am formally dismissing you. Good afternoon, Dr. Donovan."

Dumbfounded, Brian tried to muster some dignity. He replaced the envelope in his jacket pocket, turned and walked out of the office.

Dermot Browne sat down heavily in his chair and picked up the red receiver of one of the two phones on his desk. The other, internal telephone was cream-coloured. Mobile telephones were, in his opinion, vulgar accessories which should never be used in the office. He dialled a number and when the call was taken, he spoke quickly. "Put me through to Gerald Collins' chambers please." A pause, then: "Gerald, I have taken care of Donovan. Tell your beautiful ex-wife that she doesn't need to worry about any more food industry revelations from this end. The man is finished. Oh, and do come to dinner next Friday, as usual. The chef has some excellent venison in the freezer. Bring the necessary remuneration for the young lady who has been so helpful. I'm sure Elisabeth has budgeted for it. Goodbye, Gerald."

****

After clearing his desk, office cupboards, and removing the package containing the dead rats from his refrigerator, Brian drove to the council rubbish tip near his North London home. He spent half an hour waiting in the long queue of cars, and then he was able to deposit the box, plus a lot of unwanted papers and books, in the trash container.

He was still feeling numb from the afternoon's encounter with Browne, and grateful that Ruby hadn't witnessed the moment when he sat down on his office sofa and sobbed. He would phone her tomorrow and ask her to package up the rest of his belongings and have them sent by courier to the house.

Now, he had to pretend to Molly that he had done what she wanted and resigned. She, at least, would be pleased.

He parked his car outside the house, and walked around to the back door. It was 5pm, and the children should be at home, although Molly was still at work.

"Hi Amy, Hi Toby," he tried to sound cheerful as he pushed open the door, which was on the latch. The kitchen was empty, and the house was silent. At this time of day, there was always a TV or music blaring away somewhere, and signs of a meal being prepared. Today, nothing. The door to the hall opened. Brian froze. Standing in the doorway was Molly, holding a carving knife in one hand and a small silvery CD disk in the other. Her cream and black suit, immaculate when he saw her earlier that day, was creased. Her auburn hair, normally smooth and shiny, was untidy, and her lipstick smudged. Her eyes were red, and there was a streak of brown mascara on one cheek. Although she looked dishevelled, her voice was perfectly controlled: icy cold, and quiet, as if she had been practising what she was going to say for several hours.

"You unfaithful shit, Brian. Don't look surprised. Even with your limited imagination, you must have guessed what has happened. You are not the only one who receives mysterious packages. I came home at lunchtime to collect a document I needed for a dinner meeting with a client, and found this." she waved the CD at him. " I assume you know what it is. Don't worry, the knife is for my own protection: a man who would have sex with a young, innocent student is capable of anything.

"Toby and Amy have gone to a friend's house for supper. Get out of this house, now. You will be hearing from the best divorce solicitor in London tomorrow, and the children and I will be flying out to New York on New Year's Day. We are spending Christmas with my parents in Scotland. I will give you five minutes to collect some overnight things. Do you understand?"

Brian had no intention of arguing. There was no point. Jenny Lewis had obviously found out his home address somehow, and either delivered the package herself, or sent it over by courrier.

He nodded, obediently, and moved towards the doorway. Molly stepped smartly aside, and then followed him upstairs. "Don't try to take anything valuable away with you, Brian. You are in enough trouble already."

****

Chapter Fourteen

Dear Mr and Mrs O'Brien. I would be very grateful if you could come into the school later this week for a meeting regarding your son, Daryl. As you know, his class is preparing for important examinations next year. Unfortunately, Daryl does not seem to be able to produce the standard of work that is necessary, not through lack of ability, but for some other reason, which remains a mystery! He is also having problems fitting into the social structure of the school.
   We are sure these areas will be best addressed with a concerted approach by Daryl, the school staff and yourselves. Please ring me for an appointment.

   Many thanks,

   Richard Askill,
   Head Teacher
   Mitcham County Secondary School, Surrey.

Daryl stuffed the letter into the pocket of his tracksuit jacket, picked up his rucksack and walked out of the boys' cloakroom towards the school exit. He had waited behind, sitting quietly in the dark safety of the cloakroom for ten minutes, so he could be pretty sure that most of his fellow pupils had already left. He didn't want to endure the jeers of the other kids in his class as they thronged out of the main entrance. It was bad enough having to put up with it in the playground. Being called "fatty", "big bum" and "Daryl the Barrel" was part of his daily experience.

Sometimes, though, the jibes were quite good-natured, and Daryl played along with them by laughing, and jumping up and down to make his stomach and bottom wobble. The girls and boys would stand around him in a ring, applauding and shouting "Good old Daryl the Barrel, he's a star", until a teacher came along to break up the group, and send them off, giggling and chattering. He initiated some jokes himself; a well-used defence mechanism which could deflect some of the worse insults. These could be personal, even cruel. George Pearson, a tall, muscular sixteen year old, had a habit of coming up close to Daryl, kicking him on the the shins and pinching him hard, then whispering into his ear:

"You're a fat bastard, Daryl. Why don't you go on a diet? Or do your mum and dad stuff you with fish and chips every night?"

George was the school's soccer captain, and very popular, so it was impossible for Daryl to retaliate. Reporting his bullying behaviour to a teacher would be unthinkable. It was best to put up with it. Even some of the teachers made unkind comments about Daryl's weight, so whinging about being bullied by pupils was out of the question.

"Come on Daryl, we're all waiting for you. The canteen's open soon, that should be an incentive." The sports master was jocular, even encouraging when Daryl tried to play football, or keep up with the others in the weekly cross-country run. His remarks were probably well-intentioned but he certainly knew how to hit the spot:

"Pity we don't play rugby at this school, Daryl. You'd be a bloody useful front row forward, if we could convert some of that fat to muscle. Think about joining one of the local clubs. Do you good, son, and it would be great for your morale, too. It must be tough to be the fattest boy in the school."

I don't want to play fuckin' rugby. I just want to be left alone, thought Daryl as he ambled slowly across the large entrance hall to the main doors. I'm fed up with people telling me what to do, what to eat, what to think. It's bad enough being the size I am, without having to put up with all this shit. I wish I was dead, then they'd all be sorry. This fuckin' letter to mum and dad is bound to be some kind of bloody summons...what a load of bollocks. They are all stupid gits.

The fish and chip shop, "Paddy's Plaice", was about half an hour's walk from the school. Daryl usually walked home via the local park. Today, he headed for an ancient wooden bench in a secluded position, well away from the skateboard area, near the bit of scrubland where old ladies walked their dogs. No-one liked sitting there because the smell of dog faeces wafted through the air, and the bench was none too clean.

Later on in the afternoon and evening, a group of old winos usually gathered there. At 4.30pm, though, it was empty, and, although another wooden slat on the seat had broken since the day before, Daryl was able to sit down fairly comfortably. He hauled his rucksack up beside him and unzipped the jacket of his navy blue school tracksuit. Actually it wasn't quite the same sort as the other boys wore, because they didn't make them in his size. It was an extra-large gents' special from the market, with the school badge carefully sewed on the jacket pocket: another source of mirth for George Pearson. Concealed in the inside pocket were the letter to his parents, and a squashed packet of crisps, which he placed on his lap.

He scratched a large red bump on the side of his nose which threatened to develop into a monster of a zit, replaced the letter in his pocket, undid his black rucksack, and removed a can of cola, three chocolate bars and a large blue and white checked handkerchief. He spread the handkerchief on his knees, extracted his precious mobile phone from the Velcro-sealed front pocket of the rucksack, and pushed the "on" button. Pupils were not allowed to use their phones on the school premises, except in an emergency, so most of them switched on as soon as they were outside the school gates. Daryl preferred to wait until he was somewhere private.

The" greeting" message flashed up on the silver screen, and

Daryl smiled hopefully. It was unlikely that anyone other than his mum would send a text message or call him, but one never knew, and, in any case, it was good to be ready. There was this girl in his class, Helen, who might just call or text. She was the only pupil who actually talked to him as though he was a normal person, not a freak show. He put the phone back into the rucksack, and carefully re-sealed the Velcro.

The picnic lasted just three minutes: Daryl wolfed down the crisps, opened the cola can and took several swigs, then rapidly chewed his way through two of the chocolate bars. He finished the cola, and swiftly devoured the third chocolate bar. It was all done automatically, with no sign of enjoyment. Daryl had not eaten lunch because he didn't want to run the gauntlet of pupils who made comments about everything on his plate. That morning, his mother had instructed him to eat "something healthy", but had not had time to prepare a suitable packed lunch, despite being given a very comprehensive diet sheet prepared by Susan Simpson. Consequently, Daryl's blood glucose levels had fallen dangerously low, and, although he didn't know it, he was already experiencing the symptoms of hypoglycaemia: his pulse was racing and he felt hot and sweaty.

The sweet carbohydrate food made him feel slightly better. He decided to open the letter to his parents and read it. As he had suspected, it was an "invitation" asking his parents to attend school for a meeting with the headmaster. He could imagine what would take place at such a meeting. He considered what to do:

If I give the letter to mum, he thought, and they both come to the school, it will be a fuckin' disaster. The bloody parents will sound off about me being bullied, old Askill will go on about me being a "difficult" boy, and then the parents will say I'm diabetic and should be given more help at the school. It will all end in a row, and I'll be in shit again. If I get rid of the letter, Askill will just think I've got stupid parents, which I have, and he'll probably send someone round to the house. But all that will take time and I might, at least, get a bit of peace before all hell breaks loose. I can always say I lost the poxy thing, and then forgot all about it. They can't prove anything.

Once he had made up his mind to rip up the letter, he felt happier. He tore the single sheet of paper and the envelope into into little shreds, and stuffed them, one by one, into the hole in the empty cola can. He would dump it in the rubbish bin before leaving the park, along with the chocolate bar wrappings. The common assumption that overweight people are untidy and slovenly certainly did not apply to Daryl. He was meticulously careful about keeping his small bedroom, in the flat above the chippie, absolutely spotless. His clothes were always clean, and his trainers whitened.

He had learned that it was wise not to provoke any kind of criticism from his parents: they were always tired, always irritable, and both had very short fuses. So, Daryl tried to have as little physical and verbal contact with them as possible. Every night, from 6pm. to 11.30pm, they worked in the chip shop while he watched telly in his bedroom. Well-balanced meals were not an option. He simply helped himself to any food in the refrigerator. They occasionally asked him about his homework, but weren't sufficiently interested in his progress to check that he was actually handing it in, or keeping up with the school curriculum.

As he ambled towards the park gates, his phone rang. His chubby fingers grabbed at the velcro fastener on his rucksack. He opened it, took out the phone and clamped it to his ear. In a split second, his expression changed from happy expectation to sullen acceptance. "Daryl, it's mum. We've got to go to the "cash and carry" to get some more pickled onions and saveloys, so we won't be at home when you get in. Come into the shop and speak to me before you have some supper. There are some burgers and chips in the freezer for you. Are you alright, Daryl? Taken your tablets OK?"

"Yes mum, ok. See you later."

The rest of the walk home was without incident. Most of the time, Daryl kept his gaze fixed on the pavement in front of him:

eye-contact with other kids could provoke teasing, shouting, or even worse. He dreaded being gang-punched, after reading a newspaper article which told of the plight of a nineteen stone, twelve year old boy who had been cruelly beaten up. He wasn't as big as that, yet, but yesterday's weigh-in at the hospital had shown that he was gaining about half a stone a month. That stupid Miss Simpson had told him that it was all in his own hands to change things, but she didn't have to live like him with all this fatty food, and no-one who would listen to him for more than five seconds at a time. If he could go to a fat camp, he would meet other kids who would understand and the teachers there would have to listen. It would be great.

He turned into his own short street, and reached the fish and chip shop. Peering through the greasy glass window, he could see that the shop was empty, but that the large stainless steel jugs of batter were already piled up on the aluminium counter ready to use that evening. An old black van emblazoned with a three foot wide fish with huge round eyes and "Paddy's Plaice" in bold yellow letters emblazoned on its scaly stomach, was usually parked outside, but the space was empty. Paddy and Maureen were probably already down at the "cash and carry."

He walked round to the back of the shop to the small yard where Paddy parked his other car: a large, shiny silver saloon which was his pride and joy. Paddy hated having smelly raw fish, pickled onions, and saveloy sausages in his car, so the old van was invariably used for work.

Daryl wondered if his dad had left his car keys hanging on the hook in the kitchen. Sometimes, when his parents were out, he would take the keys, open the car, and squeeze himself behind the wheel. He didn't drive anywhere, of course, but just tried to imagine what it would be like to own some "wheels". The car had an automatic gear box, and Daryl had watched his father drive so often that he knew he would be able to handle the car, given half a chance. At least he had only a couple of years to wait before he took his driving test. He already reckoned he knew almost everything about driving: it was kids' stuff, really. You didn't have to be slim or fit to drive, anyone could do it. Dad was fat, but he drove everywhere. Mum wasn't allowed to drive the saloon, but she had promised to give Daryl lessons in the van when he reached his seventeenth birthday. Wicked!

He reached the narrow metal staircase which led up to the front door of the family's upstairs flat and started to climb. There were fourteen stairs, and by the time he reached the top one, his legs felt as though they would break with tiredness. Luckily, the key was under the mat.

The door opened directly into a tiny square hall. Daryl's bedroom was at the back, opposite his parents' room. He went inside, breathing heavily, and switched on the small television set surrounded by model cars, on a shelf by his bed. Without removing the rucksack from his shoulder, he flopped down on one side, on top of the muscular body of the England football captain, printed in garish colours on the thin cotton duvet cover. The bedstead made a loud creaking sound, and Daryl could feel the springs touching the floor underneath. Miraculously, his telephone rang again. He heaved his body into a sitting position, heaved the rucksack off his shoulder and onto the bed beside him, and took out the phone.

"Daryl, it's Helen here. Are you on your own? I've just had a bloody horrible fight with me mum." Helen's divorced mum was a bossy cow with short, blond and red striped hair, who wore mini skirts and drove a shiny green people-carrier to collect her daughter from school. During one of their playground conversations, Helen had confessed that she thought her mother was "pathetic", and obviously on the look out for a new husband. "Desperate for it," were the exact words she used.

"Yes, course I am. What of it?" Daryl tried to sound uninterested. "What'yer want?"

"My mum said she thinks you ought to have an operation to stop you from eating so much. I've told her that all you need is decent food and some consideration, but she says you must have bad genes, inherited from your fat dad. I said she was a rotten cow so say that, and she told me to go to my room. So, look what trouble you've got me into ...just for defending you. Why don't you do something about yourself, Daryl? You're a pain in the arse."

"Thanks for nothing. You're not exactly a bloody glamour model, yourself, Helen. If I could get rid of some of this blubber, I would, believe me. I'm sick of people nagging me all the time. How about going to see a movie on Saturday night, if you can bear the thought of being seen around with me?"

Helen's voice softened. "I'm sorry, Daryl. Honest, I would go out with you if I could. On a friendly basis, mind. I don't care what people say about you. You're ok, really. The trouble is that this Saturday I'm going to a party at George Pearson's house. His mum and dad are in Ibiza, and he's asked half the class round. Don't expect he's asked you, though. He's a pig, really, but I do fancy him. It's a shame you aren't good looking, Daryl, because you are really nice. Maybe you'll find a girl your own size to go out with. That would be good. Better go, mum's coming. Text me later if you like. Byeee."

Daryl put the phone down on the bed beside him. That was it then. Helen, his one friend at school, was just the same as the rest of them. When it came to choosing between going out with a fat fool like him, or going to a party with her other friends, there was no contest. Fat blokes missed out every time, and cocky bastards like George Pearson were the winners. His misery was compounded by the feeling of acute panic that suddenly came over him. If life was going to be like this all the time, it wasn't worth living. He felt weak and disorientated, and his head was spinning. He had to eat something.

He rolled off the bed, and lumbered over to the small pine chest of drawers by the side of the door. In the botton drawer, beneath his underwear, was an old cardboard cigar box containing four peppermint cream-filled chocolate bars. He took them out of the box, flopped back down on the bed and ate them quickly, stuffing the wrappers under the mattress. As usual, the taste of the sweet chocolate and fondant filling made him feel better. Chocolate was good to eat, made him happier and there was fuck all else in his life to enjoy. That dietitian woman at the hospital had told him to make sure he had a proper balanced meal every night. Well, what was the point of eating fruit and vegetables and stuff, when chocolate was so easy to eat. It was all food, so what was the difference, anyway?

His mobile phone rang again. "Daryl, it's mum. The van's broken down at the "cash and carry", so we're waiting for a mechanic to come from the garage to pick us up. Are you OK? We'll be at least an hour, so the shop won't open until about 7pm. If anyone turns up, tell them we'll be frying later. Get yourself something to eat. There are some cold sausages and a potato pasty in the fridge and plenty of ready meals in the freezer. Help yourself."

"OK mum, I'm alright. I'm doing me homework."

"Good boy, Daryl. See you later."

The phone went dead, and Daryl put it down on the bed beside him. Typical. He was on his own again, with no-one to talk to, and just some mouldy old leftovers for supper. It was bloody pathetic. One day, he would show them all that he was a real person, not just a fat freak. He'd take dad's car and drive it past George Pearson's house just for the hell of it. In fact, if dad had left his keys in the kitchen, he would sit in the car now, and imagine how it would feel to drive it.

Cheered by this plan, Daryl put his precious mobile phone into his jacket pocket, eased himself off the bed, and went into the kitchen. There, on the hook behind the door, hung his father's car keys. He took the keys, opened the back door, and clambered slowly down the iron staircase. Dad must have washed the car that afternoon. It stood, shiny and immaculate, in its usual place on the cobbles of the small yard, facing the road. The dirty grey double gates of the yard were open. Daryl unlocked the driver's door, and squeezed himself into the car. Paddy kept the car seat well back, so Daryl's large bottom fitted easily into the luxurious black leather seat and the belt fitted perfectly. He stretched out his legs, placed his hands on the wheel, and breathed deeply. The leather upholstery smelt wonderful, a bit like dark chocolate.

He put the key in the ignition, and turned it. The huge engine fired immediately, and began to throb softly. It was almost a purring sound, so gentle that you could hardly hear it. Paddy called his car "my other lovely lady," and joked that the vehicle was "as big and playful as my Maureen - without the nagging." Daryl looked at the automatic gear shaft, black leather tipped, and so simple to operate. All you had to do was to put it into the "drive" position, gently let off the brake, push down on the throttle and steer. It was easy.

Eating the four chocolate bars had pushed up Daryl's blood glucose level. He now felt fine: confident and reckless. He grabbed the brake with his right hand, coaxed it into the "off" mode, slotting the gear shaft into the "drive" position as he did so. Daryl pressed down gently on the throttle and the car crept forward. He made up his mind quickly: he would drive the car down the road to the park, then turn it round and come back.

A few minutes later, he was driving, really driving! It had been so simple to edge the car out of the yard, and turn left onto the main road towards the park. Daryl started to enjoy himself.

Then, the euphoria disappeared. His mood changed quickly from happy to uncertain. His blood sugar level started to plummet, and his heart started pounding. It was a familiar sensation but, this time, Daryl had no bar of chocolate or can of cola at hand to give himself a quick sugar "fix". There was a clear stretch of road ahead, with one car just a little way in front of him. Daryl knew he had to concentrate, but his mind felt foggy. He relaxed his right foot, and the car slowed down. The park was about 100 metres on the right, and he knew he must now get over into the offside lane in order to swing round into the half-circle of space in front of the park entrance. If he stopped there, it would be simple to turn the car round and come back on the opposite side of the road.

He turned the wheel to the right, then remembered that he

should have checked in the mirror first. "Mirror, signal, manoeuvre", those were the words his dad had used when he was telling Daryl about driving. "Remember, when you get your licence, son, that you must always check what's going on behind you: there's bound to be some bastard doing something stupid."

The woman driver of the four-by-four who was overtaking the slow-moving silver saloon was killed instantly when her vehicle plunged into the back of Daryl's dad's precious car and was pushed into the line of oncoming traffic. The driver of the large, articulated lorry which struck the silver saloon head-on was badly injured; his neck was broken and he suffered severe lacerations to his upper body, internal injuries, and his left leg was crushed. The height of his cab prevented him from taking a direct hit, otherwise he would have died.

The impact of the articulated vehicle, with its massive wheels, on Paddy's beautiful car was so great that it was crushed, concertina-fashion, and wedged under the belly of the lorry. It took the local fire brigade a whole day to extract Daryl's mangled body from the wreckage.

The fish and chip shop stayed closed.

****

Susan heard the news early next morning from Guy Johnson. He strode into her office at the hospital as she was sitting at her desk sipping a cup of coffee. He looked dishevelled and tired, his eyes sombre, his grey hair standing on end. His white coat, always crumpled, now looked filthy.

"So sorry, Susan old girl, one of your fat patients was wheeled into A and E last night in bits. A road accident. Two dead, ghastly mess. A young lad, too, Daryl O'Brien. Curiously, he was driving one of the vehicles. Parents distraught of course. They seemed to think he might have killed himself deliberately because of his weight problems. Seems he pinched his father's car. Sounds a bit far-fetched that. What do you think?"

The cardboard cup slipped from her fingers, and the hot coffee spilled out over Susan's desk. She leapt to her feet, ignoring the mess.

"Guy, this is terrible. What a tragedy. Daryl was unhappy but he didn't give any indication of being suicidal. I can't believe it. His parents didn't seem to understand the importance of helping him to eat properly and I'm afraid I was rather sharp to them when they brought him here the other day. God, what a dreadful thing. The poor kid. It's heartbreaking."

She sat down, heavily, and started to cry, shoulders heaving, her head in her hands. Wretched with shock and disbelief, she looked up at Guy and tried to speak coherently, but her words were jumbled. "Guy. Can't do anything. Just a child, and all so unnecessary. It's my fault. Should have been firmer. Psychiatrist needed, perhaps. How stupid. Could have done something. Useless. Sad..so sad."

Dr. Johnson spoke firmly. "Susan, pull yourself together. That's stupid talk. The boy's parents could stir up trouble if you say things like that. They are looking for someone to blame for this, and you could be the perfect candidate. I am sure you handled this case properly, and there is absolutely no need for you to feel guilty. You did your best for him. No doubt, the coroner will record "death by misadventure", and there will be no come-back against the hospital or you. All you've got to do is keep quiet. I've been involved in similar cases before, and there really cannot be any reason why you should be blamed. Make sure you do not speak to the parents. In fact, I would recommend taking a holiday. The Trust must owe you a few weeks?"

Despite her tears, Susan managed a weak smile. "You've got to be joking, I took a week's holiday in New York recently, and don't qualify for another break until spring. Seriously, Guy, do you think Daryl's parents will blame me? He was such a vulnerable kid and we've all failed him: myself included. It's horrible. I have to tell you that I have considered chucking in this job several times during the last few months. Recently, though, I decided to stick it, simply because I felt I was doing some good for my patients. After this, I am not so sure. Perhaps I would be better off taking a year out to work in a different environment, in industry perhaps.

Her voice faltered: "God, how can I even think of myself at a time like this. Daryl's parents must be going through hell. You look all in, Guy. Thanks for taking the trouble to come and tell me this. If I decide to leave the hospital, you'll be the first to know."

Guy Johnson turned to leave the office, then changed his mind, and spoke, his face etched with tiredness. "Listen, Susan, if you do go, I must warn you that industry jobs are just as ghastly as those in the health service. Industry bosses demand blood and you don't even get the satisfaction of helping patients get well. It's a battlefield out there. Why do you think I've stuck in this job for years? I'm too shit scared of working in the private sector or for some drugs company, that's why. Good luck, Susan, whatever you decide. But, no guilt. Promise?"

She nodded. As her office door closed behind the ample figure of Guy Johnson, Susan opened a desk drawer and extracted a box of tissues. She mopped her face, then the puddle of coffee on the desk.

Daryl. A child who was, albeit only partially, in her care. A child with diabetes and who was severely obese. She imagined his spotty, unattractive face, and pudgy body crushed to smithereens. Was his death directly linked to his problems? Had he committed suicide? Or was he just out "joy riding" in his dad's car? Probably, no-one would ever know. Unless, of course, he had left a note. This thought sent a chill down her spine. The phone rang:

"Miss Simpson? It's Paddy O'Brien here. You must have heard what's happened to our Daryl? Well, I hold you directly responsible. You should have arranged for him to have a stomach stapling operation months ago. Maureen and I will never get over this. I'm getting a solicitor to bring a case against the hospital for negligence. Do you understand?"

"Mr. O'Brien. First, my deepest sympathies to you and your

wife. It is dreadful news about Daryl. You must both be heartbroken. He certainly seemed to be very positive about wanting to go to a treatment centre for obese young people when we last met. What makes you think he might have wished to take his own life?"

"What are you talking about, you stupid cow? My Daryl wouldn't commit suicide. No, he was out in my car, the little bugger, and I reckon he had one of those "hypo" things you are always on about. He must have blacked out or something, and it's all your fault."

Susan could well imagine Paddy O'Brien's anguish. Although it was clear from his words that neither she nor the hospital could be held responsible for the death of a patient who had not followed any of the dietary instructions he had been given, she decided to let Daryl's distressed father continue:

"You'll have his death on your conscience for the rest of your life, you bitch. When I've finished with you, you'll wish you'd never been born. Goodbye."

She had just replaced the receiver, when Gladys knocked at the door. "Your clinic is in five minutes, Susan. Are you OK, love, you look all in. I've just heard about Daryl. Poor kid."

"Ok Gladys. I'm coming. It's appalling, isn't it? I'll write to his mum and dad tonight."

****

It was late, around 11pm. Susan's house was quiet, with no sound at all from any late-night passing traffic outside. She sat at the desk in her sitting room, an untouched glass of white wine by the keyboard of her computer. A single spot of light from the bulb of her angle-poise desk lamp was reflected in the shiny, transparent surface. Her face was still blotchy from that morning's tears, and there were dark circles under her eyes. For once, she hadn't changed into a caftan or tracksuit; she still wore the dark brown skirt and cream sweater she had put on that morning.

The letter to Daryl's parents still remained unwritten but she just completed a letter of resignation, addressed to the East Central Hospital Trust Manager.

The day's events had left her feeling drained. Her life seemed to be going in circles. After New York, she had been determined to find out about GE203, taking on the world if necessary. She had even managed to compartmentalise the brief affair with Brian Donovan: it had been firmly placed in a mental filing cabinent marked "good experiences, not to be repeated."

Despite being almost sure that their liaison was now over, Susan had imagined that Brian would continue to work with her to expose the truth about the ingredient which they both believed was being planted, deliberately, in foods in order to compromise the health of innocent people. Now, Brian had gone "cold" on his promise. His last phone call had been more than a mere brush-off; it had virtually been an admission that he was unable to continue probing GE203 because it "compromised" his position at the university. Without his scientific knowledge and contacts, she now realised, it would be impossible for her to continue.

Even Caroline Dempsey was becoming soft. Instead of revealing full details about the utter ruthlessness and money-grabbing activities of the food industry, she had diluted the message that the three of them had agreed to put over during their meeting in New York. The first article in her "hard-hitting" series, exposing the way manufacturers are allowed to fool the public with totally innaccurate labelling, had been good. The following two pieces were innocuous, with no new revelations, and hardly any pictures. It was as if she had been got at by someone - probably the advertising department of her newspaper.

None of these things would have made Susan sufficiently depressed to contemplate resigning, until today. Although unconnected with her worries about GE203, Daryl's case, and his tragic death, had tipped her over the top from a general feeling of helplessness, to a state of near-depression, and even a feeling, totally unjustified, that she needed to be punished. Getting drunk would be a sensible way of dealing with it, short-term, and she had tried, but failed, to do so...hence the untouched wine.

With her own clinical experience, and knowing (too well!) her own health history, she surmised, correctly that her "punishment" would take the form of self-denial: no alcohol, little food, long, solitary walks, days of introspection. It was a path she had trodden before: when she had compared her achievements, unfavourably, with those of her parents, after her failure to land a "glamorous" job, and during the first, horrible few weeks following the breakup of her relationship with Mark. What she really needed now was a nourishing meal, and a good night's sleep, but she knew that she would probably sit at her desk for most of the night, analysing the causes, and possible consequences of Daryl's death. Tomorrow, she would be unable to eat anything. By the evening, she would feel worse, and try to force herself to eat a meal, probably without success. It was a familiar pattern.

For the hundredth time since hearing about his death, she mulled over the conversation she had had with Daryl's parents:

I remember being very sharp with them, she thought. I criticised them both for being overweight, which was unforgiveable. Supposing Daryl took my words to mean that I thought his parents were neglecting him, and then decided to punish them by stealing his father's car? Suppose he was so miserable because of my negative attitude after his request to be sent to a "fat camp" that he did, indeed, deliberately crash the car? Or, suppose he suffered a "hypo" because he just didn't understand any of the dietary information I'd been giving him, and that caused the car crash. Poor kid. Whatever the reasons for the accident, he didn't deserve to end up like this. His life must have been a total misery.

Susan then turned her thoughts to some of her other very obese patients: John Barnard had died because he couldn't follow the diet instructions she had given him. Another patient, Valerie Tate was struggling too, and she had already suffered one heart attack. Poor old Arthur Taylor, an amputee, was confined to a wheelchair and unable to see his one foot because his stomach was so huge. He was gaining a pound a week, and his blood cholesterol was sky-high. Another youngster, Gemma Hartley had learning difficulties, and her only pleasure in life was going to a big fast food restaurant and being "entertained" by the resident clown hired each day to encourage the kiddies to eat up their burgers, fries and shakes.

She was letting them all down. The industry, and possibly even the government as well, was set on "cradle to grave" strategies to make people dependent on junk food and she was just one health professional trying to prevent people from killing themselves. It was an impossible task.

It was definitely time to change her job.

She folded the letter of resignation and put it into a white envelope, addressed it, and placed it in her briefcase, ready to put it into the internal mail next day. The white cordless phone on her desk rang urgently. It was very late for a call. Puzzled, she picked up the receiver.

"Susan, it's Brian. Are you in bed? I'm so sorry to ring you so late, but I had to speak to you. I owe you an apology and an explanation for my brusque attitude the other day. Can you speak?"

She tried to sound unconcerned: "Of course. How are you? Don't worry, Brian. I am fine about it, I promise. I must tell you though, that I am resigning from the hospital. Two patients in my care have died, and I don't feel I want to carry on there. It will do me good to get a taste of the commercial world. I've been looking through the journals and marked a couple of jobs in industry. It's funny, but one of them is with Kenley and Palmer, the company who produce one of the ready-meal brands that contain GE203. In fact, I brought one of them with me to your office and you had it tested. It seems ages ago now.

" If I get the job, I might find out something. Not that it would concern you, professionally. I must say that I'm very surpised, after what happened in New York, that you have decided to back out on this, Brian. You have your career and family to consider, but, after your brilliant lecture, I thought you were braver. I'm sorry, that was a stupid thing to say. Of couse Molly and the children must come first...I do realise that."

Brian sounded tired and his voice was quite faint. Even though the line was crackly, she could pick up the sheer urgency in his manner. "Look, I'm speaking to you on my mobile, from a hotel in London. I must warn you Susan that your phone could be tapped. There is a lot I have to tell you, but the details will have to wait until we meet up. The bare bones of it are that I have been fired, and, like you, I'm looking for another job. Molly has thrown me out. I can't say more. I will call you tomorrow at the hospital. Goodbye."

Stunned, Susan replaced the receiver in its cradle. She sat staring into space for a moment, then her mind started churning. This was crazy stuff. After a few minutes of frantic conjecture she decided that, whatever had happened to Brian, nothing had changed as far as her own immediate future was concerned. She was right to resign from her job. No doubt, she would find out about Brian's situation soon enough. Her phone tapped? Surely not: he was the one who had been given the third degree by a bunch of Chinese lunatics, not her. There was no reason why anyone would want to tap her phone. It was ridiculous.

No, he was obviously overwrought. Meanwhile, she had definitely made the right decision.

Satisfied with this reasoning, Susan picked up the glass of wine and took a sip: it tasted disgusting: slightly warm, flat and acidic. Despite the lack of response from her underused taste buds, she took another sip, and then another.

Feeling slightly light-headed, she picked up her pen and began: Dear Mr. and Mrs. O'Brien...

Chapter Fifteen

LOSE A STONE FOR CHRISTMAS ON THE PUDDING DIET

It's just desserts, girls! You can shed fourteen pounds of unwanted lard in just two weeks on the brilliant new diet plan devised by our consultant nutritionist Gilly Unsworth.
Scoff icecream, profiteroles, and chocolate mousse while the inches just melt away. The diet has been tried and tested by gorgeous Penny Briggs, celebrity icon and TV personality. She says: "Puddings were always my downfall, but now I'm in perfect shape for my New Year's Eve telly special. I'm feeling fine - and there'll be less of me in 2009!"

Why do I fall for this crap? Caroline Dempsey was sitting in front of her parents' TV set, with a tray on her knee. On it, were positioned a copy of "Gleam" magazine, open at the "food and diet" page, plus a very small carton filled with a dark brown substance that, according to the label stuck on the side, was "low-fat chocolate mousse", a spoon and a glass of water. She wondered, out loud, why she even bothered to follow stupid diets like the one in the magazine.

"I'm a sensible, critical, savvy, possibly even brilliant, journalist, yet just because I'm a bit overweight and feeling depressed, I fall for the stupid promises offered by some ridiculous magazine, and endorsed by a skinny girl who would declare that she'd slept with the pope if she thought she'd make a few quid. I must be crazy".

On the screen in front of her, the latest "lifestyle" programme was in full, moronic blast.

For some reason, the channel bosses had decided that viewers would enjoy a show devoted to evesdropping on couples arguing about their forthcoming Christmas arrangements. Subjects for "discussion" included how to stuff the turkey, who to invite to stay, how much to spend on presents. The hysteria generated by these seemingly innocent topics was considerable. One woman had just thrown the pale, sticky contents of a bowl of pudding mixture over her ranting partner. The presenter uttered the all-too-predictable line: " Well, it looks as though Harry is getting plastered a little early this year."

Irritated with herself for watching such rubbish, Caroline picked up the spoon and dug deeply into the carton of "delicious, virtually fat-free chocolate mousse". Stiff with sugar, preservatives, colourants and other additives, it formed a neat, rubber-textured ball shape in her spoon. A seasoned connoisseur of real chocolate mousse, made with double cream, dark chocolate and fresh eggs, Caroline knew that the proper stuff doesn't form neat shapes because it is too rich and delicious. It wobbles and oozes dribbly bits of chocolate.

She tasted the unappetising-looking apology for chocolate mousse very carefully. Yuk. According to the article in the magazine, you had to eat this muck three times a day. No wonder you lost weight; the food was so disgusting you felt sick all the time. She knew that the diet was non-scientific and ridiculous anyway, so why bother?

She chastised herself again: "Because you're fat, you stupid woman. You are also without a boyfriend, and your contract with the Evening Echo is not going to be renewed. In other words, Caro doll, you are stuffed. Actually, on second thoughts you are unlikely to be stuffed, looking the way you do. What's happened to you?"

She got up from the sofa, placed the tray on the table in the bay window of her parents' neat suburban semi and stood in front of the mahogany-framed mirror above the mantlepiece. She was not happy with what she saw. In just a few weeks, she had changed considerably. The fine line between "voluptuous" and "obese" had definitely been breached. Her long blonde hair hung limp to her shoulders, her eyes looked piggy, and she had two chins.

Looking down at her large bust, today covered by a sloppy red sweater, and the overhang of pink flesh above her size 18 jeans, she was horrified by the way the excess weight on her body seemed to have shifted downwards. Her thighs were so large that her jeans looked like a couple of overstuffed sausages, and even her feet, (in scruffy gold flip-flops, with matching gold toe nail polish), looked fat. This morning, her mum's bathroom scales, which Caroline rarely used, had registered 16st. 10lb. Horrible.

"Right, girl. This will not do." She spoke firmly to the sad-looking, overweight woman reflected in the mirror. "Mum and Dad are out Christmas shopping, so you've got the whole afternoon to get yourself organised. If Rob bloody Kelly thinks he's seen the last of you he's wrong. Within a month, your byline will appear in another tabloid, and you'll be riding high again. Meanwhile, he is running innocuous stories about a food industry which is obviously greedy, corrupt, and probably encouraged to poison people by this poxy government. He must have been got at by the advertising department, or someone high in the chain of self-seeking hypocrites who run this country.

"First, you need a good, nourishing meal, then some retail therapy followed by hard networking. You can do it, Caro."

Her abrupt dismissal from the "Echo" had come as a very nasty surprise. She was only employed on a three month "rolling contract.", a normal arrangement in the cut-throat world of journalism. She knew she had delivered some good work, and, until the "Hidden Killers in Your Food" three-part series had gone pear-shaped, Caroline had reckoned that she would stay on the paper for a couple of years and even, perhaps, achieve her ambition of becoming a political reporter.

On the day her contract was due for renewal, she had received an envelope from the paper's Human Resources department containing a tersely worded letter telling her that it was being terminated. The letter had been signed by someone she had never even met who operated from an office on the eleventh floor of the newspaper building. It read like an end of term school report. Only the words "could try harder" were missing: "This is no reflection on your work, but is part of a whole strategy for improving our staffing. No doubt you will be asked to contribute to the paper, but on a freelance basis. Your agreed severance cheque for two months' salary has been paid into your bank account. Good luck for the future."

Good luck, my arse, thought Caroline at the time. If they think I'm emailing any ideas to the Health Editor for her to rip off, they've got another think coming.

She pulled herself up quickly: unless, of course, it suits me and they pay me a fortune. Despite her anger, she was astute enough to realise that, in the difficult world of freelancing, it's best to stay friends with everyone who might be a potential customer.

A week might be a long time in politics, but twenty four hours was an eternity in journalism. Some people in the industry had made it to the top after being sacked several times on the way, sometimes in very damaging circumstances. She remembered one randy editor who had seduced most of his female staff, and was finally sacked after an unfair dismissal case which cost his newspaper many thousands of pounds. He was now lording it as a top columnist in a Sunday quality paper, and had recently been knighted.

She had kept her cool during the embarrassing process of clearing her desk; she stuffed the contents of her two small drawers (a pair of tights, a few stale "SuperSnacks" bars, some tissues and a bag of make-up) into a carrier bag, and crammed all the paperwork which littered the top of her desk, including that day's unopened post, into her newest fashion investment a large orange leather bag. She even managed to stay cheerful while buying drinks that evening at the hacks' favourite watering hole, an old Victorian pub near the office.

Now, she felt defeated. Her parents, supportive as ever, had been wonderful, telling her to enjoy a quiet family Christmas, relax, and start again on the career in the New Year. She tried to be cheerful when they were around, but for the last few days it had been a struggle. "Down in the dumps" was exactly the right description for the low-hanging mounds of flesh around her waist and hips, as well as her state of mind.

Caroline had never been the kind of girl to let problems get to her, even big ones, so she allowed herself another few minutes of self-pity. Then, she made up her mind, quickly. The seven day mourning period was definitely over.

She took the tray out to the kitchen, dumped the half-eaten chocolate mousse and the magazine in the bin, and rinsed the spoon under the tap. What she needed was some real food, a hot bath, make-up and shopping. Her mother, Gwen, had left some salad and a plateful of cold roast pork on a shelf in the fridge, and there was an unopened bottle of Reisling, her parents' favourite wine, in the door compartment. Oh well, it was better than nothing. Caroline put the pork and salad on a plate, opened a can of baked beans, and the bottle of wine. She laid herself a place at the scrubbed pine kitchen table, and tucked into the delicious food and the rather sweet, but quite respectable wine.

Half an hour later, with her tummy feeling comfortably full and her spirits lifted by the wine, she went up to her room and looked for a suitable outfit to wear on her shopping spree. Given her current (temporary!) weight worries, it had to be something loose and comfortable. She settled on a long gypsy-style skirt in three different shades of green, a loose black top, black boots, and an ocelot-style fake fur coat. Her new orange handbag needed sorting out, but it wouldn't take long. She emptied the contents on her bed. Most of the paperwork from the office, old email printouts and page proofs, and could go in the bin. There were one or two letters as well, which she opened. What she needed was a good old invitation to some kind of jolly public relations Christmas party, with plenty of opportunities for networking. Luckily, there were two for that evening.

She decided she would plump (the word had a special significance, she thought) for a big bash which was being thrown at the offices of Spencer and Lee, a public relations company with a whole range of clients, from food giants to sports clothing firms. Maybe, just maybe, she would be able to get some work out of one of their clients, or even make contact with someone high up on another paper who would hire her. The last idea was a long shot, as she knew that important journalists and executives who hired and fired newspaper staff were unlikely to have time to attend public relations parties. Anyway, it was worth a go.

She stared critically at her reflection in the full length mirror on the inside door of her built-in wardrobe. She didn't look too bad, but her hair needed attention. Three hours at a good crimper, some shopping, and a manicure; a certain recipe for success.

"We're back, Caroline. How do you feel? Hope you've been having a nice rest, dear. Dad's unloading the car." Caroline heard her mother coming upstairs. Gwen was a comfortable-looking woman in her sixties with blond hair like Caroline, but worn in a sensible short style. Unlike Caroline's thin, nervous father, Eric, who had always thought the world of journalism was no place for a woman, Gwen had full confidence in her talented, attractive daughter. The girl had brains, as well as looks. This job business was just a set-back, nothing else.

"I'm going up to town to a party, mum. Work thing. Shouldn't be late, but you never know." Caroline gave her mother a hug. "How do I look?"

"Lovely dear. Don't worry about putting on that little bit of weight. You can easily lose it again. Now have a good time. Your father and I are going to decorate the tree later on, so you'll see it when you get in. We've bought some new bits and pieces to hang on it, including those lovely little chocolate liqueurs you like so much. The turkey is ordered, and I'm going to make the mince pies today as well. I'll leave them in a tin in the kitchen. Help yourself to a couple if you're peckish after your party."

Caroline wished her mother wouldn't tempt her with yet more yummy, edible treats. Her whole life had been spent trying not to indulge in Gwen's temptingly light mince pies, her delicate lemon sponges, and incredible roast dinners. Maybe it was time she quit the family home and lived, temptation free, on her own. To do that, she needed money.

"I'll see you both in the morning, mum. I'll kiss dad on the way out. Bye for now."

****

Five hours later, with a glass of wine in one hand and a cardboard plateful of nibbles (including a chicken vol-au-vent, nuts, crisps, various crumb-coated bits of fish and a dollop of bright red chilli sauce) in the other, Caroline was standing by the bar in the Spencer and Lee boardroom, holding forth on the subject of food additives to a young man from an organic farming magazine.

Her afternoon's retail therapy had been fruitful: the black top she had been wearing earlier was now rolled up like a silky sausage in the bottom of her handbag. She had replaced it with a very expensive low-necked, green sequin-embroidered tunic with long, flowing transparent sleeves, which were now floating dangerously near the chilli sauce on her plate. Her blond hair was softly waved, with new silvery highlights (the result of a two hour session at a top London salon - £200, but what the heck!) and her nails were painted bright red. The effect was dazzling.

She was now in gushing mode: "My recent series in the "Echo" - did you read it?- was an eye-opener, even for me. I was staggered by the way manufacturers deliberately try to fool consumers. Did you know that there is thirty grams of fat in a salad served at the Muffins 'n Burgers chain - which they try to pretend is a "healthy option"? It's disgusting."

Her companion, a thin young man wearing a loose blue denim shirt, black linen trousers and brown immitation suede sandals, had already decided that a night of passion with this warm, cuddly-looking woman would be the perfect pre-Christmas treat.

"That's nothing, Caroline, " he said, lifting his glass of lager for a quick swig. "You really must go further and investigate the way noxious materials enter the food chain in the first place. I've just done a piece for *Earthworks* plotting the life cycle of the classic, all-American burger. Did you know that, in the US, the cattle breeders buy millions of dead cats and dogs from animal shelters and feed them to their stock, which then end up on people's plates? It is madness!"

Caroline put her plateful of nibbles down on the bar top, not noticing that the filmy edge of her left sleeve was now covered in sauce. Suddenly, the party food didn't seem so appetising. She decided that it was better to die from a heart attack induced by eating too much fat and sodium, than to linger painfully with a nasty dose of "mad moggy" disease, and reached for a small cardboard bowl containing some bright yellow tortilla chips.

"Darling," she said, " I don't think tabloid readers would be able to stomach that, but it's a great story. I'l buy a copy of your magazine tomorrow. Lovely talking to you."

She turned swiftly, leaving her companion just as he was warming to his subject. Fascinating stuff, but, frankly it was a bit stomach-churning, she thought. Anyway, chatting to mediocre journos like him won't get me any work. Come on, Caro, concentrate.

"Excuse me, may I be of assistance?" A tall, slim, balding man of about fifty wearing a well-cut dark grey suit, pale pink shirt and matching tie, was offering Caroline a pristine white handkerchief. "You appear to have some tomato sauce on your sleeve. Let me wipe it off for you before it goes all over that beautiful outfit. "

Caroline was slightly flustered, but allowed the man, who introduced himself as Lars Johnsson, the European Director of Protin-Foods Ltd, to dab her sleeve with his handkerchief. He seemed to enjoy the task immensely, and continued to dab away after most of the sauce had been removed. The crush around the bar was now intense, and Caroline found herself crammed close to Lars, who had placed one hand around her waist.

Sensing a quick conquest and a work opportunity, Caroline introduced herself as a "freelance journalist and food writer specialising in commercial projects." There was no time to lose: she had already spent a good whack of her severence settlement that afternoon. She needed a well-paid freelance commission as soon as possible to cover Christmas expenses, then she could concentrate on getting another, full-time newspaper job.

"I write about nutrition and diet, " she told him, smiling into his bulbous, rather fish-like blue eyes. "Does your company produce any booklets for commercial distribution? I specialise in writing those. I'd love to write one for Protin-Foods. It's a fascinating company. "

She did a quick mental check, thanking god, briefly, for giving her the brains to read the business pages every Sunday. Protin-Foods, she remembered, was a Swedish based company, with offices and a factory in a business park near Newcastle. They made a vegetable protein food which could be flavoured and shaped to look and taste just like meat or fish. It was not genetically modified, and the main ingredient was a kind of yeast. Lots of supermarket brands used the stuff in their ready-meals, and the company also produced their own branded products. The company wasn't quoted on the stock market, but was doing very well in Europe, with expansion plans. They had plenty of money.

"We have recently hired Spencer and Lee to help us put the healthy eating message across to consumers, " said Lars, in slightly clipped tones, with a hint of a Scandinavian accent. Caroline noticed that he had rather large, rubbery looking lips. She tried not to think about her last visit to the London Aquarium, and concentrated hard, gazing at him with her special "serious journalist expression": eyes wide, mouth slightly open, two tiny frown lines between her brows.

He continued: "That is why I'm here tonight. Lucky me, to have found such a beautiful lady to talk to. As a matter of fact, I have already asked the public relations company's account manager, Johnny Haskins, to hire someone to write a twelve page booklet giving information about our products which we can distribute in supermarkets in the spring. I'd like it to include recipes as well. You sound well-qualified. Of course, the decision will be taken in conjunction with Spencer and Lee, otherwise they'll get irritated with me! It would involve a trip up to our offices on Tyneside. Do you know the area? It's so lively. I am so enjoying working and living up there."

"Actually," admitted Caroline, "I'm ashamed to say that I don't know Newcastle at all, but I've heard it is a very exciting city. Here, let me give you my card, and perhaps you'd give me yours? I should tell you that, recently, I did write a series of articles about the food industry which were not exactly complimentary. However, Protinfoods came out of it very well; your basic product is very interesting, and maybe, with the present reaction against meat products and problem of overfishing, you will one day be supplying your foods to the United States. Is that your long-term strategy?"

"You are very perceptive, Caroline," he spoke her first name in three distinct syllables, with the second two much longer than the first. It sounded exotic. Despite his carp-like face, she decided that Lars was quite attractive, especially as she was now in with a chance of a job which must be worth, say, a couple of grand.

Employing her never-fail strategy of promising more than she was prepared to deliver (in the interest of work, of course), she eased his hand away from her waist, drained her wine glass and said: "I can't wait to dance the night away in Newcastle! Let's hope I get the commission I'm sure I will be satisfactory, in every way. How about having a chat to Johnny right now? I've met him before, a lovely bloke. He's just over there, by the window. There's no time like the present. Lars, I've got a feeling that this could be a could be a satisfying arrangement for both of us."

****

While Caroline was networking at the Christmas drinks party, Susan Simpson and Brian Donovan were re-thinking their lives, their careers, their relationship and GE203. The venue for their meeting was Susan's bedroom, where they were both lying, naked, on top of Susan's white, Egyptian cotton duvet. Her bed, a reproduction brass affair from a London junkshop, was set against a wall facing a bay window which looked out over her tiny front garden. The long, heavy, dark brown cotton curtains were closed and the room was lit by one small lamp on her glass-topped dressing table, a modern, functional piece which she had chosen to balance the decorative theme of the house. Her mother collected antique furniture, and Susan had grown up surrounded by china ornaments, mahogany sideboards and nick-nacks of every kind: her own home was simply furnished, with strong shapes and blocks of muted colour.

"I can't tell you how ashamed I feel," Brian raised his head, reached over and traced the fingertips of his left hand over Susan's right breast. She noticed that he no longer wore his thick, gold wedding band.

Brian was in a contrite mood. After meeting Susan at the hospital earlier that day, he had confessed his dalliance with the student and told her about the rats incident. She had expressed horror at both, but her real wrath had been reserved for something else: his failure to follow up on the research into GE203. Her fury had ended up, as it so often does, with a surge of intense sexual desire, and they had returned to her house, to continue their conversation. The liaison which Susan had previously decided she should write off as just a one-night stand, had now become more serious, from her own point of view at least:

"You are an absolute sod," she said, stretching her arms above her head. " The law of thermogenesis applies to all human activity:

in the last half an hour, we've burnt off at least 300 calories, now we have to burn a few more talking this through.

"This food additive is probably indirectly responsible for the deaths of many people, and you actually intended to hide your interim findings and tell me, and Caroline Dempsey, to back off. I can understand you wanting to protect Molly and the children, but this is something that you have to persue now Brian, especially as you have been fired anyway. What have you got to lose?"

He removed his hand, swung his bare legs over the side of the bed, and stood up. His freckled back, very slim waist and rather scrawny buttocks were not unattractive, Susan thought, and his penis was a healthy size and length, which certainly made up for his thin physique. She remembered one of her college pals describing a boyfriend's penis as "the kind that can go round corners without slipping out". Crude, but accurate in Brian's case.

She tried to think about the weaknesses in his character; philanderer, ditherer, a man who didn't stick to his principles? Maybe, but at least he was someone she could actually talk to. She sat up, reached for a green silk kimono which was hanging over the brass end-rail, and watched Brian getting dressed. Mark had always worn tight black and grey Calvin Klein underpants which Susan thought were a bit too flashy. Brian was stepping into a pair of well-cut blue and white striped boxers, with a Jermyn Street label. He turned and faced her with a serious expression on his face:

"Susan, the problem is that we are looking at a lot of money if we want to set up a proper study. I am now jobless, and Molly is planning to employ a top divorce lawyer. After it's all over I will probably be left without a penny, with her legal fees to pay as well as mine. Even though she earns more than me, she has a good case. I behaved stupidly, and the children have got to be looked after. The Vice Chancellor has stitched me up brilliantly within the profession: I won't be able to get another top university job anywhere in the world. I have a suspicion that the whole thing is part of the same conspiracy to shut me up. You probably won't believe this, but that girl really did throw herself at me. Browne is pally with a lot of Government people, and after the rats incident, nothing would surprise me.

"Last night, I wrote to the City University in Liverpool and applied for a teaching post in their Department of Nutrition. I'm over-qualified, of course, but it will help pay the bills. The Head of Department was a final year student when I started there. He's an old friend. A great chap, who has done a lot of work on animal nutrition. If I get the job, I might be able to carry out my own research into GE203. It's all I can do for now, I'm afraid."

He looked so upset that Susan changed her tack: "If that's really all you can do, I'll just have to be content with that won't I? I intend to apply for a job in industry, maybe in the production department of one of the big multinational food companies. The trade papers are full of them. Ironically, I'll probably earn more than I'm earning at the hospital. If I can find out something that way, I will. Meanwhile, I am going to contact Caroline Dempsey again. Let's keep in touch, Brian. Where are you planning to live, by the way?"

Fully dressed, he looked less skinny. The thick fabric of the blue denim shirt made his slim frame appear bulkier. He put his hand in the pocket of his beige slacks and pulled out a comb, white cotton handkerchief, and a green and gold plastic hotel room key-card.

"Given my circumstances, Claridges seemed a bit extravagant so I've checked in at the Victoria Thistle. The service isn't quite as good, in fact it's non-existant, but it's cheap and clean. Molly has taken the children up to her parents' place in Scotland, and I'm not invited, so Christmas is going to be difficult. I've got to see my parents. They live in Cheam and are both quite frail now. The situation with Molly has hit them for six. They are very fond of her. My mother was looking forward to seeing Amy and Toby as well. It's an awful mess. How about you - will you be going to your parents?"

Susan nodded. "Mum loves Christmas; it gives her a chance to show off! That sounds horrible, but she really is a very good looking woman for her age, and she always dresses in something stunning. She cooks brilliantly too. My brother and his wife and son will be there, and I will stay for a couple of nights. No doubt mum will have lined up some local neighbours and friends to come to her Christmas Eve drinks party. Dad can't stand that kind of thing but he just goes along with it. Her dearest wish at the moment is to see me "settled", so she'll probably invite a few spare men along. Horrors!"

Brian gathered up his car keys and wallet from the dressing table, and pulled on a black leather jacket which he'd left in a heap on the dark wooden blanket chest at the end of Susan's bed. She knew that he was struggling to find the right words to say before he left. Like an actor searching for a line, perhaps? She made up her mind to take whatever he did say with a gigantic pinch of salt. Brian was a brilliant guy, but clearly not a good bet as a long-term lover.

"It's obvious that we both have a lot of things to do at the moment. I think you are a courageous woman, Susan, and very special. I would love to see you again, but it might not be until after the New Year. Until I have settled things with my family, it would be unfair of me to burden you with my problems. Can you trust me? I really do want to continue our relationship but, for now, I think we should just keep in touch by phone. Do you agree?"

Susan stood up, fastening the long tie of her green kimono tightly around her waist. She put her arms around his neck, and kissed him lightly on the mouth. " I certainly do," she said. "You're up to your eyes in trouble Brian. Sort things out, then we'll see. Meanwhile, don't forget to get on the GE203 case again. If you get this job in Liverpool, you can do some more research. Keep me informed. That's an order, professor!"

****

The 9am. Newcastle-bound train from King's Cross Station was dirty, crowded and already running late due to heavy snowfalls in London and in the North East of England. The second-class carriage was crammed with loud-mouthed Saturday football fans on their way to a match. They were not pleased at the prospect of missing the 3pm kick-off, and one or two of them had already drunk several cans of lager. One lad, who was trying to drink and speak into his mobile phone at the same time, dropped his can, spilling the pale coloured liquid in a large puddle on the carriage floor.

Caroline, sitting just behind the football fan, watched the pool of lager washing around her feet. She shifted them quickly. Her brand new soft brown suede shoes would soak up the beer like a sponge. A bit impractical for late January, but they were so pretty and she had put them on that morning to cheer herself up. She was beginning to regret being so friendly towards Lars at the Christmas party. She'd landed the job of writing a twelve page booklet for his company, and the fee of £4000 was generous. The only problem was that he had insisted that she visit his boring factory on a Newcastle industrial estate in order to do her "research." for the project. He had suggested she took the train up from London at the weekend, when everything would be quiet.

She had a good idea of what Lars meant by research. Entirely my own fault, she thought. He's not bad looking despite the froggy eyes, but bed - well, no thanks! She knew she would now have to play things cleverly. There was a proper contract for the job, so Lars couldn't sack her without paying up, but it would make things run a lot more smoothly if she could, somehow, ease herself out of any potential bonking situation. Swedes were notoriously vain, she thought, so maybe she should pretend that she couldn't sleep with him while working for him, but might do so when the job was finished. Not too difficult to achieve.

Somewhere in the depths of the large orange leather handbag her mobile phone range. It was difficult to find, because the bag was stuffed with make-up, spare tights, jewellery and two morning newspapers, complete with Saturday supplements. She removed the papers and located the phone wedged in the toe of a pair of black silk embroidered slippers which she had decided to bring at the very last moment after packing her large suitcase.

"Caroline? It's Susan Simpson here. Can you talk? It's important."

Caroline switched into "acute concentration" mode, cupping her hand around her ear to block out the noise of the football fans. Susan sounded agitated:

"Look, we haven't spoken since Christmas, and I've noticed that your byline is missing from the Echo. Have you been on holiday, or got the push? The GE203 mystery is still unsolved, I'm afraid. I've resigned from the hospital and have applied for an industry job. I should hear about it this week, and if I get it, I hope to find out something. Brian has been fired from his college and is about to start work at his old university. My own resignation was my decision entirely, but his sacking was ridiculous. I won't go into details, but he was virtually set up by a student. What has happened to you?"

It was like listening to a different person. The cool, guarded tones were completely absent. Her voice was high-pitched, and a bit shaky.

"Susan, you sound stressed. Yes, I was kicked out just before Christmas. My contract was only short term and it wasn't renewed. They gave various excuses, but it was all very fishy. I'm sure the editor was got at by someone high up, even at Government level, who forced him to cut my articles to shreds. It's disgusting.

" Now, I'm earning a crust by doing some PR work. In fact, I'm on my way up to Newcastle to do a job for Protin-Foods, the Swedish meat substitute company. If they are using GE203, I'll find out about it…don't worry. I haven't stopped thinking about this. I'm still hoping for a world scoop!"

Susan sounded even more worried: "Caroline, don't joke. I have to tell you that this could be more dangerous than you realise. Brian has been the victim of other, horrifying tricks to shut him up.

He is now very nervous about investigating any further. I might as well tell you: his marriage has broken up and his wife and children have gone to live in New York. His career is ruined.

"Be very careful indeed. If you start asking awkward questions, you could end up in big trouble. You may think I'm being hysterical, but this Government is capable of anything. There's an article about voluntary euthanasia in one of the papers today: apparently, they're trying to get a law passed allowing it here. I've been thinking a lot about this, and I'm convinced that they are desperate to reduce the population by killing off the obese, elderly and infirm. It's terrifying.

"Try to gather any information you can using subtle methods and then come back to me. The small amount of research Brian was able to carry out before he got fired showed that GE203 is a plant-based substance that can be hidden in a "carrier", usually a meat substitute. Protin-Foods supply ninety per cent of these products in the United Kingdom, and a lot of their production is used by other companies to bulk out meat and fish ready-meals. So, you are in a good position to find out something. But do be careful. I'll have to go now. Take care, Caroline. Let's meet up when you get back. Keep in touch."

She rang off. Deep in thought, Caroline stared out of the window. A dark stain now covered her new suede shoes, but she didn't notice. She opened one of the newspapers in her bag, and looked for the article on euthanasia.

****

Chapter Sixteen

Health News: *the all-party Select Committee on Health is setting up a new inquiry into the care and medication of elderly people. An Evening Echo reporter has learned that the agenda will include a "sensitive" investigation into the religious and medical ethics surrounding the emotive subject of euthanasia, referred to as "assisted mortality".*

Questioned by our reporter, Junior Health Minister Elizabeth Collins refused to give more details. Instead, she urged the nation's elderly, especially those who are overweight, to extend their life expectancy by "eating more low-fat food products and fresh fruit and vegetables, and taking more exercise." The Committee is due to start its inquiry in Sepember.

The factory was tucked away at the end of a long, concrete dual carriageway leading off the Great North Way. It was surrounded by dazzling snow which was reflected in its long windows. The concrete and glass stucture looked like an ice palace from a Hans Andersen fairytale. The temperature was just below zero, and there were icy patches on the black tarmac road which led to the factory from the roundabout at the end of the dual carriageway. A large piece of modern sculpture, depicting a family sitting round a table, was positioned in the front of the building, on what was probably a large lawn, although it was now covered in snow.

Caroline's taxi driver cursed as the vehicle slid to a halt outside the main entrance. "Sorry about that, pet, but this snow is driving me mental. Still, it is January, so I'd better stop complaining. Here we are...all quiet on a Sunday morning, though. Not a soul about.

Looks deserted to me. Sure you'll be alright? Isn't there anyone there today?"

His question was answered as a large silver Saab pulled up behind them. Lars, who was wearing dark blue jeans, a fur-lined black suede jacket and carrying a small carton of milk, got out and came round to the cab door. "Let me help you out, Caroline. It's a bit slippery, but once we're inside the factory, I'll make us some coffee."

Caroline, somewhat unsteady in her black leather high heeled boots, allowed herself to be led inside the factory by Lars. He switched on some lights, and took her into a large ground floor office.

She performed a rapid eye-scan of the room. It was about 15 metres square. The front part, which had two large windows looking out onto the tarmac road, was a normal office with two black and chrome desks, each with a computer and telephone, steel filing cabinets, and a few modern pictures. The back wall was a single sheet of thick-looking tinted glass. Behind it she could see a vast, dimly lit area. Through the tinted glass, Caroline noticed several production lines, now quiet, a group of stainless steel containers, and what looked like mixing machinery. In the far corner, there was a round steel gantry overlooking a huge circular vat.

"This is the nerve centre of our operation," said Lars, gesturing towards the large glass window. " On Monday morning, sixty five people will be working in there. As I'm sure you know, Protin-Foods products are based on a unique substance which is made from a culture which comes from a high protein grain product. The culture grows, naturally, when it is heated slowly to a certain temperature.

"We "harvest" it, and then we add various ingredients and shape it into sausages, burger type products and chunks for mixing with other foods. It's simple, really, and the resulting product is very healthy: low in fat and calories, high in protein. I call it the "food of the future".

"We started to produce it in Sweden, but now we make it in this outlet, and are just negotiating rights to produce it in America. The US Food and Drug Administration were being sticky about it, but they have almost rubber-stamped it and we hope to start production there at the end of the year. Apparently, the President himself has been involved in their decision: he is anxious to encourage people to eat more low-fat food. What I would dearly love, of course, is a contract to supply our Protin-Foods low-fat, no meat burgers to a big American chain like Muffins 'n Burgers. That would be worth billions."

Caroline nodded. Lars was looking excited and was clearly enthralled by his subject. His fishy eyes were glittering and his thin silver hair was practically crackling with the electricity generated by his enthusiasm. He looked like a baracuda about to swallow a school of sardines. If she could keep him worked up about his favourite topic, business, perhaps he would forget about her reckless flirting at the Christmas party. He had telephoned her hotel the night before, but had not suggested a meeting until this morning. Considering that he had booked her into Lumley Castle, a fabulous hotel with four-poster beds in every room, it was strange. The hotel was a wonderful place for an affair; romantic, stunning surroundings, and fun features like false wardrobe doors leading to decadent-looking bathrooms. Maybe she had got him wrong, and he never really fancied her in the first place. Please, God!

Lars sat down on one of the two desks in the office, and motioned to Caroline to sit in the black leather chair facing him. "The purpose of the booklet I've commissioned you to write is to raise public awareness of the health benefits of our products. I plan to distribute it though newspapers and magazines, and in supermarkets. I want the tone to be upbeat, family orientated and it must include a delicious diet plan with good photographs. I liked the outline you've drawn up, and I assume you are qualified to write the diet? I also want a good breakdown of the various food lines that contain our product, and quotes from some of the manufacturers on how incredibly healthy it is. Can you do that?"

"Of course, Lars, " said Caroline, briskly. She wasn't, actually, qualified to make up a diet, but Susan would certainly be able to help her. She continued:

"I must point out, though, that most consumers couldn't give a stuff about what boring old food manufacturers think. They assume, usually correctly, that they will say anything to make money. I suggest you use real people instead. Let's get some families to endorse the diet plan, and include some photographs. People are very wary about manufactured food products, so the leaflet needs to to be absolutely clear about how the stuff is made and what it contains. Can you give me full details please? Presumably, everything is made here, so perhaps tomorrow I could meet up with your technical staff for a a full run-down of your manufacturing methods?"

Lars blinked. "Certainly. Our manufacturing director, Dr. Piers Lindstrom, will be able to help you. Of course, some details have to be kept secret, but I can assure you that Protin-Foods products contain no genetically modified or other suspect ingredients. The grain from which the culture is grown comes from a French farmer who is certified as organic - even the manure he uses to fertilise his crops is organic - and the various binding agents we use are all natural plant substances. We only use colourants and stabilisers that have been passed as fit for human consumption. They are clearly listed on the labelling as well; the goverment are very tough about that kind of thing these days."

"Now, let's have that coffee, and I'll take you round the plant. "

While Lars went off to make the coffee in the kitchen next to the office, Caroline took a good look around her, using her journalistic training to glean as much information as possible. There was no clutter of paperwork on his desk; he was obviously a meticulously tidy man. On the second desk, presumably for his assistant or secretary, there was a large blue diary. The computers were Swedish, of course, and she noticed a flat television screen on the far wall opposite the door.

She focused carefully on the labels on the drawers of each of the two filing cabinets. "Stock Control", "Shipping Details", "Customer Correspondence", "Staff Contracts". Nothing particularly interesting there. The diary might be fascinating though. Caroline toyed with the idea of walking across and opening it, but decided against it just as Lars reappeared with the coffee. He put the tray on his own desk, handed her a cup, then walked across to the second desk and picked up the diary himself. He opened it and sat down on the desk.

"I like to keep details of all my top staff's movements in this diary," he said. "Tomorrow Dr. Lindstrom is here in the morning, so if you come to the factory at about 10am, he will meet you. I have an appointment in London in the afternoon, so I'll have to leave here at about 11 am. If you want to start work on the booklet here, you can use this office. My personal assistant Marion will give you any help you need." He put the diary down beside him, still open at the next day's page. Caroline, adept at reading peoples' private correspondence upside down, saw that Lars' afternoon appointment was with Mrs. Elisabeth Collins, at the Health Ministry offices in Whitehall, London.

Trying not to choke on her coffee, she uncrossed her legs, stood up and replaced her cup on the try. "Right, I'm ready for the tour, Lars. It all looks absolutely fascinating."

He led the way out of the office, and unlocked the door into the main factory, switching on a large bank of lights. When fully illuminated, the stainless steel machinery gleamed brightly. The whole place was spotlessly clean, with no evidence of any foodstuffs, ingredients or packaging.

"Where do you keep all the stuff that goes into the products, Lars?" asked Caroline. He seemed amused by the question. "Journalists still think factories are dirty places with men in filthy overalls everywhere. It's not like that any more, Caroline. We start each day afresh. Our ingredients are stored in the large units at the back of the factory. At 5am tomorrow morning, we will clean every piece of machinery thoroughly, even though it was done on Friday night. Then, we start the culture running in the big steel cylinder you see at the far end of the space. By the time the main body of our team arrive at 7am, there is enough product ready to "harvest" to start preparing the food items. Our team work on the various production lines, shaping the product into chunks, "burgers" or other types of food, and then it is packaged automatically and removed by lorry at the end of the day."

"At what stage do you add the colourants and other additives? " Caroline wondered if she was appearing to be too interested in the additives that went into Protin-Foods. She decided to introduce another subject entirely. "Do you employ mainly women? Are they paid the same as the men?"

Lars laughed. "Of course. This is a Swedish company, Caroline. We have strict rules about that. As for the additives, they go in at the production line stage. Quality control is very strict. I can assure you that none of our products are contaminated. When you consider what ghastly things go on in poultry broiler houses and abbatoirs, it's amazing that people actually eat meat protein at all. Here, nothing suffers. "

Only the people who eat the stuff, thought Caroline.

It was obvious to her that all kinds of rubbish could easily be mixed in with the basic foods that were being made here. How was anyone to know if the labelling was correct or not? She decided to get a good look around the next day, possibly when Lars had gone to London to see Elizabeth Collins. Now there was a strange thing. Why would a Swedish food manufacturer have an appointment with a government health minister? Odd.

"Seen enough, Caroline? How are you going to spend the rest of the day? I can recommend the shopping centre in Newcastle, and maybe, later, I could come to your hotel for dinner? My wife is visiting her sister in Sweden at the moment, so I am a free man". He giggled happily, baring sharp white teeth, which made him look like a basking baracuda with his eye on a school of sleek, tasty young herring.

"Sounds good, Lars, " said Caroline, wondering how she could dampen his enthusiasm. "Come along to the hotel at about 6.30pm. and I'll book a table in the restaurant for 7pm. I have a lot of work to do tonight, unfortunately. I have a story to write for an American newspaper, and they are expecting it to be emailed at about 11pm, our time. It's a sweat, but there you are. I will be with you, bright and early, tomorrow, I promise."

Lars looked slightly disappointed, but seemed to understand that business must always come before pleasure: "You are a hard working woman, Caroline. Right, I will drive you into Newcastle and see you later on for a short, working dinner. I am sure we can organise another trip up here for you before the booklet project is over. Meanwhile, I look forward to a little more of your company. You are so different from our Swedish girls, Caroline. My wife is beautiful and blond like you, but very cool. I do admire your warmth. Wonderful."

He seemed quite content, and Caroline breathed a sigh of relief. Sunday evening would be easier than she had expected.

****

The same evening, in a small restaurant tucked away in a Pimlico side street not far from the House of Commons, Elizabeth Collins was dining with her ex-husband. They had always maintained a cordial relationship, and now that Gerald was about to retire from the judiciary, he was taking even more interest in his former wife's career.

"Thanks for sorting out that problem with Dr. Donovan for me, Gerald. The Prime Minister is delighted that the matter has been taken care of. I really am grateful, you know." She pushed her dessert plate to one side, and leaned forward, keeping her voice deliberately low. The restaurant was popular with MPs and journalists, and you never knew who was listening in. Gerald was slightly deaf and too vain to wear a hearing aid, so Elizabeth spoke slowly. He smiled, revealing brilliant white false teeth, which looked odd in such an elderly face. He had no hair to speak of, so, when he wasn't sporting his judge's wig, or one of the many elaborate music hall wigs in his private wardrobe, Gerald had taken to wearing a soft French-style beret, indoors and outdoors.

Hisi expensive Harris tweed jacket, flashing dentures, and black roll-necked cashmere sweater, gave him a rakish air, like a rich Parisien pretending to be a Basque peasant. Elizabeth was, as usual, both elegant and sexy; this evening she had chosen a black Chanel suit with a cream chiffon blouse underneath, and added just a single row of real pearls around her coffee-coloured throat. As usual, she wore very high heeled shoes, and slightly shiny stockings. The couple could have been plucked out of their seats and transferred to the Champs Elysees without looking out of place.

"It was a pleasure, my darling," said Gerald, continuing the French theme by lifting her hand to his lips and kissing it gently. "I convinced old Dermot Browne that Donovan was going to ruin the university's chances of obtaining some very useful funding from that Chinese company unless he got rid of him. Knowing Donovan's weakness for the ladies, the rest was easy to organise. It's amazing how young women these days are quite prepared to have sex for money. Lucky for us gents, though, ha ha. Oh excuse me, Elizabeth, I shouldn't have said that. Now, how are things going with your progress in the House? I want to see you elevated to ministerial level soon, darling. There should be a cabinet re-shuffle in April. Jack Barton should get rid of the Health Minister. He's practically gaga. You would make a wonderful replacement."

Coming from Gerald, critical comments about aging ministers were rich indeed, thought Elizabeth. He was seventy five and, until recently, had been sitting at the Old Bailey several times a year, his long ermine-trimmed robes covering his favourite high-heeled boots and ladies' silk underwear. Only a few months ago, he declared during a libel trial that he was "unaware" of the existence of a famous sixties pop group. The tabloids had had a field-day.

"Thanks Gerald," she said. " I'll let you into a secret: I've actually got my eye on the Foreign Office. Anyway, I'm now playing a very sensible game, and doing everything Jack tells me, no questions asked. You'll have noticed the new Select Committee on euthanasia has been set up. That was my idea. A lot of elderly people, present company excepted of course, would be better off with a bit of what we have termed "assisted mortality". They are such a drain on pension funds and hospital resources and the benefit system won't cope much longer. It's a good idea all round.

" The other project I'm working on is how to find a solution to the problem of reducing the number of obese people in this country: it's so bad for our image abroad. Healthy eating initiatives are the "top dressing" on this one, of course. We actually gave up that campaign several years ago, but we simply go on saying the same old thing to reassure people.

"Now, the best method seems to be to let people get even fatter. They then die of obesity-related diseases. There is a short-term increase in demand on hospital space, of course, but, in the long term, this policy will prove to be sensible. We have been helped a lot by the food industry. As you know, it's in the government's interest to make sure supermarkets continue to enjoy huge profits. I've taken on board one manufacturer, Protin-Foods, who have been brilliant. They are using an additive which is made from a herbal compound produced by the Chinese company who are being so generous to your chum, Sir Dermot Browne. It actually works on the brain and appetite to make people eat more. They're putting it in the kind of rubbish sold in supermarkets. Wonderful.

" They also have some other ideas on additives which might help with this project. Their European Director is coming to see me tomorrow afternoon about other ways of encouraging over consumption. He has an experimental plant near Penrith in the Lake District where all kinds of food enhancing ideas are being tested. It's well hidden and it's on the MI6 "protected science establishment" list. Fascinating stuff."

To his credit, Gerald blinked after absorbing, quickly, this fascinating piece of inside information. At his age, he had heard everything, and seen most things as well. Even his own interesting hobbies were not that unusual in the judiciary, and the rest of the establishment, from the royal family down, were all engaged in what might be termed "odd pastimes." However, this was different, and it could be dangerous.

"Elizabeth, I'm sure you know what you are doing but do make sure your security is tight, keep no written or computer files on either of these subjects, and be very careful about what you say to the press. I'm an old man now, and when I retire I won't be able to help you much, you know. Beware of letting power go to your head. The people of this country aren't all stupid...although most of them can certainly be manipulated very easily. Television is a wonderful tool for that kind of operation. But, do look after yourself, my darling."

Elizabeth smiled and beckoned to a waiter. "Some of your favourite cognac, Gerald? This meal is on me, or rather Jack. Thank you so much for being such a support. I still love you, you know. "

****

By Monday morning, the snow had started to melt, and the Protin-Foods factory was surrounded by a sea of slush. Caroline cursed as she stepped out of the taxi and tried to tip toe through a dark puddle of water on the road in front of the factory entrance. Today, she'd worn her pretty brown suede shoes, which had dried out well after being soaked with lager. Now, they were covered in grey muck. Never mind, at least she hadn't had any problems with Lars: at the end of their dinner together, he'd kissed her lightly on the cheek, and left her to get on with her supposedly "urgent" work.

Instead, she'd enjoyed a couple of hours' luxury, with her feet up in her hotel room, sipping white wine, nibbling smoked salmon sandwiches and watching TV. She'd also phoned Susan to give her

Thermogenesis

an update on the Protin-Foods operation, and to check that she would be able to help with the diet for the Protin-Foods booklet.

That morning, to make up for Lars' disappointment (and secure in the knowledge that he would be leaving for London at 11am) she had decided to dress to thrill in a plunging V-necked sweater in soft shades of beige and gold, knee-length brown leather skirt, sheer stockings, her super little shoes, and the glamorous mock ocelot coat. The large orange handbag now contained a small camera and tape recorder, plus her spiral bound reporter's notebook, and plenty of make-up and perfume.

"The complete sleuth's outfit, " she muttered to herself as she walked carefully through the dirty puddles and soft black snow to the main entrance. On the way, she noticed that Lars' Saab was parked in a concreted area to one side of the factory, next to a red Ferrari and a black Porsche. There was obviously plenty of money to be made out of food products. She wondered where the employees parked their cars. Probably at the back of the building.

Lars was waiting to greet her. He kissed her cheek, then ushered her into his office. Behind the glass wall, the factory floor was now bustling with activity: male and female workers in matching white trousers, loose tops and close-fitting hats were manning the production lines, and there were a couple of men in white rubber boots on the gantry overlooking the big steel vat at the far end. The efficient sound-proofing and the slightly sepia tint of the glass, made the whole wall look like an animated art installation.

"Meet Dr. Lindstrom," said Lars. A very tall, middle-aged man in a white coat, with thinning hair caught at the back in a short pony tail, unwound himself from one of the chairs in the office, and held out his hand. He was wearing steel-framed glasses which gave him a sinister look. Caroline took his hand firmly. She had never trusted older men who wore their hair too long. They were usually trying to hide something.

"Delighted to make your aquaintance, Caroline," he said. "I understand from Lars that you wish to know more about what goes into our products. I can explain everything. Have a coffee first with Lars, and come up to my laboratory in, say, ten minutes? I'll be waiting. Meanwhile, I must go out on the floor and check the latest batch of meat-free burgers which are going out to Allardyce Supermarkets. See you later."

Dr. Lindstrom's laboratory was on the first floor of the factory, directly above the main production department. There was a glass lift on one wall which, Caroline decided, must be for Dr. Lindstrom's personal use, and probably connected directly with the main work area. A long laboratory bench held samples of the various food ranges which contained Protin-Foods' basic product, shaped into burgers, chunks or mixed in with meat and fish to "bulk out" the meal. Opposite the door was another long bench, with four computer terminals and four high stools. He motioned to Caroline to sit on one of them, and sat on another, facing her.

"Precise details of the fermentation process which is used to make our product are a company secret, but I can assure you that it is safe, and involves just a grain-based culture and water. The process takes place in the large vat which you probably noticed through the window in Lars' office. The frothy substance that is produced is rather like the stuff you get on top of beer. We add a binding agent which is made from egg white, and then cool the basic material before adding things like colourants, flavourings and preservatives - all vegetable based, by the way - and shaping it into the finished item.

" Here's a list of some of the ingredients we use. As you can see, they all have the approval of the British Food Standards Agency. We haven't yet gone down the same route as many companies who produce so-called "functional foods" - adding things to basic foods which actually improve your health: such as plant stanols which can reduce cholesterol. That is a difficult market, and we are not ready for it yet."

He handed her a sheet of paper, which she could see was a computer print-out. She scanned it quickly.

Forgetting that she was now a temporary employee of Protin-Foods, Caroline plunged straight in. "I recognise most of these names, but what do you know about an ingredient called GE203? It's listed on many ready-meals, snacks and other products but no-one seems to know anything about it except that it appears to be legal. Do you put it in your product, or does it get into these foods by other means? What does it actually do?"

Dr. Lindstrom turned away from Caroline, removed his glasses, and then turned back towards her. He was frowning slightly and looked puzzled, but it was hard to tell whether it was genuine or not. She decided the latter.

"The ingredient you mention is unfamiliar to me. It certainly isn't put into Protin-Foods products. If it gets into supermarket items, it must be from other sources, perhaps as an extra colour additive in the preparation of vegetables, such as beans, which are often put into ready-meals and snacks. The letters usually refer to a European Union regulation, and the figures could refer to the batch. Anyway, we don't use it, I'm afraid. Try the FSA website."

"I've already done that, but it isn't listed," blurted Caroline, before deciding, too late, that she should be careful about what she said. She covered her error quickly:

"It was part of a routine check I made when I was writing a food article recently. Intriguing. Anyway, can I just interview you about the company and how this exciting product was first discovered? Were you part of the team that developed it? I've got a small recorder with me, so perhaps we could make a tape?"

He relaxed his shoulders, replaced his glasses, and treated Caroline to ten minutes of chat about how he and another scientist had first formulated the basic Protin-Food product, and teamed up with Lars to launch it on the Swedish market just ten years earlier. It was all useful stuff for the booklet, but Caroline knew that she had to probe further. For a start, she didn't believe that Dr. Lindstrom was "unfamiliar" with GE203. His body language revealed the exact opposite.

She got her chance when a call came though on the internal phone. Dr. Lindstrom took it, muttered something in Swedish, and then said:

"Excuse me, Caroline, I've got to pop down to see Lars for a moment. He is going to London for a meeting, and I have some paperwork he needs. I won't be long." He gathered up a red file from the bench and walked out of the lab. Caroline wondered if there was any close-circuit surveillance in the laboratory. She decided that there certainly would be, and her movements would be monitored. She must try to behave as naturally and casually as possible.

She replaced her tape recorder in her handbag, crossed and uncrossed her legs, looked around her and got up, with her handbag in her hand. Slowly, as if she had all the time in the world, she walked over to the lab bench where the products were displayed. There were about 20 items, all in brightly coloured sample packaging, ranging from burgers to soups. None of packaging carried listed ingredients or bar-codes, which, presumably were added by the retailer later on. She recognised a few of them, and was surprised to see a FizzCo "Super Snacks" Breakfast Bar amongst the items. She had had no idea that it contained the Protin-Foods meat-free protein. Extraordinary: why put a protein substitute into a product made from fruit, nuts and cereals? She obviously had a lot to learn about food production methods.

At the far end of the bench, partly hidden by a large plant, a luxuriant creeper of some kind, was a thin, buff coloured folder which could have been left there by Dr. Lindstrom, or another employee. Carefully, Caroline placed her handbag on the bench, over the folder, and continued looking at the food items. Then she picked up her handbag, and the folder, and clutched both tightly to her chest.

She walked out of the laboratory, and into the ladies' lavatory which was nearby. Hoping that the firm's surveillance cameras were not operating in the staff toilets, she put the folder into her handbag. She would have to look at it, somehow, before she left the building, and then try to smuggle it back into the lab without anyone noticing.

Tough, but possible. Of course, it could be a total waste of time: for all she knew, the folder could contain nothing at all, or maybe nothing more revealing than Dr. Lindstrom's shopping list.

When she returned to the lab, Dr. Lindstrom was waiting. "I popped out to the loo," she said, praying that he wouldn't notice that the folder was missing from the bench. "This has all been fascinating, Dr. Lindstrom, but could I now have a tour of the factory floor? It's always interesting to meet the people who do the important production work. Without them, there would be no profits, would there?" She couldn't resist a quick dig, but smiled so charmingly that Dr. Lindstrom relaxed his guard.

"Well said. You are quite right, of course, Caroline. In Sweden, sharing profits is a very important part of our culture, and we have continued the tradition. I think you'll find that our employees enjoy very good working facilities here. We have a fitness suite, excellent showers and relaxing areas, and our wages are among the highest on the whole of the factory estate. There is a share scheme as well, so workers feel that they have an investment in our products. I'm going to have to ask you to change out of that beautiful outfit, and put on working clothes. One of the ladies will show you to the ladies' locker room."

An hour later, Caroline's mind was numbed by the wealth of detail that had been thrown at her. She didn't care if she never saw another production line. Unfortunately, the part that really interested her, the addition of colourants and preservatives to the basic Protin-Foods formula, took place in another, closed building to the right of the main production floor. According to Dr. Lindstrom this building was out of bounds to visitors because of extra strict hygiene regulations. Just two key workers operated there, under his own supervision.

Oh really, how very convenient, thought Caroline, as she changed back into her own clothes in the ladies' locker room. That means that only a handful of the work force know exactly what goes into the products they are selling.

It was time to look at the file. She took her handbag into the ladies' toilet, opened a cubicle and went in. Fishing into the bottom of her large orange bag, she pulled out the buff folder She sat down on the lowered seat of the toilet and opened the folder.

To her annoyance, there was just a single sheet of paper inside, with just a few paragraphs of text on it, hand-written in a foreign language which she assumed was Swedish. Only one word on the sheet was recognisable, the name "Penrith", a town in the Lake District in the North West of the country. Digging into her bag, she extracted her notebook, and copied out the text carefully. Then, she replaced the clipboard in her bag, pulled the lavatory chain loudly and emerged from the cubicle, just as three girls came into the ladies' room. She smiled at them, washed her hands and emerged from the cloakroom quickly, practically colliding with Dr. Lindstrom.

"Would you like to join me for a light lunch in the canteen in about an hour, Caroline? Lars has just left for London and has asked me to say goodbye to you. He has arranged with his PA for you to use his desk. Presumably, you'd like to start working on the booklet while you are here?"

She hesitated. What she would actually like to do is, somehow, replace the folder in the lab, and then get out of the factory and head back to London. It wouldn't be difficult to find someone to translate the Swedish text. There was that journalist on the Stockholm Daily News who she'd very nearly shagged during a press trip around the fjords. He was bound to be able to do it.

One nagging worry was that her movements might well have been monitored.

"Fine, Dr. Lindstrom. I'll see you for lunch, then head back to London. It's been a fascinating trip and I'm sure you will be pleased with the booklet. I was particularly interested in the products in the laboratory. Could we go back there so you can talk me through them?"

God knows how I'm going to replace the folder but getting back to the lab is a start, she thought. Hopefully, Dr. Lindstrom will be called away again. If not, I'll just have to leave it somewhere else. This investigative journalism lark is more exhausting than people imagine. I bet I've lost a few pounds in sweat this morning. Pity lunch is bound to be reconstituted froth from the top of a vat, which has been pumped full of additives, then shaped into a chicken leg. Horrible. Thank goodness I had kippers with lots of brown bread and butter for breakfast.

Once in the lab, Caroline started praying in earnest. Please, God, let Dr. Lindstrom be called away for a while, just to give me enough time to replace this sodding folder.

By a miracle, (or maybe not: God probably had more important things to do than help her, thought Caroline), Dr. Lindstrom was called down to the factory floor to answer a technical query, and Caroline seized her opportunity to replace the folder under the large houseplant. She did it as carefully as possible, first putting her handbag on the bench, then hiding her hands under the plant while she extracted the incriminating folder. By the time Dr Lindstrom returned, her bag was zipped up and she was examining a flat plastic carton of bright orange vegetable and protein curry with rapt attention. "This looks absolutely delicious,"she said. " You'd never know that the chicken pieces are really made from Protinfoods' protein substitute. Amazing, really."

On the train back from Newcastle to London, Caroline felt she deserved a whole bottle of white wine to soothe her shattered nerves. She needed to go home, phone Susan Simpson, and then get a good night's sleep, but her first priority was to get something to drink, and eat. Finding anything nutritious was, of course, impossible, so she settled for the buffet car "special", a vast beefburger, covered in cheese, topped with tacos and chopped gherkins, plus two half-bottles of Australian Chardonnay.

This little lot must contain at least 1700 calories, and about 400 grams of fat, thought Caroline, as she bit into the gooey, crunchy, stringy mess. It tasted absolutely delicious...

Chapter Seventeen

Email to Sir Dermot Browne, The Royal College, London.
From: Chairman Tang Liu, Changjia Food Company, Chongqing Technological Park.
Date: January 31st, 2009.

Good morning, Sir Dermot. This is to let you know that a cash transfer of one million dollars has been made from our Research Account to your University Buildings Improvement Account in respect of the research you will carry out for us. We note that Dr. Brian Donovan is no longer employed at the University, but is about to take up a teaching post in Liverpool. Give him our good wishes.

You will be my guest on 5th June at a polo match at the Berkshire Polo Club. sponsored by our company, which is being attended by Princess Michael of Kent and other members of your royal family.

Tang Liu

Sir Dermot Browne rubbed his hands as he read the email, which had been printed out by his secretary and laid on the black leather blotter on his desk. A million dollars wasn't a fortune these days, but it could help repair some of the stonework on the old College building, and maybe help spruce up his own suite of offices. The Board of Governors could easily be persuaded that his wallpaper needed replacing with something a little more imposing: perhaps in crimson silk overlaid with printed gold leaf; he'd seen something suitable in the Victoria and Albert museum. Maybe a copy could be obtained? The private washing facilities could do with a new image as well. Gold taps were, well, rather flashy, but a solid marble bathroom with a classical Greek theme would enhance the whole atmosphere of the college. Moneyed people like Russian oligarchs and Chinese businessmen and ministers were now sending their offspring to be educated at The Royal College so it was important to give a good impression when they visited his offices: where better than in the bathroom?

He scratched his tangled white whiskers. It was odd, though, that Tang had made a point of mentioning Brian's whereabouts, and the polo match invitation sounded like a summons. The Chinese were becoming very powerful and pushy indeed, sucking up to minor royals. Whatever next?

Still, there were ways that men like him could benefit. He drifted into philosophical mood. One of the few good things about getting older is that there really isn't any point in worrying about the long or even medium-term consequences of your decisions: " have fun now" is a good motto for sexagenerians. What's the latin translation? He would have to look it up. He picked up the phone: "Get me Gerald Collins, please. I want to invite him to dinner on Friday. Oh, and order some venison and a whole Stilton from Fortnums, would you? Excellent, excellent"

****

Brian sat at his desk in the front room of his rented flat in Liverpool, looking out over a snow-covered Sefton Park. The room was on the first floor of a double-fronted Victorian villa, high-ceilinged, spacious and comfortable. It was furnished simply with an oak desk, and a straight-backed chair with an upholstered seat embroidered with flowers, both set in a bay window. On the far wall of the room, near the door, was a pink chintz-covered sofa. The only other furniture was a set of matching armchairs, a television, single bed and a large Indian rug, in shades of green and gold.

On the wall above the sofa was an old framed print of a gang of shackled African slaves being unloaded from a trading ship in Liverpool docks. The subject matter was depressing, but perfectly in tune with Brian's mood. Slavery, of a different kind, was a good description of his new job.

Marking new students' first written efforts of the term was always mind-numbing, especially if you were a new professor. Standards of literacy and numeracy were so low that sometimes it was difficult to fathom what on earth they meant to say, and their calculations were often just as foggy. He would have to get his group of final year BSc students to improve their spelling; not to pass their exams, as spelling didn't seem to count for much with examiners these days, but to stop him from going stark, raving mad.

His mobile phone, on the desk in front of him, buzzed loudly. He had recently decided to replace the urgent ring-tone with something more soothing. When your whole life is a mess, the thing that finally drives you round the bend, he thought, was likely to be something simple like an irritating mobile phone tone, or an odd sock lost in the wash. As he was now visiting the launderette each week, he was aware of how fragile the relationship between socks could be; they behaved like twins who hate each other; identical, but each determined to go their own way.

Cheered by the prospect of being side-tracked from his marking task, he picked up the phone. "Brian, it's Susan. Sorry to disturb you on a Monday afternoon, you're probably in college. I'm at home. Can you speak?"

"Actually, I'm in the flat marking papers this afternoon, Susan. Fire away."

"I've just had a call from Caroline, who has come up with some brilliant stuff. She's been doing some freelance work for Protin-Foods, and she reckons they are using GE203 in their products. Apparently, the company's run by a group of Swedish businessmen and they are secretive about the additives they use. She's been spying at their factory in Newcastle, and is getting some paperwork translated from Swedish into English. She hopes it might tell us something. What have you been doing, Brian? Is the new job going well?"

Better to lie than give Susan any more worry, he thought. "It's fine, really fine. I've rented a lovely first floor flat near the park, only a short walk from the University. You'll have to come up here. The students are, well, the usual mixture of bright kids and dullards. A couple of the third year BSc girls are brilliant, and probably destined for good research careers. My old friend, Gareth Ward-Thomas is Head of the Department of Nutrition.

"He's involved in some very time-consuming research on animal growth and development, which leaves me in charge of many of the day-to-day problems of the department. He hasn't been able to do more than give me lists of instructions so far, but tomorrow we are having a meeting. I want to find out what funding is available before I suggest that we conduct a proper trial on GE203. Of course, he might oppose the idea. He's well aware of my position on food additives - my Conference paper was published, in full, on the internet and in the Journal of Obesity."

Susan was irritated. "Brian, try and keep your eyes, and hands, off the brilliant students for once. Get this Gareth Ward-Thomas on your side. If he's got half a brain, he will realise that this is important. People are dying, and we need to get this awful business exposed. We need proof that the food manufacturers are playing dirty, and you are the only one who can get it. I won't be coming up yet, by the way. I managed to get an interview with Kenley and Palmer for a job in their dietetics department as assistant to the Development Manager. If I'm successful, I'll be based in Wembley. It's a hell of a commute every day from here, but the salary is excellent, and I'll be in charge of testing new ready-meals in their healthy eating ranges which will be very useful. I imagine that I'll be too whacked at the weekends to contemplate visiting Liverpool. Maybe you can come down here some time, perhaps in the college holidays?"

He sounded resigned. "I think I've learned my lesson, Susan. I don't want to lose another job. Molly has just sent me a bill for her and the children's air fares to New York. Our house is on the market, but things move slowly at this time of the year. She wants me to send her £100,000 right away for her living expenses. Luckily, I have some savings, and I've sold my car and taken out a bank loan with my half of the house as security. So, as you can imagine, forking out fifty or sixty quid for a rail ticket to London is out of the question at the moment. It's a humiliating position for a man of my age, but I brought it on myself."

Her voice softened. "Sorry, Brian. I know you're in a lot of trouble. Look, give me a ring tomorrow after your meeting with Gareth, and we'll have another chat. By then, I should have some more news from Caroline. Take care, love."

She rang off, and Brian picked up his pen to continue marking the student papers. He couldn't concentrate on the task, and spent half an hour just staring out at the gradually darkening landscape: the bare trees in the park looked beautiful with their crisp covering of snow, and the street lamps glowed softly. It would have been wonderful to have Susan with him, but she deserved someone better . The thought was depressing, and Brian decided to abandon his work for the night, and watch something frivolous on TV. Tomorrow, he would try to get Gareth interested in GE203.

****

Since their student days together, Gareth Ward-Thomas had changed. A lot. He had aged much more rapidly than Brian. Admittedly, he was four years older and now fifty five, but the years had been very unkind to him. As Brian entered the laboratory-cum-office where Gareth worked, his friend stood up slowly and carefully, revealing a loud yellow and black checked waistcoat undone over a grey flannel shirt which was straining over his pot belly. His head was almost completely bald, his shoulders rounded, and his eyes, tinged with yellow, looked tired behind brown horn-rimmed spectacles A dark green tweed jacket hung on a plastic coathanger hooked over a large blackboard, fixed to one wall of the office.

"Hello Brian. Sorry I've been too busy for a proper meeting before. Take a pew. Great to have you at Liverpool. London's loss is our gain. I've read the paper you presented at the New York Obesity Conference, by the way. Made a few waves, didn't you? " He chuckled, and sat down heavily. The straight-backed metal chair made an ominous twanging sound. When it was designed ten years earlier, the average weight of a male was 13st. Gareth weighed over 20st.

He gestured to Brian to sit by his side.

"To be quite honest, you only touched the tip of the iceberg there, boyo. The manufacturers put all kinds of muck into food. In fact, these days food isn't even food - it's just chemicals. When you start making dead chickens and dead horses into feeding stuff for cows, slaughter the poor beasts, then chop bits off, and mix them up with twenty or thirty flavourings, colourants and preservatives, you're bound to be in trouble. What are governments doing about it? Sod all. My area of work is in pig food, which is pretty well-funded, and I'm delighted to tell you that I only use the best organically grown ingredients, plus a few herbal compounds to fatten the little buggers up. It must have been hell to have to work for so many greedy multinationals, knowing that they all they care about is profits. How did you cope with it?"

Brian shrugged. "I didn't. I loused up. That's why I'm here. No disrespect intended. I'm delighted to be doing some useful work and the students seem a decent enough bunch. Actually, Gareth, I haven't quite given up on "making waves" as you so kindly put it. A couple of friends and I have decided that the only way to stop this collective poisoning of humanity is to prove that a specific additive, which we have identified by the way, is being deliberately added to food to make people fatter. The big question is why is this being done? We are convinced that there is more to it than just for profits. We also believe that he government are directly involved. It seems illogical that they should want people to get fatter, given the amount of extra strain obesity-related diseases put on the Health

Service, so there must be another motive. I want to set up a proper study on the substance we've isolated, and hope that you'll be able to help. Is there any funding in the university's kitty for this kind of thing?"

Gareth roared with laughter. "Not a bean, I'm afraid. Unless you can get the cash from someone else, no chance. How about approaching Greenpeace or one of the other direct action groups for the money? You'd have to do it carefully, though. This is supposed to be a forward-thinking university, but the hierarchy are a bunch of reactionary old farts. You just can't get rid of them. Given that research of that nature is hardly fashionable these days, questions are bound to be asked. On the whole, Brian, I don't think it's on, unless you do it somewhere well away from the university itself. I couldn't let you neglect your students, so your time would be limited."

It was just the kind of reaction that Brian had expected. "So, where do you do your own research? I imagine you test your pig food on rats before you give it to pigs? Or are the clinical trials carried out directly on the pigs? Animal foodstuff regulations are a lot tougher than those for human food, so I imagine you have to be very thorough?"

Gareth nodded. "It's a joke really. Since the BSE scandal you would have thought that animal feed would be very carefully monitored. It is, up to a point. For instance, premises where it's prepared are scrutinised regularly for hygiene standards, and every new product has to pass rigorous tests before it's allowed on the market. Yet, food producers are still using animal products to feed other animals, and there is little control over what goes into the stuff we end up eating after the animal is slaughtered. It is scary. My testing is done on rats here, and then in a specialist feed testing unit in the heart of the Lake District. The company that makes the feed keep about 20 sows and their litters there for constant testing. Since the foot and mouth disease epidemic, a lot of farmers had to slaughter all their pigs, so a couple of them are very happy to be financed by Wilkinson's Animal Feeds who make the finished foodstuffs."

He noticed the look of mild disgust on Brian's face, and added: "Don't worry, they are well looked after, and the feed is good stuff. They are simply weighed and measured to see which formula produces the best yield, in terms of size and meat quality. It's ok, really Brian. Otherwise, I wouldn't be involved. Come and have a look at the rats I'm using for the initial tests and I'll show you some of the ingredients I put in the various feeds. We keep them at the other side of the campus, in a secure unit. You'll need that overcoat. It's freezing out there."

He eased himself slowly up from the chair and walked across the room to collect his tweed jacket from the coat-hanger. It slipped and fell on the floor and a large bunch of keys dropped out of one pocket, jangling sharply on the hard wooden floor. Gareth tried to bend down to retrieve his jacket and the keys. He straightened up, gasping for breath and obviously in pain. "Pick those up for me Brian, old mate. I'm afraid I am not as fit as you are. Years of sitting on my backside and university food have taken their toll. The old ticker is a bit slow, angina they tell me, and my back's a killer. It's a blasted nuisance."

Concerned for his friend's welfare, Brian stepped forward quickly, retrieved the keys and helped Gareth into the jacket. "Sit down for a minute, Gareth. Then we'll go to see the rats. There's no hurry."

"No, I'm fine. Let's go." He walked slowly to the door which led outside, and opened it carefully. An icy blast of air nearly knocked him over. He fastened two buttons of his jacket, only partly covering his enormous stomach, pulled up his collar and stepped outside. Brian followed, shuddering in the freezing temperature. It must have been minus two or three, he thought. The path which led to the building where the experimental rats were kept had been cleared, but was still icy in patches, so it took the two men five or six minutes to reach the unit. Gareth's hands were so cold that he spent a few moments unlocking the outer door of the small, concrete building.

Inside, the temperature was about 60 degrees. Compared with the bitter air outside, the atmosphere in the small lobby felt like a sauna. There was a a small office on one side. Gareth opened the door, switched on a single lurid fluorescent strip light and led Brian inside.

Brian took off his heavy navy blue cashmere and wool overcoat. "Thank God it's warmer in here, Gareth. Couldn't you get some kind of covered passageway built between your lab and this unit? You'll kill yourself if you keep coming back and forth in this weather. That jacket's not warm enough. Get yourself a decent coat. You must take care of yourself. For goodness sake, man, you are a nutrition scientist. Why on earth have you let yourself put on so much weight?. You, of all people, should know how dangerous it is when you've got heart trouble. Sorry, I'm being too personal. Forgive me."

"No worries, boyo. It's a familiar story, I'm afraid. Since Janie, my wife, died from breast cancer last year, I've let myself go. I don't give a damn whether I die or not, to be quite honest. The kids are at university in Wales, and don't need me. I eat boring, fatty takeaways, just like the students. Have you noticed how overweight most of them are? The rats here enjoy a better diet than us. Tell that to the animal rights people! Come on, I'll take you in."

He led the way out of the office, and, using a large key from the same bunch , unlocked and removed a padlock on the the inner door. Dim strip lighting suspended from the high, black painted ceiling, revealed a dozen or so large steel cages, each containing ten or twelve white rats. The cages were stacked in two rows, one on top of the other, with a narrow walkway between them. At the far end of the unit was a long wooden bench. On top were four large square containers and a number of smaller, round glass jars.

Gareth pointed to the nearest cages. "These little beasts are the control group; they're being fed on a basic grain food. The chaps in the far cages get the nutritionally enhanced feed. I am trying several different compounds at the moment, and two more are in the final stage of testing at the pig farm. One of my earler compounds is already being used by pig farmers. I gather that they're delighted with the results they're getting. As you can see, Brian, our ratty friends who're being fed on the best grub are a lot fatter and stronger looking than the control group. They get weighed and measured every day, are given plenty of water to drink, room to exercise and the temperature and light are kept at constant, pleasant levels. It's just like being in a health farm! The students have nicknamed this unit "The Rodent Riviera."

Brian could see that some of the rats were, indeed, almost twice the size of the control group. A few of them were so large that they could hardly stagger around their cage. They looked like small, white kittens.

"So what exactly are you using to fatten them up, Gareth? Is it a hormonal compound?"

"No, but it does seem to have a real effect on the appetite centres of the animal's brain, as well as increasing the body's efficiency at storing fat. As I said before, I'm using all natural herbal ingredients, mainly from China. After my tests are completed here, I add them into the pig food, which as you know is mainly vegetable based. It's a bit like muesli. They also get fed on non-animal protein chunks, and we can easily make the herbal mixture into a smooth serum which can be injected into the protein material before it's formed into chunks and flavoured and textured to taste and look like turnips. Pigs are surprisingly discerning you know - unlike so many humans! They love turnips - must be in the genes. I work out the correct proportions for each foodstuff, and sample bags are sent to the pig farm. Take a look at the herbs I use." He gestured towards the bench at the back of the unit.

Even before he looked at the items on the bench, Brian knew that he had now found out, for certain, why Tan Liu was so worried about the searching questions raised by his own controversial presentation in New York. Tan's firm, The Changjia Food Company was supplying the herbal compounds which were being used to fatten up pigs, and probably humans as well and poor old Gareth was, unwittingly, being used to test them.

Quickly, his excitement turned to frustration. It was going to be difficult, if not impossible, to prove that the "fattening up" additives were also being mixed in with non-animal protein products destined for human consumption.

His doubts were further justified when he saw that there was no brand name anywhere in sight on the bench. The various herbal ingredients were loose in their containers: no packages, no handy loose invoices, absolutely nothing to identify their country, let alone company, of origin. They looked like any other dried herbs, the kind of thing you might see any day on the shelf of a pharmacy or health food shop.

"Who's your supplier, Gareth? And what is the active ingredient?" Brian spoke casually, trying not to sound too curious.

"I know what you're thinking, boyo," chuckled Gareth. " It's all right, really. They are imported from the Changjia Food Company, but all the relevant European Union controls are in order, and are licensed only for use in animal feed. The active ingredient? It's called Guaria Engorgia, and comes from the cellulose-like leaf and stalk structure of a very rare plant that's grown in a remote part of Sichuan Province.

"The locals have been feeding it to sickly pigs for years, but it has only just been properly cultivated and harvested for medicinal use. The Changjia people are the only food company currently licensed to sell it. It works in two separate ways: there is a definite effect on the appestat centres of the brain, which stimulate and increase the desire for food. Interestingly, it also seems to increase the animal's enjoyment of the food, and makes the rat, or pig, crave more of the same compound. We've found that our rats have been gobbling up twice as much food as they actually need to survive. Pigs, with their much greater body size, tend to eat about a quarter more than usual.

"I've been testing various compounds and mixtures all using different types, crops and vintages of this ingredient. There must have been over two hundred so far. It's been a long, long job. Of course, the University benefits a lot. As you know, these big animal food companies pay well for their research projects. I've been working for them for five years, and they've been delighted with my results. The last few compounds have been particularly successful. I've been refining them so that the pig farmer can decide just how much yield he wants, the fat content of the animal, life expectancy, and so on. It's fascinating."

"So, you've actually been to the experimental pig farm then? " Brian felt his heart racing. At least he now knew what the initials "G.E" stood for: Guaria Engorgia. How come the Food Standards Agency hadn't identified this name when he had asked for information?

"Yes, once or twice. Sorry, old mate, I can't tell you exactly where it is. The animal rights people are so damned agressive these days that everyone working for Wilkinson's has to sign up to their secrecy rules. I've signed on the dotted line, and if I breach that obligation I would lose the university a lot of money, and probably get fired and lose my animal research licenses as well. Otherwise, I'd have loved to have taken you there to see our perfect porkies"

Brian had to ask the question:

"Gareth, surely you must be worried that the meat people eat from these pigs will contain traces of this stuff, and cause health problems? Quite apart from increasing people's appetite, you might be mucking up their brains. It could be catastrophic."

Gareth looked hurt: "There is no evidence that this would happen, Brian. By the time the pork gets into the food chain, Guaria Engorgia has virtually disappeared. It's only used in very tiny quantities anyway. You'd have to eat pork three times a day to get a micro-milligram of this stuff into your gut, and then it would quickly be excreted via your body's own elimination systems. Think about all the other additives in meat: they don't cause problems, do they?

"To my mind, the most dangerous additive on the planet is High Fructose Corn Syrup - it's in everything from burgers to salad dressings, and screws up yor metabolic regulating hormones. Yet, it's legal. That's the stuff you should be trying to ban, Brian. Not my pig food."

He took off his glasses, put them down on the bench and rubbed his eyes. He looked old, and very, very tired.

Brian realised that it would be unfair to try and convince Gareth that the work he was engaged in was unethical, dangerous, and probably had already been, albeit indirectly, responsible for some premature human deaths. In any case, he had absolutely no proof that this was true. Looking at his friend now, he felt sure that, as academics are so well able to do, Gareth had convinced himself that the research was useful, valid and the consequences of its commercial use were really not his affair. Probing him on the whereabouts of the experimental pig farm was also stupid. Gareth wouldn't tell, that was certain. Why upset the man? Especially when he was going to have to establish a working relationship with him.

He was suddenly overwhelmed by concern for Gareth, and consumed by guilt. How could he have neglected this friendship? Had he been so wrapped up in his own career progress that he couldn't be bothered to stay in touch? It was easy to blame the pressures of work, marriage, rearing children, but that hadn't stopped him from being in regular contact with influential old pals who could help him in his own research projects. Just because Gareth had spent most of his career in the academic doldrums: working at the same university and plodding along with his life, he hadn't bothered. Before today, Brian hadn't even realised that Janie, Gareth's wife, was dead. It was appalling.

Gareth was re-adjusting his glasses and walking back to the steel door. "Come on, mate, let's get out of here. I'll be working in this unit most of tomorrow with a couple of post-grad kids who've been helping me, so I could do with a breather tonight. We'll take a taxi into town, head for a restaurant and have a good meal. We can discuss your schedule for the next two terms over a decent bottle of burgundy. You are the first excuse I've had for a proper night out for months."

****

An hour later, fortified by two pints of stout, Gareth was in garrulous mood. He had given Brian a thorough run-down of the academic and social scene at the university and warned him about the many political traps that it was possible to fall into.

"Keep your nose clean, and do everything through me, " he now advised, leaning against the dark brown oak bar of one of the city's oldest hosteries. "The Vice Chancellor and Dean are both after knighthoods, and are more interested in exam statistics than the welfare of the students and staff. I gather that your wife has left you, but if you're after sex, keep away from the female students. These days, you have got to be careful about that sort of thing. Once bitten, eh?"

Gareth laughed loudly, and took a long drink from his pint glass. "Sorry, Brian, that was unfair. Is there anyone new in your life yet. Anyone important, I mean? Or is that question impertinent? Are you still heart-broken because your wife has left?"

"I've got to be honest, Gareth. I miss the kids every single day, but Molly and I were virtually finished. The marriage was over before she went to America. There is someone else, but I'm going through a real crisis at the moment. I don't think I can commit to anything. You know what it's like."

Gareth looked serious, and shook his head sadly. "No, I don't, boyo. Janie and I made our vows the day we got engaged, and never wavered from them. Even now, I am still committed to her. You wouldn't understand, Brian, but I cannot ever contemplate having sex with another woman, ever again. According to my doctor, I won't have to worry too much about being frustrated in old age because

I'm unlikely to live that long. I'm not religious, but I am holding out some kind of hope that Janie and I will meet up somewhere again. Does that sound stupid and sentimental for a scientist?"

"Not at all," said Brian. "Come on, mate, let's go and get some food now. You're unlikely to die tonight, so we might as well have a good time. While we eat, I'll try to convince you that Janie would want you to take care of yourself and live a bit longer. You've got a lot of work to do."

Gareth smiled, put down his empty glass on the bar and belched, softly. "Don't be a boring old fart, Brian. There's no point in preaching at me. I'm a lost cause. Let's eat."

****

At precisely 9.16 am next morning, one of Gareth's post-graduate students found the body. Gareth was lying, spread-eagled on his back on the concrete floor of the rat research unit. The position of his body indicated that he had been just about to give the creatures their first feed of the day. One of the cages was open, and there were some spilt grains of feed on the floor.

Later that morning, the male, post-graduate student gave a short statement to the police:

"I arrived at the building, knocked at the door of the unit and there was no reply. The padlock was undone, but the door was locked - there is a Chubb lock which can be operated from both sides. I knew Professor Ward-Thomas had come down earlier to do the first feed, so I was slightly concerned that he didn't hear my knock. I thought maybe he was too busy to respond, so I waited and then knocked again. By this time, I was a bit worried. We all think very highly of Professor Ward-Thomas, and I was worried that something could have happened to him.

" I knew the Professor kept a spare key in the bottom drawer of the desk in the office, so I was able to unlock the door. I walked in, and that's when I saw the fat rats waddling along the floor. I slammed the door shut behind me so none could escape, then ran towards the bench where the feed is kept. The Professor was lying there, wearing his white overalls and lab shoes. He looked as though he had just opened one of the cages and was about to put the food compound into the feeders. His face was very contorted. It was awful. Poor man. He must have suffered a massive stroke or heart attack. We will all miss him."

Later, the student gave a full statement at the local police station. He signed it carefully: Jim Wang, BSc (Hons).

****

Brian found out about Gareth's death an hour after the body was discovered. He was addressing a group of first-year students on the subject of the importance of hydration for marathon runners, when the door of the lecture room opened, and the college secretary appeared.

"Can you come outside, Professor Donovan? I won't keep you a moment." She looked upset, so Brian apologised to his students and joined her, closing the door behind him.

"I'm sorry to have to break this to you suddenly, Professor, but Gareth Ward-Thomas died this morning. He's been taken to the city hospital. I know you were a friend. I am really, really sorry. The Vice Chancellor will be telling the students at a special meeting this evening. Of course, with the grapevine in operation, most of them will know by then. The police were called, but it is absolutely clear what happened. Poor man, he was in the lab with his rats at the time and had a massive heart attack. What a terrible way to go."

****

Chapter Eighteen

Email to Caroline Dempsey:
From: Kimi Skaarsgard, Stockholm Daily News.

Hi Caro, I"ve translated the memo. See the attachment. It sounds as though these people are running some kind of experimental farm in the Lake District. I'm in London next week - let's meet up. You owe me a large lunch. You might be on to a good story here. My favourite shoe fetishist could clean up with this one!
    Cheers, gorgeous: Kimi.

Caroline was sitting in front of the small oak desk in her bedroom wearing a loose black cotton wrap and her black silk slippers. She was feeling exhiliarated. Her first real piece of investigative journalism had paid off. The memo which she had so painstakingly copied out in the lavatory at the Protin-Foods factory, was a printout of an email from Lars to Dr. Lindstrom, asking him to send a large consignment of product to a pig farm near Penrith. The name of the farm was not given, but, when Caroline examined the full, if brief, text on the attachment, there were some clues as to its location.

She clicked onto the attachment icon on her laptop again, and re-opened the text. It read:

Piers: can you please ensure that a batch of 550kilos of our basic product gets transported to the pig farm next week? The professor has produced some more of the special additive, and it is at the farm ready to be put into the product. Then, as usual, the treated product will be returned here for processing into low-fat ready-meals in the normal way. It might be best if you take the batch up there yourself. Don't worry, the roads near Penrith are passable, despite the terrible weather. I gather that the farm looks very attractive in the snow, and the lake is quite spectacular. Very much like home in fact. Enjoy the trip. Lars. .

So, the farm was near Penrith, and there was a Lake nearby as well. Caroline pulled out an old school atlas from the pile of reference books under her desk, which somehow were often more useful for research than trawling through the myriad of information on the internet. She opened it quickly at the section on the North West of England. Ullswater was the nearest lake to the town, so presumably the farm was somewhere amongst the rolling fells and hills that surrounded it. There couldn't be many pig farms in the area. Since the outbreak of foot and mouth disease a few years earlier, most of the farmers had cut their losses and switched to other businesses. Large-scale piggeries were a thing of the past. It shouldn't be too difficult to find the farm, surely?

She reached for the telephone on her desk and dialed Susan's mobile number. It rang briefly, then she was connected to the message service.

"Hi Susan, where are you? I've got something important to report. Ring me back as soon as you can. Biting her lip with frustration, Caroline tried Brian's number. He answered, brusquely.

"Hello, who is it?"

"Brian, thank God you're there. It's Caroline. Sorry to sound dramatic, but I'm on to something important. Can you talk?"

"Yes, but make it quick. I'm in alone in the staff room between lectures but someone could come in at any moment. A colleague who was working on GE203 has just been murdered, I think. It's been made to look like a heart attack, but I'm certain it's suspicious. What is your news?"

"That's it! It's the link, Brian." Caroline sounded excited. "Protin-Foods are running an experimental farm of some kind near Penrith in the Lake District. I think that's where they inject GE203 into the meat substitute that's put into the ready-meals. I found a memo which proves this when I was at their factory in Newcastle. Anyway, it's a long story, but the gist is that Protin-Foods are up to their neck in all this. Their big boss was actually at a meeting with Elizabeth Collins, that sexy Junior Health Minister, earlier this week. God knows what they are planning next. I am trying to contact Susan today, and I suggest we meet at her house this weekend. Can you come down for the day on Saturday? Meanwhile, I will do more research on the internet to find out where the farm is. Probably well hidden, but there will be clues I'm sure. What do you think?"

Brian felt cold and shivery. This phone call was dangerous. Gareth's death had been no accident: it was more likely that his old friend had been given some indetectable drug or been frightened so badly that the shock triggered cardiac arrest. Maybe Brian himself would be the next victim. He could hear the sound of footsteps approaching the staff room door. He had to make his mind up quickly:

"Yes, 1pm. I will be there. Goodbye."

Caroline punched the air, and shrieked out loud. "Yeees!" Now all she had to to was get hold of Susan, get her to agree to the meeting, find the location of the farm, and then... what?

She slumped back in her chair, and considered. They could, she supposed, break into the place, take photographs, locate computer information or even better, written records, and then persuade a newspaper to publish the story. In your dreams, girl!

For a start, the farm was probably guarded day and night and, even if they did get some evidence, who would use it? After her experience with Rob and the Evening Echo, it was likely that every editor in London was being nobbled by the Government to suppress any more juicy stories about food additives. No, that wouldn't work.

She logged off the computer, and reached for her battered black leather contact book as she often did when she needed inspiration.

Although she kept most of her most important contact numbers stored in her mobile phone, and also had a very smart chrome-trimmed personal organiser to impress fellow hacks, the old, dog-eared, spiral bound book was her "bible".

During her time on the Evening Echo, she had met a lot of weird and wonderful people, collected dozens of business cards, and "cold-called" hundreds of individuals for information. Each telephone number, email address, if any, together with a few important facts was listed, alpabetically, in the book. Sometimes, the names were famous, or semi-famous. "A" list celebrities didn't give out numbers, but most of them had a sister, brother or former lover who could be contacted, and who might be co-operative if there was some cash in it, or they had a debt to score. The "B" list kind were often only too keen to give their mobile telephone numbers to journalists. Any publicity was good publicity.

Many of the people in the book were agents, photographers, public relations contacts, officials, or bright secretaries who often knew a lot more than their employers. Some were simply "useful", such as a night club owner who could always be relied upon to produce some glamorous girls to give their opinions on the latest sex toy or designer diet, and a middle-aged woman who worked in a department store who had been particularly helpful when Caroline was researching a story on counterfeit goods. Others were the kind of informants who needed to be approached with care, such as those working in Government department or royal households.

She settled back in her chair and started to go through the book. Maybe a name, a note or just a couple of words would give her an idea of how to get this story where it belonged: in the public domain. It was worth a shot.

When she reached the letter "C", two entries nearly jumped off the page. Against the name "Les Cunliffe" she had scrawled the words "ex cop, was banged up for fraud, takes cash. Drink and recreational drugs habit." plus a mobile telephone number. A little further down, she spotted the heading "Consumer Journal, British" with the name of the editor, Mary Hawkhurst, written alongside.

There were three numbers for Mary: office, home and mobile, plus an email address.

Caroline's mobile phone, on the desk beside the computer, blared out its latest, tuneless ring-tone.

"Susan here. Sorry. I was using the landline. I've just been told that I've got the job I was after at Kenley and Palmer. The Development Manager rang to tell me and we had a very long chat. I start tomorrow. It's good news, although I'm not looking forward to the daily commute."

Caroline was impatient: the details of Susan's new employment were not exactly top of her list of important topics for discussion.

"Tell me about it when we meet. I've asked Brian to come down to your house, Susan. Sorry, but I had to make the decision quickly. He is up to his eyes in shit at the university and I've got a lot to report as well. We must get organised urgently. 1pm, Saturday. OK?"

"Fine. I'll do lunch. All fresh, non-adulterated foods from the local farmers' market, OK?"

The joke went down badly. "Come on Susan, when you hear what we've both got to tell you you won't be laughing. See you then. 'Bye".

After the call, Caroline took a piece of blank, A4 paper from the pile by the side of her printer, and wrote down the two names she had found in her contact book, with a few notes beside them.

Les Cunliffe: knows everything about breaking and entering premises. Could be persuaded to give some tips on how we can get into the pig farm. We don't know what it's going to be like, or what security they have there, but any advice invaluable at this stage. Cost? Reckon on £100. Risk? Nil. No credability with the police these days.

Mary Hawkhurst: great campaigning journalist. Built up the circulation of the British Consumer Journal from 50,000 in the late nineties, to a very healthy 1.5 million now. Monthly. Required reading. Reports on car safety, pensions frauds, filthy hospitals, and misleading food labelling. Made newspaper headlines. Stories always embargoed to give maximum impact. Never lets go. Hated by most government ministers. Would need to see hard evidence of malpractice before running anything in the Journal.

Caroline folded the piece of paper in two and considered: it was now Thursday. She would wait until Saturday before even considering approaching either of these two contacts. No doubt Susan and Brian would have some ideas of their own. One thing was certain, though. They *had* to get into that pig farm, somehow.

****

The only similarity between East Central Hospital and the Kenley and Palmer factory was their size. Both were enormous, but while East Central consisted mostly of large grey Victorian buildings, the factory was ten stories high and built of stark white concrete. Curiously for such a large building, it was completely circular, with just a few glass and concrete satellite structures dotted around its perimeter.

As Susan drove the green Renault into the football pitch sized carpark at the side of the main building, she decided that her new place of work looked like a gigantic Polo mint. The architect's intention must have been to subject the staff to as much inconvenience as possible: finding her way around this ghastly building would be a nightmare.

For the first time in her working life, she reflected fondly on her outdated office and the depressing wards of East Central. At least it had a heart. This place looked like a white cage, designed for hamsters scurrying around a massive treadmill.

It was a good 15 minute walk from her space on the outer row of the car park to the main door of the building. As it was pouring with rain, Susan was glad she'd remembered to bring a large umbrella. She was wearing a long, shiny black raincoat, which suited her dark hair and pale complextion. She made a mental note to set out from home at least 2 hours before her starting time, 9.30am. God. Four hours a day in traffic jams. Hell. Maybe she would test the public transport system and see if it was bearable. At least she would be able to do some reading. Wembley tube station couldn't be far away. Perhaps that would be a more tolerable solution.

Thinking about the horrors of travelling to and from the factory and avoiding the puddles in the tarmac carpark kept her occupied during the walk, so, when she reached the large main entrance, she was taken aback by the size of the reception area. It was like a small cathedral. Three glass and plastic chandeliers, each about three metres in diameter, hung from the atrium roof, illuminating colourful murals depicting the cultivation of various ingredients used by Kenley and Palmer: sugar and banana plantations manned by bronzed local workers gathering the harvest: fields of wheat with jolly-looking red combine harvesters chugging up and down; groups of cheery, leather-faced Mediterrean workers picking olives, lemons and oranges.

Maybe they forgot to include some pretty pictures of scrawny battery hens couped up in filthy cages, thought Susan. After all, chicken has to be one of the most-used ingredients in the company's many food products. Her new employers were obviously adept at presenting the best possible public image. Or, to put it another way, they had a glossy way of hiding the less-acceptable face of food mass production techniques.

Her unflattering conclusions were confirmed by the four middle aged female receptionists who were dressed in identical blue blazers and bright yellow shirts. The Kenley and Palmer logo, large red K and P letters entwined on a bright green backround, was embroidered on the top pocket of their blazers. Sitting behind their long, curved black marble desk, they looked like a row of tropical parrots on a perch.

In the middle of the white tiled floor was a large circular table with a display of packages and cans, placed in geometrical patterns.

Small groups of people occupied the seating areas around the sides of the hall. Some were waiting patiently, others were speaking in hushed tones, as befitted the church-like atmosphere.

"A temple of hommage to human greed," Susan said out loud, as she approached the reception desk.

"Not quite, but I know what you mean. You must be Susan. I'm Don Fellows, the Development Manager for the Ready Meals Section. I thought I would come down and meet you here on your first day. It's hell trying to find your way around this place at first. You'll understand the system by tomorrow."

The speaker was a tall, fair-haired, middle-aged man in a dark grey suit. Susan flushed. She had been so occupied with looking around her that she hadn't noticed him approach. Her comment had been stupid. If she was going to be an effective "industrial spy", and keep her job as well, she would have to be more careful. She smiled quickly, and held out her hand.

"Sorry about that. But the place does look more like a place of worship than a factory. I'm sure it's great to work here, everything's so bright and shiny."

Don laughed. "You get used to it. The factory was built ten years ago when the company aquired several smaller food producing operations. We wanted everything in one place, and, at the time we were trying to show off to our shareholders. I'm pleased to say that we are now making even larger profits. Pleased, of course, from my own point of view as I'm due to retire next year. At least my pension is secure.

"Anyway, I digress. Let's get you a pass and take you up to our labs and offices. Most of the product assembly is done at ground floor level, and we have our laboratories on the top floor. I want you to start work immediately - testing a new line of six products we're launching next year. They're being aimed at the children's market, which, as I'm sure you already know, is highly lucrative."

Half an hour later, Susan was sipping a cup of coffee in her new office, and examining sample dishes from the "Activity Kids" range of tasty teatime ready-meals. According to Don, the name was meant to impress parents, not children. The Kenley and Palmer marketing people had found, during research, that parents were attracted to food product names that suggested participation in some kind of activity - even if their offspring were actually couch potatoes.

Don had explained how this worked. "The idea we are planting in parents' minds is that all you have to do is place a dish of "Activity Kids" cheese and bacon flavoured spaghetti hoops in front of little Johnny, and he will suddenly be transformed from a spotty, fat twelve year old into a football hero. Our TV advertising will endorse this idea by incorporating a series of cartoon characters who morph from blimps into sporting superstars. It's all great fun."

He went on to explain that the concept, name, marketing strategy and product placement had all been organised, the TV airtime booked and the commercial film was ready to roll. As it was scheduled to be shown during adult evening programmes, the company were still abiding by the Government's rules. Now, all that was needed was for the products to be finalised, and to make sure that they passed the health and safety standards required. Susan's job was to analyse and test the recipes, and work out exact quantities for each of the main ingredients in each product. It was long, tedious, analytical work, and the deadlines Don had given her were very tight.

She put her coffee cup down, and moved over to her well-equipped workbench. As she reached for the first food sample, a disturbing thought crossed her mind: she was now directly involved in effectively ruining children's health.

****

"I suggest we all pool our information, separately, and I take notes. Then, we can work out our next move or moves, although I must say that I've already more or less decided what they should be. I just hope you both agree with me."

Caroline had taken charge of the meeting. She was sitting on one of Susan's brown leather sofas, a clipboard on her knee, with legs crossed to show off her new mulberry leather boots. That morning, she had dressed for action: wide black goucho-style trousers, a cream cashmere roll-necked sweater which clung to her magnificent bosom, topped by a mulberry coloured woven wool poncho. Her blonde hair was tied up in a loose knot on top of her head To complete the "investigative journalist" ensemble, she wore large black-rimmed spectacles. Despite her good intentions, she had gained a few pounds recently. She had an array of equipment, including a tape recorder, camera, magnifying glass and large brown leather brief case spread out beside her. Consequently, she took up most of the space on the sofa.

Brian and Susan, who both looked tired and nervous, sat on two low, matching chairs facing her. They both wore casual jeans and sweaters. Susan's blue roll-neck looked two sizes too big for her. She clutched a mug of coffee in both hands, taking sips while she gazed at Caroline with intense concentration.

Caroline continued, clipboard in hand, referring to typewritten notes as she spoke.

"Here is the situation, so far. We have proved, to our own satisfaction, that the government are in collusion with a company, Protin-Foods, to put a substance known as GE203: sometimes referred to as "Greed Enhancer." but more often under its natural name, Guaria Engorga, into foods which are destined for the lucrative "healthy ready-meals" market.

"The reason they are doing this is not known, but we suspect that it could be to increase the obesity levels in this country, thus encouraging earlier mortality. We know that Lars Johnsson, the European Director of Protin-Foods, has had at least one meeting with Elizabeth Collins, the minister who is in charge of various areas of public health including the provision of hospital beds. She recently intitiated an inquiry into euthanasia, which she charmingly referred to as "assisted mortality", another indication that the government wishes to reduce the population to ease the appalling strain on the health service.

"We also know that the British Prime Minister, Jack Barton, is facing increasing pressure from various charities and senior citizen groups to come clean on the real state of pensions, whether publicly or privately funded. It is suspected that the lack of funds and suitable provisions by companies has now become so serious that he will soon announce plans to put back the official retirement and pensionable age to seventy.

" So, there are now three sound reasons to try and reduce population levels. We also know that at least two of the big supermarket chains make regular, substantial donations to government funds.

"The development and production of GE203 is as follows: it is derived from a wild herb-type plant which comes from a remote part of China, and is harvested by a division of the Changjia Food Company who are importing into this country. Changjia also make various confectionary products and fast foods which are exported to the US and other Western countries. There is also a growing market for these items in China, itself, where the high-fat, high-sugar Western-style diet is becoming more and more popular.

"Changjia employ various "heavies" who are not exactly shy about piling on the pressure or threatening violence when it comes to protecting their interests - and their profits. Because of their huge commercial power, they are also capable of using very large bribes to get public figures, such as University Vice Chancellors, to get rid of anyone who speaks out against them."

Brian managed a quick grin, and opened his mouth as if about to speak. He changed his mind, and allowed Caroline to continue.

"The Chinese herb has been developed into GE203, ostensibly to be included in pig food. The scientist who has worked on this is Brian's colleague, Professor Gareth Ward-Thomas, who is, unfortunately, now dead, probably killed by one of Changia's thugs. Professor Ward-Thomas had no idea that his researches were part of a scheme to place GE203 into Protin-Foods' non-animal protein replacement product. One of the effects that he has noticed on the rats who ingest this stuff is that they develop a desire to consume more and more of the "host" food, which, in the case of rats, is a form of grain. Pigs, I presume, would eat it in a swill of some kind, and, of course, when we're talking about humans, it can be hidden in anything from a burger to a cereal bar."

Susan put down her coffee cup and held up her hand. "Caroline, can I just add something here? In my new job, I'm working on a range of children's teatime meals, which aren't yet on the market. These also include some of the Protin-Foods meat-substitute among the ingredients. These meals are being carefully targeted towards parents who want their kids to be more active with TV, magazine and newspaper advertisements. It looks as though they'll be disappointed. Once a child has become hooked on this rubbish, he or she will want more and more, and get fatter. It's just the kind of thing that the company concerned would do. They seem to think that food for humans is all about effective promotion, pretty packaging and making huge profits. After just a day I realised that they don't give a damn for their consumers' health and wellbeing. It's terrifying."

Caroline nodded, and turned over to the next page of notes on her clipboard. " If you think that's terrifying, be very, very afraid, Susan, because it is nothing compared with what I have to say next. I'll continue.

"The emailed memo I copied at Protin-Foods proves that GE203 is put into their product, and maybe other items destined for human consumption, at a pig farm near Penrith in Cumberland, probably quite close to Ullswater. The next bit is supposition: I imagine that the farm would be quite large, with a section where the pig experiments are carried out, quite legitimately by Wilkinson's the animal feeds company Gareth was working for. So, there will be a complex of pig pens and buildings. In one building, which presumably is on the same site, GE 203 is definitely being put into the Protin-foods product, which is delivered in batches, and then returned to their factory in Newcastle. It is probably going into other foods as well. "

"I did some research on the internet. First, I looked on Wilkinson's own website. They are an old-established company, who supply animal feed to many European piggeries, farms, and broiler houses. They started up in 1850, and remained under the control of the same family until five years ago, when they were bought out by Magnum USA, the American chemicals and fertilizers giant. However, they still remain virtually independent, on paper anyway.

" Because of the risk of animal rights demonstrations, the company don't list an expermental piggery among their facilities in the United Kingdom. However, they do mention a rest home for former staff near a village called Westover, which is about five miles from Ullswater. They don't give the exact address but the place is called Heaven's Rest, which I think is absolutely ghastly. If you happen to be a clapped out old pensioner who's spent their life slaving in an animal feed factory and has just arrived there for a couple of weeks' holiday, you'd imagine that the place might be your final destination! Anyway, it might be near the pig farm. Someone who works there must know something.

"I suggest that one of us, probably me as I'm the one who's almost unemployed at the moment, goes up there to find out more. I'll hire a car and you two can chip in to help with the cost. I will also get in touch with an old contact who might be able to to give me a few helpful hints on getting into into our pig farm once I've located it. Frankly, that is the part I won't do alone. You've both got to come with me, so that we can all go down for trespass together. Or, hopefully, find some evidence that will prove what is going on. I have already earmarked a consumer journal with an editor who, I know, would publish a report on this, provided we make it stand up. What do you say?"

This time, Brian was able to speak. "Given that Changjia have already threatened me, sent me a package of dead rats and murdered one of my friends, I think that being sent to jail for trespass is probably the mildest thing that could happen to us.

"If we get caught, we'll probably be turned into pigfood ourselves, Caroline. Or they could easily arrange some kind of accident. Walkers and climbers die every week of the year in the Lake District. Even on the journey down here, I am sure I was followed. I'm not joking. Are we really ready to do this?"

Susan looked at him in horror. "Why didn't you mention this before, you stupid idiot? Who followed you? What happened?"

Brian shrugged. "Well, he looked like a backpacker and it might have been a co-incidence that he was on the same tube train from King's Cross to Victoria Station, and then caught the same main line train as me. He wore a hooded coat, with a woolly hat underneath and sunglasses, so he could have been any nationality. I thought I had managed to give him the slip by jumping into a cab at the station, but when I knocked at your door, Susan, I saw him at the end of the road. He must have leapt into another cab and followed me. It couldn't be mere co-incidence."

Caroline's mouth dropped open and she dropped her clipboard on the sofa. Susan stood up and started pacing the floor.

"Brian, this is terrible," she said " I agree with Caroline that we've got to go on because it's obvious that this is the only way to get this appalling conspiracy out into the open. Stay here tonight, and we'll talk it through. If Caroline is willing to do the intitial investigation into the location of this pig farm or whatever it is, that is brilliant. The man who followed you might still be outside, so I suggest that we wait until it's dark, and she leaves by the back door, goes through the garden, and into the road in front of the railway line at the back of the house. She can take my car, which is parked there. We can eat first. What do you both say?"

" If I'm to be murdered by an oriental hit-man, I would prefer to enjoy a good meal first," said Caroline, grinning. "Don't worry, Susan, I can see that you two anorexics would like a night of lust together. Go for it. I doubt whether you'll have time for many more until this thing is over. They say that the Lake District is notoriously cold, damp and unromantic in winter...Gawd help us!".

****

Four hours later, Susan and Brian were lying in Susan's comfortable brass bed for the second time. Because of her new, longer working hours and the added pressure of travelling to and from her new job, Susan had abandoned any attempt to tidy up. The cotton sheets were greyish and rumpled, there was a pile of unwashed underwear in one corner of the room, and she had dumped the entire contents of her handbag on the dressing table; including her mobile phone, keys, a grubby handkerchief, packet of tampons, a blackened banana and a half-full bottle of pale pink nail varnish which was covered in sticky yellow flesh from the squashed fruit. Brian's jeans, sweater and underwear were in a heap on the floor, and her own clothes were still on the bed, hastily removed before they both dived under the duvet.

"They say that fear heightens all the senses," said Brian, stretching his thin arms above his head. "What we've just been doing felt so good, Susan, that I might even invite our backpacking villain inside to give me another scare. I bet he's still lurking outside. When Caroline phoned to say she'd arrived home safely, I was relieved, of course, but it does mean that he's probably still around somewhere. I'll have to order a cab to take me back to the station first thing in the morning. I've got to be in college at 8am on Monday and still have lectures to prepare. Still, we've got time for a quick..."

His words were cut short by Susan, who raised herself up on one elbow, placed her hand over his mouth, then climbed on top of him, with her knees either side of his hips.

"No thanks, mate. I want something *very, very slow* now. I'm going to be the one who takes the lead this time and you are not allowed to utter a word until I've finished. Nod if you understand. If not, you're going to get out of this bed and leave immediately, without a taxi. Yes, or no?"

Brian rolled his eyes and nodded. When Susan removed her hand he opened his mouth to speak, then changed his mind and grinned instead.

Twenty minutes later, they were both exhausted...and satisfied. Susan lay on her back, and stretched her legs and arms. Brian, by now lying on his stomach, appeared to be asleep. "Open your eyes, Brian, I know you're not really snoozing" she said, giving him a pinch on one scrawny buttock. We have got to have a serious talk. What are we going to do? We're in a mess. If we get through all this, what are your plans? I can't just go on having one-night stands with you. It's just not my style. I've been badly hurt in the past, and I refuse to let myself love someone who doesn't love me. I'm not going to let you have any rest until you discuss this with me, sensibly. Do you hear?"

Brian turned over and looked at Susan, who, by now, had covered one leg, and her breasts with a portion of the rumpled sheet. "I see you are trying to divert my attention from your gorgeous body, Susan. Quite right too. I can't be expected to think clearly with your delicious breasts on display.

"Actually, Susan, it's something I have been doing a lot of lately - thinking, that is. Before Gareth was killed we spent a memorable evening together. We got pretty pissed of course, but we also had a chance for some serious discussion. He told me about his own happy marriage, and commitment to his wife. I admit that, at the time, I felt that he was on another planet. My own marriage was over, and I had never had the courage to commit to anyone properly. As you know, I could never resist a beautiful woman, or even a fairly attractive one, come to that.

"Now, though, I've decided that I must change. You probably won't believe a word of this - and why should you? I can only say that this business, the humiliation of losing my job at The Royal

College, even the break-up with Molly, have affected me in a sharp, brutal way which has probably done me the world of good. They have certainly shaken me out of my middle-aged complacency and made me think in a very different way.

" You are a wonderful person, Susan, with more integrity in your left nipple than I have in my whole body, and I would like to promise you that you have my love, and fidelity. You may not believe it, but it's true. You mentioned the word "love" just now, so I hope you feel something for me. My divorce should be through later this year, and then I would like you to share my life. Do I have a chance?" He collapsed back on his pillow, apparently exhausted by this outburst.

Susan didn't move. She appeared to consider his proposal very carefully. "Look Brian, last time you came here, I decided that you were a great lover, a brilliant scientist, a wonderful talker, someone I could admire and have fun with. I also thought you were a serial philanderer, a ditherer, and a man who was unlikely to stick to his principles. Now, I'm not so sure about the last three.

"If I've been wrong about you, or you really have changed, and we both get through all this without getting killed or going to jail, I will consider your proposal. However, you must be faithful, positive, and vow to help Caroline and I to prove that the government is deliberately, and wickedly, manipulating people's food, in order to shorten lives.

"Now, I'm going down to the kitchen for a bottle of champagne and two glasses. In the morning, you can order a taxi to the station, then go back to your university and practise looking at all the female students *without planning how to get them into bed.* Understand?"

****

Chapter Nineteen

"Around Ullswater, the second largest lake in the English Lake district, are some of the top UK hotels, and three rosette restaurants, country house hotels and cosy farmhouses offering homely fare with bed and breakfast, plus a wide selection of self-catering holiday cottages, discreet camping and caravan sites and wonderful wedding venues."
Lakeland Tourist Board Brochure.

If only the sun was shining, it might indeed be a wonderful place for a wedding, but in pissing rain, this place is the pits, thought Caroline. Give me good old Knightsbridge, any day of the week.

She was sitting on the patchwork quilted cover of her single bed, flicking through the brochures and leaflets which, until half an hour ago, had been arranged in a neat fan shape on the small, octagonal table in front of the boarding house window. She had swept them to one side to make sufficient space for her large leopard-skin printed plastic make-up bag.

Her new, dark green Barbour raincoat, buckled rubber boots, brown leather gloves and waterproof slouch hat were spread over a long, creaking old-fashioned radiator which stretched along one wall. She had unpacked her small (ish) suitcase and now her clothes were neatly arranged in the large shiny mahogany chest of drawers: 2 red satin slips, six pairs of black lace knickers, matching bras, stockings, suspenders, tights, long black and green skirts, jeans, and a selection of low-cut sweaters and bright silk and cashmere scarves.

Caroline had read enough Sunday supplement features to know

that country women wore practical clothes on top, and naughty bits underneath. Fine, she would abide by the rural code. The main problem when packing for this expedition had been to select the correct, and practical, footwear: hence the rubber boots, a pair of sensible (and very heavy) climbing shoes, and a pair of black stilletos for indoor wear.

She had also brought with her the almost-complete copy for the Protin-Foods booklet, which she intended to work on. Her "cover" story would be plausible enough: she was a journalist researching a series of travel articles about holidays in the United Kingdom for a woman's magazine, and needed some local "colour" and photographs.

The grey stone guest house was small, square, and cosy. It was one of a row of twelve similar cottages in a cobbled side street in the village of Westover, about five miles South of the eastern side of Lake Ullswater. Caroline had picked the cottage for its location and size, not that there had been much choice. At this time of the year, most bed and breakfast establishments in the area were closed.

"Would you like a cup of tea, dear?" The door handle turned, and the landlady, Mrs. Bonnet, appeared. She was a sturdily built woman who, as far as Caroline could tell, lived alone with her dog, a yappy little West Highland terrier. Caroline hadn't seen any sign of a male presence in the house, so concluded that Mrs. Bonnet was either widowed or divorced. It would be fun finding out. Mrs. B was certainly fond of bright clothes, which contrasted gaily with traditional washed-out, chinzy decoration in the guest house. Her very tight white jeans, fluffy pink slippers and bright green sweater stood out against the shadowy background of the landing, she was wearing nearly as much make-up as Caroline and reaked of Opium perfume.

She continued to speak, while removing one fluffy slipper. She scratched the sole of her foot carefully, before replacing the slipper on her foot

" It's raining cats and dogs out there. I hope you don't have to go far today? There's one good Indian restaurant open at this time of year if you want a decent meal, or the Wordsworth pub does good bar food. There's a quiz contest on tonight. Have you parked your car in the car-park or the square at the end of the road?"

"I'd love some tea, Mrs. Bonnet. I left the car in the square, as your road is so narrow. It really is a lovely village and I'm not going to let the weather spoil my stay, even though I've got to work. I'll definitely give the restaurant a try and maybe include a write-up in the article I'm doing for the English Travel Magazine. I've already got some local information and a map of the area from the tourist office in Penrith, but I'd be really grateful if you could help me on one point. This is actually quite a personal thing. My aunt, who died recently, spent some time staying at a place called Heaven's Rest near here. I'd love to see it. Do you know where it is?"

Mrs. B. looked amused. "Well, you'd have be really fond of your old Auntie to go there. The place is hell to get to. It's about five miles from here, right up on the top of West Hill not far from Hallin Fell, overlooking the Lake. The road to West Hill is signposted down at the crossroads. Unfortunately, it's more like a track at the top, and in this weather, it's probably just a sea of mud. They don't seem to take many guests now, although there are a few long-stay residents, I gather. "

Caroline tried not to sound too interested. She got up from the bed, walked over to the window, and pulled back the pale pink and green floral curtain. "I must say that it doesn't look too promising out there. Maybe I'll go tomorrow or even put it off until my next visit up here. Auntie Hilda spent two weeks there in the summer a couple of years ago, and said it was beautiful."

Mrs. Bonnet shook her head . "Not at this time of year, it isn't. The lake is almost invisible on a day like this and the building is one of those awful Victorian monstrosities built by prosperous businessmen from Carlisle and then left to crumble. The firm who now own it, Wilkinson's, have done it up, but the last time I was up there, a couple of years ago, it was very bleak. There was a thriving pig farm just behind the house until two years ago when foot and mouth disease took hold. The farmer was a fishing pal of my late husband. The man was nearly bankrupt: practically suicidal, the poor bastard. So, he sold up and I believe he now lives in Bournemouth. Billy, my husband, God rest his soul, never did get to the bottom of who bought the farm, but people do say that there is something a bit odd about the place. Be careful if you go up there. I won't say any more, but just don't trespass."

Caroline kept her voice light: "Why, am I like to get shot at? "

Her new landlady suddenly looked serious. "People around here are very sensitive about that kind of thing. Farmers, and other landowners, get fed up with the hoards of climbers and tourists who tramp across their land. There, I shouldn't have said that. Actually, we just love townies coming here! I'll get your tea directly."

She grinned, turned, and closed the door. Caroline punched the air. Yes! She hadn't even had to try hard. Already, she was virtually certain that Heaven's Rest was the place she had come to find. Well, maybe not the rest home itself, but somewhere nearby must be the farm or factory of some kind where GE203 was being fed to pigs and put into foods for human consumption. All she had to do was go up there and take a look. Then, if it did seem very likely that it was the right place, she could at least find out what the layout of the place was like from the outside.

The weather was the one big obstacle, but perhaps that might be an advantage. She turned towards the window again, and checked her watch. It was now 2.30pm, and raining hard. By 5pm it would be dark, but there was plenty of time to go up and take a look and the four-by-four vehicle she had hired was fitted with excellent, all weather tyres. Why not?

"Here's your tea, dear." Mrs. Bonnet was back. "I'll give you a front door key, so if you do go out, you can come back when you like. I'll be in the pub for the quiz night later on. Might see you there. A good looking girl like you coming in to the bar at this time of year should shake them all up a bit. That's the trouble with this place: too many cars and people in the summer, dead as a dodo in the winter. Have a nice afternoon if you can in this awful weather. I'll be in the kitchen downstairs when you go. Bring the tray down if you don't mind."

She put the tray on the table, on top of the tourist leaflets, and went back downstairs. A faint but pungent whiff of Opium was left behind in her wake.

****

According to the weather forecast on the car radio, the wind off the coast of the North West of England would be rising to Force 6 that night, and heavy squalls of rain would sweep in from the Irish Sea, across the Lake District to the Pennines.

"They're a bit late with that piece of information. It's all happening now," muttered Caroline, crossly.

She was sitting, huddled, in her hired motor which was parked in a crude, stone bordered gravel layby about four and a half miles up the steep road which led to West Hill.

The big question was whether to continue on up the road, which had been getting narrower and narrower as she drove, or to head back towards the village. It was only 3.30pm, but it was almost dark, and the rain was lashing against the dark green car, streaming down the windscreen and making large puddles on the steaming bonnet of the vehicle. She could just make out the rough stone walls either side of the road, its steep, deeply rutted surface, and the rivulets of water running down either side. It looked very forbidding.

She decided to make a phone call while she made up her mind whether to proceed, and fished into her very damp leather bag for her phone and contact book. It would probably be impossible to get through, but it was worth a try.

"Cunliffe." The gruff voice at the other end of the phone was immediately recognisable. Les Cunliffe had always been a terse, surly bloke, and Caroline wondered if the ex-cop would give her an earful of abuse when she answered:

"Les, it's Caroline from the Echo. You probably remember me: we got some expert advice from you during that series of celebrity house break-ins up in North London. I was the junior reporter on the job. How are you?"

His reply was terse and to the point: "What do you want, and how much is in it for me?"

"I'm doing an investigative story and need to get some evidence, which might involve entering some premises. I'd like some ideas on that. In fact, I'm sitting in my car near the actual premises now. Say, £100 in cash, at the usual pub next Wednesday? I just need your experience and tips. There are three of us on the job. Can you help?"

"I remember you: big knockers and a mouth to match. Mind you, I liked your style, girl. OK.

" The first rule of the game is preparation. Do your homework. Where are you? Just give me the details of the terrain, no names, no involvement. Keep your car out of sight, go round the location on foot. Have a good excuse ready if you're picked up. Look for likely entrances, such as kitchen doors, low windows, etc. Pace out measurements if you can, and draw a plan later. Note any electric wires, guard dogs, buildings that might house security guards or equipment.

"Is there any chance of you entering legitimately? The simplest, and often most overlooked, way to case a building is to get someone to open the front door, then spin them a line which gives you time alone to rob the place. We call it "distraction burglary" in the trade.

" The downside of that approach is that you are then known to the occupier, but I presume that when your story comes out everything will go public anyway. If you can get in, and then snoop around you'll be able to find out a lot more than if you just look through windows. In that case, you've got to have a really good story ready and stay absolutely calm. Are you still as excitable, Caroline? I seem to remember that your report on the celebrity break-ins was ridiculously lurid: your readers must have had nightmares."

The rasping, yet almost inaudible chuckle at the end of the line reminded Caroline that Les was in very poor health.

She decided not to rise to the bait. "I've changed a lot since then, Les. This is important to me on a personal level, and is so hot that there will be no need to hype it up. I do have a good cover story, and I think I'll come back tomorrow morning and use it to gain entry. I've had some experience of operating covertly just recently, so I should be able to hack it.

"But, as I'm reasonably near the premises, I think I'll walk up and take a quick look. It's up an unmade road, Les, the light is going fast and it's still pissing down, so it's unlikely that I'll run into anyone. What do you think?"

"I presume you are sensibly dressed? Take a torch, but don't use it unless it's absolutely necessary. Keep to the side of the road. If you see a vehicle approaching, go into the bushes, or hide behind a wall. Do the minimum amount of research tonight: get the atmosphere, and general layout of the place, then scarper. Good luck."

"Thanks, Les." Caroline wondered if she had made the right decision. Having come this far, she was reluctant to turn round and go back to Westover, even though she was now incredibly hungry and cold. Her journalistic curiousity won. She opened the glove compartment of the car, and took out a torch, which she stuffed into her rucksack, checked the fasteners on her coat, and tucked her hair up into the waterproof slouch hat.

Finally, she pulled on her gloves, opened the door, and stepped down, her new boots making squelching noises on the gravel. It was bitterly cold, but the rain had eased to a fine drizzle, and, despite the gloom, it was easy to see the unmade road, boarded by a grassy bank, scrubby bushes and low rough stone walls on either side. She closed the car door quietly and locked it, tucking the key into a pocket on the rucksack, which she hauled onto her shoulder. It wasn't very heavy as she had pruned down her equipment to the basics: a small tape recorder, digital camera, notebook, pen, boarding house door key, wallet, tissues, comb, lipstick, and an "economy size" bar of fruit and nut chocolate.

She set off up the road, keeping to the right hand side, as close to the grassy bank as possible. The stone wall was broken up by small gaps at intervals of about 150 metres. The lane seemed to be fairly straight, so she hoped that she would have enough time to dash through a gap in the wall if she spotted the headlights of any approaching vehicle. If not, a rapid dive into the bushes would have to do.

The half-mile walk uphill to Heaven's Rest proved to be arduous: the rain had started to pelt down again, and Caroline's boots, although waterproof, did not grip the uneven, slippery surface very well. After just a hundred yards or so, she felt exhausted: the combination of unusual exertion and straining to keep upright was a killer. It was almost dark, so she followed the grassy bank carefully, hoping against hope that no-one decided to drive down the hill.

She made a pact with God: *if I get through this in one piece, I really will shed a couple of stone and join a gym. OK, I know I've made this vow before, God, but this time I mean it. Sorry for being such a lazy, selfish cow. I'll improve, honestly.*

After she had stumbled along for about 20 minutes, the road widened and there was a tarmac surface which, although cracked and full of pot-holes, was, at least, a bit easier to walk on than the unmade track.

As she rounded a corner, she saw some lights glinting dimly through the bushes about 25 years further along the road. She thought quickly: if this was Heaven's Rest, should she just have a quick look and go straight back to her car as she had planned...or, knock at the door and see if she could talk her way in?

The decision was made for her. She was nearly blinded by a pair of dazzling white headlights, as a vehicle came down the hill towards her. There was no time to hide behind the stone wall. She made a rapid calculation: she would bluff her way into the house.

Caught in the glare of the lights, Caroline stepped out into the road and waved her hand at the car, a brown Range Rover. It stopped and the driver wound down his window. It was so dark that she couldn't quite make out his features, but he was wearing a tweed cap and dark jacket. She stepped closer to the vehicle and peered in, smiling in what she hoped, was a rueful way.

"Can I help at all? Have you broken down? "

He must have been about sixty, with a sandy-coloured moustache, and rough brown skin. His eyes, shaded by the cap, looked kind.

" What a lousy night." She tried to sound bright and breezy, although her teeth were chattering. "I'm on my way up to Heaven's Rest. My hired car was making strange clanking noises, so I decided to leave it in the layby about half a mile down the road, and walk. Not much fun, but I'm sure the trek is doing me a lot of good. Sorry to wave you down but I just wanted to know if it's much further. If it is, I'll abandon the idea until the morning, and get my car back to the village."

"You're in luck," said the man. "The house is only another fifty yards or so, and they're just serving tea. Are you visiting one of the guests?"

Caroline stopped smiling, and tried to look sad, with some success. A stray whisp of saturated blond hair sticking out from under her hat had curled around her cheek, and rivulets of rain dripped off the brim of her slouch hat, mixed with her brown mascara and ran, muddily, down her nose.

"It's a pilgrimage, in a way," she said. "My mother's sister died recently, and she once stayed at Heaven's Rest. It was quite a few years ago now, but she loved the scenery up here. I was in the area so I decided to come up and see for myself. We were very close. I suppose I could have picked a better day for it."

"Well, continue walking, and I'll phone them up at the house, and tell them to expect you," the man said "Sorry, I can't offer you a lift, but I'm the only doctor on call tonight, and I've got a patient waiting for me in Westover. What's your name?"

She thought, quickly. There was a chance, albeit a very slight one, that this country doctor might have heard of Caroline Dempsey, the journalist.

"Caroline Osborne," she said. "Thanks for that. They're probably very busy, but all I want to do is just get a bit of the atmosphere there. It will make me feel closer to Auntie Hilda. I'll drive up tomorrow to look at the view, but I've come this far, and I feel I ought to try and get to the house today if possible."

Caroline turned away, and continued to walk up the hill. She glanced back and saw the internal light in the car go on and the doctor speaking on his mobile phone. Well, she had burnt her bridges now, all right. The next few hours would be critical .

****

"What a shame I wasn't the Director of Care when your aunt stayed here. The place changed hands ten years ago, and there is no-one still around from that time, I'm afraid. "

The speaker, a trim-looking woman of about fifty, with iron grey hair cut into a mannish "short back and sides" style, was wearing large tortoiseshell spectacles on a chain around her neck. She fingered it, nervously. Her uncompromising hairstyle, and no-nonsense outfit: black skirt and red jacket with black buttons, gave the impression of a woman in control, but the constant movement of her thin hands, twisting and untwisting the gilt links of the chain, implied that she was ill-at-ease.

She sat, in large red velvet covered arm chair in front of a big open fire, facing Caroline,.who had adopted a lounging position in a matching chair, in an attempt to look relaxed.

Caroline's wet raincoat, hat and boots were draped on an old-fashioned clothes airer in front of the fire. The room was obviously some kind of lounge, with a dozen or so solid-looking armchairs, draped with multicolour hand-crocheted blankets, arranged in companionable groups. Two elderly women were sitting in one corner drinking tea and talking softly. In the centre of the room was a large table scattered with dog-eared copies of Lakeland Life.

The decoration was standard country hotel; red flocked wallpaper, shabby Indian rugs, and on the walls, gilt-framed pictures of mountain scenes dotted with sad-looking cows and sheep. Caroline wondered what the back of the house looked like. From the road, it had been impossible to see beyond the imposing, somewhat forbidding, red brick facade.

The Director of Care, who had introduced herself as Judith Allsopp, crossed her legs carefully, and handed Caroline a cup of tea from a silver tray on the mahogany coffee table by her side.

"We don't have many people staying here at this time of year, but we are usually nearly full between April and October," she said. " It's good that some firms still care about the people who work for them. Our clients are mainly elderly folk now; the kind who laboured on for thirty or forty years. Younger people don't stay in their jobs long enough to benefit from the company perks, and most of them wouldn't want to come here anyway. I assume your aunt worked for Wilkinsons at some stage?"

Caroline shifted her substantial bottom from side to side in her chair, and leant forward towards her companion. She knew she had to get this right, or ruin the whole mission. She was already experiencing a ghastly gnawing sensation in her stomach, and regretted not eating her emergency fruit and nut chocolate bar on the walk up to Heaven's Rest.

Trying to ignore her fluttery nerves, and sugar-cravings, and thinking about the advice she had been given by Les Cunliffe, Caroline decided that she would try the "distraction burglary" technique. She launched into a story which she hoped would convince Judith Allsopp that she was genuine. She spoke slowly, trying to inject a note of sadness into her voice:

"Well, as far as I know, Aunt Hilda was a packer in one of the Wilkinsons' Midlands factories for about 25 years. Payed a pittance of course, but that was typical in the late forties and fifties. She never married, and when she was crippled with osteoporosis, she was helped quite a lot by the firm's personel people, so that was good.

" I remember her telling me that she came up here a couple of times, and my mother says that Auntie really loved the place. She died last month, and, as I was working in the area I decided to come up and have a look. Thank you so much for helping to dry out my stuff, and the tea. I really am most grateful."

The Director of Care smiled. "Well, you are very welcome to come up tomorrow, in daylight, and admire the view from the terrace on the second floor, which your aunt enjoyed, I'm sure. It's quite spectacular on a fine day. The Lake, and surrounding hills, the colours. It's quite superb. Shall I call a taxi to take you back down to the village?"

Caroline thought quickly. Better to get as much information as possible now than to wait until tomorrow when checks could have been made about herself and her fictitious Aunt Hilda. Les Cunliffe was right, you had to seize opportunities when they presented themselves in this game, otherwise you were lost. She thought, briefly, about her mum and dad: they had been thrilled when she decided to become a journalist. Her mother had fondly imagined that Caroline would get a job on an upmarket woman's magazine and spend her time interviewing international celebrities. She had tried not to show her disappointment when Caroline had strived, and succeeded, to break into tabloid journalism. Caroline wondered what she would make of this particular project. Well, at least the surroundings were genteel enough.

"Could I have a quick look around, now? I've got to work tomorrow, and I would just love to soak up a bit of the atmosphere while I'm here. If you have time, of course."

She offered up another prayer, this time vowing to lose three stone. Judith Allsopp delivered:

"I am very busy today, but I do have half an hour to spare after I file my daily report. We have just eight guests at the moment, and two are long-stay, so it won't take long. Doctor Brewster, who you met on the way up here, has been treating one old gentleman for bronchitis. He is recovering nicely, which is good news. I'm sure the change of air does them all the world of good, even at this time of year."

"We have a staff of four on duty at all times, so this operation is not very cost-effective in winter. Between you and me, I do worry that Wilkinsons will close us down one day and simply use the house as an office with residential facilities for current staff. They test a lot of their animal feeds at the farm behind the house, so it would make sense. It's a shame, but there it is. I could always go back to working for the public sector, although the money isn't very good in hospital administrative jobs, despite what people think. I ran two care homes for one local authority for ten years and got paid a pittance. Both places were a disgrace, as well. I never received enough money even for essential repairs, and I had to employ foreign staff, low-paid of course. At least here I feel that the residents are having a good time and eating well."

Caroline was astonished. For some reason, this hard-faced woman was opening up to her and feeding her information. She decided to use an old journalistic trick: sharing grumbles about employers was always a good way to establish a bond with someone you wanted to trust you. Once hooked, they invariably revealed more than they realised.

"It's the same in journalism," she said, nodding sympathetically. "I work freelance, and write travel stuff now, but when I was on a top paper they simply wouldn't pay me a decent salary, although I worked all the hours God gave. I asked for a rise, but they refused to cough up. Everyone thought I was earning vast amounts, but I was struggling along on a junior reporter's salary. Freelancing is tough, but at least you don't have to deal with money-grabbing overpaid executives. They make me sick. Do Wilkinsons expect you to cater for the people working at the farm as well as your elderly residents?"

"No, but we do occasionally put up special guests, usually foreign clients who want to see round the farm. They keep themselves to themselves, though. Their rooms are at the back of the house." She paused, and stood up, letting her hands fall to her sides, releasing her spectacles which lay, glinting, on her chest. For the first time, she smiled, revealing large, horsey front teeth.

"Make yourself comfortable here, dear and I will be back to show you round in about 30 minutes. I'll get the tea things removed, and you can relax. It's good to talk to someone new, believe me! "

Caroline sensed that Judith Allsopp could become a useful ally. Despite her starchy appearance, she seemed to genuinely care for the people staying at Heaven's Rest.

Now, all Caroline needed to do was to get a good look around, and try and work out something about the layout of the farm, and any other buildings at the back of the house. Maybe Judith's office contained some kind of plan of the whole area. She decided to wait for 15 minutes, then take a walk around. She could always pretend she was trying to find the loo.

After ten minutes spent trying to concentrate on a two year old copy of Lakeland Life, Caroline put on her still-damp boots, picked up her ruckstack and walked out of the room into the large, square hall. The two old ladies in the corner were now dozing in their chairs, and didn't notice her movements. The high ceilinged, black and white tiled hall was empty, but the door facing the lounge was open, and she could just make out what appeared to be a large dining room. At the back of the hall, on the right hand side was a wide staircase partly covered by a shabby green carpet. She walked swiftly across the tiled floor, and up the stairs.

As she turned the corner towards the the large open first floor landing, she nearly jumped out of her skin when a tall walnut grandfather clock against the opposite wall emitted six ear-blasting "bongs". She felt a pang of sympathy for the old dears who were trying to rest. Presumably, though, they were deaf as posts and wouldn't be disturbed.

Two corridors stretched either side of the landing, papered with the same red flocked design as the lounge and punctuated with solid doors, painted cream and numbered in blue plastic. The door next to the clock had a curling yellow cardboard sign tacked to it, with the words "Director of Care" printed in large black type capital letters. The door was very slightly ajar.

Caroline knocked, and pushed it open. Judith Allsopp was sitting at a large desk, her glasses now resting on her nose, speaking into her mobile phone. On the desk were a small computer terminal and keyboards, and a stack of papers and files. She looked up at Caroline, obviously irritated to be interrupted, said "I will call you back later, John." and placed the phone on her desk.

"I'm so sorry. Can you direct me to the loo, please?" Caroline said, apologetically, hovering on the threshhold of the room. "I'm a bit desperate I'm afraid, and there didn't seem to be a cloakroom downstairs." As she spoke, she tried to scan the small office It was at the front of the house, with two windows: one bay, one long and high, overlooking the road, and presumably the Lake as well. There was a row of grey metal filing cabinets on the left hand wall, with a big plan of the building and surrounding area, including various blocks and outbuildings, hanging above it. She could see that some of the rooms in the main house had a yellow label drawing-pinned onto them with the name of the current occupant printed in blue felt-tip pen.

Caroline's heart drummed in her chest, and seemed to perform a double somersault. What she had to do now was to photograph the plan. She promised herself a large, creamy lamb korma, mushroom fried rice and a garlic naan at Westover's one and only Indian Restaurant if she could just entice Judith Allsopp away from the room long enough to take a snap. The diet could start tomorrow.

Judith Allsopp's face softened, and she smiled." I should have told you. The visitors' cloakroom is right at the back of the entrance hall, underneath the staircase. "I'll be down in just a moment.."

"Thanks. Sorry to have disturbed you. I suppose you email your report. Computers don't seem to have cut down the amount of paperwork we all need, do they? It's so stupid."

She turned and went out, closing the door behind her. This was going to be a challenge. Cloakrooms seemed to be the places where she did most of her strategic thinking these days. Oh well, they were as good as anywhere. She made her way downstairs.

****

The plan she concocted in the antiquated downstairs loo was full of cracks, rather like the ancient wash hand basin where she was rinsing her hands.

The only thing she could think of to do was to go for "distraction " technique once again. While Judith Allsopp was showing her around the upper floors of Heaven's Rest, she would pretend that she could hear some kind of commotion going on in the lounge downstairs. A loud thump, like someone falling over, for instance. It would take some time for Judith to investigate and, with the Director of Care suitably occupied, Caroline could pop into the office and take a snap of the plan on the wall. Easy, peasy.

Except of course that Judith might lock her office door before showing Caroline around. If she swallowed the bit about the commotion, she might easily contact another member of staff to investigate. However, short of actually mugging the woman, Caroline couldn't think of any other way to distract her for long enough to get the picture taken. It would just have to work. She wrapped her small digital camera in a handkerchief and put it into her trouser pocket before emerging from the toilet.

As she sat in the lounge waiting for her guided tour, Caroline glanced at the two women who were still dozing in their cosy corner. She hoped, fervently, that they wouldn't decide to go up to their rooms. With no-one actually in the lounge, it would be hard to convince Judith Allsopp that there had been some kind of accident.

A few minutes later, Judith strode briskly into the lounge, glasses once again dangling around her neck:

"Right, Caroline. Let's start at the top of the building and work our way down. It's on three floors, as you've probably noticed. I'll show you one of the empty rooms, and you'll see how comfortable they are. No wonder your Aunt enjoyed staying here. The second floor has a large conservatory which looks out over the lake. The view is absolutely spectacular during the summer, although we don't use it much in winter because of the heating costs."

She led the way back upstairs, to the first floor landing. The door of her office was now closed, and Caroline sent up her third prayer of the day: " Dear God, I'll forgo the garlic naan, if the door is unlocked. Please..."

The third floor consisted of eight large bedrooms, a linen room and small kitchen, all connected by a long corridor. While being shown around, Caroline made all the correct, complimentary comments, but her heart was fluttering and her palms sweaty. She knew that she would have to make her pitch when they went down to the conservatory on the second floor.

The huge room had a glass roof which projected out over a balcony area. Caroline could see that it would be a marvellous place to sit, with its potted palms, basket chairs, and airy atmosphere. She imagined her fictitious aunt reading, or doing some embroidery while gazing out at the Lake and surrounding fells. She almost believed her own colourful story. She walked forward, kicking the side of a large brass jardiniere containing a tall ficus plant.

"What the hell was that?" she said.

"What was what?" replied Judith Allsopp.

"A noise downstairs, like somone falling out of a chair."

"I didn't hear anything except your boot making contact with the flower holder, " said Judith. "Are you sure?"

"Certain", said Caroline. "I do hope one of the old ladies sitting there hasn't taken a tumble."

"Wait here, " said Judith Allsopp. "I'd better take a look." She walked quickly out of the room, her neat black high-heeled shoes tip-tapping on the wooden floor.

With, at best, about one minute to get her picture, Caroline counted twenty, then half-ran out onto the landing, and down to the first floor. She tried the office door, and it was open. She went in, closing it gently behind her, removed the camera from her pocket, pointed it at the notice above the wall, and took three flash pictures. She opened the door and ran back upstairs. The whole operation took no more than 30 seconds.

When Judith Allsopp returned to the conservatory, Caroline was sitting in a basket chair looking out at the blackness. Her face was pale, and there were tears running down her cheeks. They hadn't been difficult to produce. Her covert actions, and dashing down and back up the flight of stairs, had reduced her to a state of emotional and physical exhaustion. She made a mental note to order the garlic naan at the Indian Restaurant after all. God would understand.

"I can almost imagine Aunt Hilda is with me, " she said, in a choked voice. "I'm sorry. I feel a bit overcome by this. Were the old ladies all right? "

"Nothing to worry about. The noise you heard must have been the central heating. It makes a racket every so often. The two guests were just about ready to go back to their rooms. They are quite sprightly, but I took them along to the lift. I do hope this little tour has helped with your grief, dear. Come down now and have another cup of tea while I call you a taxi. "

****

Chapter Twenty

London: Reuters. *The Government today issued new guidelines for doctors treating elderly, terminally ill and morbidly obese patients. In order to avoid bankrupting the NHS, these patients are not to be resuscitated if they do not respond to treatment within a reasonable time. The "cut off" point for non-resuscitation is up to the discretion of the patient's doctor, but medical bodies such as the BMA have been warned that there would be targets set for each hospital. Moveover, it will no longer be possible to keep coma patients on life-support systems.*

As the population is aging, and seven out of ten people are classified as overweight or obese, these guidelines are expected to raise fierce opposition. Unveiling the new proposals, Junior Health Minister Elizabeth Collins said: "This is a sensible measure which will free up more hospital beds for those able to benefit from medical care."

"I suppose she means people like her: young, strong and selfish". There was more than a hint of bitterness in Brian's voice as he spoke out loud. He was sitting alone in the lecturers' common room during his afternoon break, reading the paper. No one else was around to hear his comments, but he was sure that most of his colleagues would agree with him. The next step towards wiping out a good chunk of the population would be legalising euthanasia, which a Government Select Committee was already looking into. Obesity was increasing rapidly, thanks to the policy of introducing GE203 into foods. In ten years' time people would soon be lucky to live past the age of 60.

"Well, at least it will solve the question of what to do about finding enough money for pensions," Brian muttered, folding the paper. His mobile phone rang.

"It's Caroline. I'm driving down to see you tonight. Get in touch with Susan and tell her to arrange to take some time off next week. Two days should do it. The job is on."

Before Brian could reply, the phone went dead.

The excitement in Caroline's voice was a giveaway: she must have found out how to break into Heaven's Rest. From now on, the three of them were going to need a lot of luck, and courage.

Not for the first time, Brian wondered if he would come out of this nightmare alive. The man who had been following him in London had not reappeared but it was difficult to tell whether there was someone monitoring his movements at the university; students came and went and there were so many of them, of every nationality, that it was impossible to be certain if he was under surveillance or not. There were certainly at least fifty Chinese students at his college: any, or indeed several of them, could working for the Changjia Corporation.

After his final lecture of the day, Brian walked back to his rented flat, looking nervously over his shoulder from time to time during the half-hour journey. Once safely inside the flat, he went over every inch of the place looking for any sign of bugging devices. Not that he had much idea of what he should be looking for. His total sum of knowledge about such matters had been gleaned from the occasional film or television programme. The incident of the rats was no fantasy, however. He decided that he would have to meet Caroline somewhere different.

****

"At this rate, I will soon be the size of a house. I had a big Indian blow-out in Westover last night, and now you're expecting me to eat another one." Caroline had removed her raincoat, and was sitting on the grubby green velvet bench-seat facing Brian, uncomfortable on a hard wooden chair. The restaurant was long and narrow, and, thankfully, apart from Brian and Caroline, it was empty. Their table was in a corner, away from the street.

"I had no choice, Caroline. It's safer here than at my flat. Mondays are quiet, and we should be undisturbed. The kitchen is right down the end of a corridor, so once we've ordered we can talk properly. If you're really worried about your weight, which I sometimes doubt, order the Chicken Shaslik and plain boiled rice."

Brian was irritable, and in no mood to be side-tracked by Caroline's fixation with her size. He had worked with many people who were too ill or too ignorant to control their weight, and was not about to be sympathetic to the bleatings of an intelligent woman who could easily lose a stone or so if she controlled her excesses. She had already told him about her trip to Heaven's Rest, making it sound like a story from a kids' adventure novel. Caroline's habit of milking every event for maximum drama was beginning to get on his nerves.

"OK Professor, point taken," Caroline looked crestfallen. "But, I really do want to slim down, you know. It's bloody hard when you are a manic, driven, sex-starved, comfort-eating woman like me. Have some sympathy, please."

They lapsed into an uncomfortable silence until the waiter came to take their orders. After the food arrived (Chicken Shaslik for Caroline, a Prawn Vindaloo for Brian with plain boiled rice and a side-salad), Caroline delved into her leather bag and produced an A4 size piece of paper. She moved the dishes of food to one side, and spead the plan on the white tablecloth.

"I had this plan scanned and printed from a photograph I took at Heaven's Rest. It's brilliant, though I say it myself. You can see the main building, the farm where I gather that Wilkinson's keep their pigs for testing the animal feed, and a couple of other buildings behind the main farmhouse. I would bet my life on those buildings being the site where the foods for human consumption are contaminated with GE203. Your pal Gareth never got to see that side of the business, poor man.

"According to the scale of the plan, the two buildings must be about 30 metres square. They are very neat looking, in contrast with the farmhouse which is all angles, so I reckon they are modern, like a couple of rectangular warehouses. There are two doors marked on the first building, three on the second, and, as you can see, there appears to be a fence around the whole perimeter of the farm and the two buildings.

"This, I suppose, could be electrified. There is one gate marked, right at the back of the complex, opening onto a narrow road which appears to run almost parallel to the one I used, with an irregular strip of unmarked land in between the two. I seem to recall a fairly high hill behind the wall bordering the road I walked up, so it's probably a grassy fell, quite open and bleak. Not much cover for covert operations, I'm afraid."

Brian studied the plan carefully. "The other side of the road could be a better approach route. It might be wooded, you never know. So, supposing that we reach the fence, what do you propose that we do to gain entry? Being electrocuted is bad enough, but there might be guards or guard dogs."

"I'm pretty sure there are no dogs. On the night I was there, I didn't hear any dogs barking at all, and the inmates of Heaven's Rest wouldn't be happy if there were dogs around. I remember newspaper stories of cases where animal rights protesters have successfully claimed damages from companies who set dogs on them, so I would imagine that the security is electronic; close circuit TV, infra-red cameras, that kind of thing. Unless we had someone on side who knew exactly how to de-activate electronic surveillance we would be finished straight away. The warden woman, Judith, is disatisfied with her job, but I don't think she could be bought, even if we had the money to do it.

"The best plan is to try and con our way in again, this time as some kind of client. What about using Susan? She works for a company which puts GE203 into their products. Once she gets into the complex, maybe she could just walk into a warehouse and fool whoever's in charge into believing that she's been sent by her company to check out production methods. After all, they are big players, and are just about to launch a new range of kiddies' foods which contain the Protin-Foods meat substitute, doctored with GE203.

"As we know, Protin-Foods sent their development scientist up there with a consignment of their product. Perhaps Susan could have samples of the new Kenley and Palmer range with her, and just wing it somehow. We will need photographs, and copies of the client list, but the fact that she is working in the food trade and is able to give full details of her experience at the plant will lend authenticity to the story and pictures we give to the consumer journal.

"Susan will lose her job of course, but she has taken that into account, and, after all, we have both already lost ours. I know it sounds weak but what do you think?"

Brian was silent for a moment. His feelings for Susan were so new and intense that the thought of her being put at risk was almost unbearable. He had done a lot of soul-searching since their last meeting. His years of selfishness and weakness couldn't be wiped out but with her help he knew he could change into a better person. The process had already begun. Scientific training might have turned him into a cold, calculating human being who could only evaluate a problem according to the sum of knowledge available. Luckily, the warmth and freedom of his upbringing had left him with a valuable legacy: imagination.

So, while calculating, quite coldly, what he had to do to keep Susan, he was haunted by a grim picture of the affect that his possible future actions might have on both of them. Losing her was unthinkable. Therefore, casual flings were out of the question, and his priorities were now absolutely certain. The three people who mattered most in his life were his children, and Susan. He also had to help expose this appalling food scandal and help to bring to account those responsible. Nothing else, including his own safety, was important.

"It could be very dangerous for Susan. I should do it myself, " he said. "The problem is that I am now known to Changhia's people, and the staff who run the Heaven's Rest set-up have probably been briefed about me. You have already been warned off indirectly by your editor, and are also known to people up at the house.

" Susan is the only one of the three of us who hasn't yet been targeted by Changjia, either directly or indirectly, but, for all we know, she may also be on their suspect list. We will have to think this through very carefully. I've asked Susan to come up to Liverpool tomorrow. She is going to plead sickness for a couple of days. Book into a hotel tonight, Caroline, and we will have another meeting when Susan arrives. Let's sleep on it."

****

Susan was thin and pale, and was suffering from sore throat and a persistant cough which just wouldn't go away. She knew full well that her resistance to infection was low for the very good reason that she was eating poorly. Her appetite seemed to have disappeared, and she now had to force herself to sit down to a nutritious supper. She often threw away more organically grown vegetables and omega-three rich oily fish than she actually consumed.

The first couple of weeks at her new job had been very difficult: the daily commute (by car, as her single attempt at using public transport had proved to be far too time-consuming), the pressure to complete her work quickly, and the draining effect of her surroundings were all hard to cope with. After years of trying to help people beat their diet problems, she did not feel comfortable working on a project which she knew could harm children's health. Memories of the meeting she had with Daryl O'Brien and his parents kept popping into her head. Had he lived, the poor child would probably have been given the very products she was helping to make. His mother had always been influenced by TV advertisements for processed, brightly packaged foods laden with additives, despite Susan's advice to serve simple, fresh meals.

She decided to find a cab at Lime Street Station, Liverpool, and go directly to Brian's flat. She had intended to phone him first, but it was too cold to hang about. The wet weather had eased a bit, but there was still a chill, damp wind, and the dull lamps outside the station were reflected in the dark pools of water which sloshed around in the gutter by the taxi stand. As each vehicle approached, a spray of filthy liquid shot up into the air, and the thirty or so waiting passengers were forced to stand well back from the road.

As Susan pulled her black raincoat more tightly around her legs, she realised that she was facing a nightmarish couple of days. Caroline had insisted that she brought samples of all the children's foods she was working on, hinting that she would need them when the three friends tried to get some concrete evidence together about the food-tampering scam. God knows what would happen.

Then there was the problem of Brian: his declaration of intent had sounded plausible, and she wanted to believe him. It was probably too early to even think about their future together, if indeed it was even remotely possible to plan such a thing, yet she couldn't help imagining what it might be like to share his life. He was the one man who had touched her heart, and her soul. She could not envisage living without being able to talk to him, be with him.

At last, she reached the head of the queue, and, somehow, managed to cram her large suitcase into the next cab. It was fitted with a steel grille between the driver's and passengers' seats, to stop drunks and muggers from attacking the poor man. The effect on the passenger once the door slammed shut was rather like being locked in a padded cell, which just about summed up Susan's own situation. There was no escape from her feelings: Brian, with all his faults, was the love of her life.

"Where to, love? Can't hang about long. You're my last fare. "When Susan gave the cabby her destination, she heard him say "fuck it!" softly, but he didn't refuse to take her. Things are looking up, she thought.

****

Caroline had exchanged her four-by-four hire car for a sleek silver Mercedes saloon; the type that food companies issue to middle management, and Susan drove this flashy vehicle up to the main entrance of Heaven's Rest, while mentally rehearsing her cover story.

She was now Susan Dearing, Product Manager of the baby and junior foods division of Kenley and Palmer, and had come to the Lake District to see the establishment which was producing one of the ingredients for her new line of "Activity Kids" ready-meals. She had a case containing samples of her products with her, a business card, and the right clothes for the job: straight black skirt, cropped cream jacket, black roll-necked sweater, boots, and black raincoat.

Persuading Susan to take on this difficult and probably dangerous role had been easy. She was up for it, provided Caroline and Brian waited for her outside the back gate of the complex.

If, and it was a big "if", she managed to get into the building where the GE203 was being put into the Protin-Foods basic product, and could also find a list of customers who used this vegetable based protein substitute, and then copy it, she would have to make a quick getaway. Hopefully, she would be able to exit via the rest home, but if it was necessary, or possible, to go out the back way, she wanted to be sure there would be a car there.

Stage one was successful.

Judith Allsopp looked surprised to see her, but glanced past her at the impressive car, checked her up and down, and swallowed her story. She ushered her across the chequered ground floor of the rest home to the large double back door.

The Director of Care then told Susan to wait by the door while she telephoned the experimental food plant and made contact with the operational staff. Susan stood, clutching her black briefcase tightly, her heart pounding, while the stern-faced woman went upstairs to her office.

Judith returned after a couple of minutes, looking puzzled:

"They said they were not expecting you, so it looks as though someone in your office has their wires crossed. But Julian Churcher, who is the operational manager, and on duty today, is coming up in a Range Rover to collect you and take you to the experimental and production part of the complex. No doubt, you can sort out the muddle between you. He'll be up here directly. Just wait. I've got to go back to check on some of my clients. Nice to meet you." She turned, and went back upstairs.

After ten minutes or so, one of the double doors opened, and a man appeared. Susan's palms were sweating, and she shifted her briefcase into her left hand, and held out her right, glad that she hadn't removed her black leather gloves.

Julian Churcher was a short, dour-looking, toughie of about forty five with a bald head and beer gut. He was wearing a padded black jacket over a roll-neck sweater and baggy jeans, an outfit which gave him the air of an off-duty night club bouncer. He eyed Susan up and down as if she was a prime piece of fillet steak, and shook her hand briefly.

" Hello there. Well, I haven't got anything in the diary about anyone coming up from Kenley and Palmer, but you look a lot more attractive than some of the men who hold down the top jobs in the food industry. I'm just a humble technician so you can imagine how snotty some of them can be.

" Your company is, indirectly, one of our best customers, so I suppose I'd better lay out the red carpet. Sorry, the passion wagon is a bit muddy, but we have to drive around the piggery before we get to the food section. Don't worry, everything's spotless once we get there. You'll have to get out of those smart clothes and put on sterile gear before we look round, but the plant is heated, so you won't feel too chilly when you strip down to your Janet Reger undies. You look like the kind of woman who wears silk next to her skin."

His leering grin made Susan wonder whether she was likely to be raped, then turned into pig food. The prospect of spending even a couple of hours in the company of this sexist pratt was daunting. The word "swine" came to mind.

"Don't worry, I am used to wearing industrial whites at work," she said coolly. "I look forward to seeing the plant. We are investing heavily in this new range of foods, and I want to be sure that the right quantities of each additive goes into the products. The additive you put in here is useful, but we can make the foods without it if necessary."

After a bumpy journey around a potholed perimeter road which skirted several pens of squealing pigs, a farmhouse, and a couple of old, tumbledown barns, Julian pulled the Range Rover over onto the concrete forecourt of a large rectangular, single story concrete and steel warehouse. It appeared to have three doors. Another, similar building was directly opposite.

Julian waddled over to the central door, a large steel affair, tapped a code onto a security panel, and pushed it open. Inside, he repeated the procedure on an inside door, and led Susan through a narrow lobby into a dimly lit corridor.

"I'll go first. Watch out for the rats!" When he saw the look of horror on Susan's face, he threw back his head and roared with laughter, his vast paunch heaving up and down with the effort involved. "Don't worry, love, I'm only kidding. The animal research is all done in a lab elsewhere and on the pig farm. The sows and their litters are treated royally, believe me.

" We just add the goodies to the food here - for pigs and humans. You'll find it's a boring place, but as far as quality control goes we're the best. Our machinery is a made in the Far East using the latest technology. Our computers, storage vats, injection valves, packaging are all top of the range."

"There are two changing rooms, here, one each for women and for men. Although, as I told you, we don't show many women around the plant. Take everything off except your underwear, put on the whites, then go through the double doors you will see leading from the changing room into the plant itself. They're easy to operate, just like the kind you get at banks. I'm sure you have the same sort at your factory? You can bring your briefcase and valuables with you, but switch off your mobile phone if you don't mind. I will meet you through the other side. OK?"

He turned and disappeared through a door marked "Male Staff only".

The female changing room was small, icy cold and smelt of disinfectant. There were six sets of white overalls and disposable hairnets in sterile packs, stacked on a chair and a couple of coat hangers hung on a rail which ran down one side of the room. Six pairs of white mule shoes, also in in plastic bags, were piled on the floor. Judging by the small number of outfits for women, they were obviously not expecting many female visitors. No wonder Julian was so excited by the prospect of showing her around.

Shivering, Susan took off her raincoat, and then stripped down to her white lace bra and pants. As she struggled into the baggy overalls and mules and tucked her hair into a net, she glanced down at her thin legs, and bony hips. She must have shed at least half a stone since leaving East Central Hospital. The part of her brain that still clung to her old, anorexic habits kicked in and, just for a split second, she felt quite pleased about her weight loss. Then, common sense took over, and she decided that her body wasn't becoming "lovely and slim." It was becoming emaciated and ugly.

She put the worrying thought out of her head, and opened her briefcase. Inside were the sample packs of the "Activity Kids" range, a small camera, and tape recorder, both supplied by Caroline. She put the camera into a side pocket of the case, out of view, and snapped it shut. She switched on the tape recorder, and tied it around her waist with the piece of tape she had brought with her. The folds of the baggy overalls concealed the slim recorder perfectly.

****

"You look charming, Miss Dearing, like a sexy nurse."

Julian Churcher was waiting in the large white-walled room beyond the double doors. It was about 20 metres square, and lit with fluorescent panels in the ceiling, reflected in six gleaming steel vats which were against the far wall connected by thick copper tubing. There was a faint buzzing noise, as if a pump was being used.

Julian stood in the centre of the room, leaning against a steel counter stacked with boxes. In his white overalls, he looked like a beached whale. His face glowed bright red, and he was breathing heavily; each breath ended in a high-pitched wheezing sound, clearly audible above the noise of the pump.

Susan hoped that this was due to the physical exertion involved in changing from his outdoor gear, and not excitement at the prospect of jumping his visitor. He could easily, she conjectured, have been drinking. There was no smell of beer, but it was possible that he had a taste for vodka or tequila. It must be very lonely looking after this operation, with no other staff to talk to. She hadn't expected this at all: her mission to find evidence was becoming more dangerous by the minute.

If she was going to find records of some kind, and photograph them, she would have to distract Julian somehow. A plan formulated in her mind: it was very, very risky, but it might just work.

"How many staff do you employ here Mr. Churcher?" she asked, as she walked towards him and placed her case on the counter. She tried to sound as casual as possible.

Julian leared. "Sorry, love: it's just thee and me today. We have two assistants who come in to load foodstuffs, such as the Protin-Foods product you use in your range, into the vat over there. the additives go into the smaller vat in the middle, and are piped into the bigger one. Then it is mixed well, and is pumped into the third vat, over there, and then pushed down the covered shaft over there into large containers, also made from stainless steel, which are sealed automatically on that machine." He indicated a large pulley and ramp, covered with dials and handles, currently idle.

"Everything is fully automated until a batch is ready and then it is either collected by the company concerned or we arrange to have it shipped out by lorry. We do, of course, keep all the products totally separate, and there is a day-long cleaning process used between each batch. It wouldn't do to find a bit of pig food in your low-fat curry would it?"

Susan attempted a girlish giggle, and launched into a speech she had prepared during the drive up to Heaven's Rest:

"What do you know about the additive you put into the food here? I gather from my colleagues at Kenley and Palmer that it is marvellous stuff, and does people, and pigs, a power of good. Functional foods are so popular these days. Without added vitamins and minerals in cereals and bread, most people would go short of even the most basic nutritional requirements because they just won't eat fresh foods.

" It's great that we can add plant stanols to food to lower cholesterol. I am very excited about working on these. Here, have a look at the range." She opened the suitcase and took out three meals in bright "Activity Kids" wrappers: burgers with mash and carrots, spaghetti Bolognese with cheese sauce and lamb cutlets with chips.

"Kids will love these, and their parents will be thrilled that they are getting all the right nutrients. The range is a sure-fire winner."

Julian's face was still red. His breathing was more regular, but he looked terrible. His forehead, and chin were covered in sweat, his lower lip glistened with saliva and his podgy fingers in their white latex gloves looked like a pile of *Boudins Blanc* in the window of a French *charcuterie*. Clumsily, he picked up the pack containing the lamb and chips meal, and turned it over.

"You're a nice girl, but naive. Look at the list of additives in this muck. There are, oh, about twenty five of them, and the lamb comes right down at the bottom of the list, which means that there is only a small amount of meat protein. So much for building strong little bodies. You'll notice that your favourite healthy ingredient, the Protin-Foods meat substitute is in there, and it has had the GE203 added to it - right here in this room, as it happens."

"Well Miss Dearing, I have to inform you, strictly off the record, of course that GE203 isn't just a natural, herbal compound containing vital minerals which are good for people and pigs, it is also an appetite stimulant. The effect is cumulative: the more you eat, the more you want. It comes here from China, and is refined in a university lab. I'm afraid you are being duped by your bosses at Kenley and Palmer. They are simply trying to make their customers eat more and more. Oh, and is it legal? You might also be interested to know that we are very popular with the Government here. Apparently, they are very happy to encourage people to eat more and die young."

As she listened to this tirade, Susan decided that Julian definitely was drunk. His voice had changed, become thicker, and slurred. She hoped to God that the tape recorder was working properly and picking up everything he said. She glanced round for an escape route in case he became violent, and noticed, for the first time, that there was a metal door in the wall, next to the pulley and ramp Julian which had pointed out earlier.

"You are joking, of course," she said tartly. "I was told that GE203 was an additive approved by the Food and Drug Administration in the US, and by our own people. It is a mineral supplement that helps give the non-animal protein more food value, adding amino acids and other nutrients that would otherwise be missing in a vegetable product. It's ridiculous to suggest that the Government are trying to fatten people up. What nonsense."

Julian threw the ready meal pack down on on the table, and lurched towards her, placing both hands heavily on her shoulders.

"Believe me, you bitch. I don't tell lies. You're the first person who's come up here who didn't know the score. You must be a spy of some kind. I was a stupid idiot to let you in."

He pressed her backwards, so her hips were rammed up against the metal counter. She could feel and smell his hot, rancid breath on her face. "Well, little lady, don't think you're going to get out of here in one piece without paying the appropriate price. I've fancied you from the moment I saw you on the CCTV camera before I picked you up in the wagon. If you are nice to me now, I might let you get out alive. The Chinese arm of this operation can then send someone to finish you off at their leisure."

Pushing her shoulders down, so she was forced to lean back onto the counter or fall over, he threw himself against her. She ducked her head forwards, and his slobbery mouth made contact with her forehead. Summoning up all her strength, she brought up her knee hard against his crotch and pushed as strongly as she could. He yelled, let go of her shoulders, and fell backwards, his legs buckling.

His head struck the concrete floor with a loud crack. Expecting him to get up, she reached backwards and grabbed her black briefcase, wrenching her arm in the process. Somehow, despite the pain, she heaved it up, ready for the next bout.

It never came. Blood was pumping from a two inch gash on Julian's head and he was clutching his chest and moaning with pain.

"Help me, you cow. My fuckin' ticker is packing up. Get an ambulance, quickly. There's a land line in the office over there. Use that. Mobiles are useless round here." His voice tailed off, his face turned ashen, and his eyes began to roll back in his head. As spasms of pain wracked his body, his left leg and arm twitched repeatedly.

Susan had seen enough heart attack cases in the ER department of East Central Hospital to recognise a massive myocardial infarction when she saw one. Unless Julian received medical attention quickly, he was dead meat. The nasty crack on his skull wouldn't kill him, but his morbidly obese body probably would.

Still clutching the case, she ran to the office door, pulled it open, snatching off her protective headgear as she did so. The room was small and stark, just a single desk with a telephone, and a flat-screened PC, mouse, printer and closed circuit TV screen, which, thankfully was switched off. Probably, Julian had already decided to make sexual advances to Susan and didn't relish the idea of being recorded in action. What a bastard.

Quickly, she threw the case onto the desk, opened it and took out the digital camera, then switched on the computer, which booted up rapidly. A clutch of icons appeared on the swirly blue and green screen. Now, all she had to do was find a client list of some kind, and take photographs, or, better still, a print -out.

One of the icons was marked "Documents." She clicked onto it , and a list of files flashed into view. She ignored one marked "Animal Food Consignments, January 2008," and opened " Retail Consignments, January, 2008". A large chart appeared on the screen. It was headed, "Protin-Foods Protein Substitute with Added GE203: Goods Despatched"

Underneath, was a chart listing the client and quantity of product sent out. As Susan skimmed down the column marked "Client", she felt sick with excitement, and relief. It contained seven names, in alphabetical order: Allardyce Superstores, Associated Dairy Products, FizzCo UK, Kenley and Palmer, Preswick Foods, Underhills Fast Foods. Rapidly, she pressed the "print" button. The printer clicked and whirred, and a print out of the chart appeared. She ripped off the piece of paper, folded it and put it into her case, then took out her camera. A few shots of the office, and the production line would be a good idea, to complete her evidence. She finished her work, switched off the computer, then made her way back to the production centre.

Julian Churcher was now lying, immobile, in an untidy, slumped, semi-foetal position. Susan fought back her instinctive urge to go and check whether he was alive or dead. Instead, she took photographs, dozens of them: the warehouse machinery, loading bay, stainless steel ramps and pulleys. She snapped two of the boxes on the counter where Julian had been standing. Both bore the Protin-Foods logo. It was irritating that there was no evidence of the food additive around: no vats with "GE203" stamped on them. However, she did have the tape recording of Julian's outburst. It would have to do.

Getting out of the complex was her next problem. Susan decided not to try and connect with Brian and Caroline in their waiting car. God knows what infra red or other security devices there might be along the back perimeter fence. It was best to play it cool, and go out the way she had come in - through the front door of Heaven's Rest.

After changing back into her clothes, and checking that the recorder had done its job (it had, thank God), she set off to walk the half mile or so back to the rest home. If she met anyone on the way out, she would somehow bluff her way through.

The wind was now blowing strongly, and it was pitch dark. The gloom was broken only by a very weak light from the lamp above the door. Susan set off, round the perimeter track, skirting the second warehouse. The rear of the farm buildings had to be nearby, although it was impossible to see very much. Some dim lights glowed in the distance, which must, Susan decided, be the windows at the back of the rest home.

The mud was now oozing over her boots, and her fashionable long black mackintosh was not very effective at keeping the wind out, which was lashing her hair and face, although it did help her to blend into the dark landscape. As she approached the first barn, she could just make out a large pen behind it. Cautiously, she stepped off the track, and walked carefully alongside the barn, as close to the crumbling brick wall as possible.

"Fat little sods can hardly walk. You've given the blighters an overdose, Dave."

"They love the stuff, mate, you can't stop them from eating it.

Anyway, this lot's due for the chop tomorrow. Put them out of their misery. Lock up now, and we'll get some tea. The sow's OK. She's got her brood for one more night. Sweet dreams, old girl. Your babies will be off to the abattoir tomorrow, and then we'll get you a good-looking bloke to put you in the family way again. Lovely life, eh?"

Susan froze. The two men were only fifty yards away. She stood, listening to her own heart pounding, for two or three minutes, while they finished locking up the pigs, and moved off. It seemed like two or three hours.

Once she was sure they had gone, she continued towards the light. When she finally reached the back door of Heaven's Rest, she allowed herself a brief pause. It would not do to walk through the house looking filthy. She pulled a handkerchief out of her pocket, and wiped the mud off her boots, dragged her fingers through her windswept hair, and straightened her coat.

She rang the bell and waited. Judith Allsopp appeared, looking harrassed. "We've had a terrible afternoon, I'm afraid. One of our old ladies was taken ill suddenly. I would love to offer you a cup of tea, but the doctor is here. Do you mind if I just see you out?"

"Not at all," said Susan, smiling sympathetically. "I've had a very interesting afternoon. Mr. Churcher has just driven back to his office. I must say, he doesn't look very well. Carrying a lot of excess weight, I'm afraid."

Judith Allsopp led her quickly across the chequered hallway, and opened the front door. "Have a good journey home. I'm glad you found the visit worthwhile."

****

Chapter Twenty One

British Consumer Journal: *Press Release: April, 2009 issue. "Don't Buy These Foods." Potentially harmful additive found in dozens of popular ready-meals and snacks. This story is strictly embargoed until 00.01am, Monday March 31st, 2009 For interviews with Dr. Brian Donovan, Head of Nutrition and Dietetics, Central University, Liverpool or Mary Hawkhurst, Editor of the British Consumer Journal, telephone 00 -44.(0)207 919 4500 or email Britishconsumerjournal@telcom.uk.*

"It looks good, very good, but I reckon we will all have to leave the country when the Press Release is issued on Friday." Caroline was sitting in one of the chintz-covered armchairs in Brian's Liverpool flat, holding a proof copy of the April, 2009, edition of the British Consumer Journal in one hand, and a triangular slab of cheese-topped pizza in the other. Her pink-painted lips were glistening with grease from the pizza, and her eyes shone with excitement behind her large, black-rimmed glasses. She put the rapidly cooling pizza down onto the flat cardboard carton on her lap and examined the four page article.

It contained photographs of all the products that had been "doctored" with GE203 at Heaven's Rest, pictures of the plant itself, a detailed appraisal of the dangerous properties of GE203, their possible long-term effects, and an interview with Brian describing, in detail, how the substance had come into the country, been tested at the university, and put into foods.

The conclusion at the bottom of the piece was that twenty two products, which all contained the substance, should be withdrawn from supermarket shelves at once. Among them: the three ready-meals which originally alerted Susan to the possibilty of some kind of weight-enhancing ingredient, and the FizzCo" Super Snacks "breakfast bars. The "Activity Kids" range by Kenley and Palmer, were also mentioned, although the article pointed out that they were not yet on the market.

Caroline closed the Journal carefully, and licked her fingers. She looked at the greasy slab of pizza on her lap, and decided against finishing it. She leaned over with difficulty, and placed the carton carefully on the worn Indian carpet.

"I'm only joking of course. We will have to be very careful, though. When the shit hits the fan, all three of us will be in demand, and therefore more exposed and vulnerable. I don't suppose the Changjia Corporation will be very happy about this. You will be running around like a blue arsed fly, from TV studio to TV studio, Brian. Can you cope with all this pressure?"

Brian looked like a man who would force himself to cope, somehow. Like Ashley Wilkes in *Gone with the Wind*, he seemed to be overtaken by some kind of moral dilemma, while, at the same time, trying to be brave.

Caroline wondered, not for the first time, what Susan actually saw in him. Right now, he was about as inspirational as a wet fish. He was sorting through students' exam papers at his desk, his face even paler than usual. Large blue veins stood out on the back of his thin hands. The black jeans and red cashmere roll-necked pullover hung loosely on his bony frame. He stopped shuffling the papers, put the cap back on his fountain pen, and placed it on the blue blotter in front of him.

He sounded mildly annoyed: "When I suggested that we used this flat as a base for a few days while we wrote the technical article for the Journal, I didn't mean that you could turn into a fast food restaurant, Caroline. You are supposed to be reporting a major food scandal, and yet you still can't control your appetite for mass-produced rubbish. If you want to be credible, you should get your own diet under control. There, I've said it. No doubt Susan will be more sympathetic. Get her to give you some phone counselling. Since she got the sack from Kenley and Palmer, she has been looking for more lame ducks to help. She'll be back in the Health Service in no time. Sorry, Caroline, but you do ask for it.

"In answer to your question, I relish the idea of giving the media the information they want. The tabloids will paint the worst possible picture, but for once I'll enjoy reading nightmarish headlines.

"I just hope that the companies responsible for this will go out of business, but I doubt it, somehow. They will simply withdraw GE203 from their products and look for something else they can do to foods to make us eat more. They are completely without scruples, or morals. Remember when Muffins 'n Burgers got together with The World Youth Health Council to promote "good nutrition" for deprived kids? Considering that their product is responsible for obesity and Type 2 diabetes, their actions show the utmost contempt for children's health. No, we can only hope that our discovery makes ordinary people sufficiently angry to boycott these company's products...for a while, anyway."

Caroline stood up. She was hurt by his comments about her figure, but her generous spirit won the day. Brian needed reassurance. She walked over to his desk, placed the Journal in front of him, and put her arms around his shoulders, her tight black sweater straining dangerously over her breasts. The safety pin which held her long red velvet skirt together popped into view as the sweater slid up, over her bulging midriff which was partially, and ineffectively, covered by a black, lacy camisole top. Soft mounds of flesh had pushed their way through the delicate fabric, like lumpy custard forced through a sieve. Brian was reminded of the time one of his London students set him up with a "roly-poly gram" on his fiftieth birthday. It had been one of the most revolting experiences of his life. Embarrassed, he pulled away.

Undaunted, Caroline adjusted her sweater and skirt.

"I'm not offended, Brian. I know I'm a fat slob, but a lot of men do find me attractive. I will change, I promise. I'll put this muck in your kitchen bin, and get going. My train back to London leaves in an hour, so I haven't got long. It's been great to work with you. Presumably, you'll come down to Susan's house before the weekend, so you're available when the Press Release goes out on Friday, and for BBC Radio Four on Monday morning? Be careful, won't you? Changjia are bound to be after your hide. They can't do anything to prevent the story appearing, and it might look suspicious if you do disappear, but we can't rule out some kind of attempt to keep you quiet."

She saw the brief look of fear in his eyes, and switched rapidly to practicalities:

"When I was working on a burglary story for the Evening Echo, one of the old lags we consulted for background material told me that the best way to be invisible is to keep changing direction and clothes. So, my advice is to use a hire car to get you down to Birmingham, then take a train to Bristol, then hire another car, and drive back to London, and so on. Take various hats, scarves and coats with you, and keep swapping. Alternatively, hire a bodyguard. I can probably fix that, but it's bloody expensive."

To Brian, the idea of being "minded" by a burly bruiser was not appealing.

"For God's sake, Caroline. That would look even more obvious. I'll try your other idea, though. If I do meet with an accident, Susan will give all our data, the tape recording, and the computer print-outs to a doctor friend of hers from East Central Hospital. He's sufficiently anti-establishment to relish the whole story, and will be able to put them in the right hands. Let's hope it doesn't come to that."

****

After Caroline's departure, Brian switched on the TV, and called Susan on his mobile phone. He had given up worrying about the possibility of his phone being tapped, but at least one precaution was worth taking: if the flat was bugged, it would be difficult for anyone to hear the call above the caterwauling group of gyrating kids entertaining screaming fans on Top of the Pops.

Even so, he spoke softly. "Well, Susan. We've done it. Mary Hawkhurst has made our story the main article. Well done, for getting all the evidence together. I'll be with you tomorrow night, if that's OK? The Press Release and early copies of the Journal go out to the newspapers, radio and TV stations on Friday, so we'll have one night together before things start happening. I don't suppose I'll see you for some time after that."

He heard Susan sigh wearily. She sounded absolutely shattered, for good reason. After the Heaven's Rest adventure, she had received a call from Don Fellows, her boss at Kenley and Palmer terminating her contract. He told her, tersely, that she would receive three months' salary in lieu of notice, and instructed her not to return to work. Whether Don was "in" on the GE203 business, or not, it didn't really matter. His company had been named and shamed in their article, so she was now officially labelled as an "industrial spy", or would be once the story hit the national media on Monday.

"I'm not exactly likely to be going anywhere, Brian. My name is on the article in the Journal, as well as yours. My extremely short career in the food industry is definitely over, but I will probably still get employed in the public sector in some sort of lowly capacity. I'm thinking of going abroad to work, perhaps in Africa or South America. The World Health Organisation are looking for dietitians to go to Peru to help launch a nutrition programme. I'll see you tomorrow, then. Bye."

Her voice tailed off towards the end of the sentence. Brian's hand was shaking as he switched off his phone. He was scared for his own skin, but Susan was in a terrible position as well. He would offer his sympathy tonight, if he managed to get to London in one piece. Remembering Caroline's advice, he packed a suitcase with enough shirts and underwear for a few days in London, plus a selection of other clothes: a couple of woollen ski hats, a raincoat, an old leather jacket, several roll-necked sweaters and a couple of heavier, cream Arun-style knitted pullovers which he hadn't worn for years.

Molly had always loathed Brian's "woolly jumpers" as she called them, comparing these ubiquitous garments with the sweaters worn by Scottish actors in television dramas. She referred to them as "those boring pullovers loved by TV Highlanders and off-duty estate agents." Brian thought she was pathetically snobbish about her Scottish roots. Bagpipes and haggis were also on her "impossibly touristy" list.

She had insisted that it was imperative to dress fashionably at all times as there was always a possibility of meeting one of her important clients, even during a family walk in the park on a Sunday afternoon. So, at weekends, Brian dutifully put on his well-pressed jeans and leather jacket, tasselled loafers, cashmere socks and became the perfect accessory for his ambitious wife. It was ironic that his life might now depend on the old clothes that she had scorned.

He realised that, for the first time in weeks, he had allowed himself to think about Molly. She was probably very happy in New York, and he had absolutely no doubt the children were having a good time as well. They sent him long emails describing their school life, baseball matches, movies, and other American treats, and he'd noticed that expressions like "gee, dad" and "man, that was some experience" were appearing more frequently in these cheerful accounts. They never mentioned being homesick, although Amy had asked when he was "coming over to the Big Apple". No chance, not now….or perhaps, ever.

He snapped the suitcase shut, put on a brown overcoat and brown and black striped scarf, and walked back into the sitting room to collect his briefcase. As he turned the key in the lock on the flat door, he could hear the land line phone ringing inside. He decided not to go back.

****

Susan had taken the unusual step of phoning her parents. Since returning, unscathed but very shaken, to her South London home after her Lake District adventure, she had become nervous and restless. She needed comfort, but as Brian was not with her, the only way to get some kind of reassurance was by re-entering that ordered world of her childhood.

Visiting her mother and father was out of the question: she knew she looked very thin, and would be subjected to cross-questioning about her diet, her exercise routine, even her bowel movements. Her mother, the former aerobics teacher, was still obsessed by "healthy living", and her father was an active ski-er and golfer. Talking to them on the telephone was the only way to get the comfort without the criticism.

Her mother answered:

"Hello darling. How lovely to hear from you. Are you all right? How's the new job going. We'd love to see you for Sunday lunch some time. Could you make it this week?"

"I can't mum, unfortunately. I'm fine, but I've been involved in some nutrition research that's proved to be very important indeed, so I wanted to warn you that I might be mentioned on the TV news, or in the papers. It's a good piece of work, and I'm proud of it, but there could be some kind of backlash action, maybe even to discredit me. You know what these multinational food companies are like. They'd say anything to please their shareholders."

The response was encouraging. "Darling, whatever you've found in your research, I'm sure it's one hundred per cent accurate. If you've discovered something that will upset the big food companies, good for you. They make too much money, and feed us rubbish. That's why there are so many fat, unhappy people in this country. Your father and I eat only organic these days. Most of the stuff in the supermarkets is stuffed full of poisonous additives. How's your love life, by the way?"

Susan considered whether to spill the beans. Why not? Her mother was obviously in a receptive mood.

"I've been seeing a wonderful man, a professor of nutrition. He's involved in the same piece of research as me. He's separated from his wife. She lives in New York. Don't worry, I'm just taking one day at a time. He hasn't moved in. I'm only just recovering from my last experience of co-habitation!"

"Good. Try not to rush things, Sue. You're such a giver and men take advantage of that. Your father will be delighted that you're happy again. He's at the golf club at the moment. Give us another ring tomorrow at about 7pm. He'd love to talk to you. I must dash now, darling - it's my yoga class, followed by a massage and facial. God knows why I bother at my age, but you've got to keep on trying, haven't you? I'd hate your father to wake up next to a fat old bag. Anyway, that's my excuse for spending so much time and money at the health club. Do you blame me?"

The "little girl" voice which had suddenly developed at the other end of the line amused Susan: she went along with the daughter-as-mother role-play:

"Good for you mum. You always look great, and dad's a very lucky man. You're a tonic. Have fun, and I'll catch up with you both again tomorrow night."

The short conversation with her mother cheered Susan up so much that she decided to pull out all the stops for her visitor. Brian was going to enjoy the best night of his life. She ran a bath, scenting the water with some bath oil left over from Christmas called "Poison" - a pungent, sweet smelling French perfume. It seemed appropriate. She stripped off her jeans, sweater, socks and underwear in the bedroom, and pulled on her green silk kimono. It was still chilly. She made a mental note to light the fire in the sitting room.

As she hung the robe on the back of the bathroom door, she couldn't avoid seeing her reflection in the shiny metal-framed mirror over the white bathtub. Her thin body looked gravely undernourished and gaunt, with a concave stomach, prominent hip bones, and scrawny elbows...just like the pictures of anorexic girls she had studied at college. Her face was thin too, and there were dark circles under her eyes. Her cheekbones were almost jagged, her eyes too bright, and her dark wavy hair looked sadly in need of a good cut.

Automatically, as if she were back at school, she pulled back her shoulders. Her small breasts rose very slightly. Pathetic. She spoke out loud, to her reflection. "Well, you could always get a job as a Vogue model if no-one else will employ you. All you need is a load of concealer under your eyes, a reliable cocaine dealer and a good agent, and you'll be in business."

The ridiculous idea of someone with her knowledge and training becoming malnourished suddenly struck home. There was no need for this self-punishment. She wasn't a little girl desperate for her mother's approval any more (in fact, the reverse was now true). She resolved to improve her own nutrition standards, starting with tonight.

She also thought about Caroline. The poor girl had the opposite problem to her own. When the going got tough, she got stuffed. The sexual implication was true, as well. Susan smiled. Poor Caro was a generous girl who sent out so many erotic messages, in her dress and mannerisms, that it was no wonder that she attracted the wrong kind of men.

She stepped into the bath, lay back in the scented water (the exotic, heady smell had diminished to a chocolatey odour which wasn't unpleasant.) and thought about a menu for tonight. Poor Brian was, like her, badly in need of nourishment: physical and emotional. Well, she'd start the meal with a pasta dish: spaghetti carbonara with cream, bacon and pine nuts. Plenty of carbohydrate to fuel their muscles, and animal fat to help put some weight on their bodies. Then, they'd have Beef in Red Wine, Pommes Lyonnaise and broccoli. Loads of protein, iron and other minerals in that lot. Finally, inspired by the bath oil, she decided to serve a warm chocolate sponge soufflé with pistachio icecream. Not a lot of nutritional value, but the sheer pleasure of eating it would do them a power of good. They'd drink a good champagne, and a couple of bottles of Burgundy. About 4500 calories each, and an orgasm in every mouthful. Yummy. God, she was sounding just like Caroline.

Contemplating a longish session at the better of her two local supermarkets (the organic section wasn't too bad there, and they had a decent meat counter), Susan allowed herself another ten minutes of wallowing, and then stepped out of the bath. It was hard not to look in the mirror, but she tried to ignore her reflection. It was too disturbing.

She rubbed some "Poison" body lotion into her body, and pulled on her robe. The bedroom looked a mess, and she tidied it carefully before selecting an outfit for the evening: a long black velvet skirt, a new black lambswool cardigan edged with pearls, long pearl, thirties-style earrings from her favourite charity shop, black patent high heeled shoes. Tucked at the back of her underwear drawer, she found a flat cardboard box containing a red silk bra, knickers and suspender belt, plus a pair of nude-coloured, lace-topped stockings, a never-worn gift from Mark, presented to her just before he left.

Mark, true to his calling as a marketing manager, had been much taken by the instant visual appeal of saucy, brightly coloured underwear, which she had never been keen on, preferring sleek knickers and bras in white or cream, with discreet trimmings. He hadn't managed to get Susan to parade in the red silk underwear, and she had tucked the gift away. A few days later, he had left her.

Now the set of garish matching silk garments might be useful. She tried them on in front of the long mirror. Her body was so spare and white, and her face so pale that she looked like a dancer from the Moulin Rouge or a Vogue model on a photo shoot. The bra was a bit too big, but, after a filling meal and a few glasses of wine Brian wouldn't notice. For a moment, Susan wondered whether she had gone completely mad, and then remembered her intention to work in the Third World. She might just as well enjoy some craziness while she could as red silk undies would certainly not be appropriate for her new life in Peru or Zaire.

It was now 2.30pm, and she had a gourmet dinner to prepare. She stripped off the silk underwear. It was time to be practical.

Two and a half hours later, she had completed her shopping, the beef was simmering away in the oven and the potatoes layered in a dish, ready to be topped with cream and bacon lardons before cooking. The chocolate sponge souffle and spaghetti carbonara, both "last minute" dishes, could wait until later. The meal would be the most complicated one she had prepared since Mark left, and she was already regretting having her bath so early in the day. She'd need a shower before Brian arrived.

She was just trying to fasten the fourth and last of the suspenders into the flimsy lace top of one stocking without ripping the delicate fabric (a job so fiddly and time consuming that she began to wonder if Brian was worth all this trouble) when she heard a loud knock at the back door, which led out into her garden. She managed to finish fastening her stocking, eased down her skirt, slipped her feet into the shiny high-heeled shoes, and walked slowly downstairs: running was out of the question in this get-up.

"God, you look a sight." She spoke without thinking. Brian, did, indeed, look extraordinary, standing there on her back doorstep in the pouring rain.

His face was partly-covered by a navy blue ski-hat, the kind with a peaked cap built into the design, and a zip fastener under the chin. He was wearing a heavy brown raincoat with a protective extra layer over his shoulders, which would have suited an Australian farmer. Rain was running down the coat in a steady stream from collar to hem. Either he had put on about five stone in weight. , or he was wearing two large sweaters underneath this long, flowing garment and, she conjectured, he probably had a cushion tied around his stomach as well. She could just make out a pair of red tracksuit bottoms and black training shoes beneath the coat. The bit of his face that she could see was streaked with mud. His eyes looked red, and there were mud-encrusted circles beneath them.

"Come in, and tell me everything. It's obviously been a terrible journey. Did you hire a car or come by train?" She took his arm, and led him into the kitchen, where he collapsed heavily onto the one chair in the room, a large high-backed pine junk shop bargain, with a bright peony-splashed tapestry cushion on the seat. The ancient wood groaned under his weight.

He pulled off the ski hat, his soft, thin hair standing on end. "It's taken me nearly 24 hours to get here. I hired a car in Liverpool, then drove to Bristol, and caught a train to Reading, " he said. "I hired another car, drove to Brighton, and then took a train to Gatwick Airport. Then I got the Express train to London, and came the rest of the way by bus. I don't think I was followed, unless the Changjia mob employ people who can melt into thin air. It was Caroline who advised me to keep on changing my clothes. A brilliant idea, but I can tell you that it isn't easy. People give you odd looks when you disappear into a lavatory cubicle at an airport wearing jeans and a jacket, carrying a suitcase, then emerge five stone heavier wearing a stockman's coat, and ski hat. Anyway, enough of my troubles. Something smells wonderful. Give me a drink, please, Susan. I need one."

He leaned back, and stretched his feet out in front of him. Beneath the chair, a large puddle of muddy water was beginning to spread out over Susan's beautiful cream and brown quarry-tiled floor.

She side-stepped the puddle and kissed his muddy cheek. "I will, but I want to see a strip show first. Start peeling off all that gear. You can have a hot bath and then we'll eat."

For the first time since he had dripped his way into the kitchen, Brian noticed how beautiful Susan looked. As she bent forward to open the fridge door, he could see that her dark cardigan was undone to just above her breasts, and she was wearing a red bra.

After his exhausting journey, sex was the last thing on his mind, but, the signs were that it was right at the top of Susan's agenda. Glancing around the small kitchen, he saw that there was a fairly complicated meal in preparation: a chopping board on the black marble work top with small chunks of some kind of green vegetable, broccoli perhaps, two opened bottles of red wine, several casserole dishes, and some smaller dishes containing olives and cashew nuts. The delicious aroma coming from the oven seemed to be a combination of meat, wine, and some kind of creamy sauce. Susan had laid on all the right ingredients for a fantastic night.

He hoped he would be up to expectations; he had never experienced erectile dysfunction before (in fact, he often had to concentrate hard on chemical equations to calm himself down), but he was so, so knackered. The idea of making love to Susan tonight was, at the same time, appealing and appalling.

As he flopped in the chair (flop being the appropriate noun and pronoun - there was the complete lack of activity in his lower regions, which were still numb with cold), he wondered how on earth he was going to hack it. Shock tactics might warm things up. If he waited until the end of the evening, he would be too exhausted to do anything at all. It was now or never.

"You seem to be in the mood for a good laugh, and it's exceptionally warm in here, so I'll strip. But then, I insist you do the same. Now, do I get a glass of champagne, or not?"

Susan had already extracted a bottle of pink bubbly from the fridge. She turned towards the sink, and opened the cork with a loud popping noise, then poured the foaming liquid into two tall glasses which were standing, ready, on the draining board. She handed him a glass.

"This is all you're getting until I see what you're made of, mate. I want to find out how the cushion is fixed around your waist, and what you've got on underneath all this clobber. Then, if I'm happy with your strip show, I'll do the same. We can always eat in our underwear. There's a log fire burning in the sitting room. Just a second, I'll put some music on. What would you like? Ravel's Bolero, or the March of the Toreadors from Carmen?"

There was nothing else for it. Brian put every other thought out of his head, stood up, and began to unbutton his sodden raincoat. He wished that his doctor sister had given him some tips on how to cope with this kind of situation. All those years ago, her advice on the "G Spot" had been invaluable, but now he was over fifty, frightened and tired, and was expected to perform a ridiculous erotic dance. What did women want, these days? Sex and power? To humilate men, or tame them...or what exactly?

Did it really matter, anyway? Today he might have been invisible to Changjia's men, but from tomorrow onwards he would be in the limelight with nowhere to hide.

If this was going to be his last shag, it would be a good one.

****

All characters and companies mentioned in this book are entirely fictitious.

mobile telephone number was written on the outside of the file. Susan ran her fingers over the file, almost lovingly. She had liked Brenda: the woman was gutsy, willing to learn. All she needed was to talk to someone who cared enough.

Susan spoke out loud to the empty room. "If I can't ever be happy again, I will be useful instead."

She went back to the kitchen, file in hand, and walked over to the phone which was hanging on its cradle on the wall. She picked it up, sat down at the table, and dialed Brenda's number.

A woman's voice answered: "Hello, who's that?"

"Hello. Is that Brenda? This is Susan Simpson. Remember me? I'm the dietitian who helped you lose a bit of weight last year. I've been doing other work, but I've been wondering about you. How is it going? "

The reply came quickly: "Lousy. I'm fatter than ever. You leaving the hospital really buggered me up. There's no-one who really cares about fat people these days, just sharks who want to make money flogging us poisoned food or charging us a fortune to tell us what we already know. There should be someone out there we can trust. Considering most people in the country are now grossly overweight, it's a disgrace. What do you want, anyway?"

Susan paused before replying. The woman was obviously desperate. She was right, too. Everyone had failed her.

If Susan took her case on again, it would be hard work and, then, inevitably, there would be many others to help, as well.

But what was the alternative?

There was none.

****

truth, and another for the quacks who spilled out rubbish on TV and in the papers. If she strayed over the line, she would be struck off, disgraced by her professional body…yet they could peddle daft ideas which people lapped up eagerly, without anyone challenging them.Crazy.

Since she had arrived at her parents' home, she had lost all track of time. Her parents had been solicitous, caring, quietly watchful. Her mother had swiftly swapped roles again, slipping back into solicitous, maternal style. In her view, it was absolutely clear that Susan needed time to recover. She must rest, and gather her strength.

She glanced up at the large round pine-cased clock on the newly-painted white wall. Her mother's latest attempt to bring "peace and calm" into the home was to paint all the walls in white or cream and get rid of most of her ornaments and other knick-knacks. Actually, in mum's defence, Susan now thought, it really does look good. Bless her for trying so hard. Even now she was out being pummelled and pounded into shape. The woman was a marvel.

It was 2pm. Susan remembered that 2pm was the precise time when the afternoon obesity clinic had always started at the hospital. If she had still been working there, her first patient today would have been Brenda Jones, the middle-aged mum with suicidal tendences, high blood pressure and broken marriage. Poor thing. She must weigh a ton by now. Her own problems, and grief, seemed to fade slightly; it was true that there is nothing like work to ease the pain of tragedy and disappointment.

Almost as though she had been programmed to do it, Susan got up and nearly ran upstairs to the spare bedroom where she was currently sleeping. Her old hospital briefcase was by the window. For some reason, she had brought her patient notes with her when she made her hasty retreat from her own home.

She opened the case, and thumbed through the grey folders inside. She drew out the one marked "Brenda Jones". Brenda's smug expression was talking about the news story Brenda had just read. Apparently, there was a big fuss about it. Brenda sipped her tea and wondered if she had the energy to fetch some biscuits from the tin on the dresser. She decided against trying. It was perfectly possible that she could fall over and get stuck on the floor. Best to wait until the boys came home. They were good kids really, and would phone if they were going to be late. She took another sip of tea.

She considered for a moment. It was fine and dandy to make a fuss about corrupt and wicked food manufacturers, but what about helping poor sods like me who are already too fat to walk? Shifting loads of weight is difficult. I bet that girl on TV thinks fat women are stupid idiots who stuff themselves with food all day because they have such boring lives. Not true. I was doing very well, thank you, with that woman at the hospital, whatever her name was. I just needed a bit of support. Then, she goes off...just like that. No wonder I look like shit and feel like it too. There is no-one I can turn to.

****

In her parents' kitchen, Susan was watching the same mid-day news programme. There were plenty of doctors and nutritionists making vitriolic accusations against the food manufacturers and supermarkets, and a promise of more of the same in the evening edition, after Parliamentary Questions in the House. No mention, of course, of Brian. His death was just an "accident". No one was to blame, no mud would stick, no epitaph for a good man who, she was certain, was murdered.

She shuddered. There was nothing she could do except mourn, and pray that the pain in her heart would somehow, some day, ease just a little. Perhaps she really should go abroad, or even switch to another profession. Dietetics was a joke. There was one set of rules for professionals like her who really cared about scientific just like his Dad, Martin. It was having the kids so close together, Brenda thought, that had made her put on so much weight. There had been no time to go on a proper diet between pregancies.

Slimming clubs hadn't helped either; going out on a Monday night just to get weighed and listen to some old boiler talking about calories had seemed like a waste of time, and led to rows with Martin. It was the start of all their troubles. She had become fatter and fatter and, until that nice hospital dietitian had taken her in hand, she had even thought about topping herself.

Well, the dietitian had abandoned her. Just when the diet plan she'd given her had started to work, the bloody woman had left the job. Of course, the weight had piled back on again, and now she was gross. The doctor had given her a right going over when she went to seen him for some blood pressure pills. What did he expect? To cap it all, according to the daily newspaper, it appeared that supermarkets were selling foods which actually fattened people up like pigs. No wonder she, and millions of other women like her, were obese. It was obscene.

The kettle boiled, and Brenda put the tea-bag into a white mug with a brown stain on the bottom. The milk smelt a bit off, but it would do. With difficulty, she walked two paces back from her position at the sink to the table, mug in one hand. Since her legs had swollen up so badly, it was difficult to move. These days, she rarely went out. She would have to clear up a bit before the lads came in, but that could wait for half an hour.

She paused to switch on the TV, and then sat down hard on the grubby yellow cushion on her kitchen chair, her mobile phone on the table in front of her. Everything in the narrow room needed washing, cushion covers, the floor, the curtains, but she didn't have the energy to do any household jobs. What with the bills, the kids, the fuckin' neighbours, and the chronic aches in her swollen legs, life was becoming intolerable.

The TV news presenter, a girl of about thirty with red and brown streaked, fashionably-chopped hair, creamy make-up and a

Chapter Twenty Four

"I was ordered to cover up food scandal" Top FizzCo man speaks out. Evening Echo Exclusive, by Caroline Dempsey.

In an astonishing interview, Bruce James, former Marketing Director of Fizz-Co UK has confessed that he was complicit in a plot to fool the public about the safety of "Super Snacks", a range of so-called "healthy" foods. He has implicated the British Government, and Washington-backed American food watchdogs, in the scam, which appears to have been initiated, on both sides of the Atlantic, in order to to encourage people to become "hooked" on junk food.

Protin-Foods, who supply meat-substitute to many big supermarkets and manufacturers, are also accused of knowingly "doctoring" their products with GE203, a Chinese herbal substance used to fatten up pigs. Kenley and Palmer who make the new "Activity Kids" range of foods, are involved as well.

In the House of Commons, questions have been tabled from opposition MPs who are demanding an explanation from the Minister of Health.

When Brenda Jones had finished reading the article in the Echo, she heaved herself up from the kitchen table, and made herself a cup of tea. Avoiding the pile of washing in the sink, she refilled the kettle and switched it on. The draining board was stacked with dirty crockery, smeared with the remains of last night's supper: tomato sauce, greasy residue from fried potatoes, ash from a cigarette stubbed out by Ashley, her 16 year old son. Disgusting.

The three of them would be home, soon. Ashley was the eldest, then came Sean, and finally William, the 13 year old who looked

fascinating, it was a turn-on. He was showing considerable courage, too. It just shows that you can't dismiss people, she thought. Intriguing. She leaned forward and kissed his cheek.

"Come on then, mate, we'll book into the Savoy. We might as well do it in style. Let's make this a night to remember." Reluctantly, she extracted her hands from Bruce's still-warm grip, stood up and pulled off her scarf, revealing her goose-bumped cleavage, and the deep V-neckline of the flimsy sweater. The jet crucifix moved and re-posititioned itself, at a slightly crooked angle, just above the spot where Caroline's pale flesh met the ribbed edge of the soft woollen garment.

For the first time that afternoon, Bruce smiled.

****

"What came up at the conference was astounding. Apparently, the use of GE203 has the American Food and Drug Administration's backing, which means that it must have been approved by the President, or people very close to him. I made all the right noises, but decided, on the spot, that I was going to resign."

"So, have you done so?" Caroline kept her fingers crossed under the table. If Bruce had already resigned, she wouldn't be responsible for causing his demise at FizzCo. So she could write her article with a clear conscience. It was a purely selfish thought. She quickly regretted it, and fingered the crucifix, hoping for instant forgiveness from the Almighty. This would never do...she was going soft.

"No, but I plan to do it tomorrow, if I'm not sacked first. I discussed it with Ellen, my wife, over the weekend, and she was horrified. The company has given her a lifestyle she enjoys, and educated our children. According to Ellen, resigning over a matter of conscience is a self-indulgence I can't afford. For once, I rather hope that I can do the deed myself before the vipers get me, although it might end my marriage. God, she'll take me for everything, and quite rightly too. I am in a big mess."

He took another sip of coffee, replaced his cup on the table and took hold of both her hands. She noticed that his own hands were large, and warm, with well-manicured nails.

"Sorry, Caroline. Your hands are freezing cold. It's getting late. Let's go to a pub and continue this conversation, and then have dinner somewhere. Maybe we ought to check into a hotel if you want to interview me properly. What do you think?

To her own surprise, Caroline found that she could imagine nothing better than to spend the evening, and possibly the night as well, with Bruce. When they had first met, she had made an instant judgment required by her trade, despising him for his brashness, his obsession with profit, and the stereotypical "marketing executive" image he cultivated.

Now, to her surprise, she found herself becoming attracted to him. Witnessing his "Road to Damascus" experience was not only listed among those which had been adulterated with GE203. I was horrified. Don't make that face, Caroline. I might be prepared to mortgage my granny's soul for my company, but I'm not a complete idiot. It's one thing to hype up products a little, and exploit as many human weaknesses as possible when trying to sell them, but this is different. I suddenly realised that the firm I've spent most of my life working my balls off for is knowingly trying to turn people into food junkies.

"The formulation for these products is decided in Baltimore, but our manufacturing and nutrition team must know what's in the stuff. So, of course, I sent emails whizzing around the building trying to find out more. There was a deathly silence from all concerned, and I then received an email myself, from my boss over in the States, Charles Henderson. The gist of it was that I should stop digging for dirt in the company, and concentrate on covering up the scandal: if I had to bribe any journalists or government ministers, fine. He still doesn't realise that not everyone will do anything at all for money. It might be possible to bribe a politician, but journalists are a different breed. Once a story is in the public domain, even in a small way, it's impossible to kill it. I sent him back a grovelling email, saying I would do my best, and another one came straight back telling me my job was on the line if I didn't manage to turn things around without losing sales."

Caroline nodded. "Bloody Hell. Sounds worse than working for a newspaper. So, did you resign, or what?"

"No, I thought I'd try and find out just why the "Super Snacks" products had been doctored, so I asked him for a conference call to get a take on what we should do. The story has already appeared in one American paper, the Wall Street Journal, but only as a diary piece. The Americans are jittery over share prices, so Charles agreed to a conference call with both of us taking part, together with the Director of manufacturing for FizzCo, USA. He is American as Co USA and my own Chief Executive, Simon Tate. He is American as well, so you can see that I was completely outnumbered.

She climbed the short flight of stairs up onto the terrace, and walked towards the second man. He looked up from his paper, and took off his glasses. Caroline was stupefied: it was certainly Bruce, but his substantial body seemed deflated and his own hands were shaking as he reached forward to take hers.

"Bruce. What on earth is wrong? You're not about to be executed for treason. It can't be that bad, surely?"

She plonked herself down on the flimsy wooden seat opposite Bruce and put her purple handbag on the table. She had brought her tape recorder and a camera. She'd prepared herself for some very hard work, extracting a good story from Bruce. To that purpose, she had dressed fairly conservatively today: long black skirt and boots, fluffy dark blue low-necked sweater, fake fur coat, her glittering black jet crucifix and a very expensive, gossamer-fine long, black cashmere scarf: if Bruce was going to confess, she would make it easy for him.

But now, it looked as though she would be counsellor instead of confessor. Bruce needed some coaxing if he was going to come upwith the goods.

She reached into her handbag for her purse.

"I'll go inside the cafe and fetch us both a coffee and a large brandy, and then we'll talk." she said, as gently as possible. "You look as though you could do with a warming toddy. Don't move. "

When she returned, he had hardly moved at all. She sat in silence while he gulped down the brandy and took a sip of coffee, holding the glass with both hands. His voice was husky, like someone in the first stages of 'flu:

"This is all off the record at the moment Caroline, but I promise I will give you a story by the end of the day. Is that a bargain?"

She didn't hesitate. "Of course, Bruce. Just tell me everything, then we can decide between us how to play it. You can trust me."

"Well, I've certainly got nothing to lose. Anyway, just listen, please. It started on Friday. I received my usual early copy of The British Consumer Journal and saw the "Super Snacks" products

The Crime Editor had been sceptical. He favoured waiting for the official police report, and a statement from Brian's wife. Both items would come in later that day.

She finished the chocolate cake, and stood up. It was time to decide what to wear. Bruce James was going to get the treat of his life.

****

The terrace was slightly raised above the pathway around the long, irregular shaped lake. A few Canada geese, their feathers ruffling in the strong wind, were marching in grey formation along the grassy banks of the lake, and a couple of dark-headed moorhens paddled under a low weeping willow tree on the edge of the water. The miserable weather had kept most tourists away from the park that day.

A young Japanese couple were leaning over the parapet of the iron bridge, laughing together, while the boy took multiple photographs of a solitary, mallard duck who was parading in front of them, enjoying the attention. In their bright jackets, knitted caps and jeans, the pair looked as though they'd worn the wrong costumes to a performance of the Mikado. Caroline felt a pang of envy. It would be nice to be part of a couple again.

She shivered as she scanned the bleak cafe terrace. She noticed two men sitting alone. One, a young man, wearing a dark anorak and baseball cap, was probably a student. The other, much older, sat huddled in his chair, his head poking forward, scanning a newspaper spread out on the table in front of him. His shoulders were hunched. His black raincoat and the table top hid his body, so it was impossible to see if he was stout or slim. She remembered that Bruce had a florid complexion and luxuriant hair, but this man's skin was sallow and pale, he wore dark glasses and his hair was covered by a black homburg hat. It was old-fashioned, the kind that an old man might wear to a funeral. Not Bruce's style at all.

pink cashmere sweater which had fitted her perfectly when she bought it a year ago, but was now easing upwards. The trouble with cashmere, she thought, is that it is inclined to shrink after a few washes.

Knowing that this was just an excuse, a way of avoiding admitting, even to herself, that her waistline was expanding at an alarming rate didn't help. How could she address her weight problem when her whole life hung on this story? It was alright for those women who dealt with stress by eating less. Susan was one of those, she could tell. For women like herself, life would always be lived before, after and between diets. It was unfair, but that was the waythings were. Maybe her next love affair would be with someone who didn't care how fat she was. Unlikely that such a man existed, but it was possible.

Cheered by this thought, she took a sip from the coffee cup on her desk, and a bite from the large slice of chocolate cream sponge which her mum had just brought upstairs to "keep her going."

When Bruce eventually spoke, she could hardly recognise his voice. The booming, imperious, confident tone he'd used last time they met was replaced by a strangled wimper. It almost sounded as though he had been crying. Surely not?

"Caroline. I can't discuss this on the phone. I do want to talk to you. I'll meet you in St. James' Park at 4pm this afternoon. There is a tea pavilion near Horse Guard's parade. I'll be inside. I must go now. I have a conference call to Baltimore in a minute or so. Goodbye. "

He rang off. Caroline was astonished and exhiliarated. Bruce would hardly go to all the trouble of meeting her at a cloak and dagger location unless he was going to say something very interesting indeed. This was going to be one corker of an interview, guaranteed to put her back into Robbo's good books. It was an easier option, too, than trying to dig deeper into the possible causes of Brian's death. She had put the word out to the paper's crime reporting team that she did not think that it could have been an "accident".

and TV stations and tell them that, as of now, you are contracted to me, personally. I really am sorry, you know, Susan. Brian wasn't the type of man that I'd go for, but he was a good person and truly loved you. He told me so when we were working together last week. Good Luck."

She rang off. Susan sat up, replaced the handset on its stand, and then, remembering, took it off again.

****

Once she had ended the call to Susan, Caroline dialled another number, this time to the Hertfordshire headquarters of FizzCo. She asked to be put through to Bruce James, and after a few seconds' wait, the switchboard operator connected her to his personal phone. She was expecting to be fobbed off with a directive to talk to the press office, or one of Bruce's two secretaries, so this was a surprise. She had nothing to lose, so she plunged straight in:

"Hi Bruce, it's Caroline Dempsey here from the London Evening Echo. You probably remember me from the "SuperSnacks" press launch and the New York Obesity Summit? Have you got anything to say to me about some of your products being laced with a potentially addictive, and highly dangerous additive? Are you withdrawing them from sale?"

At the other end of the line, Bruce coughed a couple of times. Caroline waited patiently. It was clear that the coughs were a time-buying ploy while he decided on a suitable, corporate reply. He had probably been given several legally checked choices by some slimy, toupee-wearing lawyer at the FizzCo US headquarters in Baltimore. The company were hit with serious allegations about food safety all the time, always managing to emerge whiter-than-white. To them, this was just another day's work, a minor hitch in their global expansion programme.

She settled back in her chair, shifted her larger-than-ever bottom to a more comfortable position, and pulled down the pale

The telephone on her bedside table rang. Without thinking, she got up from her seat, walked over, picked up the cordless receiver and sat down on the bed. This was the last call she would take, and she would slam the damn thing down if it was a reporter. It was a reporter, but a friendly one: Caroline.

"Susan. You've obviously heard about Brian. I am so sorry. He was a brilliant bloke and I know I am probably the last person you want to talk to, but we have to stick together now. There is no way we can prove he was murdered, although we both know that he probably was, but at least we can continue to expose this appalling scam. I've been in touch with Robbo, my old Editor at the Echo. He's had that slimey bastard Ronnie Adams on his back all weekend threatening to tell advertisers to pull their ads, but he is going to run our story anyway. I'm working on it at home at the moment.

"The British Consumer Journal feature gives our discoveries credibility, and Robbo is fed up with Ronnie's bullying. He's asked me to write a follow up tomorrow. I am going to get hold of some of the manufacturers whose products are involved if I can. Bruce James, who heads up the FizzCo marketing operation might just speak to me. Can I count on you, as well? Will you give me an interview, and appear on TV if necessary? You know Brian would have wanted us both to carry on fighting these bastards. We have to do it, Susan. Are you still there..?

Susan collapsed back on the bed. Her legs felt like cotton wool, her head throbbed and she had a searing pain in her stomach. She felt as though every bit of strength had left her body.

"I will do it Caroline, but you have to help. Tell your editor that we have a contract if you like. I cannot deal with the media pack, baying for my blood. Is that understood? I am going to leave this house tonight and move in with my parents for a while. Don't tell anyone where I am. I will call you when I get there. OK?"

"Fine. Do be careful, Susan. Get over to your parents' house as quickly as you can. I will phone round the red-top picture editors

Chapter Twenty Three

Mystery Death of Top Scientist - London Evening Echo exclusive.
Leading nutrition expert, Dr. Brian Donovan, fell to his death under a tube train in London early this morning. The accident happened after Dr. Donovan gave a radio interview blaming food manufacturers and the government for adding a dangerous substance to foods. During the interview, Dr. Donovan said he had recently been involved in a secret investigation into GE203, an additive which increases appetite, and, consequently, causes rapid weight-gain. A Department of Health spokesperson told The Echo, that Dr. Donovan's allegations are now being investigated at the highest level.

Dr. Donovan is separated from his wife, Molly, who lives in the USA with the couple's two children.

Police do not suspect foul play. It is understood that Dr. Donovan was very distressed about his personal life before the accident.

Susan sat by the window of her bedroom, the open newspaper on her lap. The watery, late afternoon sunshine shone weakly through the dirty smudges on the glass, and she could see the lean branches of the budding cherry trees in the road moving to and fro in the light wind.

So that was it, then. Brian was dead. Their last few days together had been just that...their last few days together.

The article was short, but tomorrow, or even later tonight, the media would be hot on the trail. Reporters would be banging at her door, her parents alarmed, her whole life taken over by grief and worry.

board, a train was due in just one minute. Brian worked his way towards the front of the throng. The board was just above his head. He craned his neck to look upwards. Details of the first train had disappeared, replaced by a row of pulsating yellow stars which sped along the black surface like a frantic column of giant ants. He felt the crowd surging forwards, and then a sudden, hard thud in the small of his back.

The train driver slammed on the manual brake but, even as he pulled the lever downwards, he knew that he couldn't prevent the ten tons of solid metal from hitting the man on the line.

****

expected, and now he was heading for his next appointment, this time with a large television network. Given that he was accusing the government of plotting to poison the population, the first interviewer had given him an easy ride. The anchorman, a seasoned veteran of early morning news programmes, seemed to be very cautious in his approach.

The previous day's papers had been equally circumspect. Most led with the story on crime figures, giving the GE203 revelations just a few column inches of space. Brian and Susan had found this surprising. Maybe the GE203 story would build. It certainly wasn't shocking the nation yet. Brian felt a lot happier. Perhaps his life was no longer in danger. The Changjia Corporation and the government might just ride this crisis, and become more responsible. He smiled to himself: in this crazy world, anything was possible. At least he now knew that Susan would be there for him, whatever happened. They were together.

He suddenly wished that he had taken up the TV network's offer of a car to take him to their studio. Every taxi was occupied. He would have to take the tube. He put his hand in his pocket and pulled out a couple of coins. The interview was at 8am, so he had plenty of time. The studio was in Soho Square, just off Oxford Street.

He turned into Bank Station, feeling the welcome rush of warm air as he forced his body against the tide of passengers coming out of the main exit. He would have to change at Tottenham Court Road, but that was fine.

"Oi mate, look where you're going." A young man in a knitted hat, tracksuit and trainers stepped back as Brian pushed by him.

"Sorry, just got swept along by the throng. I'll be more careful. in future".

The man seemed satisfied with his reply. He nodded curtly, and walked away, towards the exit. Brian made his way down to the platform. It was heaving with jostling bodies. According to the words and figures which flashed up on the black information the Environment. If the people who found out about this can't be discredited, we'll have to get rid of you, and probably the Chief Executive of the Food Standards Agency as well. Don' t worry. A few years in the wilderness, as a back bencher, or leader of some kind of health quango, and then you'll bounce back. You're young enough to stand it."

Elizabeth could feel her body shaking. She had to make a big effort to keep her voice steady.

"Jack, if I didn't know you better - much better - I would think that you were prepared to sacrifice my loyalty and friendship to save your own skin. Well, I have to tell you that women are not like men. The games we play are very different. I am not prepared to spend a "few years in the wilderness" as you so tactfully put it. I haven't got time. If I am blamed for this, I'll take you with me.

She turned to face Adams, thrust back her shoulders, and forced herself to look straight into his bulbous eyes:

"Ronnie, if you are going to try to dig the dirt on me don't bother: I'll give you every last, delicious, pornographic detail myself."

She turned and walked out of the room, almost bumping into Marigold, Jack's smiling, blond, buxom wife, in the doorway. Marigold stepped back, and greeted Elizabeth warmly.

"Sorry, Liz. I didn't realise you were here. Have you got to rush? Jack works you too hard. Come down to Chequers soon. we can catch up with some gossip. I'm sure you have masses to tell."

****

Brian hurried out of the Central London radio studio into the freezing cold, blustery morning. Mondays were always crazy: traffic screamed past, city workers rushed along the pavements, cafes and snack bars were packed with people attempting to propel their alcohol-impaired brains into the working week by sipping from bucket-sized paper cups full of strong, American-style coffee.

The 6am radio interview had been less traumatic than he had

His tones were more East End than Whitehall:

"Hello, gorgeous. You've got us into a bit of a fix here, darlin'. We'll have to put out a spoiler quickly. We'll kill the immediate impact of this with a much meatier story: Jack's going to get the Chief Constable of the Met to push out some scary crime figures this afternoon. If people are worrying about being stabbed in the back on their way home from work, they won't be so bothered about being killed off by the food bosses, especially as it's only a long-term danger.

"The Sundays will want to use the food story big, but, hopefully, we can head off most of the impact with some well-placed threats to editors. They all need advertising to survive , and the big players involved in this spend millions on press, TV and internet advertising. I've been looking into the background of the editor of the consumer journal, and found out a few things we can sting her with. The journalist involved in the story, Caroline Dempsey, will be an easy girl to fix, as well. She's relatively inexperienced and has been known to offer sex in exchange for a lead. We could dig up something or other, I'm sure. The professor is quite likely to have a nervous breakdown or top himself. He's quite flakey, I gather."

Jack's expression was calm but, as usual, he looked as though he had just jumped out of bed. His jacket was lying across the back of a chintz-covered sofa, and his sleeves were rolled to the elbow. His trousers were rumpled, and his brown hair was standing on end.

Elizabeth didn't know if she was meant to respond to Ronnie's precis of the situation and his bold ideas on damage limitation strategy or not. She decided to remain silent. Jack looked straight at her, his eyes suddenly cruel:

"Ronnie always has a solution, doesn't he? That's why he's lasted so long. He's wonderful. Well, Liz my girl, if his ideas don't work, you'll have to fall on your sword I'm afraid. Sorry, not a good analogy for a woman minister.

"Adding this GE203 stuff to foods could be explained away as a joint cock-up between your ministry, and the Department of job. If necessary, she would have to use the "S" card: there was no way a Prime Minister could survive a sex scandal involving one of his own ministers, not while he was in office, anyway. There were plenty of examples of PMs in recent times who had managed to get away with extra-marital affairs when they were in power, but the evidence had always come to light after their term of office. To be caught bonking a minister while actually governing the country might take some explaining. She gave herself a mental pat on the back for her astuteness in starting their affair, and finishing it so neatly.

Jack's brief kiss on her cheek was cool. She could smell his favourite aftershave, a sharp lemony scent from Floris in St. James's Street.

"Come into my Private Office, Elizabeth. I am sure you know what this is about. Ronnie is already in there. The press are onto it, and are demanding answers from the Food Standards Agency. there is an embargo on the piece in the Journal until Monday, but the Sunday papers are bound to carry something. We need to be very clear about our strategy here."

He turned and led the way into the high-ceilinged room. Ronnie was standing by the fireplace at the side of the room., one hand in his trouser pocket and the other resting on the thick, marble mantelpiece, next to a happy, smiling photo of Jack in the Downing Street kitchen, preparing breakfast for his wife and kids, who bore startled expressions as if this didn't happen very often.

Ronnie stared hard at Elizabeth. Not for the first time, she was reminded of Toad of Toad Hall, without the jaunty cap and the jocular manner. Ronnie was short, fat, and wore round glasses which made his face appear distorted: his eyes looked larger, and more protruding than they really were, and his cheeks were puffed as though he was trying to attract a lady frog for some watery games in the garden pond. The elastic in his blue braces and the fabric of his pink shirt were severely tested by his high, rock-solid stomach, and his pinstripe-clad legs tapered off to a neat pair of feet, encased in shiny black shoes.

briefcase, and left the flat. For once, her nose was shiny, her lipstick smudged, and there was a streak of dirty black newsprint on her cream silk camisole.

In the taxi, Elizabeth studied the feature. Dempsey and Donovan: they sounded like a television detective duo. Maybe they would be easy to discredit. Probably. It was best not to panic.

The very overweight driver was holding forth. She tried to ignore him.

"You all right for time, love? It's not far, but the traffic's hell today." He was obviously looking for conversation, and when there was no response from Elizabeth, he continued anyway, with a long rant which he delivered in a series of gasping, short sentences:

" Looks like one of those pension demonstrations again. Poor buggers, I feel sorry for them. You work bloody hard all your life, then they leave you without enough money to buy a few groceries and have a decent holiday. I blame this Government. They're a load of sheisters. Sorry, love, as I'm taking you to the Ministry of Health I suppose you must work for them. Make sure your own pension is well tied up, darling. Otherwise, you won't be able to afford clothes like those. You look smashing.

The rasp turned into a throaty chuckle and the sweaty rolls of flesh at the back of his neck stretched and contracted as his massive, rounded shoulders heaved up and down.

****

At 9.15 am. Elizabeth made her way across Whitehall to Downing Street. She walked with the confident stride of a woman who knows she is going to win. She had decided to face it out. Without actually giving his blessing to the policy of allowing companies to add GE203 to foods, Jack Barton had been complicit in the arrangement. The Prime Minister wanted people to get fatter, become sick and die: end of story.

Right. She wasn't going to carry the can for simply doing a good desk and went through them. The nationals were all carrying stories about the latest pension crisis developments: a large engineering firm with branches all over the UK had capped pensions, and raised retirement age. There was indignation from the unions, and moving stories from workers who faced an uncertain future.

The early copy of The British Consumer Journal was right at the bottom of the pile. As soon as she saw the cover picture, she knew she was in for a very hard day indeed. It was a lurid close-up of a pig, with its muddy snout deep in a murky trough containing dark yellow and brown swill, and several brightly coloured food packs. It was a disturbing image, which readers and national newspaper editors would find it impossible to ignore. Elizabeth knew she was in just as much shit as the pig in the photograph. The cover lines were equally arresting: "*Don't Buy These. Harmful Additive found in 22 popular ready meals and snacks.*" "*Why is Pig-Fattener hidden in our Food?*"

She turned to the Contents page, and then glanced quickly at the feature itself. She would have to read it properly in the taxi...she was already running late.

The article was spread over eight pages, and included twenty two pictures of packs of food, what looked like a food processing plant and a house called "Heaven's Rest", which appeared to be somewhere in the Lake District. There were standard head shots of Lars Johansson, the European Director of Protin-Foods and Bruce James, Marketing Director of Fizz-Co UK. The main article, on the first spread, had two authors, a journalist called Caroline Dempsey, and Professor Brian Donovan. The name rang alarm bells.

He was the maverick academic who had given the lecture at the New York Obesity Conference, accusing the Government of ignoring the obesity epidemic and encouraging multi-national companies to peddle fast food. Gerald had promised her that he had been disgraced, and no-one took him seriously any more. Well, the Editor of The British Consumer Journal obviously did take him seriously. She gathered up the papers, stuffed them into a large

After reading it through, twice, Elizabeth forced herself to remain standing. She placed her hands on the desk-top, squared her shoulders, and reached for a pen and notepad. She would deal with this shock summons efficiently and logically. She made a vertical row of bullet points on the pad and scrawled a note by each one:

* *Ronnie Adams in attendance, so this must be a media matter.*
* *Curt tone to message...this is a fuck-up of some kind*
* *Instruction to bring obesity data: maybe a shock story has appeared, or is about to appear in one of the papers?*
* *Inquiry about meeting food manufacturers. Shit: the last one I met was Lars from Protin-Foods. No minutes kept.*
* *This has to be about fattening food additives.*
* *Jack is going to make me carry the can for something very serious.*
* *I've got to be available all day: does he want me to resign?*
* *The bastard!*

Her hands were trembling as she replace the pen on the table, ripped off the top sheet of the pad and screwed it up into a ball. She hurled it, with as much force as she could muster, at the photograph of herself and Jack, taken at the previous year's party conference, which was prominently displayed on her desk.

The front door bell rang. The papers always arrived just before she left for the Ministry, together with any early copies of influential magazines, health reviews and journals like Nature and Science. They were all required reading, and Elizabeth tried to pick out, and scan the most important articles while she was travelling to the office. It was such a short journey from Victoria to Whitehall that she usually hailed a taxi outside her block of flats. She opened the door. The papers were in a neat bundle on her doormat; the Times, Guardian, Telegraph, all the red-tops, and a few journals at the bottom of the heap. She grabbed the bundle, rushed back to her prime ministers. She stood up, brushing the liquid with her hand. The single drop of coffee became a long, dirty-looking streak. Well, she thought, it would probably come out at the cleaner's. It was time to get dressed. She liked to check her emails at 7.15am, and then set off for her office at 7.30am. She took the coffee into the small galley kitchen off the sitting room and walked back into her bedroom. When she had chosen this flat, the large bedroom with windows overlooking Westminster Cathedral had been the biggest selling point. Although the sitting room, kitchen and office were all pokey, the bedroom was magnificent.

In the centre was an eight-armed crystal chandelier, another gift from Gerald. The walls were panelled in oak and there were two large built-in cupboards either side of the tiled fireplace. It would have looked rather like a gentleman's club bedroom, if the bed had been a sturdy English mahogany antique. Instead, it was Italian, uncompromisingly modern, built from stainless steel, and big enough to sleep four friendly people. Elizabeth smiled to herself as she removed the robe and laid it carefully on the black leather bedspread. This bed had alway been a talking point between herself and Jack: when they had time to talk during their necessarily short encounters at the flat. Frequently, there had hardly been time to reach the bedroom, let alone start a sensible conversation.

Ten minutes later, she walked back into the sitting room. This time, she was wearing a new beige and brown pin-striped Armani trouser suit. She had softened the hard lines of the suit with copper coloured wedge-soled high heeled shoes and a cream silk lace camisole. As a contrast to the muted, coffee and cream effect, she had painted her lips and nails to match, in a vivid magenta pink.

She strode through the room to her cubby hole of an office and switched on the computer. As the internet server kicked in, she could see that she already had 23 emails. She would deal with most of them when she arrived in her office, but one email almost shot out of the screen and hit her in the face: it was from Jack. She clicked onto the message.

she had handled the delicate matter of the obesity crisis. People were getting fatter by the day, which is exactly what Jack, and the President of the United States wanted.

The next set of projected life-expectancy figures for the UK would be interesting: they would show, for the first time since the second world war, that people could expect to live slightly shorter lives: the Government's Actuary Department which carries out demographic forecasts and advises ministers on pensions were due to report in the autumn, and Elizabeth had a "mole" in that department.

There was about to be a reversal in the trend towards longer life expectancy in the United States as well. Obesity-related diseases were now beginning to take their toll on the American population. Right now, hospital beds were full of these cases, but the numbers of morbidly patients actually living through their treatment for such problems as diabetes, heart disease and cancer was decreasing, and doctors predicted a sharp downturn in the number of beds required. Pension fund managers were also predicting a decline in payouts to the over-seventies, possibly during the next ten years.

It was all encouraging, and Elizabeth had no doubt that Jack considered her to be a very clever girl indeed.

She lent back slightly in her leather armchair, and the coffee in her white china cup slurped into the saucer. A drop of the hot, dark liquid splashed onto her emerald green silk robe, a present from her ex-husband Gerald. Although they had been divorced for over a year, he still lavished gifts on her. The robe had been a Christmas present. When she had unwrapped the tissue wrapped package during Gerald's annual Boxing Day gathering of judges, ministers and models (he served "nursery" food, cottage pie and spotted dick washed down with pink champagne), she had wondered if Gerald had ever worn the robe before giving it to her. The vibrant colour was his favourite, and he had two pairs of thigh-high leather boots to match!

Irritated, she put the cup and saucer down on a low side-table stacked with books about foreign policy and biographies of former

Chapter Twenty Two

Email from The Prime Minister's Office
Time of Message: 7am.
Date: Friday, 28th March, 2008
To: Mrs. Elizabeth Collins, Department of Health, Whitehall.

Please attend a special meeting at 10 Downing Street at 9.30am. today. Bring all relevant documentation and computer files on your Department's campaigns to combat obesity, and minutes of any recent dealings with food manufacturers. The Prime Minister and Press Secretary, Mr. Ronald Adams, will be in attendance. Please make sure you are available for the rest of the day.

Elizabeth sat in her tiny sitting room in the flat in Victoria, South West London. She was sipping her early morning cup of Fortnum and Mason's special brew Columbian coffee. She felt elated. Her plan to extract herself from the relationship with Jack Barton had worked. They had not made love since last November, in Washington, and their meetings were now strictly for business. Although it was delicious to keep the frisson of attraction alive with eye contact, and, very occasionally, a kiss on the cheek, their affair was over. While it lasted, the fling had been fun, and very useful.

She had learnt a lot from Jack and of course their previous intimacy would prove a useful lever when the time came for a Cabinet reshuffle later in the spring. He knew full well that she wanted a proper, ministerial role. A black, female Foreign Secretary would be popular and appropriate and she felt well-qualified for the job. Jack could hardly ignore her qualities, especially after the way